The Hunt for
Gilligan Rose

Doug Booth

What does each of us see when we gaze into a mirror, beyond our simple reflection?
We see what others cannot: We see the truth.

D Booth

The Hunt for Gilligan Rose

One
Emma Rose

Emma Rose was born to the wrong parents at a time when the world was rigid with postwar righteousness, ripe with ill-conceived values thought by the majority to be moral and proper. She was born at the wrong time into a world that was not yet ready for her. She was the by-product of an uninspired correctness, conceived by an unremarkable couple who married and gave life because their brothers, sisters and neighbours married and gave life for the sake of correctness and the approbation of one's brothers, sisters and neighbours.

Mr. Rose married Emma's mother to prove to the world that he was not a homosexual or otherwise deviant or deficient in nature, that he was a normal and well-adjusted man in all ways, and that he was virile with strong procreative abilities. He wanted boys. He wanted sons, two or three. What she gave him instead was Emma, a beautiful baby girl who ruined any possibility his wife might have of ever producing a son.

What he could not prove, however, was that he was intellectual, enlightened, or free-thinking. He thought what others thought because he was afraid of what they would think of him if he did not. And what did they think of him now, now that his wife after so many years of faithful and dutiful marriage could not manage to bring another child into the world, a male child, despite his frequent and vigorous attempts with her?

He was a cabdriver, working whenever he could, earning as much as he could to keep pace with the Joneses as best he could, never quite able to accept his family's deficiencies. When other fathers played hockey, he drove his cab. He possessed no son to be a man with. When other fathers played catch in the driveway, he drove his cab. Playing catch with Emma would have drawn attention to his wife's imperfection for which he would have been ridiculed. And so his life went each day, six days a week from breakfast till dinnertime.

Mrs. Rose stayed at home. Men worked, women stayed home to care for the family, to suckle and nurture their children at a time when breasts were, at best, unmentionable, their various shapes transformed into a common and acceptable form and size by armour-trimmed foundation garments in the name of decency. Instead Emma's first taste of milk came from a rubber nipple, the same formula all the mothers dripped into their newborns' mouths. To think that her neighbours would even imagine her exposed breasts pressed against her baby's ready mouth was appalling. Some would think entirely degenerate if not sinful beyond redemption in the eyes of the same white and English-speaking God they all went to appease each Sunday.

As an infant Emma never cried, not even when her first soft teeth began piercing her tender gums. Her green eyes were so bright and happy and the terrible twos the other mothers endured were a remarkably tranquil time for Mrs. Rose. Emma never screamed or screeched. She hummed. And when she could sing, she did, or believed that she did. But she hummed and she sang alone. And so went her life through to her first day of school, absorbing colours and sounds into her mind and textures hot and cold into her fingertips. And she would dance, in a world of her own, twirling in circles, every morning and afternoon, whenever a song came through the radio because Mrs. Rose never played the hi-fi when she was alone. She was a housewife and dancing with her only child was a distraction from her chores. Her husband insisted that his home would be the cleanest on the street.

She never hugged little Emma because she had never been hugged as a child, seldom hugged as a wife. In fact intercourse, in the dark with the blinds closed tight, the way their neighbours had intercourse, was difficult from one twin bed to another and quite perfunctory as befitted the times. Mr. Rose had his schedule and Mrs. Rose had hers. Separate beds seemed to make sense, pushed together and concealed under a single and much larger comforter to keep up appearances when company came because they had nowhere else to place the coats and hats.

In truth separate beds made life easier for both. Mrs. Rose changed at the end of each long day to greet her husband at the door and prepare his dinner: out of one apron into another, out of one housedress into another. Mr. Rose never changed. He hung the one tie he owned on the doorknob each night before dinner, ate his meal and fell asleep on the couch snoring contentedly while his wife did the dishes and planned her next day.

Each morning he had a clean white shirt to wear and once each week, on Saturday, she would iron his pants. That was Emma's life, sitting on the floor looking up at them, learning to live in her solitary world, to sing in her mind and to dance alone in her room.

Emma began school in her fifth year of a passable existence, eager to learn, unaware that her mother had never really explained why water was clear, why the sky was blue, why the sun was hot or why she could cover the sun with her hands yet never ever touch the sun. Or why the moon was so bright when the sky was dark all around, or what kept the stars in the sky from falling and sprinkling the ground with silver. She didn't know that her mother didn't know, though she didn't mind with so many other fascinations to discover.

Throughout her elementary years Emma went unnoticed by a system more concerned by the length of her tunic than the depth of her curious mind. Teachers worked nine-to-five. They had a job to do, like a store clerk or a hairdresser. Extra-curricular was a term not yet invented and special care for exceptional children existed solely in the minds and aspirations of a few radical forward thinkers. No one ever asked whether Emma could sing or dance. No one ever thought to consider whether she was happy or sad...or why. And when she graduated into high school, as was expected, they forgot her entirely. She was no longer their problem.

She was also becoming a young woman; her body was in transition, flourishing more quickly than other girls her age, growing taller than other girls. Yet all she knew was that women were dirty once each month and no one was ever to know. Bleeding was a woman's bane, a misery to endure, a secret penance, an unspoken burden. That's what her mother knew. And when Emma asked why, her mother didn't know.

What her father knew was that she was no longer a child. She scarcely resembled the little girl who once crawled on the floor, falling when she tried to stand, giggling, tugging at his pant leg until he shooed her away with his foot, her white face smudged with pink cheeks. She was tall, her baby fat was gone and, where she was once as flat as a boy, she had breasts that were suddenly a woman's breasts and he began giving her the attention she deserved, attention she had never known or known to miss.

He began letting her stay up late, first on Saturdays after her bath and in her pyjamas to watch the late-night movie. Then Fridays after her homework was done and often on Sundays when she would usually fall asleep on the couch, depleted from her mounting burden of weekend chores.

Not far from her thirteenth birthday he told his wife that Emma was too young in her thinking and that soon people would come to believe that she wasn't right in the head. Then what? What chance would she have of finding a boyfriend and eventual suitor? People would soon believe the whole family was not right. She was still sleeping with a teddy bear and wearing pyjamas with prints of puppies and kittens. That, he decided, must change.

When the big day finally arrived, when Emma became a teenager on a Saturday she would never think to remember, she bathed after dinner and changed into her first pair of baby dolls and fluffy slippers. She was allowed one glass of sparkling white wine with her birthday cake as she ensconced herself into the corner of the couch opposite her father and did her best to stay awake.

Mrs. Rose finished her glass of faux-champagne that was ginger ale mixed with gin and went to bed early, Mr. Rose promising to follow once the movie was over, which, for him, was over once his wife was gone from the room. He spent the next ninety minutes watching his daughter sleep like the innocent baby she was, once in a while wetting her lips with a tincture of soda and gin.

He tried to wake her, whispering as quietly as he could, though she wouldn't stir. He moved closer, putting his hand to her calf, closing his fingers gently against her warm skin, whispering to wake her. Still she did not stir and he thought to move his open hand lightly to the top of her bare leg. He couldn't remember his wife's skin ever seeming that soft, smooth or warm. He inhaled a deep breath and went higher, resting his hand against her buttocks, pressing, massaging her soft flesh through her silk barrier, his breathing the loudest sound in the room. He was lost in time, excited and bold, unafraid, and when her eyes fluttered open he stood, sweeping his daughter into his arms, carrying her to her room where he laid her down and kissed her goodnight, washing the sweet taste of her birthday cake from his lips before he went to his bed.

That night was Emma's turning point more than her thirteenth birthday. From that night her mother knew instinctively to dislike her, to loathe and despise the younger and more beautiful woman in her home. Worse yet, if she did nothing to cease or reverse her daughter's scandalous flaunting in front of her weak husband Emma would soon become a harlot, a whore, easy prey for any boy on the street to debase and deflower. Decent young women did not strut about the house exposing their nubile bodies in revealing underwear or enticing silk nighties in front of their fathers. But Emma did. She had no reason not to.

Once, midway through the year, quite by accident, when her mother had gone to bed early not feeling well, Mr. Rose happened into the bathroom while Emma was bathing, covered to her shoulders in fragrant white suds. That was the first time he had seen her so vulnerable, though, by then, Emma was accustomed to falling asleep under his caressing touch and thought nothing of him washing her back with a soft cloth while she hummed. She had long since forgotten how he had neglected her throughout her first thirteen years.

When she was done, and the protective bubbles had vanished, he held out a towel to her as she stood, giving her privacy to dry and dress herself in her newest teenage ensemble as he faced into the mirror. After which father and daughter sprawled on the couch with popcorn and Coke, anxious for the movie to begin, once Mr. Rose first checked in on his ill wife to confirm that she was sleeping and not in the least way in need of his attention. He found her contentedly sleeping, her breathing relaxed, and later that evening, tucking his exhausted daughter into her bed, Mr. Rose remained a while longer to watch her in peaceful slumber.

From then on bath-time intrusions were commonplace while her mother did the dishes, her father putting her to bed most Saturdays, many Fridays and often on Sunday, each weekend sitting by her bedside while she slept, waiting as long as he dared.

By her fourteenth birthday Emma had no boyfriend. Other parents in the neighbourhood thought she was too strange for their sons. She was different, talking to flowers and singing on her way home from school when she was alone, skipping when she was alone, twirling herself in circles in the middle of the street or chasing butterflies across their lawns when she was alone. She wasn't right, not for their sons. The girl was peculiar, not at all like the others. She belonged in a home for the bewildered, not on their street.

In school the other girls didn't want her around. They were ungainly, when she wasn't. She excelled in the gym and in her dance class where they could barely take two steps without tripping and falling. Much worse, as they witnessed each week in the locker room by the gym, was that Emma was already wearing a bra filled with her breasts whereas the other girls scarcely had a need and those who couldn't wait for nature's design would undress behind curtains. Not to hide their deprived chests, rather to conceal their ample and secret supply of tissues intended to disguise the temporary shortcoming. As well, Emma had hips; the others were shapeless, doing their utmost to fabricate their own reasonable facsimiles by tightly cinching their waists with sashes.

Emma didn't care either way.

As for her father, Mr. Rose increasingly found his wife irritating and increasingly he would sit in the kitchen by himself and drink in his own world. She was boring. She was drab, constantly wearing the same housedresses, the same aprons, her hair forever knotted into a bun like a dominating mother superior or schoolmarm from what he remembered of his seven years of learning. He couldn't recall the last time he'd seen her naked in the light of day, or when he had wanted to, but when he did, he clearly remembered, he brushed away her image with thoughts of his daughter standing in her place. What his wife first believed was renewed interest and lustful attention on his part towards her, his natural need for more intercourse with her, was in fact vicarious love-making with Emma.

He wanted more time with his daughter. They weren't that many years apart, he justified. She was fourteen; he was thirty-seven. At her eighteenth birthday, her majority, he would be forty-one and still a young man. So what was the big deal? And Emma had not once pushed his hand away or whimpered in fear. She was a loving girl, a special girl. She enjoyed their times together as much as he did. He could not and would not allow her to transmute into what her mother had become.

Mrs. Rose understood that she couldn't compete. Her daughter was beautiful; she was thirty-six and being attractive to a man was impossible after preparing twenty-one meals, shopping for groceries and clothes for three, cleaning a house, washing and ironing for three and making certain everything was ready for their work and school each day. She knew she was no longer desirable, no longer pretty, that sex with her husband had nothing at all to do with love. At week's end, when he was increasingly ready for intercourse she wanted to sleep, thankful that, at least then, whenever he chose to pull the sheets away from her bed and her nightdress to her waist, he had the most work to do. Nature's single kindness to womankind, she believed.

Had she suspected, she might have made herself more attractive, more available to him at a time when other mothers her age were beginning to work outside the home, wearing miniskirts and provocative blouses, shopping arm in arm with their daughters. But she didn't suspect, her mind dulled by drudgery and daily routine. She had lapsed into a lethargic state of uncaring that she would never think to regret.

Several months from her fifteenth birthday, Emma

continued hugging her mother every morning before walking the one mile to school, and every evening before her bedtime, though she never felt her mother's embrace. She never considered that she loved her mother or father. They were simply her mother and father and she saw each one in a different light. The same way she saw girls and boys at school each in a different light. Yet she did believe, she thought, when she did think of him, when her mind wasn't filled with fanciful images of ballerinas and fairies, the mysteries of caterpillars and butterflies, green grass or the warmth of the sun, that her father was the most different. She thought so.

Her mother was neither beautiful nor plain. At best she was handsome. She was her mother. What Emma didn't like was when her mother was not well, a condition which was more and more frequent. At first she wasn't well on the weekends, now she was increasingly unwell most nights of the week.

One Friday night, when Mrs. Rose wasn't well at all, Mr. Rose gave Emma a gift. Emma liked surprise gifts the most and ran to her room to change into the satin slip before the late movie began and, as usual, after she'd fallen asleep, her father waited for the movie to end and carried Emma to her room, leaving her for a few moments to remove their glasses from the living room table and rinse them clean to spare his wife the extra work in the morning. When he returned to check in on her, to see that she was safe, he found her sleeping soundly, purring. Mr. Rose stepped in and closed the door, his eyes adjusting to the dark.

He left her one hour later, believing he'd been gentle and kind, taking her satin slip with him, closing his mind to his wife who could never again be more to him than an uncaring spouse, a vessel to visit once in a while, and mother to his darling Emma. In the morning, while Mrs. Rose prepared a Saturday breakfast of ham and eggs, toast and jam, Mr. Rose went to wake his daughter, handing her a set of baby dolls from her dresser drawer, asking her how she felt.

She felt tired, she told him, not the least bit curious about her gift that was missing. Did she hurt anywhere, he asked? She answered matter-of-factly that she did not, and for that he seemed pleased. When she was dressed they went together into the kitchen.

Each night for a month Mrs. Rose continued her ritual of going to bed early, feeling somewhat ill and despondent for not knowing why. And every Friday, Saturday and Sunday Emma would fall asleep on the couch in a new satin slip, each week a different colour that her father would take with him when he was finished, leaving her to dream. Until one Sunday morning when Mr. Rose awoke with a start, thinking the worst, hearing his wife's piercing shriek, his mind clouded, his eyes blurred, his young daughter's body naked and pinned under his in her bed, her teddy bear wrapped tightly in her arms, her brightly coloured slip crumpled on the floor.

At first Mr. Rose was defensive. He had heard his daughter calling out for her daddy, he explained, and he went to her heedless of his nudity, filled with concern. She was afraid. She had been dreaming badly. All he wanted was to comfort her and he must have fallen asleep. He hadn't meant to, he insisted. He was so very ashamed, though his body told his wife differently.

She didn't believe him and rushed to the bed where she pressed her fingers into Emma's pubic hair, pressing the tips into her daughter's moist curls, smelling them, leaning forward and smelling her breath before running from the room sobbing hysterically.

Mr. Rose told his daughter to dress, however to stay in her room. Her mother still was not well. With his wife in the kitchen he was deaf to anything she screamed regarding their daughter. The girl, he insisted repeatedly to equally unhearing ears, was going through a stage and needed her father. She had no friends; he was a male figure for her, his body a simple matter of natural female curiosity. Seeing him naked she had wanted to know why he was different. They had simply spoken about his body and hers. How else would she learn? How else would she know what questions to ask, what was right or what was wrong? Mr. Rose hastening to add that he hadn't done anything wrong, nor would he ever. She must have undressed after he had fallen asleep. Besides, he ranted on, his face increasingly red with a rage that was his one defence; the fault was hers, not his and not Emma's. Emma was a woman, a beautiful and young woman, not lazy or unsightly, not a housewife whose time had long since come and gone. Emma had stopped being a child and a daughter a long time ago. She was everything his sad wife was not. He discovered during their time together that he loved Emma more that way than he ever would as a father. How could he live without being with Emma who loved him?

The kitchen instantly became a maelstrom of flying plates, pots and pans, knives and forks, spoons and bowls hurled viciously in one direction and, before she was finished, her husband was cowering on the floor and bleeding from his face and his hands.

In her room Emma sat cross-legged on her bed, listening to the din, unperturbed and dressed in her slip, smelling her fingers as her mother had done, smiling with wonder as the woman, crazed and distraught, crashed through the door. She was horrified by what her daughter was doing, leaping at Emma, stripping her naked and dragging her by the hair to the bathroom.

Emma remained in the bath until noon, deep heated water added to an empty tub every half-hour, scrubbed continuously by her mother's gloved hands gripping a coarse brush, her young skin scraped raw. She was made to lean forward without saying a word each time the tub drained completely, so that her broken cavity would be flushed and cleaned and made pure with an enema of burning detergent squeezed from a bottle into her body by a mother's unloving hands.

Strangely, her mother didn't take a moment to realize that Emma wasn't crying. Not once. Nor did she resist. More importantly, in the first few moments of her fitful rage, Mrs. Rose could easily have drowned her daughter. She should have known all along, she muttered. Her daughter was no good, a troubled child destined to become any man's vessel and die with her legs spread apart in the street if something wasn't done soon.

When she was done, her arms too tired to erase whatever trace might remain on her daughter of her husband's vile act, she forced her daughter forward onto her knees once again and beat the girl's buttocks with the long handle of the brush until at last Emma did cry.

For a week Mrs. Rose excused her daughter from school. Emma ate her meals in her room and slept with her mother, never going out, never allowed to speak with her father, wondering why she could not, wondering quietly what she had done.

During the days of that consequent week Mrs. Rose went about doing her best to right what was an irreparable wrong. She should never have had a daughter when she knew all along that what her husband wanted was a son. What happened wasn't her husband's fault, she knew that as well. Lust in men was a natural inclination. The fault was hers and Emma wasn't at all free of guilt, flaunting herself, lying with her father on the couch until all hours, her nubile and corrupt body practically naked, tormenting and taunting him. She was old enough to know better, to know what she was doing, being wicked with her own father.

Unfortunately for Emma, as her mother soon discovered to her dismay, she was growing into an era when orphanages were being forced to close, a new concept of foster homes taking over. However who would want such a sinful and devious child? If Emma could so wantonly debase herself with her natural father, why would she not with any girl's father or any good husband? No foster home would take her. She was unruly, demented in her thinking and lascivious in her nature, difficult to explain. She was a danger to herself and to others who would not know to be wary. Their eyes would be blinded by her youth and her body, her allure and her charm, their senses numbed by what they would imagine of her and the all-consuming command of her deviant adult mind. There was but one way to save her, to redeem her.

Doctor Zeke Phillips was her last hope, concurring that Emma was indeed a difficult and troubled child, clearly in need of long-term specific therapy based on half-truths and what he saw of a young girl peering from the window of his office to talk with butterflies and birds in the trees. Though to his credit, his thorough evaluation of Emma was completed without knowing the full extent of the girl's dilemma, without the slightest knowledge that her father, for well over a year, had been her persistent lover, culminating his unnatural desires months earlier and throughout the subsequent weeks until awoken one morning. Much to his discredit however he did understand that Emma was being committed involuntarily by her mother without any understanding of what that might mean, without her father to controvert the legality of the private proceeding for better or worse, without any legal representation or appeal by a kinder and more understanding court than her mother. The good doctor quite simply needed another patient to fill his quota. Another had recently died and Emma fit the profile and temperament of a distraught and dysfunctional child perfectly enough to satisfy the state examiner who, likely as not, would never see her.

Formality was requisite of course, paperwork attesting to the child's immediate need of professional care in order to reintegrate her into society at some point in time, in the future, though to specify a precise date was unwise, premature, Doctor Phillips cautioned. The cure of such deeply-rooted lunacies, he explained, was indeterminable; a gradual process of extraction and correction, supplanting the girl's inherent aberrant behaviour with acceptable societal norms. The therapy would be extensive. He would incrementally penetrate her subconscious mind as profoundly as her illness would allow, each session probing more deeply, methodically exorcising the corruption of eccentricity and anti-social behavior from her thoughts, purifying her mind and her soul.

Mrs. Rose was unquestionably free to visit with her daughter each Sunday afternoon between noon and four. In short, Emma Rose was being committed without the slightest knowledge of what was happening to her, or what would happen to her.

She spent her last night at home in her mother's room, sitting cross-legged on her mother's bed hugging and talking with her bear. She loved her bear.

That night, she didn't eat supper. Her mother didn't feel like cooking when gin was so much more appealing than mashed potatoes and sausages, certain to help her forget her failure as a good wife, overlook her husband's single immorality and her blatantly promiscuous child.

Emma fell asleep hungry, and awoke hungry, her skin damp from summer's thick heat. She wanted to bathe, her mother refusing her. Her body and mind were soiled beyond cleansing. Her clothes for the day were set out on the bed and when she was dressed she went out into the hall. Her father was gone, the smell of bacon and eggs permeating the house. She saw a single suitcase at her mother's feet by the door of what had once been her bedroom. Her stomach was empty, though somehow she intuited that her mother would not let her eat breakfast. She didn't think so.

No words were spoken as they stood on the stoop by the

front door, as though waiting for the milkman or the baker to pass by. No questions were asked by a young girl weeping. Nor were answers considered to questions unasked by a cold heart uncaring. They simply stood side by side, mother and daughter dissolved, watching the unsmiling man and woman come closer.

Emma would never see her mother or father again. To one parent she was dead, to the other, best forgotten

*

The institute where Emma Rose was housed, where she would live out her life because no one ever left the institute, wasn't an asylum, not in the strictest sense, not for the truly insane. Behind the thick, black bars of the wrought iron fence, behind the brownstone façade and the barred, dull windows that were only ever washed by occasional torrential rains, the austere rooms were private and quiet places, safe retreats for vivid imaginations or private fears.

Emma's eyes soon cleared and she came to love her room. The pictures on her four walls painted in her mind, for her eyes alone to see. Real pictures required nails and hooks and wire and Emma was not allowed any of that. Her walls were bare, the finish rough from several layers of whitewash. Her bed was constructed of welded steel tubes, unpainted and bent into a low profile, made without screws or springs. Her mattress was twelve inches of hard foam, yellowed with age and smelling of sweat which, in the oppressive heat of summer, made the cool granite floor more appealing. She loved her room. Most of all she loved her window that she could see through when she stood on her bed. She loved the greens of summer as much as the amber gold of autumn, the snow white of winter and springtime raindrops that would turn the cold pane into a mirror when she would comb her bright red hair with her fingers or make funny faces at herself or wonder whose face that really was.

Throughout the winter months she was given two sheets

to sleep under, to keep her warm, though at the first hint of spring one was taken away: an unnecessary and costly luxury. She had no dresser because she didn't wear clothes. She had no clothes. She no longer knew what that was like, to wear clothes. She had forgotten, though she never thought to remember exactly when. Her wardrobe was a thin, shapeless gown made of cotton and tied at the back of her neck and at her waist and each night she would undress and fold her gown neatly at the foot of her bed before crawling naked under her sheet to curl into herself and wait for her brightly lit room to abruptly go dark. She never waited long. She hated the dark. She hated the dark because of the faces.

Underpants were not allowed. They weren't necessary. But she didn't know that because she didn't know or couldn't remember what underpants were. Eighty-two Emmas lived behind the narrow doors dotting the abandoned corridors of the institute, eighty-two private existences brought together once each day to huddle alone in unsheltered corners to stare from, or be studied by, uncurious eyes while others walked in wide circles or stood as they were in the middle of the room.

The women spent their private time together each morning after a breakfast of cereal and milk, porridge in the winter; the men each afternoon after a meagre midday meal of watery soup and a thin slice of white bread that was meant to eat, not to enjoy. However supper was served in their rooms, segregation deemed a good thing, the meal consisting of potatoes and thick slices of meat, carrots or peas on paper plates and watered-down milk in thin paper cups. Sugar in any form was never allowed, coffee and tea were forgotten or never known and Emma hadn't used a knife or a fork in years. She didn't know what they were. She didn't know to remember. All she knew was a plastic spoon and to eat her meat with her fingers.

The administrator was of the opinion, and Phillips

concurred, that keeping the male population from the females made wearing underpants both an unnecessary cost and time-consuming: money better spent elsewhere, time better spent cleaning patients and not their soiled clothing. Patients, male and female alike, inclined to relieve themselves irrespective of their thinly cloaked nudity or whereabouts, were simply deprived of their three hours each day, shut into their rooms for a week

Emma knew men. She knew the doctor and she knew Tommy. Tommy was gentle and kind. She thought so. She liked Tommy. He always gave her candy and made her feel good. She knew she had a father once, long ago, and a mother. She knew because she was alive, though neither one ever crept into her mind to love her or make her feel good, random and fleeting memories evaporating on special nights when, in her bath water, or in her room before her single light went dark, in a way, Tommy reminded her of her father. She thought so.

She knew men lived behind some of the doors, though she wasn't exactly certain which doors. She'd seen them, men, there, those times she was taken to see the doctor or for her bath, or for the toilet, though not often and never the same ones. She didn't think so. They weren't like Tommy. Tommy was big. He was caring and he was thoughtful. The other men had dirty faces and bad eyes, looking at her in a way she didn't like whenever they saw her, touching themselves where she knew they were different like Tommy and making strange expressions with their mouths and their faces that she didn't like.

Emma Rose was nineteen. She had no memory of her past, none that she ever thought to remember. Nor did she know of tomorrow, or the day after. She didn't know hours, days, weeks or months. Or she didn't care. She didn't know the seasons; she knew dark nights and bright days, the cold of her frost-covered window and the warmth of the sun passing through her window for a short while each summer day as she would sit in its path on her floor with her gown pulled to the tops of her bare legs.

She knew what she saw and what she felt. She knew she was beautiful because Tommy told her so whenever he came to secretly give her candy with her medication, without saying what beauty was or what beauty meant. She knew her dreams and often she would awaken afraid, afraid of the dark, not understanding where the images had gone, how the people had gone from her locked room or that dreams were never real.

That was Emma's world and had been since the day the woman and the man came to her home to take her away, the day she turned to see her mother gone, no one standing at the door with tears in her eyes calling her daughter back.

She put her tray aside and smelled her hands. She seldom ate all her meat at dinner. She didn't like meat, though the doctor didn't seem to care. So neither did she, she justified in her head. She never wiped her hands with her napkin, or on her gown. She wiped them on her bottom sheet at the foot of her bed because she didn't have a pillow and she knew that whenever she was taken to bathe she would return to sheets that smelled fresh and were folded precisely.

She would save her napkins religiously after each dinner, stacking them in the corner of her room, and when she determined in her mind that the pile was as high as it should be she would have a new and clean place to lay her head. Tommy didn't mind at all and often he would bring her an extra few dozen to make the pile higher and her room more comfortable. In the other far corner of her room, away from her bed, she kept the thin paper cup after each dinner. She was permitted three trips each day to the toilet. Those were her only two possessions.

Emma was slim and 5'8". Her skin was so white as to appear translucent, taking on the hue of whatever light she was near. She didn't know that Thursday night was her bath night, or why. She didn't know that the doctor went home each day at five or that the administrator went to his home at four. She didn't know that only one nurse was on duty or that the woman spent her time between dinnertime and lights-out administering bedtime medication to the patients, sometimes in the company of the other male orderly on duty besides Tommy and sometimes not. Whenever she came into Emma's room she came alone, often later in the day before Tommy arrived for work, Emma never knowing or caring why Tommy wasn't with her.

All she knew was that sometime soon after her last bath Tommy would come to take her for another and give her more candies. She never knew exactly when Thursday night would come, or when he would open her door without knocking to see her sitting cross-legged on the floor or on her bed. Or even whether he would take her for her bath because sometimes, not every night, he would come in to make certain she was well, that she hadn't dirtied herself where she had hair, and to bring her a clean gown and a candy. She always had the cleanest gown when she went for her breakfast and her lunch, spending her three hours sitting by herself in a corner making music in her mind. She no longer knew radio, records or dancing in her room with imaginary friends. She no longer knew pretty dresses, soft sweaters or any pretty thing.

She didn't flinch. She simply looked up from beside her neat pile of napkins and saw Tommy.

She never smiled. She never felt happy, though she never felt very sad. Neither did she have much reason to talk when she wasn't with the doctor or with Tommy. The nurse never spoke to her. Nor did she think she liked the nurse very much. She liked Tommy. She thought that everyone must like Tommy.

Two
Tommy Dune

Tommy Dune was born into an ordinary family at a time when doing the right thing meant not having sex in the backseat of your father's car. However if you did, because she was as much to blame as you, or as eager as you, then marrying her was somewhat preferential to a charge of statutory rape and the girl being sent away to visit an aunt while you sit in a six by nine cell wincing at the persisting sting of fifteen deep lash wounds on your back that would never completely heal, never let you forget her. For that reason and none other Tommy Dune was born.

Neither parent was extraordinarily gifted, each one marginal at best in their thinking and their lives as one day slipped unnoticed into another. His father drank himself into another and better world each night after work, often rising late the following morning, often drinking himself out of a job, returning home dejected to spend his days in the comfort of that better world until his unemployment cheques expired.

He didn't love Tommy. Nor did he love his wife or show either one the least affection. The bourbon helped him forget.

Tommy's mother stayed at home for as long as he knew her. She was a housewife trapped in the drudgery of an era when that's where she belonged. She was unskilled and uncaring, going about her days in a housedress, existing vicariously through soap operas on a black and white television, her mind numbed to the past, blind to the future. She hadn't given a moment's thought to her youthful spontaneity in years, or how she would grow old. A single mistake had ruined her life. She had not one reason to dream.

Then he was handsome and she was, if not gorgeous, certainly not unattractive, so enamoured and swayed by his frequent attention when the other boys scarcely glanced her way. Now she couldn't remember the last time they had gone together to bed for mutual release, having convinced herself years earlier that they had never once made love, not that first night in the car, not since bringing Tommy home. She resented her husband. Too late she'd realized that he'd been handsome in her eyes alone and Tommy was the result of her wanting to be as popular as the other girls.

She didn't love Tommy. She never had. She couldn't. Why would she when she had wanted him aborted? However his parents were poor and hers were Catholic who threatened to reward their daughter's depravity with the cloistered life of a nun were she ever to find the means to kill or abandon her child on the footsteps or an orphanage.

Their single commonality, one which they would often discuss when Tommy was elsewhere, was Tommy's eighteenth birthday, his coming of age and their deserved emancipation.

The date was more important to the couple than Christmas, birthdays and the long forgotten romance of Cupid's arrow. They wanted him gone; good riddance to a ne'er-do-well burden, the father blaming the mother, her blaming him for their strife, and when the day finally did arrive Mr. Dune hadn't slept a wink the night before in his easy chair and Mrs. Dune kept busy throughout the early hours packing Tommy's duffel bag.

For eighteen years Mr. Dune had saved a dollar each month and grudgingly gave his son 216 one-dollar bills without so much as a handshake. Mrs. Dune gave him seven sandwiches and seven TV dinners, enough to see him through his first week of independence. She couldn't take him into her arms, or kiss his cheek or bring tears to eyes that hadn't smiled in years because of him. They were rid of him at last. Or was he rid of them? Either way, Tommy hadn't taken a dozen steps before hearing the door close behind him. He shrugged and went forth into a new life.

He didn't attend class that day, the last week of the school year, a week of exams. He was aware, as were his parents and his teachers, that he would repeat grade ten again and again which the school would no longer tolerate. He had already repeated grades five, eight and nine; though despite his shortcomings he also knew that something bigger and better was waiting for him.

Tommy Dune wasn't stupid; he just wasn't smart and somewhat disinclined towards remedying the deficiency. His strengths lay elsewhere. He didn't so much drop out from high school; he simply never went back, dreaming of becoming a doctor, thinking he would take special courses at a local trade school to achieve his dream of several months, soon discovering the flaw in his thinking. Then he thought to become a nurse, thinking of the girls in his class and how they went to talk with the nurse, how they all whispered and giggled when they returned to class. He could do that. He could become a nurse and see all the girls naked, like the ones once in his class that were four or five years younger. He knew he could do that and not waste another year when he already knew all that he needed to know. All the nurse ever did to him was to take his temperature, grab his balls and tell him to cough.

He wasn't smart enough for the older girls in grades eleven and twelve, his former classmates who ridiculed him: the school dunce, the zombie, the freak, the only boy in school who never attended school dances, who never had a date, who every day sat by himself in the cafeteria watching them, looking at their legs and their chests.

The Hunt for Gilligan Rose

They all knew what he was thinking; telling their boyfriends who never did anything about Tommy because Tommy was big and everyone knew that dimwitted dunces were unnaturally strong. Worse, he was too old for the younger and more impressionable ones who were either afraid of him or eager to tease him, wanting to be seen with an older man on a dare, ready to pull up their hems more than they should or unbutton their blouses more than they wanted because other girls were watching and daring. But the other parents also knew about Tommy and his parents.

Tommy Dune liked girls, girls younger than him. From his first attempt at grade five he was always the oldest boy in the class. Young girls were the only girls he knew, though he never did have a date and he sat alone to eat his lunch because no one wanted to sit with him. His mother had always taken the least that she could from the house money to buy his clothes and shoes from bargain basement outlets. He never wore sweaters; he wore long-sleeve white shirts, grey continental pants gathered at the waist with a belt that he'd grown into and then out of, white socks and thick-soled shoes that were laced and permanently scuffed.

Now that would all change. He would become master of his destiny. At eighteen, as hard as he tried, he hadn't once seen a naked girl, not a real girl. He'd seen pictures, sure, in the magazines under his father's workbench. He knew what they looked like under their tunics, what they wore, what they could do, though he hadn't yet touched one, not anywhere, especially the way he knew the other boys did each day after school.

He would though, he promised, very soon, because he was now his own man. He was free to live his dream.

The night he left home he ate his first sandwich amidst a cluster of trees at the far end of the schoolyard, in the dark with nothing to do except think about the girls in his class. He had no books, no transistor radio or magazines. All he could do was to imagine them naked before tucking himself into his pants.

When he woke he relieved himself in the creek by the trees, eating his second and third sandwiches while he watched everyone he'd once known, or at least recognized, filing into the building to affirm on paper how much they had learned over the previous nine months. He chortled. Now who was ridiculing whom?

By his second evening his meagre sandwiches were gone. He was thirsty and went away with seven tasteless dinners wrapped in tin foil with nothing to heat them with in the rising temperatures of a new summer. He spent the day by the creek during class time, hiding in the weeds and tall grass during recess and lunch because he had nowhere else to go. The town where he once lived until his coming of age was small. Everyone knew Tommy Dune. Everyone knew he would become like his father in the shortest possible time: an indolent layabout whose wife was no better. They all remembered the class slut who had to drop out.

He had to leave, to escape, which he did after a second night on the soft grass that wasn't soft enough to cushion the hard ground beneath. He woke early, his clothes damp with dew, to a breakfast of shoe-leather beef strips, spongy mashed potatoes and glutinous gravy that was an unpleasant shade of brown, clotted and cold.

The hours passed slowly until once again, and for the last time, he watched those who despised him pass through the doors eager to prove what they knew, others clearly afraid they could not.

When the first bell sounded, and the second, he sneaked into the building, feeling elated, on the edge, into the boys' locker room to shower away two days of grime and change into fresh clothes. Until the thought occurred to him: The gym instructor had gone home a week earlier, his work year complete, and Tommy had the place to himself. Smiling, achieving a wonderful dream, one of many random thoughts, he hurried into the girls' side where he stripped away his clothes and showered in an open stall until his skin was pink and the water began to cool.

Towelled and dry, dressed and ready for the day ahead, he stuffed as many dry towels as he could manage into his duffel bag and he left. An hour later he was at the bus station, an unsightly cube of a building with a single wicket, an office for personnel and one genderless washroom for anyone to share.

During his time by the creek Tommy decided where his destiny resided. His future was clear in his mind. He was en route to achieve greatness amongst half a million other souls on the banks of the Hudson, not 200 miles from an oxidized statue of freedom he knew nothing about, where he would arrive with 200 dollars in his pocket to take on a world he knew nothing about. He was excited. He had plans, great plans. He was going to Solaceville.

He arrived in the dark, near midnight, an eerie time in any small city when signs of life remained hidden until early morning, albeit not too early. Amber streetlights bathed sombre brick and glass buildings in sepia, traffic lights flickered from red to green to yellow, directing invisible cars along empty streets. Neon signs everywhere in shades of mauve and pink told him where not to go. Everything was closed. Returning uncertain to the bus station, that was also closed, this time in neon yellow.

So he wandered aimlessly. There was no difference for Tommy between left, right, straight ahead or behind. He'd never been to a town bigger than where he was born. He had never in his life left the town where he was born, where he had failed so well, where he would venture no farther than the lake where he would swim for a while, pretending to leave, retreating behind the trees and the tall bushes to watch the girls through his father's binoculars.

He didn't know the place, though what better time to see his new home than when he was alone, he thought, doing basic arithmetic as best he could as he wandered aimlessly. As best he could tell, he had sufficient funds to last ten days in a boarding house if he ate one meal a day, a month if he could find a youth hostel that would ask only a few dollars each night, more than enough time to find a job that would pay his way through trade school and establish a career.

That, however, didn't quite work out as he'd planned.

Tommy discovered quickly by the end of his first week that food was expensive and that hostels didn't operate on a first-come, first-served basis, rather a first-come with five dollars for the night, first-served. He also learned that Laundromats were coin-operated and that grade nine was an academic standing worth fifty dollars a week, which excited him, until he learned about taxes and tuition.

They laughed at him when he asked with genuine yet curious seriousness to be enrolled in a doctor's course. When he mentioned his interest in nursing, expecting them to greet a new student with arms opened wide, they practically launched him through the doors onto the street. They had no time for him.

Despondent, he went to the army thinking he would like to carry a gun. He'd seen all the movies and knew he could do that. The recruitment sergeant listened for as long as he could bear, gripping Tommy's neck on the way to the door, where he pointed Tommy towards a cluster of bikes, not quite certain the kid could cross the street on his own.

That afternoon he landed the job, which he lost five days later. He had forgotten to lock his bicycle to a lamp post, returning to the street after delivering the day's first parcel to discover the bike and his carry bag filled with more envelopes and parcels were gone.

That Friday was Tommy's first night in an alley. He had nowhere else to lay his head and no money, his first week's pay garnisheed by his apoplectic employer. Tommy had been in Solaceville two weeks, despondent and disillusioned, completely bereft of his hopes and his dreams.

The next day he panhandled. He was clumsy. He made twenty dollars, twenty-three on the Sunday. On the Monday, with twenty-five more in his pocket, he went to an army surplus outlet where he bought fatigues, solid boots, sunglasses, a new bag and a knife. He'd always wanted a knife. Then he went to a barber who shaved his head to the scalp and to the Y where he paid three dollars for a shower and five for a bed. When he woke, he threw what little remained of his past into the garbage and left to work on the street.

Strangely, with his new clothes and his new look, his income dropped to under ten dollars and he determined to find a better, more lucrative part of town, which he did on the Wednesday, on a street corner in the centre of town, changing his life forever. The intersection was the busiest in the city, hundreds of cars in line behind red lights each morning and afternoon. That's where he saw them and watched them. The guy, he thought, was seventeen, maybe eighteen. The girls seemed more like fifteen and sixteen, all three making money, right in the middle of the street without begging, without the side glances or the sneers from passers-by.

The guy was dressed in black jeans and boots, a black tee-shirt and a braided wristband that Tommy thought was cool. The girls were wearing low-cut fatigues, green like his, army boots and white cotton halter tops twist-tied under their otherwise bare breasts. That was all. And they were sexy. Their midriffs were bare, and most of their backs. They were smiling, tucking money into their pockets and waving at each new car. The guy was equally busy, contentedly filling his pockets with change. Yet they were three, and Tommy saw that the intersection was comprised of four corners.

He watched them until they were finished, until the last

cars made their way through the green lights, and went to the guy because he was a guy. They spoke for an hour in the park, each one feeling out the other: one surviving with street smarts, the other beginning his new existence with no smarts. The girls laid on their backs in the grass, their knees in the air, opening, closing, their flat bellies rising and sinking, listening quietly, nodding when asked by the guy if they agreed.

That night Tommy slept in a warm bed after a few beers and a meal of hamburgers and fries cooked by the girls. He'd never tasted beer. His life was coming together. He was becoming someone. Starting the next day he would pay a quarter of his earnings to the guy for his part of the rent, another quarter to the girls for his food and his beer. The girls themselves were to share.

The small four-room flat was over a corner store, one room boasting a king-size bed not much smaller in size than the room, a sitting room with a sofa, recliner, ghetto blaster and portable coloured TV, a bathroom with a curtain for a door and a kitchen with dishes piled high.

Life was good and getting better. He'd known for a long time what girls looked like under their clothes, often at night imagining a girl in his class undressing, never dreaming that he would see girls undressing right in front of him and climbing into bed naked between him and some other guy, never dreaming that he would have sex with any girl so soon, let alone two, one right after the other.

By morning Tommy was a new man.

He spent a year on the street, cleaning car windows for someone's loose change, a fortune for him. He made a good living, not once remembering his parents who had never once thought to see the good in him. He and the other guy changed apartments twice: out of necessity: Once when the girls thought to become pregnant in the same month and again when, due to bad weather, their incomes were disappointing to them as well as the landlord who had more reliable tenants waiting.

Undeterred, they would always find another low-rent four walls to make their own, more girls on the run to shelter with promises of money and fun with no one belittling or denigrating them, constantly nagging, criticizing and spying. Besides, they weren't girls; they were women, young, hot women who didn't need caring parents harassing them every minute. What they needed was a life and all was well with the two most recent inductees until the late spring when midway through rush hour traffic the guy complained to Tommy that he didn't feel well. That he was going home early, that Tommy should stay with the girls until the end of the business day.

When the last quarter went into his pocket Tommy sat on the curb waiting for the girls who soon came by to tell him they were going shopping for groceries and that he should go home without them. He did, to find his friend gone along with his personal belongings, the girls' bags and his own duffel bag where he'd hidden three thousand dollars. He was broke, and the fridge was left empty.

For the next month he slept alone with nothing nubile and naked to keep him warm, barely able to make ends meet, though correct in his thinking that his former friend had taken the most profitable corner for himself.

He was being forced to make certain changes. He went to the Laundromat twice that month, not once each week, and he ate one cold meal a day when a beer or two wasn't more important. His cigarettes were never new, they were butts coated with foreign spit or lipstick and the girls who needed a place to sleep that was warmer than the night air and softer than a sidewalk were never as young or as pretty as his previous acquaintances. He missed them all very much.

To improve his conditions he began spending his nights searching for kindness in lieu of a handout, not far from the doors of what he believed were expensive restaurants, appearing better than a panhandler, more like a man down on his luck.

His life was improving. He could afford three small meals a day and had decided that the least ugly girl in his bed, as long as she was young, was better than none at all. He liked girls in his bed very much and the younger she was the more he liked her. Then one night he stepped in front of a well-dressed and unattractive man who exited the restaurant without a companion. The man was Doctor Zeke Phillips of The Philips Institute who, on a whim, asked Tommy to walk with him to his car. That night was eight years earlier; the closest Tommy would ever come to achieving his dream.

Then he was bald by choice, now his hair was cut short which was Phillips' choice. And he was big: 5'11", weighing in at two-twenty, wearing his whites at work as proudly as any marine might wear his dress blues.

He wasn't lazy. He was a chronic underachiever who, because of the good doctor, had hit pay dirt. He was in the right place at the right time and was now the institute's senior orderly, much less capable though with more seniority than the nurse who had quickly learned to despise him. He worked 4:00 PM to midnight because he chose to, explaining to Doctor Philips that doing so allowed him to interact with the members of his early morning and day teams before and after each shift. The doctor didn't care either way.

He no longer rinsed bedpans or hosed wet or dried excrement from between the buttocks and thighs of miscreant patients. Nor did he clean vomit from spongy mattresses or mop urine from the floor. That was the work of lesser men. Besides, he'd learned very quickly that most people, either by accident or with a purpose, shit themselves during daylight hours.

He lived alone without a girlfriend. He hadn't needed one for a long time. They were initially expensive for one thing without any guarantee of convincing them into bed. Most often, once they discovered that he worked at the insane asylum, albeit as the Chief Administrator, even the homeliest and most eager fled and left him to pay the bill. Those who didn't were difficult to be rid of in the morning.

Each afternoon he would leave for work dressed in a suit and a tie, the same suit and tie, each night returning home to an empty apartment with barely a crease in either one. He never sat while riding the bus.

His single white shirt was washed, bleached and ironed faithfully each Saturday morning when he had little else to do. Many in his building believed Tommy was a doctor, without the slightest knowledge that he carried his sandwiches along with his daily supply of soft drinks and candies in his little black bag. Thomas Dune, MD, embossed near the handle in large gold letters for all of them to see, which is why he never sat on the bus. Though, once at the institute, inside his private domain, his secret went directly into his locker that he sealed shut with a key.

Satisfied most often with his day, he lay in bed most nights with a healthy measure of undiluted bourbon, like father like son, a taste he believed went well with his suit, gazing at the pages of glossy magazines, at one-dimensional bodies of naked women he could never afford, women he didn't have to afford because the prettiest of the women housed at the institute liked him. He made certain that they liked him. They liked that he photographed them as they bathed or lay on their beds. Photos of their naked bodies ready for him on clean sheets and with their legs open in shallow bathwater lined his walls because he would treat those young women so well bringing them candy and sometimes even a Coke or a Pepsi.

They were his girls. He made them feel good.

The others were work, his job. He didn't care about them and they didn't care about him. If and when he saw them naked he was never aroused. They were unkempt and filthy, as vulgar as the male patients who were the domain of his underlings. He didn't like touching men at all, or old and homely women.

His favourite by far was Emma Rose. She'd been his charge since the day she arrived. She was young and pretty, like the girls who once slept in his bed for free. He enjoyed bathing with her the most, her photographs the most prominent on his walls, her eyes watching him, her breasts and her open legs taunting him, drawing him to her.

Three
Emma's Bath Night

Tommy looked down at her. He was always anxious for Thursday night, for her. She was his girlfriend. But he wasn't stupid. He knew he couldn't take her to a movie, sit in the park with her or buy her flowers. Anyway, those things were not important to Emma. She wanted nothing more than what was his alone to give her: attention, love and the warmth of gentle touches, fleeting and intimate moments together as often as he dared.

Deep in his heart he knew the other girls did what they did for the candies. He had no delusions. But Emma was different. She cared about him and he would never tell her about the others, that he went to them the same way because he couldn't be with her every night as he was with the glossy girls in his bedroom, the girls in the magazines stored under his bed because he couldn't help himself. He'd liked pretty girls ever since he could remember and she was the prettiest of them all.

None of them, the patients, ever had visitors. Family and friends, if there were any, would never want even the most distant stranger to see them passing through those eerie front gates into a nuthouse, a loony bin. Everyone on the outside knew the institute was crammed with lunatics aimlessly wandering the halls, their brains dulled by electric shock, anxious to escape because they would never be released. That's why he told everyone in the free world that he worked at Solaceville General Hospital in a private ward that didn't exist.

Emma knew to stand, to take his outreached hand. He was taking her for her bath. She wouldn't lie down with her knees far apart for him to see that she was clean, or raise her arms so that he could change her gown. That would be another night, but that evening she would have clean sheets and she was happy. Clean sheets hid the unpleasant smell of her bed…for a while. She formed a little smile. She liked going for her bath. She thought so.

She would lie in the steaming water and turn pink, patting away trickles of sweat from her cheeks, the tip of her nose and her chin, wiping frothy white foam from her face when near the end of her bath he would wash and rinse her hair. Sometimes, every once in a while, more white foam covered her to her boobies, foam that smelled nicer than her clean gown and sheets; other times she would wash her hair herself with soap while he sat watching her from his white chair. She very much preferred the shampoo. Other times, she remembered, she thought so, the deep water was clear and she could see herself from her toes to the patch of red curls swaying lazily in concert with the soothing current between her thighs. She wondered about that.

Bath times were from 8:00 AM until 8:00 PM seven days a week and usually lasted ten or fifteen minutes. Emma's bath time began at seven and lasted the full hour. She liked taking her bath. The room was never as bright as hers and was warm, except in the summer when Tommy would open the window and make the water not so hot. On bath night she was also allowed to pee one extra time.

She didn't like the hallways, especially the one that led to her room. They were long and green and the floors looked wet and slippery even when they were dry. They smelled awful, like the doctor's office, like the times they washed her room when she was gone. That was the only time she didn't love her room. Nor did she like the big room where she ate her two meals. She liked eating alone and being alone. She saw that the other women didn't like her, sneering at her, pointing at her. What she did like was that Tommy would often stay and watch her eat supper, the evenings he brought her clean gowns.

She held his hand tightly once in the hall. She didn't like seeing the end that was so far away, or the rows of ominous lights on the high ceiling above, one over every door. She didn't like the small squares of tinted glass she thought were pasted to every door like hers, or the empty eyes peering through them at the sound of Tommy's footfalls thumping along the floor, the dark grey faces pressed against the glass so that one eye could see into the hall to watch her passing by.

The bathroom was different. The door had no window. Inside was a toilet, a sink, a gurney and a shower inside a stall with no curtain. In the corner, by the window, was a bath with legs shaped like thick, gaudy seashells. The piping was open, the ancient brass discoloured. The faucets had achieved the same condition over time, the yellowed white porcelain scarred with black pot marks where the thin veneer had chipped away.

She looked at him, her eyes bright. Her bath was a time she could be happy. The water was clear. She smiled her delight and Tommy locked the door behind him.

Sometimes, she remembered, she thought so, the times she was allowed to pee, Tommy would wait outside the door in the hallway. That was then. Now he did not. He stood inside with her, in case someone would want to come in. And that way, he would tell her, she would have more time because no one would know she was outside her room. He was considerate that way.

There were more places to pee than to bathe and although the rooms were as small as closets Tommy would make certain she was safe. She was in his care and sometimes Tommy would also relieve himself when she was finished.

The first time she thought what he was doing was funny with whatever the thing was. She thought so. And one time, longer ago than last week, he let her touch what she thought was a big finger, which she thought was silly, happy that she didn't have one the same. And she told him so. She had long ago forgotten her father altogether.

She remembered, at first, whenever that was, not that she cared, that Tommy would sit in a chair watching her bathe, and that he would talk with her. Later, he explained, because she had already seen his pee-thing, which was good because they were friends, and that he was seeing her taking her bath, that she should see him. So that she wouldn't be nervous, and he gave her a candy. That night, and for many nights, he stood in the shower watching her as she sat, kneeled, rolled and splashed in the water. He enjoyed taking pictures.

She wasn't afraid. She was happy having a friend, someone who didn't look at her with bad eyes or laugh at her like the other women who sometimes tried to touch her boobies or pull at her gown to her see her secret red hair. The other women didn't like her and she didn't like them. She liked Tommy. He told her things. No one else ever spoke with her. She could ask him things, like why she had hair at the top of her legs and why his pee-thing was different from hers. He showed her why no one else should ever see under her private red curls, what would happen to any man who would see that part of her because she was so pretty.

From her bath that first night of revelation, seeing what he had waited so long for her to see, what was happening to him, to his pee-thing, he longed to be with her.

Sometimes he sat in his chair, though he preferred to stand in the shower, stepping out every so often to take pictures. Until the time, last month or the year before that, or maybe soon after she arrived, he wanted to wash her hair unlike before and she felt him behind her, in the water, stroking her hair and her back. She wasn't afraid at all.

She untied the strings at her neck and her waist, letting the gown drop to the floor. She knew she would leave with one that was clean. She went to the toilet and when she was finished she sank herself into the hot and unscented water.

Those hours always went so quickly. She liked the touch of his hands, the way he cupped her boobies, pulling her back against him, pulling at her little pink crowns, the way he would let her sit on his legs, touching their noses, her body swaying dreamily with the gentle rush of the water, or facing away when he would run his hands over her bum, searching every part of her, lingering, closing his eyes. Or when her bath time was almost over, the way he would guide her onto her knees, the way he felt, the way she felt, the way she often had to take deep breaths and stop her toes from curling. She couldn't like anyone as much as she liked Tommy. She didn't think so.

Tommy climbed from the bath at 7:50, drying and dressing as the tub drained. He knew the nurse was fully aware of his times alone with Emma, the candies, the same way he knew of her frequent intimacies with one female patient in particular who was off limits to him. He took his time. When he was done he went to Emma who was standing in the tub, dripping, smiling, patting what she'd known for a while was a source of well-being when she was alone with her eyes closed to the dark.

When she was dry, her hair combed out, he kissed her. She was, after all, his girlfriend. In her room he gave her more candies, unwrapping each one, sitting on her bed, watching her suck them one at a time until she wanted another as she stood smiling down at him. She liked Tommy. She liked him very much, wanting him to stay a while longer. Her body was tingling and she hated the dark. She wanted to close her eyes to the light, not for her room to be dark, to make herself feel the way Tommy had shown her.

She folded her gown at the foot of her bed and lay by his side with her eyes closed.

*

That evening was in mid-April. Emma's bed was made up with a single top sheet and Tommy wasn't expecting to stay. When he did leave near 10:00 to flip the switch that would darken the rooms and most of the corridor on the third floor where Emma lived, he took the candy wrappers with him. In his mind they were lovers. In Emma's mind she somehow knew that Tommy would always come to her to bathe her, to make her heart beat faster and to make her body warm.

As for the other women whom he considered not quite as pretty as Emma, he continued to visit them in their rooms with his camera and candies and to bathe them from outside the tub on his knees so that he could help wash their hair and make certain they were clean in all places. Yet none was as lovely as Emma. They were older, in their twenties and thirties. They knew why Tommy came to see them, to give them candies, to comfort them, to make them feel good once they took their medication. Besides, he wasn't ugly or mean and they had nothing else to do, no one else to pretend with.

Tommy was good for them, a frequent escape from a dismal world where the living often wished they were dead.

Four
Doctor Zeke Phillips

Doctor Philips owned the institute, leaving the day-to-day operation of the three-floor complex to his administrator.

He was late fifties, tall, and gaunt. His skin was pallid, his eyes sunken and streaked with thread-thin red lines most of the time. His nose was long and narrow, his nostrils thin with thick gardens of coarse hair that were long one week and cut short the next. The hair on his head was an orangey-yellow, completing a wrongful depiction of who he was and what he might be that was cadaverous at the best of times. He was also single and wealthy, the beneficiary of old money, money dug from the ground by hard labour and sweat, his future secured by virtue of a German's true aim and a bullet delivered precisely to the centre of his father's uncovered head.

Part of his wealth was a parcel of land of some 100 acres on the shores of the Hudson and a convent left abandoned since the Sisters of Charity years earlier fell victim to a world deficient in what they believed.

The Phillips Institute was privately managed on behalf of the state, established some thirty years earlier when society, or those who controlled the minority who constituted the lowest common denominator of society, decided in law that not all criminals were insane. Truth be told, more space was desperately needed in prisons for the true criminal mind. Lunatics and social misfits of the day, those who existed nowhere save in their own dark and clouded worlds, were an inconvenience as much as they were an expense. No one was quite certain what to do with them. No one wanted to deal with them, except a young doctor who came forth with a plan, a man who in no way concurred with the consensus of the day.

No, Doctor Zeke Phillips declared, these still feeble minds could not yet be set free to meld with or deal with the suspicions and fears of a society not yet cured of its own pre- and post-war paranoia in a country where neighbours remained uncertain of neighbours, cautious of every word they spoke. But yes, he assured them, one day each man and woman under his care would find a new home, live a new life, once probed by modern techniques, his and her aberrant minds understood and altered, his and her failed human condition corrected for all time.

Science and psychology were emerging hand in hand from the ignorance of dark years into an époque of enlightenment. This when a much younger Doctor Phillips believed he could make a difference, that he could rid the human subconscious of private demons or implant reality where only fantasies existed.

Work on the convent began a week later.

Now he knew differently, certain in his own conscience mind that demons could never be suppressed or expunged, equally convinced that fantasies were, without the slightest doubt, if not a cure against demons, the human psyche's single defence against such intrusions. All he could do was take notes, write and submit reports. The brilliant career he had once studied toward and envisioned diminished by those he had once hoped to set free. Now he laboured for no other reason than to fill the void that was his life.

He was, in point of fact, the headmaster of a school without learning for the incurable...with one possible exception.

The good doctor's research was funded by the state whose examiner was a good and close friend who often summered at Phillips' country estate: one thousand dollars each week per patient, tax-free, for clothing, food, basic amenities and comfort, the man's bi-annual report largely based on Phillips' considered findings and conclusions. The closest the bureaucrat ever came to the institute was to the front gate from which vantage he was able to evaluate the condition of the property which the state had agreed years earlier to maintain, being that the residents of the institute were wards of the state under the doctor's care and not private patients.

Phillips saw each patient every other week for thirty minutes, noting the constant battle between their progress and their regression, a few of whom had been with him since day one. On occasion patients did leave the institute, freed of their malaise, their troubled minds purged of horrid spectres, in a hearse, delivered without ceremony, tears or regret to nameless graves marked by wooden crosses in a place without trees where others would not have to worry about their loved ones sleeping forever with the souls of mindless ghouls. And on those occasions, without any delay or ceremony, another resident would inevitably arrive.

Of course he had his favorites, a certain few whose evaluations he looked forward to: some of the older men, some of the younger women, without exception following their bath time when they were cleansed. However those who were bathed at night would see him in the morning.

The male orderlies were all young by necessity. Strength was a prerequisite for the job and what healthy man could accompany any young woman, despite her obvious deficiency, to her bath without looking or wanting to touch her? He knew very well that certain of the orderlies, at least the most senior, took advantage of the younger female patients. To dismiss such encounters from his mind would be to his discredit, though he had little choice other than to accept what he knew to be true.

Female orderlies were impossible to recruit, potential

candidates invariably scared off by what they witnessed and what they had heard. So what was he to do but expect a certain amount of innocent touching? Nor was he oblivious to the fact that relationships would without doubt develop over time. Nor did he see a problem with coital interaction given the proper safeguards and requisite discretion, never once questioning a patient or orderly as to the possibility of such informal occurrences.

Urgent and spontaneous need anywhere would most often trump regulation while suppressing rationale.

More importantly, not one of his patients received visitors. So what was the harm? What mattered was that the patients were calm and that the younger ones amongst the female population were content, that they were happy. That was the real human condition and he suspected that Tommy Dune was no better than any other. If anything he had probably and regularly been much worse. He was the most senior, most of his subordinates not lasting more than a year or two on the job. He was the most senior by reason of his never having left and the good doctor suspected that Tommy had his reasons.

He hadn't been hired for his intellect. That he would never aspire to any but the lowest of expectations was obvious from any distance. He was given the job because no one else had applied and the tightly run institute was understaffed.

But this particular situation Phillips never expected. Why now? Why after all these years, and right in the middle of summer vacations? He didn't need the aggravation or the undue stress. He dropped the girl's file on his desk. Phillips never lost his composure, a character flaw that would have disastrous consequences amongst so many frail minds.

He seldom remained in his office past five. However this day in July he did, instructing his secretary to summon Orderly Dune to his first-floor sanctum. He wasn't happy. He didn't want to lose Dune. The man followed instructions and never complained despite being more important in his own narrow mind than in Phillips'. But the doctor had to do something. Even with his well-cemented connections and good friends he wouldn't explain his way out of this. The choice was entirely Dune's as was the consequence.

*

"Sit down, Tommy."

Phillips poured a brandy, one.

Tommy Dune was smiling. He liked the doctor, his saviour, the man who pulled him from the gutter. Being invited to sit with him in his office was a rare privilege.

"Good afternoon, sir. Thank you for thinking of me. I hope you had a good weekend."

"Thinking of you, is that right?" Phillips examined his snifter, swirling the liquid, sighing a deep breath, sitting side-saddle on the edge of his desk. "I've been thinking of you since Friday morning and, no, I did not have a good weekend at all."

"I'm sorry, sir."

"Sorry, you say. Indeed, sorry about my lost weekend or sorry that one of your charges is currently with child?" He reached for the file. "Miss Emma Rose, a girl who believes that butterflies are angels, a girl who dances with fairies in her room, making music without singing in an otherwise capricious head, a girl who believes her pubic hair is intended to conceal her vagina from the leering eyes of men, lest like magic they become, what did she say, like a stick. Miss Emma Rose, youthful in body and mind, is now three months pregnant." He sipped the amber liquid, pleased. "Would you care to explain that one?" He sipped more brandy, giving the red flush on Tommy's face time to ripen, studying the instant machinations erupting in a frantic mind behind eyes too filled with shock to blink. "And don't think to bullshit me, Tommy. In five years, excluding your time off, you alone have been her primary caregiver beyond serving her breakfast or lunch, the one orderly whose care she's enjoyed or tolerated in quiet desperation. Not one other entry from any other orderly exists in her file. Why is that?"

"There is no quiet desperation, sir. No, that's not Emma. Sir, I don't understand what's happening here. There must be some mistake. She's pregnant? She's our youngest charge. The same way I was the youngest orderly when Emma first came to us, when I already had three years of experience on the job, three years of solid training and guidance from you, sir. I did what I thought was best. I knew she was afraid, that she needed someone more her age to care for her. She felt good with me, almost right away, like we had a common bond. You know the turnover here is bad, sir, and Emma doesn't like new faces. She doesn't like men."

"With one notable exception, or is there something about pregnant that's a mystery to you?"

"No sir."

"Tommy, I shall be interviewing the other orderlies based on this discussion. So please choose your words well. The last thing I want is to involve the police."

Tommy Dune's chin sank into his chest. He wasn't smart enough or quick enough to invent a plausible lie. He was what he was. He needed his job.

"Sir, please believe me, I was only with her that way once. I didn't mean for anything to happen. And, sir, for a short time she wasn't a patient. I could see the difference in her eyes. We shared something special."

"Spare me the details. I'm more concerned about what you were seeing through your eyes, and how frequently."

"One time, sir, I swear."

"So you're admitting to raping a pretty young girl on a whim."

"She's of age, Doctor Phillips. She's legal. Technically it's not rape. She consented."

"You might have an arguable point, Tommy, were it not

for the contents of her file which indicate the girl is incapable of coherent thought, that she lives in a fantasy world."

"What we did, I don't know, seemed so natural. And, sir, I've never seen her so peaceful. I could tell that in her mind she was in another place and time."

"Possibly because you over medicated her with malicious intent. And make no mistake, Tommy. What you did to the girl is most assuredly rape. That is precisely how I view your ill judgement and that's how the newspapers undoubtedly will, and the police, that you intentionally raped and abused a mentally deficient girl in your care, that you availed yourself of the poor creature's innocence, stealing her virginity, the one possession that was hers to cherish in her miserable world. This isn't good, Tommy. The reason our female patients wear gowns and nothing else is not to facilitate sexual intercourse with our staff."

Tommy was frightened. Remaining calm was impossible. Rape carried a severe prison term and cons didn't take kindly to rapists or child molesters and he'd done both. That any normal man would have done the same wouldn't matter.

"It wasn't that way, sir. Things happen. Because she's different, that doesn't mean she doesn't have feelings. Times have changed. I didn't rape her. Our feelings were mutual."

"Mutual, you say. A weak defence at best. Spontaneous for you, possibly, which I feel inclined to disbelieve at this point. Not so for Emma Rose, and certainly not mutual. What you saw in her eyes, if anything at all, for I daresay your preoccupations lay elsewhere, was simply a response to a heretofore unknown sensation. She has no understanding that she's been here five years, which is more likely our doing than her lack of cognizance. What she doesn't see doesn't exist. When she doesn't see you, you don't exist. When she doesn't see me, I don't exist."

Phillips went to refill his snifter. "In truth, what need has she to recall the events of today when they will in no way differ from the events of tomorrow? With that in mind, Tommy, I must strongly advise that you contemplate contacting legal counsel. This institute will not in any way intercede on your behalf. We must, you understand, distance ourselves from such unabashed wrongdoing. Or must I remind you of the contract you signed, asserting that you are of sound mind and good intent?"

"I've been a good employee, sir, reliable since my first day. I can't afford to lose my job. This is all I know. I didn't rape her." Tommy clasped his hands together. "I couldn't rape her, not the way I feel about her."

"The way you feel about her. Let's leave that one alone, shall we? What's more likely is the way you felt with her. You and I know what you did, and why. The girl's a beautiful airhead, a vulnerable waif in a universe she doesn't comprehend or, better said, in a world that doesn't comprehend her. If she were wealthy, she would be eccentric, whimsical. However she is not rich, so she's borderline insane, a danger to herself, supposedly, which I intend forthwith to determine more accurately. And you're probably the envy of every orderly in here on her bath night or whenever you choose to entertain yourself with her. To propose that you molested her on a single occasion after five years when she is so readily availability to you is preposterous." Phillips went to the high-back leather chair behind his desk, sitting pensively, rubbing the crystal snifter between his open palms. "You're not losing your job, Tommy. You're good at what you do, and you're reliable. You do as you're told. You follow procedure. Or you gave me cause to believe that you did. We need you here. That said; you have caused me to lose faith in you. A faith you must now work diligently to restore to its previously high level. What did you possibly imagine I could do with a pregnant girl, not to mention the resultant child? And were anyone to learn that I aborted the girl, I would certainly have to hang myself. I would be ruined." He sipped his brandy. "Do you begin to comprehend the issues at hand, Tommy?"

"Sir, I have no family. All I've ever wanted is to make you proud of me. No one else has ever cared about me the way you do."

"I asked you when you came in here not to spread the bullshit, Tommy, and in this brief time we're up to our knees. So let's cut the crap, shall we? What I will now tell you, Tommy, is the considered end result of my weekend spent thinking of you, which was unpleasant in the extreme. Please understand, Tommy. This is not an order, merely a suggestion to better serve a mutual dilemma caused by you, one that you must seriously contemplate this evening. You must also contemplate the singular alternative."

"Sir, I don't understand. I want to."

"First, in effect immediately, you will no longer take responsibility for Emma Rose's care. She is no longer in your charge. I also discovered upon closer review of your reports a telling fact which I either previously overlooked or ignored, which is that you have an indisputable preference for working with our young women. For that reason you are forthwith reassigned to the morning shift and forbidden from interacting with Emma Rose other than in the company of other staff upon pain of dismissal and arrest for her rape. You will also, beginning immediately, advance your career by removing your youngest patients from your duty roster and replacing them with the oldest residents of the institute regardless of gender or age. Perhaps washing the aged will assist you in diminishing your carnal appetite. To that end, your previous patients will, in the very near future, be examined for any impropriety. In short, Tommy, to you and all others who may have offended, they are off limits and I shall be taking measures to see that they are."

Tommy's instincts cautioned him not to react to the

affront. "Sir, I understand. You're punishing me for what Emma and I did together. I swear, though, I have never touched those other women. But Emma, she won't like that. She won't like someone else caring for her. She'll regress. And, sir, I wasn't Emma's first. "

"Emma cannot regress, quite simply because she has never advanced. I spent the entire day Friday with her. She is here, Tommy, because no one knew what else to do with her. Her single fault is naïveté and youthful exuberance. She merely seems the way she does because she has nothing good to remember and, in her mind, this is her life, her yesterday, her today and her tomorrow, which to her is the same without the slightest delineation. Though I daresay, with all due respect, Tommy, the girl is much brighter than you."

Tommy thought his head might explode. No way was the girl smarter than him. "Sir, you're losing me."

"Simply put, you raped her in my house. She wasn't your charge, she's mine. They all are. You might well go to prison for your deviant behaviour, however I would suffer the severest repercussions and I would prefer that not happen. In short, Tommy, no legal reason exists or can be argued for Emma Rose to endure further confinement within these walls. Nor can I possibly explain her condition without, in turn, explaining your irrefutable participation which, according to her files, would make you decidedly guilty of raping a poor, psychologically disadvantaged girl. You see my quandary. You get the picture." He put up his hand, beginning to tire of the interview. "Emma Rose is quite sane, Tommy, guilty of a fanciful mind better suited to a more forgiving and tolerant world which we are beginning to grow into. Emma Rose will have her child off campus, so to speak, with you, her husband, in your home where you will live happily ever after. Or she will have her baby here and you will spend the next fifteen years in a cell applying anti-inflammatory creams to a ruptured... Well, need I be graphic? You are quite handsome, Tommy, and in remarkably good shape. I daresay you would make some fellow a desirable cellmate."

Tommy coughed, practically whining. "Sir, you want me to marry her?"

"No, Tommy. You want to marry her because you have a common bond, the way you feel about her, the way you feel about each other. Of course I will spend the next several days modifying her file accordingly, to reflect a gradual improvement in her condition sufficient to warrant her release. As will you with my supervision. The wording must be precise. Emma Rose has lived here these past five years because nobody wants her, for no other reason, her dossier composed by me to substantiate a condition that does not exist. I simply had no choice. Can we for a moment imagine the cruel existence she would have lived on the street at the hands of vagabonds and malfeasants?" Phillips despised himself for the lie. He swirled the amber liquid. "That the question is rhetorical goes without saying, the answer all too unimaginable: a desperate and unenviable one as you well know by memory of your own formative years. So, yes, Tommy, very shortly you will have lovely Emma Rose to yourself, and her baby…your baby."

"Sir, Doctor Phillips, this can't be real."

"Emma Rose is perfectly fine. Her single dilemma is her lack of education and I am quite certain that eventually she will see fit to amend the insufficiency. I find the girl quite delightful. Had I been much younger at the time, and married, I would have adopted her myself. I can't imagine why her mother, in the absence of her father, would ever have thought to commit her to these dungeons lest they be deficient themselves. So you see, Tommy. Not only did you rape the girl, you set her free. And what do you mean to imply, that you are not Emma's first?"

"Sir, that first night she didn't cry or act afraid. She was weeping gently. She was calm, like she was expecting me. I thought she would be afraid, but she wasn't, not once. She was smiling, sir, because I was gentle and, sir, Doctor Phillips, when I left her, she said 'goodnight, daddy'."

"That despicable news doesn't surprise me, Tommy. I never met the man, a convenient oversight on my part and the mother's, despite having his signature on file. So Emma Rose does have memory, albeit well-contained. Very interesting, very much so, as is your Freudian slip regarding your first intrusion into her innocence, which, to me, implies a second, third, and many more illicit visits whether prior to or subsequent to her fertilization...or both, which I believe is more representative of the truth and entirely reprehensible." Phillips couldn't resist a telling smirk. "How intuitive of the girl, in retrospect, that she should call you daddy."

"Sir, I don't even have a girlfriend. What do I know about being married, about babies?"

"I daresay you've likely never needed a girlfriend Tommy, not with the abundance of available female companions and desirable attributes here at the institute. Nor will you, not unless you relish an immediate cessation of your freedom. However you do now have a fiancée, a very lovely one." Phillips leaned forward onto his desktop, crossing his arms. "Emma Rose will be released on the first of September, released into your care by our agreement, although officially, as determined and signed by me, she will not require you or anyone else as her guardian. She shall be responsible unto herself and you will be married the following Saturday, four months prior to your acquisition of a son or daughter. Let me be the first to congratulate you, Mr. Dune."

"Sir, please don't do this." Tommy's mind was racing. He was leaning forward, mimicking his boss. He was desperate. "Listen, I could take her over the weekend to another city, or tomorrow. I've never once taken a sick day. No one would have to know about the abortion, or that she even left here. You don't have to release her, sir. She can stay at the institute. She's happy here. She's content. She doesn't know better. If you would let me take her out for a day or two this would go away. Who would know?"

"Tommy, I do what I do not for the money, rather to fill my days, which wasn't my original motive years ago. By my own admission I have allowed myself to incrementally become jaded by what I do, detached from my once single-minded determination to make a difference. However I find what you just said quite contemptible. Emma Rose does not belong here. She's here because at fourteen she was considered difficult, unmanageable, quite unsuited to fostering, and now that she has passed her majority she is even less desirable as a daughter. She is completely competent, yet by virtue of her incarceration here and her tender age, unable to live on her own. You are her way out. You don't have a choice in the matter and, furthermore, if you choose to decline my offer of freedom in lieu of incarceration, I will this very day begin interviewing each of your previous charges to ascertain the degree to which other delinquencies have taken place…in conjunction, of course, with the police. I daresay the findings will be quite interesting."

"You don't believe that Emma is my one and only mistake."

"No, I do not. Despite our turnover, that you have systematically availed yourself of our youngest and prettiest patients is disgraceful and I hold myself in the highest contempt for not previously perceiving your intent."

"I just can't take her home, just like that. She hasn't been outside in five years. She has no clothes and I live in a bachelor. I can't do this, Doctor Phillips."

"Ah, but you will. As I have said, I spent the weekend ruminating over your predicament, which is now mine thanks to you. I will advance you six months' salary, Tommy, as well as your year-end bonus, reducing your paycheque by fifty percent over the next twelve months which should allow you to seek out more suitable living quarters. As for Emma Rose, until her departure date I will take her personally under my wing. She will leave with me at day's end and return to the institute with me each morning. She will learn to dress herself and enjoy a new wardrobe. She will learn to bathe herself and to sit properly at a table with proper utensils. Until then you will meet with her regularly each Friday in the garden by my window when your shift has concluded and prior to her weekend."

"I want to be sick, sir. This isn't right. What you're doing is wrong, for me and for her."

"Which clearly implies that what you told me a few moments ago is untrue, that you do not like the girl, you simply wanted something as yet untouched...the warmth of virgin flesh." Phillips drained his glass. "Either way, Tommy, the girl goes free. I've decided that much in her favour. The questions are: where do you go, how quickly and for how long? Please understand; I am not releasing Emma Rose from here to live in the squalor of a dilapidated tenement. She will live comfortably with a husband of long duration, or until she chooses otherwise of her own accord. To that end I will maintain an ongoing interest in her well-being and at the first sign of a sudden flight from responsibility on your part I will most assuredly press charges on behalf of the institute. I owe the girl that much."

"This is a lot to digest, sir." Tommy paused, slouching into his seat, rubbing his face hard. "Okay, I'll do it."

"That's excellent, Tommy. I had no doubt that you would and I anticipate receiving my invitation to the wedding very shortly. I shall be mailing them out in a few days. I suppose your parents won't wish to attend, or any of your co-workers as I expect they shall be somewhat displeased with you very shortly. Once they hear of certain new safeguards in the planning as a result of your indiscretion. Do you have friends you would care to invite?"

"No sir. I'm thinking something fast, like a judge instead of something religious. I don't believe in anything like that."

"A good choice, Tommy, and equally binding on your part. I would say a far better venue for standing before an officer of the court to hear the verdict read aloud. Indeed a life sentence without any chance of parole, at least while I remain alive, Tommy, though much more agreeable in so many ways. Don't you agree?"

Tommy nodded, exhausted. "Yeah, I do."

Phillips glanced at his watch. "Thank you, Tommy, for doing what is right. I'll make the arrangements and keep you apprised."

"Does she know…that she's pregnant, that we're getting married?"

"She does not. I am aware of her condition, as is the nurse, and you know. That's it. That's it, Tommy. Understood?"

"Who would I tell?"

"Good boy. Emma Rose will learn of her new dual status this evening at dinner with me, as my guest, as she enjoys the first of her new wardrobe and the strangeness of fine dining. And if I might anticipate an obvious thought forming in your mind, Tommy, my home is well-equipped to ensure her privacy during her bath and after. I have no intention of misusing the girl. Nor will she any longer interact with other female patients during the morning group time or at lunch. She will spend her mornings in the garden, where she is at this very moment, or in my private study relearning the basics of reading and writing, relearning everything she's forgotten while incarcerated here. Her instruction begins tomorrow under the tutelage of a good friend. And you must understand this; your limited time with her at week's end will be closely scrutinized from this very window. As I have said, the girl is now free…either way." Phillips stood. "Good day, Tommy."

Five
Thirty-two Years Ago

That Monday Emma ate breakfast in her room, on her bed, her legs crossed, puzzled, yet unconcerned that she was alone and not with forty other women. She ate lunch on the floor of her room where she thought she would stay, waiting to pull her gown away from her legs to feel the warmth of the sun. That didn't happen and the man who opened her door was not Tommy Dune.

He took her from the room she loved and led her along the corridor she didn't like for the last time, down the stairs and along the first floor to a bathroom where she began to untie her gown thinking her bath time had come, curious that the room was bright with sunlight when she was accustomed to bathing at night with Tommy when, most times, there wasn't any light in the window. Yet this man was telling her not to undress and she saw no water in the tub, no fresh gown on the wooden chair painted white.

He left when the nurse came in. Neither one was smiling, neither one spoke. The orderlies never smiled and she didn't like the nurse. When the man was gone Emma went to the gurney. She pulled herself onto the cold stainless steel and lay back to stare at the ceiling. She tugged her gown to her waist and opened her legs. That's what the nurse always wanted her to do. That's why she didn't like the nurse, but doing what the nurse told her made her life more pleasant because sometimes the nurse wasn't nice. She didn't think so. And she was never to tell Tommy, the woman told her each time, or Tommy would be angry with her and never again bring her candy. The nurse never gave her candy.

This time, however, the nurse didn't touch her that way, instructing her instead to sit properly and to remove her gown.

That Monday afternoon Emma was dressed in new jeans, sneakers, socks and a bright red raglan sweater. For the first time in five years she slipped into new panties and struggled into a bra with the help of the nurse. Her normally straight red hair was clipped into a ponytail with a plastic barrette and she was fascinated by the white leather band of her new watch.

She spent what remained of the afternoon in the garden, caressing the manicured grass, pressing her palms against the rough bark of the huge oak, inhaling the scent of Doctor Phillips' prized tulips and lying on her back to gaze at a single cloud in an otherwise bright blue sky.

Doctor Phillips went to her at five once he was finished with Tommy Dune and sat with her for a while, explaining to Emma that she was leaving, that she had proven herself capable, certain he was doing what was right and pleased with the way she looked in her outfit. The more pertinent details could wait for a more propitious occasion.

The last time she'd driven in a car was the day she arrived at the institute, afraid of what was happening to her. Now she wasn't afraid. She'd spent five seamless years being told what to do, discovering not too many days or weeks after her arrival the futility of arguing or crying; now he was telling her that she was leaving. So she left with him and listened quietly as they drove the short distance to his home, turning her head this way and that in wonder. When they arrived he waited for her to decide when to go in and when she did he let her wander and touch whatever she wanted.

A bachelor throughout his life Phillips was an adequate

cook, though not once had he thought to entertain at home on his own, engaging a catering service when he did. His home was his private place. Instead he ordered a pizza which Emma wanted to eat on the living room floor with her ice-cold glass of Coke and her legs crossed, her eyes glued to the television.

When the last bite was swallowed, her second glass empty on the floor, he gave her another tour of his home, taking her into each room and finally into her room where she saw her bed and her private bathroom. Both were very clean, she thought so, though neither one smelled of harsh disinfectant. She went to her bed, glancing over her shoulder at him, smiling when he smiled. She pressed her hands against the mattress, twirled, and let herself fall backwards with her arms stretched into the air.

She had no reason to hurry. She had not one pillow; she had two that were thick and soft, and beside them was a teddy bear that she adopted immediately.

He pointed to the dresser, suggesting that she look into the drawers. She did. Then he opened the closet, where she saw dresses and sweaters and shoes. She went to where he stood, stepped inside and touched each one as though each piece had feelings.

In the bathroom were a toothbrush and toothpaste with red stripes that made her giggle. She'd forgotten what a comb and brush set was. Or had she ever known. She didn't think so as she tried each one. By the tub, on a small table with wheels, she saw oils, salts and shampoo in a plastic bottle she could see through, inverting the bottle, seeing the minute bubbles float upward to the bottom, tracing the path of the biggest bubble with the tip of her finger.

Again he let her wander and touch as he set about pouring her bath, adding a capful of oil, somewhat shocked when he turned at hearing the toilet flush to see that she was sitting unabashedly on the toilet without her sweater, her jeans and panties bunched at her ankles, working to push them past her sneakers.

Tommy Dune flashed across his mind as he knelt on one knee in front of her, helping to set one foot free, then the other, tugging at both her pant legs at once, hearing her giggle, expelling from his mind the last time he'd undressed a woman. He pulled away one sock, then the other, taking her hands and helping her to stand. His heart skipped a beat. Seeing her that way wasn't right. Yet he knew in his mind and his heart that his intentions were pure. He unclasped her bra, telling her in a gentle yet firm voice that from that moment on she would bathe and undress in private, though he could not deny the girl was well-formed and difficult to ignore. She was not at the institute, he told her. Those days were over. She once again had the unequivocal right to ask questions and say no.

Her parents were inconceivably cruel, he mused, to so callously abandon such a lovely and delightful child for no other reason than her buoyant innocence and boundless imagination. Or had they? Now that he suspected what was likely the vile truth. Quite possibly Mrs. Rose wasn't entirely candid when first they met, choosing to commit an innocent daughter rather than see a guilty husband sent to prison for the most loathsome of criminal actions and, in so doing, giving up whatever security he might provide her. Who, then, was the worst offender? Clearly they each deserved the worst possible life.

He helped Emma into the tub as best he could without seeing more than he had of a flawless female nude. When she was settled he walked from the room pointing to her towel on the rack and her robe, saying that he would be downstairs in the parlour if she cared to join him to watch television. Passing first though her bedroom, he went to the dresser to select a pair of pyjamas and placed them by the teddy bear.

An hour later he returned to her room, concerned that she might be timid, uncertain of what he might expect, or of what she might expect. She was fast asleep in her bed, her jeans and her sweater, her panties and bra folded neatly by her socks and her sneakers at the foot of her bed, her head buried snuggly into the pillows.

Emma Rose was content in her sleep, nose to nose with her new fluffy friend, the room softly lit by lamps on either side of her bed. He left them on, padding quietly to the bathroom. The tub was empty and clean, the towel returned to its proper place. Then he knew; he had done what was right. He left her door ajar and went to his bed.

*

The next morning he noticed that Emma had closed the door. He called her for breakfast without hearing an answer. He called her again, and a third time before climbing the staircase and tapping his knuckles lightly against the door. Again she didn't answer, and when he stepped in she was sitting in her pyjamas on the window sill. She had turned out her lights and was weeping quietly, murmuring secret thoughts that were unclear from where he stood. He knew from her file that she hadn't wept once, not since her first few days at the institute.

Bathed by the sun she was radiant, much too good for the likes of Tommy Dune, he harboured no doubt. Yet what choice did he have? She could not remain long-term in his home. He had no means of caring for a baby, let alone the inevitable enquiry he would undoubtedly undergo regarding the undeniable coincidence between her unforeseen recovery, when she was expected to live out her life at the institute, and his incongruous largesse towards her.

*

Emma woke once through the night, believing that she was dreaming. Her room was softly lit and her door was open. She wasn't lying under a thin sheet, curled into a tight ball for extra warmth; she was floating on a soft, warm mattress under a sheet, a blanket and a comforter. She threw back her covers and went to the bathroom where she sat to pee, scanning the room. She hadn't done that by herself in such a long time. She hadn't been dreaming at all. She didn't think so. She did smell of sweet flowers and her skin was so smooth. She patted herself dry and went to the mirror. Much better, she mused, than seeing her face always speckled with raindrops in the window. She was pretty. She hadn't seen her face so clearly for such a long while.

She went to the dresser where she opened all the drawers, taking her teddy bear with her. She went to her closet, pressing each fabric to her cheeks. Nothing was coarse and nothing was faded. She went to the door and closed herself into the room, closing out the dim yellow lighting from the hallway. In bed she lay facing her new little friend, the lights on, not wanting to sleep. She wanted to see him. She had a lot to talk over, hoping she would never wake up.

But she did, the sun shining through her window, her issues unresolved, remembering the previous day in the doctor's garden. Such a strange feeling, she told herself, to have something to remember. Or was she asleep in her room, dreaming of the day before, the pizza, the Coke, and her soft cozy bed? Suddenly she couldn't be certain and pinched herself, which didn't do any good at all. What if she was pinching herself in a dream?

She slid from under the covers, staring at the closed door, the door she'd closed herself. When had she last closed a door herself? She didn't know or didn't remember. She was hungry and wondered who would bring in her meal. Scanning the bedroom and the world through the window for as far as she could see from her perch, she no longer liked her room at the institute. She didn't think so. She wanted to stay where she was, inside her dream that didn't have a single one-eyed face to make her afraid.

She knew it wasn't true, that she didn't have things to remember. She just didn't say that she did. Why would she? Who would believe her now when no one did then? She did.

She remembered things, things that happened so long ago. Or she had, once, for a short time: the arguments, the screaming voices, the pushing, dragged to her room without any supper, looking to her father for help, incurring a heartless slap when what she wanted from her mother was a loving embrace. She remembered her father, in the dark, when later he came to her room to comfort her, to make her feel better, to make her feel good, warning her not to tell her mother because her mother really did hate her and that he was the one who truly did love her. She remembered. She remembered his voice and his breath. She did, until they faded from her memory at last. Or had they died and somehow she knew that they were dead. She thought so.

She remembered the last day, or she had for a while: a bright sunny day that was warm, without the slightest breeze, tears cascading down her cheeks, the strange man who wouldn't answer her questions holding one hand, and the stern, unsmiling woman the other. She remembered turning, at the car, searching through blurred eyes for her mother and seeing no one.

She remembered the gates, and how slowly they opened as though they wanted to scare her, to make her afraid, and the unsmiling men dressed all in white who took her from the car. She remembered them that first day, and Tommy who watched her undress and who took her clothes away without saying a word, and her favourite saddle shoes, her clean socks and her underwear.

She remembered that she had cried, that Tommy was seeing her naked and throwing her clothes into a bag, though not when she might have stopped crying. She remembered that Tommy had become like her father, in a way, though much nicer. She thought so, though she couldn't remember when exactly that was or might have been. Tommy never pushed her or covered her mouth in the dark. And when he did leave her room before the lights went out, she never felt sad, not like those times with her father. She remembered them all looking at her. She remembered her first gown opened from her neck to her bum, and the cold of the steel table on the back of her legs. She remembered the nurse and her hot breath that smelled.

She turned to the door, unafraid. People always came through her door.

*

"Emma, my girl, what's the matter. I've been calling you for breakfast. And why are you crying? This should be a happy time for you, without any question. You should be gleeful at the prospect of your newly found freedom."

She hadn't said a word since leaving her room the day before, Doctor Phillips seemingly unaffected by the need to maintain the one-sided conversation. She turned her attention to the window, ignoring her wet face, more intent on saying the words in a way that she thought was right. She didn't want to make him angry.

"No, Doctor Phillips."

"That's not quite a complete sentence, Emma. To what are you saying no?"

She remained as she was.

"No, I don't want to go back to the institute."

"But we must, so that you might begin to reacquaint yourself with the world and meet with Tommy this Friday. I assure you, you will return here with me each night without fail."

"This is the world, Doctor Phillips. Can you see everything that I can see? From my other room I can only see your big oak tree through thick bars when I stand on my bed and the windows are so dirty."

"Yes, indeed. Well, I assure you, we will return here together in a few hours to sit where you are or to do whatever you please."

She shook her head. "But not if you die. You're very old, Doctor Phillips. You can die and no one would know to bring me here. Who would take care of me then? What would happen to me then?" She pressed an open palm to the glass; the pane was warm from the morning sun. "Last night in the bathroom you said I could say no." With her other open palm she smeared her tears. "I want to stay here in my new clothes and sleep in my nice bed. I want to say no."

Phillips pondered the minor dilemma for a moment, conquering his uncharacteristic urge to chuckle, unaccustomed to acquiescence. Though, from the mouths of babes, he did feel very old now confronted by her youth.

"Indeed, Emma, I understand. And you are quite correct in asserting your right; I applaud your resolve despite your much appreciated concern for my premature passing. Of course you may stay here, in the short term because your destiny lies elsewhere. You have seen the institute for the last time. I daresay I have exceeded my time there as well. In that particular aspect of my life I envy you. Your tutoring will take place here beginning tomorrow. Today will be ours for shopping and lunch at an eatery of your choice. However may I first join you for a moment before our breakfast to explain a matter of urgent importance?"

Her eyes brightened, not her face. "I'm not going back, Doctor Phillips, not ever?"

He coughed, smiling. The girl was refreshing, though he couldn't suppress the barrage of worrisome thoughts and images assailing him. Had he been wrong all these years, so blind? Perhaps he was, though he was not prepared to accept any punitive judgement from within his own mind before further reflection. Or was Emma Rose an anomaly, a prisoner of her fanciful mind as much as she was a free soul confined by prejudice and fear? He had much to consider.

"No, my girl, you are not returning to your recent past, not today, not ever. You are meant to reside elsewhere in your life, to do other things. We all have our time, Emma, however long we must wait to accomplish our destinies. Today is yours…and breakfast awaits us. However first we must talk."

"Do you want me to take a bath first?"

"No, I do not. That practice was a matter of policy, regrettably without exception. Not every resident at the institute is as delightful as you were."

Emma slid onto the floor, grimacing, rubbing her backside. "My bum hurts. I've been sitting here for a long time. Do you ever sit in the window, Doctor Phillips?"

"I did once, as a boy, though not here and, as you have rightly determined, a very long time ago. I fear that now, to do so, I would find myself tempted to contemplate a more pragmatic application of the ledge despite its close proximity to the ground below. We all have our crosses to bear, Emma."

She furrowed her brow, unconcerned. "Is this when I should dress in my new clothes, before breakfast?"

"Yes indeed, though not at this precise moment. Dressing oneself is a private matter." He sat in a chair, leaning forward onto his elbows: his signature posture when conducting a therapy session, or a habit borne of a profession he'd grown to dislike. "Now, Emma, before our day begins I must talk with you about Tommy."

She went to the bed forgetting her hunger, wiggling into the centre, crossing her legs. "I like Tommy. Will he miss me? I think so. He was good to me, Doctor Phillips."

"Tommy treated you differently from other patients, Emma. He is very fortunate, as you are, that his deep feelings for you did not manifest at an earlier time as they have now."

"Doctor Phillips, I'm crazy, remember? What is manifest?"

"To my discredit, I have never thought of you as crazy. Eccentric, yes, without any doubt, and a slight possibility does exist that you are a danger to yourself in an uncaring world. But those possible few who would do you harm are the ones who deserve imprisonment, my girl, not you. Nor are they likely to ever cross your path. For that reason you are free to live and to make your own choices. However, of necessity, I must first make one important choice on your behalf. Let me get to manifest in a moment."

He paused, watching Emma dreamily caress her arms and her legs, most probably unaware of her smile, he thought.

"Can I wear my pyjamas all day?"

"You may wear them as soon as we arrive home, or whatever else you wish to wear." He took a moment to compose his thoughts, straightening; never once throughout his career considering that he would one day delve into such a difficult conversation with a patient, let alone in his home and in a bedroom. "Emma, at night when Tommy was with you, once, or more than once, he came to think of you more as a desirable young woman than a patient. I'm talking about one time or several that he joined with you in a familiar way, touching your body with his the way a husband joins with his wife. He might even have hurt you without meaning to. Sometimes…"

"You mean my bath time, don't you, Doctor Phillips, or in my room before the light went out. Tommy told me not to tell anyone, or else I could never feel that way again."

"Your bath time, Emma, what do you mean? And please tell me the truth. I won't be angry with Tommy whatever you tell me. I like Tommy also."

"Tommy always came into my bath with me; I think so," she shrugged, "for a long time, to make me feel good. I like Tommy, Doctor Phillips. He would bring me candies and clean gowns and sometimes he would stay with me after my bath until just before the light went out."

"You mean to say that he was in your bed, Emma? It's alright to tell me. I've spoken with Tommy. He is aware of our conversation. And, yes, he likes you too. He does miss you. So please tell me, Emma. Was he in your bed?"

"Yes."

"Many times?"

"Yes, I think so."

"Do you remember how often?"

She shook her head. "But, Doctor Phillips, I do remember that I feel good with Tommy." She shook her head again. "But I don't like the nurse with black hair. She doesn't hurt me, but she doesn't make me feel good like Tommy. Her mouth smells. She told me that I could never tell Tommy or she would send Tommy away because men are dirty."

Phillips grimaced. "Emma, that nurse, you're talking about when she would come to your room with your medication."

She nodded, hesitating, pursing her lips as though uncertain what to say, cupping her breasts. "Yes, many times. She likes to touch me here and I knew to lie down so she could see that I was clean under my gown." She made a face. "She doesn't touch me like Tommy, Doctor Phillips."

"Forget the nurse, Emma. Let me deal with her, which I will. I assure you. In the meantime Tommy is the more important issue. What he did to you was wrong, Emma, very wrong indeed. He knows that and now he wants to do something very good to correct his misjudgement. He wants to be with you all the time, Emma, forever. Do you understand what that means?"

She shook her head. "No, Doctor Phillips. I don't want to go back, not even for Tommy."

"And you will not. You know that. What I mean to say, Emma, is that he wants to marry you. He wants to become your husband. He wants to live with you in your own home, a comfortable home with a garden and trees. Unless you wish to invoke you right to once again say no. I will honour any decision you make."

"I will marry Tommy, Doctor Phillips, if you want me to. I know what that means."

"What I want is not the issue at all, Emma. What you desire is what matters. This is not my decision alone. You must be certain."

Her brow creased.

"Doctor Phillips…"

"What is it, my girl? You may ask or say anything. This is not a time to hide your feelings or hesitate to seek answers."

"Tommy never yells at me now. He never hurts me. But when he marries me he will. I think so. I remember, Doctor Phillips."

"Tell me what you remember, Emma. Take your time. Breakfast can wait a while longer."

She did take her time, reaching for her teddy bear, staring intently into its black plastic eyes; Phillips sitting patiently, watching, wondering what deep or dark thoughts were forming in her mind.

"Before the man and woman took me away, for a long time, I think so, they were yelling. My mother was yelling and my father was yelling because he liked to make me feel good like Tommy when I was tired and already in my bed to sleep. But my bed wasn't cozy like this one. I don't think so, and he didn't like to make my mother feel good. She was yelling at him that she wanted to know why." She hugged her bear. "That morning, I remember, Doctor Phillips. They were yelling and using bad words until he went to his work and when he was gone I came out from her room. I wanted to hold her hand because I knew I was going somewhere alone for a very long time and I was scared. I was crying, when I didn't want to cry. She was telling me to stop, but I was going to the institute and I didn't know what that was. Nobody told me. She didn't want to hold my hand and when they took me away she wasn't there. When I looked for her, she wasn't there. She was gone too. That's what I remember, that she wasn't there."

"How often did I probe, Emma, to understand what you remember or what you could not? Yet you remained silent when all this time you knew, you remembered."

She nodded. "I'm not really crazy, Doctor Phillips. I don't think so. I don't remember everything. I remember my father like I remember Tommy. Tommy made me remember, but I don't recognize them in my mind anymore. I don't think I like them anymore. I don't think so. I knew then, in the car, that I would never go home. I didn't think so. So what reason did I have to remember?"

"Your logic is not without merit, my girl. Your father fornicated with you and your mother discovered his incest. That's why she sent you away." He inhaled a deep breath. "Your dislike of them is well warranted, Emma, exceeded only by my disgust of them for their equally despicable roles in your abuse and my own inability to perceive the obvious truth. I apologize profoundly for my neglect. What your father did was wrong, Emma, appalling beyond the most scathing reproach, wanting to make you feel good in that particular fashion. What Tommy did was wrong as well, though he wishes now to correct his misconduct and make you his wife. He won't yell at you, Emma. No one will ever yell at you and, most certainly, I promise you, no one will ever hurt you. You have my word. I will never cease to make right my heretofore unintentional mistreatment of you. I give you my solemn word."

"Then he can marry me. I would like that. I think so. I do like Tommy, Doctor Phillips."

"And he likes you very much, Emma, though I lament that your decision is a much more complicated one than simply liking the young man. You see, when Tommy was making you feel good, not to discount his selfish well-being, which would be impossible to deny, and one time in particular which was his deserved undoing, he also succeeded in inadvertently accomplishing the unexpected. Better said, Emma, so that you will not misinterpret the facts in any way... he made you pregnant."

Her reaction surprised Phillips. She had none, her expression impassive. "He gave me a baby."

"Yes, he did indeed, albeit a most inopportune gift at best, Emma. And quite frankly, one you need not keep."

"Did my father want me to have a baby? Is that why he made me feel that way?"

"He did not. That was decidedly not his intent, I assure you. What your father did, and what Tommy did, was wrong for the same and very different reasons, though let us not belabour either malfeasance. More importantly, the primary difference, Emma, between the two is that Tommy, because of his actions, has set you free, which does not oblige you to have this baby. Either way, you are free. Do you understand?"

"I want the baby, Doctor Phillips. I think so."

"Unlike many, Emma, I give no credence to the concept of a woman's principal purpose being one of procreation and the proliferation of an already burgeoning population. Unless you are very certain in your mind that you like Tommy, the baby can be removed from this difficult equation in very short order. However should you not want the baby I would suggest that you do not marry Tommy. In fact I would not allow any such union. I have no doubt that many men will soon knock at your door, competing for your favour, charmed by your good looks and carefree manner. Of course, I would see you through the first difficult years of readjustment. I believe, Emma, that I shall always somehow be attached to you if you would allow me to become your friend...in the most paternal sense, of course."

"I would like you to be my friend and my father, Doctor Phillips. Will having a baby girl hurt very much? Do you think so?"

"No more or no less than a baby boy, Emma. I will arrange for the best care. You need not worry."

"Thank you, Doctor Phillips." Emma Rose giggled, wiggling from the bed with her bear. "My stomach is making noises. I'm very hungry, Doctor Phillips. Can I have my cereal now?"

Phillips couldn't believe the happy sound. What terrible thing had he done to this innocent girl for so long? What had he done to so many?

"One does not learn to become a young lady by eating pizza on the floor, Emma. I have in mind a much finer breakfast than cereal. I shall leave you to your preparations and see you downstairs when you are ready. Take whatever time you need."

She shrugged, and he understood why. After five years of nakedness under a thin, loosely tied garment Emma Rose was accustomed to people in charge of her seeing her body. She would learn, he thought, and quickly, about propriety and so many other facets of her new life and her new world. She was not the same girl whom he watched in his garden from his office window twenty-four hours earlier. That Emma Rose would never return. Of that he was certain. Of that he was thankful.

Six
Emma's First New Day

When Doctor Phillips left her room that morning Emma Rose pulled away her pyjamas, folding them and placing them neatly at the foot of her bed. The clothes from the previous day she put where she believed they belonged in her closest and in her dresser.

She chose a particular pair of panties because they were pink and soft, though not the matching bra because she didn't like them at all. She chose blue ankle socks that she did like and a bright red skirt because of the colour and the cool silkiness against her skin. Finally she pulled a V-neck cotton sweater over her head that was the same shade of cinnamon as her teddy bear, completing the look with black penny loafers.

She was satisfied and went downstairs with her hair combed into matching ponytails swaying from either side of her head.

Phillips was taken aback. He stood speechless. He'd never seen such a palette of odd colours on one person. Were the clothes years older and threadbare she would have looked the part of a homeless street urchin. They were going shopping, not to a circus as the premiere performance and he marched her upstairs to her room where he introduced her to pantyhose, laying a pair on the bed. He selected an emerald blouse to contrast her skirt, and the bra whose matching panties he determined were missing from the drawer.

She was to remove her shoes and socks, her skirt and her sweater and recommence her day, first with the pantyhose and skirt, per his somewhat comical demonstration, and attach the brassiere to the best of her ability before calling him to assist her in the event of any undue difficulty. Then he left her, returning some fifteen minutes later to clasp her bra and leave her once more after pointing to a pair of low-heeled leather pumps that matched her skirt.

When, closer to the lunch hour than breakfast, she finally did join him for the first meal of the day, she was a vision to behold with her red hair combed out and her green eyes sparkling.

By day's end Emma Rose had a wardrobe the envy of any young woman and Doctor Phillips was out several hundred dollars. He enjoyed her company to such an extent that he remained home with her on the Wednesday, delaying her first day of studies until Thursday. He took her to a spa where he spared no expense and to dinner in a fine restaurant where she looked divine in her new ensemble and her hair swept into a European updo. What he did not allow her was wine.

Strangely, though not in her mind, when at home, when the evening was over, she hesitated, waiting for him at the bottom of the stairway. He smiled and shooed her to her room. When she was gone, when he heard her door close, he went to his bar for a brandy, delighted as he savoured the warm liquid to hear the bathwater running in her room. Emma Rose was adapting well. She was going to do well.

The next day her studies began in earnest from early morning till late afternoon when he arrived home. Friday she studied until four, when Phillips arrived home early to escort her to a restaurant where she would meet with Tommy Dune. Phillips intended to keep his promise to her. She would never again see the institute. Neither would the black-haired nurse whose breath smelled of other women and who was sent home the day before without financial consideration or references.

And so the summer went quickly for Emma, more quickly for Tommy Dune who was given an unexpected reprieve by Phillips. The good doctor would keep Emma in his home another two months. She was already displaying her maternity and he had no faith in Tommy Dune's ability as an expectant father. The wedding was delayed and Emma's wardrobe required certain and undeniable modifications.

She was learning, absorbing, compensating for five years of life in a vacuum, anxious to tell Doctor Phillips each evening about her day, each morning about her wonderful dreams, about the world she was discovering and verbs, about long division and why the sky was blue.

Of course he was fascinated with each revelation. He was becoming attached to the girl, desperately reviewing and examining his decision regarding Tommy Dune each night in his study and in his bed after Emma was fast asleep in her room.

She wasn't the same girl at all, though she hadn't lost her flightiness, her capriciousness, her love of life. She loved to dance and sing in his home and often she would discuss profound questions aloud with herself, sometimes asking his opinion, though not always. Furthermore, and much to his relief, she had learned to coordinate colours and to clasp her bras without his awkward assistance, though on the weekends she would join him in the living room to watch movies in her pyjamas and fleecy robe with a big bowl of popcorn between them.

At first she was uncertain, images of her past conflicting with her present, though he never insisted one way or the other. She was free to join him, or not. He never once tucked her into bed, or thought to do so. He never once knocked on her door to wish her goodnight and never once intruded on her privacy except when called upon to critique her choice of wardrobe for her then twice weekly meetings with Tommy Dune, at which time, most times, she was dressed.

He adored the girl, at times consumed by doubt, on his knees with self-recrimination and deep regret, the double-edged sword of right and wrong levelled at his neck.

Increasingly he considered the marriage unwise, searching his mind each day and night for a single and selfless reason to annul his first thought. She really had little or no reason to marry Tommy Dune. Several weeks earlier Emma's release papers were approved and signed by the courts. The court's original record of her commitment was eradicated forever as a result of her then adolescence, her documented freedom in addition which any and all records of Emma Rose's forced incarceration at the institute were now under lock and key in the private study of his home. She was free to live her life and expunge her past in all ways save the deepest recesses of her mind.

No one present at the final hearing was aware of her condition. She wasn't there to be seen, poked or prodded. Neither were they aware of Tommy Dune's crime, his debauchery curtailed too late.

Were anyone to discover the rape, the consequences would be disastrous. The institute would be closed or handed over to the state, all manner of criminal charges would be laid and the residents would suffer indeterminable setbacks. Prison sentences would be meted out were the abuses ever to be unearthed, his amongst them as would befit his previous and careless disregard.

The public would never understand. Human beings were by nature carnal, undeniably disposed to do wrong when discovery and retribution were unlikely. And those two elements of the human condition when combined with the vulnerability of weak minds and the corporeal urges left unrestrained by those weak minds would ultimately and inevitably culminate in undesirable yet understandable consequences. To believe or hope otherwise was pointless. The public, in their misdirected righteousness, would certainly not understand.

For that reason alone Tommy Dune was not in prison, protected by mutual guilt.

Increasingly Phillips thought of Emma as his daughter, on more than one occasion pondering that he might make the relationship legal; give her a real family, a father who cared about her, which he knew was not realistic. He couldn't now protect her forever when, in her past, he had done so little towards that end. One day she would leave him, with a child she would soon bring into the world. And how, in her innocence, would she manage to guard the secret of how, who, when and where that came to be once on her own. And, once spoken, how would she explain the complicated truth from within an uncomplicated mind.

She was decidedly attractive to men passing her by on the street, garnering second glances by reason of her beauty and not her apparent maternity. Without Tommy she would be free to meet men of better standing. And then what? Their conjoined worlds would fall apart, ripped asunder by innocence. His good name would be smeared. He would be imprisoned with a dozen others and Emma's convenient release would be overturned. She would be returned to a state-run institution to live out her life in a colourless world, forgotten. She deserved more. As much as the world would not understand, none was more myopic in their common beliefs than the state.

Tommy, he had always known, was her way out.

As much as Phillips had helped Emma, Emma was leaving her indelible mark on Phillips. He began wearing more modern suits and coloured shirts, replacing his laced Oxfords with more elegant loafers. His hair was less severe and dyed to a light shade of brown, his face tanned to a more natural hue by virtue of his time with her spent walking and talking in the summer and autumn air. He appeared ten years younger and felt that many more.

He was a new man, rejuvenated with a fresh mindset. The austere beds at the institute were fitted with new and comfortable mattresses, pillows and warm blankets. New gowns in vibrant colours were issued with fleecy slippers and soft music permeated the corridors and common areas. Breakfast now included toast and butter, lunch included a sandwich with a more nourishing soup and dinner was being served in the main hall at six for the women and 7:30 for the men. Furthermore, once each week, in groups of eight, the residents spent their morning or afternoon in the garden if they so wished.

All this was the doing of Emma Rose

For her twentieth birthday Doctor Phillips took her to an exclusive restaurant for dinner and gave her two gifts. One was a promise that she would never be alone, the other was a bank account opened in her name and containing ten thousand dollars which her future husband was never to know about. The fine dinner was their last together for a good while. In the coming week Emma Rose would marry Tommy Dune and the good doctor would reluctantly give her away.

Seven
Not Much Choice

Tommy Dune wasn't happy. Phillips was treating him like errant child, watching him, spying on him, questioning others about him behind his back, his subordinates who no longer respected him. He wanted to run, to return to his life on the street, to hide, to do anything but marry a lunatic whose kid probably wasn't his and probably wouldn't be right in the head either. He was trapped with no escape, with no choice except to respect the doctor's wishes and do what he was told.

Since his invitation to Phillips' office in July the mean age of his patients had climbed by forty years and more. He no longer cared for the prettiest and the youngest, rather the oldest and most difficult. The bodies were limp and wrinkled, orifices loose and discoloured. Breasts were empty and flat, the men no better or worse than the women, scrotums and labia discoloured and sagging with age.

When once he sat to watch his young patients on the toilet smiling, he now stood watch over grimacing faces so that old men wouldn't defecate purposely on the stainless steel seats or old women urinate down their veined legs as they stood laughing, wanting to piss like a man. He no longer looked forward to attentively bathing younger and smoother bodies before rubbing each one dry with equal keenness. Those days were gone for everyone, he suspected.

Instead he had bedpans to empty and clean, bedding soaked with urine and stained with feces to change, though he no longer had foam mattresses to replace and lay in the sun to air. He had loose mouths putrid with cavities and impacted with particles of food to clean, dentures to extract and to brush before refitting them into gaping and hollow mouths, no longer tender lips to kiss or firm breasts to fondle and caress, giving pleasure and comfort to those in his care. He now had toilets to examine and flush, discoloured and pot marked buttocks to examine from bodies hunched over, when once he was more giving of his time and attention with smooth backs to rest one hand upon while the other probed with unhurried pleasure.

Tommy Dune no longer brought his camera to work tucked into his little black doctor's bag. In fact his albums, magazines and photos of Emma and others once taped to his wall were gone from sight, hidden in boxes marked 'private' and stored in the basement of his new home.

What reduced the sting somewhat, if not the intended humiliation of his fall from grace, was Phillips' unexpected proposition that he would co-sign the mortgage on a larger and much more comfortable home. In addition to which he would furnish the interior throughout on condition that, in the event of a divorce, separation or annulment initiated by either party, or his untimely death, the house would become Emma's free and clear, duly signed and witnessed. In effect he was making Tommy either a devoted husband for life or an eventual indentured second party. Tommy agreed not knowing better. He didn't think not to. Though he might have had he known the true nature of Doctor Phillips' mind.

Emma visited her new home on several occasions like a curious child, a few hours each time since his September reprieve, greeting Tommy as she would an older brother or cousin, not once as an eager bride-to-be or lover. She was more excited about the child and that once the baby was born she would learn to drive and become independent, able to go wherever she wished, free to visit Doctor Phillips at his home whenever she wished. She would also return to school at night since Tommy was now working days. Decisions he had no voice in, which he was determined to change once he was the man and she was the wife.

She chose the colours and Tommy painted the walls on his time off. She chose the furniture and he placed each piece wherever she thought was perfect with the help of Doctor Phillips, always Doctor Phillips. They were never left alone. Phillips was constantly with her, when all that Tommy wanted was Emma Rose in his bed, Emma Dune who from that coming day forward would honour and obey him, and to see her naked body once again the way he remembered without the hideous bulge.

He hadn't touched a woman younger than sixty in four months and with the tight control Phillips was keeping on him, his finances no longer a private matter, he could barely afford ten dollars for a single private dance once a week with a couple of beers let alone a whore for the night. But he knew Phillips wouldn't hesitate to ruin his life, not that he hadn't already. Everything was about Emma, Phillips' pride and joy who could do nothing wrong, when before the shit hit the fan he scarcely gave her thirty minutes every other week.

She wasn't the same girl. Each time he saw her she was more like Phillips, acting as though she'd never been locked in an asylum reliving the same day over and over again, as though she was normal when she wasn't. Nothing about her was normal. All he ever did was to make her feel good. That's all he'd ever done. She liked sex. So what if she didn't understand. She liked when he was inside her, calling her little girl. She liked when he squeezed her tits and pinched her nipples. She liked his hot breath and the passionate probing of his tongue. So did the others. He was a good lover. He knew what women liked, what she liked, their bodies together pushing the hot water to and fro in the tub while she purred, his hands sweeping thick suds from her cleft where they joined to her shoulders and again into the water where he groped for her breasts.

She wasn't innocent and she certainly was no virgin, calling him daddy those nights when he left her room, crying softly because she hated to see him go earlier than he wanted to darken the rooms and corridors he knew that she hated.

He'd come a long way since first meeting Phillips on the street outside the restaurant. He had a good life. Now he was broke each week before and after his payday, living by himself in a house he despised, sleeping in a bed by himself when he knew damn well that Phillips would not have the girl alone in his house for so many months without getting something worthwhile from her in return. For all he knew, Tommy increasingly suspected, the child wasn't even his. Maybe Phillips had been doing the girl in his office all along during their so-called closed sessions, promising her freedom in return while he, Tommy, was a convenient way of getting Phillips off the hook. Who knew? Who could know? He wasn't the only one fucking insane patients. Other orderlies had the same young females to care for on their shifts with even more opportunity now, not to mention the nurse who got her kicks every day. Sex at the institute was common, expected, the women's sole link with the real world, their pasts, and by the next morning not one of them ever remembered, their blank minds too preoccupied with breakfast or going to the bathroom. So where was the harm?

Maybe he could disappear, run and hide. Why not? Get the hell out. Phillips wasn't that wealthy or ready to plunge his institute into a scandal.

The wedding was in two days, November 15th, with Phillips acting as witness, best man, father of the bride and Tommy had no doubt who the godfather would be. He would never be free of Phillips, nor had either one thought to invite him to her birthday party for two.

Phillips took her shopping again. He bought her a dress, shoes, a coat and a hat for her big day, the whole nine yards, yet nothing for him. He was left to buy a new suit from what was left in his depleted pockets for a one-hour trip to City Hall because Phillips didn't think his other suit, the one he wore to work, was appropriate. And, what was worse, after a single night in a hotel room paid for by Phillips, she would be of little or no use to him for another couple of months. She wasn't even allowed to drink, which meant he couldn't drink, get drunk to forget. Screw that, he thought. What the hell was he expected to do with a pregnant woman on his wedding night? Phillips hadn't even authorized time off, no honeymoon, not until the kid was born, claiming that Emma had been through too much in too short a time, her own private honeymoon of sorts. So who was talking bullshit now?

Eight
Emma's Secret

In Tommy Dune's rapidly deteriorating thought process, he had no sooner fallen into bed Thursday night, his anxious mind somewhat calmed with hourly and significant doses of bourbon, than he was waking Saturday morning to a life he'd never imagined and never once in his life desired.

He downed three straight bourbons for breakfast before showering and dressing in a new suit he could ill-afford amidst all his other current and overwhelming expenses. He downed three more substantial bourbons without the benefit of water or ice for lunch and another before getting to the City Hall alone and on time.

There was no stag the night before with his buddies. He had no buddies; no naked girls leaning this way and that, stretching this way and that on stools, taunting him, inviting him to touch, to explore their bodies for 100 dollars extra, their bare breasts inches from his face, their asses gleaming with artificial sweat, their scent tempting. There was no raucous humour or good-natured slaps on the back from his male co-workers, his underlings vying for his attention. Friday came and went the way Thursday came and went. He worked, he went home, and he drank himself into a stupor that imitated sleep.

All that was different was the invitation to Doctor Phillips' office at 11:55 Friday morning before the good doctor went home to his live-in, pseudo and capricious daughter.

"Come in, Tommy, and sit."

"Thank you, sir. I know this is about tomorrow." He paused, his head pounding. His amber breakfast hadn't helped. "I'm ready."

"You look terrible, Tommy, very much so. I believe the common expression is 'like shit'." Phillips took his seat. "Let me be very clear, Tommy. Tomorrow is Emma's big day, not yours, not mine. It's never the man's day, irrespective of your current and prolonged bout of self-pity which I expect you to confront and conquer by this time tomorrow. What you're doing is the right thing, very gentlemanly of you, I might add. And for that I congratulate and commend you."

"You didn't give me much of a choice, Doctor Phillips."

"Quite the contrary, I did give you choices, Tommy, and you chose correctly. You've been with us at the institute for nine years now. You possess a clear understanding of what it's like to live in a closed cell twenty hours each day, to have someone watching you every moment without the slightest privacy. At least here our patients enjoy their own segregated worlds. Can you imagine sharing fifteen years in a nine by six cell with a man or men not as pleasant as you?" He waited. "I didn't think that you would. You chose the right path, Tommy: a beautiful young girl, a family and a wonderful home. Tomorrow you stand before a judge as a free man. Things might have been much worse for you."

"I'll be a good husband."

"I have no doubt whatsoever. And in order to assist you in that challenge I have made arrangements for a substantial increase to your current remuneration as well as your immediate promotion to Chief Attendant. I will not hear of Emma going without. She's lived a deprived life sufficiently long. Now she must enjoy her home and her child. However, a single word of caution and please do not misconstrue me. You are Chief Attendant as a convenient means of justifying your new income as well as certain bonuses you might expect. This I do for Emma, not for you. Are we clear?"

"How much, sir?"

"Ah, spoken like a true family man." Phillips paused. "The adjustment is twenty-five percent." Phillips leaned forward. "Tommy, I abhor colloquialisms. I have since a very early age when severe and immediate corporal punishment was exacted as a result of every wrong word uttered. I tell you this so that you will understand that when I say to you... do not fuck up... that I mean precisely that."

"Sir, Doctor Phillips, thank you." Tommy Dune's mouth was dry, his entire body screaming for moisture. "Emma is a beautiful woman, and the baby is mine. The one time we were together was special for us, for me and for Emma. I know, sir, that our life will be that way all the time. Thank you for helping us."

Phillips knew better, not once but countless times. The more time he spent with Emma eating pizzas on the floor, hot dogs in the park, cooking dinner together in his previously seldom used kitchen, he had gleaned abundant amounts of information about Tommy Dune from an innocent source.

"What I do, I do for Emma. Do wrong to her or the child and I will see you in prison and the marriage terminated by annulment or divorce. Despite your newfound wealth, Tommy, you continue on probation in my mind. You did a terrible thing, an atrocity not yet expunged from your record, despite the black mark being known to none but the two of us. Let us maintain status quo, Tommy, for your sake and no one else's."

"Tomorrow, sir, she'll be my wife. What happened here is in the past."

"Tomorrow Emma will be your wife, not she, and, yes, your debauchery is most assuredly in the past...unless reawakened by thoughtless disregard on your part. I will join you and your bride for dinner and drinks after the ceremony, Tommy, leaving husband and wife to spend the rest of the evening as they should. Be careful with her, Tommy. Be kind and gentle. The girl is in her seventh month. I fear that as a result of your previous enthusiasm towards her you must now restrain yourself until the child is born. Quite the irony, don't you think?"

"I'm thinking differently than I did a few months ago. I'm ready for marriage, sir. I've changed a lot."

Tommy Dune was a liar, and not a very good one. The meeting was over.

"I think of the girl as my estranged daughter newly found, Tommy. If not for her and her unexpected freedom, her escape due in large part to your vile crime against her, I daresay the institute would have remained in a darker époque for a very long time. The sad part is that the residents neither know nor care about her inadvertent benevolence towards them." He glanced at his watch. "See that your condition tomorrow at this time, Tommy, is not as apparent to me as at this present moment. I will not see her day ruined. Good day."

Tommy knew to stand and leave.

In the corridor outside Phillips' office he checked his own watch, angry: four more hours before he could have a stiff drink. He felt like a schoolboy dismissed by the principal after being strapped. He hadn't shared a moment alone with Emma since her release, always in public, now he was being told not to touch the woman that would be his wife until her kid was born.

*

When Tommy's silhouette faded from behind Phillips' door, the doctor went home, making stops at the haberdasher for his new suit and tie, his barber, and a tanning salon. Over the summer months, exposed to fresh air and the warmth of the sun that was at first foreign to him, he'd grown accustomed to a less pallid appearance.

At home Emma was sitting on the couch reading,

neither waiting for him nor expecting him. Time still had no relevance for her despite her watch. She was preoccupied with living and learning. That she would have a baby in two months might have been two years or two days. That she was getting married the next day and would be with Tommy alone the next night was far less important to her than the page she was currently engrossed in.

Doctor Phillips seldom spoke of Tommy at home with Emma. The thought of giving her away was akin to abandoning her when all along he felt he should have made a pact with the devil, freed Tommy Dune from his guilt, freed Emma from her imprisonment and helped her to live her life until such time as a more deserving young man discovered her.

When he came in she slid from the couch to greet him with a tight hug: the extent of their father-daughter symbiotic relationship. She'd made two decisions. The first was that she wanted pizza on the floor for their last dinner at home together. The second was a secret that he couldn't guess and she wouldn't tell.

That night Doctor Phillips did tuck Emma into her bed, kissing her cheek, waiting for her to fall asleep lost in time. He would miss her terribly and, he believed, he would quickly discover how much he would despise being alone. Much worse, however, was a thought he hadn't once contemplated until then: How would he tolerate seeing Tommy Dune every day knowing that Dune was with Emma every night? He closed the door unable to force the thought from his mind. What had he done?
*

The next morning he found Emma in the kitchen cooking breakfast, wearing a tee-shirt. She'd given up wearing a robe, telling Doctor Phillips that it made her look all puffy and fat and, despite his best arguments, she'd won out.

If not yet a consummate chef, she was learning to navigate her way through his pantry. She was ready for her day. She had begun taking showers because of her size and because Doctor Phillips was adamant that helping her in and out of her bath in her natural state was not in any way appropriate behavior. That was his perspective. Emma's was that she liked her bath time even more since being in his home. She missed the hot water and the scent of her salts and her oils, the tingling sensation and her soft fleecy towel. She had spent so much of her life without privacy, her most intimate moments observed by orderlies who were men, that she saw nothing wrong with someone she did like seeing her naked.

"Anyway today is different, Doctor Phillips. You told me that it's my day. So I want my bath and, besides, you're a doctor." She looked down, exaggerating, trying to see her toes. "If I can't see anything, how can you?"

"Let's see how the day progresses, Emma, after your appointments that will transform you from a scruffy urchin into a beautiful bride." He inhaled a deep breath, taking her in from her head to her toes. She was far from scruffy. "You have come a long way, Emma. You should be proud of your accomplishments."

"I like reading the most. And I think I will like being a mother, once she comes out of me. I think so."

"And what if she comes out as a boy?"

She shook her head. "She's a girl, Doctor Phillips. I think so."

"Emma, let me say before you leave me to begin another chapter of your new life that I am truly sorry for all that has happened to you. You should by now be a talented artist or musician, not a young mother and wife and I shall miss you profoundly."

"Five years wasn't a long time, Doctor Phillips. I met you and I met Tommy." She patted her belly. "And now I have her. I have a family, Doctor Phillips. I don't think of that place anymore, or my room. I like my room here more." She served his plate. "I was never crazy, Doctor

Phillips. I don't think so. Because you don't understand, or they don't understand you, that doesn't mean that you're crazy. I didn't understand. Nobody ever told me. Besides I had nowhere to go. I don't see them anymore in my head, or hear them. I don't think of him in the dark anymore and I don't cry anymore before I go to sleep. And I'm not afraid of the dark anymore, Doctor Phillips, not when I can see the light in the hall. I remember when I used to cry because of what he said each time."

"Which was what, Emma? What did he say?"

"That we couldn't share our special secret or something bad would happen to me. He told me that my mother would send me away to an orphanage and no one would know to look for me there. That's why I cried when they took me away. That's why I didn't want you to die, Doctor Phillips, why I didn't want to go back with you to the institute because you might die."

"Yes, I remember, because I'm old."

She hugged him. "I'm glad that you didn't die."

"I share your delight, my girl." He grinned without humour. "Emma, I wish you had told me. How differently your life would have evolved. I might have done something, brought him to justice. Now, after so many years..." Phillips paused. "Your father, Emma, is dead. Not a loss to mourn, I'm sure. He died three years ago and I can only hope that one day you shall be as free of your inner torment."

She shrugged, not thinking to ask about her mother, carrying her plate to the table. "I don't care that he's dead. You're my father, Doctor Phillips, and I want my bath when we come home. The rest doesn't matter. I know you're not like him." She giggled. "And I won't wear a bra under my dress, Doctor Phillips. I won't."

"Thank you for that confidential information, my girl."

"I don't like them. I'll wear a camisole instead, like the women in my magazines." She put her nose into the air. "I want to be elegant today in my new dress."

"And you shall be."

*

Emma knew what to expect later that day, after her wedding and dinner, when she would be alone with her new husband. Doctor Phillips had repeatedly explained in detail over the previous several weeks that, despite her marriage, becoming a wife did not negate her right to say no. She also knew that Tommy was to deprive himself of her until the arrival of what Emma was certain was a girl.

More importantly, and what astonished him, was how resolute she was that no one would hurt her daughter, especially Tommy. But Tommy, she knew, wasn't like that. She didn't think so.

They were home shortly after noon. Home, he thought. His house hadn't been a home for more than a few months and once again the place would become a collection of four walls and not much more. He would miss her, her relentless whimsicalness, her twirling in circles, her conversations with birds and butterflies in the park. If that was insanity, he thought each time, let the entire world become insane. He'd also begun devoting more time to his patients. Since September one other woman and a man were released into a halfway house and were doing well on their own. Though there was never a shortage of new arrivals to choose from, which he did on a much more selective basis, more often than not refusing to incarcerate minds that were free.

Because of Emma Rose, Doctor Zeke Phillips was a much happier man, though not entirely comfortable as he climbed the stairs to her room. Emma wanted her bath and stood waiting for him in the middle of her bathroom with a large towel, the one he insisted upon, draping her front from her shoulders to her knees. He could manage with seeing her backside, he believed, from which angle Emma didn't appear at all like an expectant mother.

Her skin was the whitest he'd ever seen, grinning at the

memory of her sitting on the toilet their first night together, a night that at times seemed so long ago and other times not. The contours of her waist and hips weren't in the least affected by her maternity. She was slim, a superbly sculpted young woman and that any man could think to abuse her was an abomination.

One leg went over, her first foot splashing through the water. She was laughing, giggling, not the least embarrassed or afraid. He was a psychiatrist, he told her, not an orderly, which was patently apparent to each of them with her one leg in the tub past her knee and the other foot still on the floor, her towel half in the water and half on the rim of the tub.

She couldn't reach out with her right hand to the far side. That small hand was busy cupping her towel to her breasts. Neither could she use her left hand to grab the rim between her legs because the good doctor was holding her forearm in his left hand, his right hand on a hip that he was doing his best to forget was close to forty years younger than him and decidedly bare. However if he didn't let go she couldn't raise her other leg, and if he did let go she would need both her hands to support herself, unable to ease herself backward into the water and onto her bum.

He understood. They were at an impasse, Emma much more amused than Phillips whose thoughts had travelled beyond the moment to when she would later call upon him to extricate her from the tub.

"This isn't working very well, Doctor Phillips. Maybe we should have my wedding here."

"Not appropriate humour, my girl. I don't believe the groom would appreciate knowing that I'm seeing the nether regions of his lovely bride in their entirety."

She dropped the towel onto the floor. "Then we won't tell him, but my bum's getting cold so let go of my arm and let me hold onto you while you lift my leg over. You're not very good at this, Doctor Phillips."

He did as she asked, thanking her for the instruction, letting her attach her hands and her arms firmly to his bent over neck, wanting to laugh at the ridiculous sight as he raised her remaining leg over the rim while securing her in place with his other hand to her waist.

He was squeezing perhaps a little too hard, she knew, though she didn't mind. She knew he didn't want her to slip and hurt herself and she was having her bath which was more important than anything.

When she was settled on the bottom, the water to her shoulders, her breasts covered by a snowy field of suds, she asked him not to leave, to sit on the toilet. She wanted to talk with him. She had things to say. So he did, sitting patiently, not feeling the least bit out of place leaning forward with his elbows on his knees, his fists together under his chin, waiting for her to speak. When she hadn't said a word after ten or fifteen minutes, seeing her smile and her eyes brighten, he asked why she hadn't said anything at all. Perhaps she couldn't find the words, he suggested.

She had found the words, she replied, the tiniest tears sparkling in the corners of her eyes. She'd said everything she'd wanted to say, just not out loud. She did, though, have one last thing to say, something very special.

"And what's that, my girl?"

"Thank you for being a good father." She put her hands to either edge of the tub. "And now I have to get out, Zeke. I'm very sorry, but I guess if you can see me naked I can call you by your name. I think so."

"I never thought that you should or should not, though I like very much that you do. However might I suggest that we keep your logic as to why between us."

He hurried to reach out for her as she made a first effort to stand, easing her from the clearing water, holding her arms, the remnants of suds thinly coating the natural highlights of her body, the rest of her glistening with scented oil.

Again she held him firmly with her arms and her hands at his neck, his hands planted securely to her hips, succumbing to the natural order of things, taking her in despite his greatest effort not to look until her feet stood side by side on the tiled floor when he would happily and necessarily let her go to reach for another dry and fluffy towel. The girl was a beauty, too good for the likes of Dune who, from that day forward, would be subject to the doctor's closest scrutiny.

He turned from her, giving her privacy, emptying the tub as she patted her front dry. When he stood Emma was the one facing away, holding out the towel.

"You can dry my back, Zeke, because I don't want to look silly and I know you're not bad."

"Thank you for your confidence, young lady, though not a duty I ever thought to perform as father of the bride."

Do you think Tommy will like me the way I am?"

"A sightless man would find you delightful as you are, Emma. He is, after all, the unskilled architect responsible for temporarily reconfiguring your heretofore enviable dimensions. You will always be the prettiest girl wherever you are. So, yes, he will like you and very soon your stomach will be flat again and your life will be normal for once. However I must conclude, Emma, judging by the size of you, that you should expect a rather hefty male child and not a little girl as pretty as her mother." He tossed towel across the tub. "Call me when you're dressed. My weak heart has tolerated quite enough of the nubile female form for one day."

He turned and walked out through the bedroom into the hall, as surprised as he was pleased that his heart hadn't failed while assisting her with her bath, not to say his pulse wasn't somewhat quickened. Emma followed, walking to her dresser. Phillips hadn't closed the door, neither did Emma. She hadn't closed the door since discovering she could trust him, though she couldn't help giggling at the thought of teasing him. Sometimes Zeke could be so straitlaced.

She peered into the mirror, at her belly. She was big, very big... huge. Zeke couldn't be right, not about this. She didn't think so and she began dressing first in underwear that she hated: silk bloomers meant for an old lady and a camisole that rested on the top of her belly and not her once slim hips. She sat by her bed slipping first one foot into her stay-ups, then the other, stopping to catch her breath, wanting to cry. She looked horrible and felt worse. She went to the closet, tugging her silk dress from the padded satin hanger and over her head.

In front of the mirror she whimpered and called out to Zeke who moments later stood in her doorway with his mouth agape.

She was a sight, a Kodak moment, standing in the middle of her room with her dress gathered at her waist, unzipped and shapeless, hanging loosely from her shoulders, the bottom edges of her silk undies showing intricate lace, her stay-ups bunched at her ankles.

"I can't reach my feet anymore."

"Perhaps, my girl, this is why I never married. Quite possibly in a dream long since forgotten I once envisioned my future. And why are you crying?"

She pointed into the mirror, giving him a look that only a sane and beautiful woman on the verge of calamity could create with her eyes and her lips. He agreed with a straight face as he knelt at her feet, uncertain about how high to tug or what to do when he got there. The question was foolish and uncaring.

"You'll always remember me with a big belly, like this, in my horrible underwear. I'm ugly, Zeke."

"I assure you, I will not. I already possess a sufficient workload with the psychoses of others. I have no need to develop my own. Now would you please move this foot a little to the left and this one to the right so that I might return to my brandy?"

She did, turning twice to see herself in the mirror, approving his work before dropping her hemline so that he could zip the back of her dress and leave her.

Thank goodness, he told her, walking through the door, that she'd gone to the spa that morning for her hair and her make-up. He had that much to be thankful for.

When Emma came down in her white, knee-length dress tied with a bow under her breasts, her arms gloved to her elbows, her white satin shoes glimmering, she was a vision. Her earlobes were dotted with glittering diamond studs, her cloche the perfect detail to complete the elegance of days gone by that she so badly wanted to live for a day, her neck left bare as he had earlier requested of her.

"My girl, you are a nymph of the highest order."

"Is that a good thing, Zeke?"

"Yes, that is a very good thing."

"Then thank you."

"Emma, this once belonged to my mother. Now it belongs to you, as do I." He clasped the diamond pendant at the nape of her neck without further ado and kissed her cheek. "You must remember without fail that you have a home here with me, a safe place to stay whenever you need me," he patted her belly, "along with whatever this might be."

She had nothing to add to the moment. She'd never owned so much as a girl's glass bauble, now she had diamonds. She wrapped her arms around his neck and lost herself in time.

Together they left the house and arrived at City Hall not long moments after the groom who stood ready, per Phillips' previous instructions, to open the door of the limo. Thirty minutes later Tommy and Emma were husband and wife in everyone's mind but Tommy's who knew he was the man of the house, if not the owner and despite her last minute affront.

That night man and wife left the restaurant together, alone for the first time without supervision. Mr. Thomas Dune and Mrs. Emma Rose crossed the street hand in hand to the hotel as Doctor Zeke Phillips arrived home in a taxi to clear his mind of intrusive images, stunned by Emma's second secret, her secret decision, marvelling at her resolve and acuity. Before the judge Emma had declared that she liked Tommy very much and that she would marry him. However the child, her little girl, would be hers alone.

That night Zeke Phillips didn't sleep. The next day he wasn't at their home to greet them, nor was he expected. He spent the day in Emma's room wondering what he had done, not quite believing what she had done on her own without consultation.

Though once each week he was invited to dinner and he accepted. He called Emma at home several times in between to follow her condition and joined them at Christmas with a bonus cheque for Tommy and his arms filled with gifts for Emma. In the final few weeks, distressed by her fatigue, he hired a live-in nurse to stay with her as Tommy did his best to play his role as a caring husband.

On the worst day of winter thus far, at three in the morning, Phillips was shocked awake by the shrill peal of the phone at his bedside. Amidst a violent maelstrom of snow and ice assailing him, howling winds battering him, slick ice-covered roads threatening to destroy his chance of being with Emma when she most needed and wanted him, Zeke Phillips sped from the road, his European sedan spinning out of control, leisurely, as though riding a deadly merry-go-round, every degree and second imprinted and erased from his memory.

He never arrived. He spent the night and early morning trapped upside down and snow covered in a ditch, the wrecked vehicle eventually discovered by police. Phillips was found disoriented and injured, wet, cold and distressed, worried for his daughter and her baby.

He arrived at Solaceville General strapped to a gurney, not yet aware of the birth or that he would not see Emma until much too late to reverse her determined mind, to prevent her from making a horrible mistake, one that would ruin, alter and shape countless lives beyond her lifetime, much too late to save Gilligan Rose.

Nine
Last Year: July 15th

Trans-Global Airlines enjoyed a deserved reputation for offering their passengers not only the finest in-flight service, but the most beautiful attendants. And she was the most beautiful by far. She was striking; her beauty unapproachable, though many had tried and many had failed.

She had travelled the world as a flight attendant for ten years, working her way up from regional short-hauls to Senior Flight Attendant on international flights onboard mammoth 380s. She was thirty-two and looked twenty-two. She stood a straight six feet in heels, four inches less when she wasn't. Her skin was translucent, emitting a natural glow, her hair lustrous and full, the deep red of a setting sun, her eyes bright and clear, piercing yet warm, despite the icy hue of a rich emerald green. Her lips were pouty and full, wet with a mahogany gloss, her fingers slender and smooth, tipped with the same shade of lacquer.

She was single, never once thinking or believing she would marry. Her job was her life which she lived all but five or six days a month and not for the money. When she wasn't living in Long Beach, California her home was in Paris, France. She spoke fluent Castilian as well as flawless French with a Parisian flavour because her adoptive mother, whom she never once loved, was French and her interim father who paid for her to be his daughter, whom she never once trusted, was Spanish.

She was then Collette Salazar. As a teen she spent half her summers in Spain, yachting on the Mediterranean in tiny string bikinis purchased by her father, hating the feel of his palms slippery with cream sliding across her back. The other weeks she spent on the French Riviera, ignoring boys, finding young love one year at summer's end, too late to let love flourish, her memory of tender moments stained by the sudden creak of an unoiled hinge, her father's eyes leering through the half open door, her face coated with pungent juice, the girl squirming from under her nude body to cover her own vulnerability. That was the moment she knew, certain beyond any doubt, the man ignoring their shouts, refusing to leave, stepping instead inside her room to watch them dressing, pleading with them sardonically not to hurry. He liked what he saw. He would like to join them. He should. So would his wife. That was the moment Collette knew. No man would ever see her that way again.

She never saw him or his wife again. She left them months before her eighteenth birthday because she didn't need their money. She traded New York smog for the joie de vivre of Paris, years later moving to Long Beach, California to begin her career. She decided on a seaside condo with a view of the ocean from the twentieth floor of a complex where the young and upwardly mobile with disposable incomes to match their good looks and long hours could enjoy each other's attention.

She didn't. She lived alone. On her days off she spoke on the phone.

She seldom went out and had never danced, not even at school, the envy of all the other girls and conspicuous by her absence at the prom because she liked those other girls more than she liked the boys. She didn't know how to dance and she never sang or giggled with glee. Her work was her life as much as her façade, a way to pretend she was all that she wanted to be. At home, alone, she didn't know who she was. What she did know was that as far into her past as she could remember she had never been truly happy a day in her life. Perhaps that's why she painted.

She hated the dark and slept alone in her home with a light by her pillow without a young lover to share that part of her life or her bed. She hated the dark more than she hated all men, more than the one who came to her each night in the dark of her dreams.

She didn't like their bodies, the way they sat with their legs spread apart or the way they walked about bloated with arrogance or with the slumped shoulders of the downtrodden. She didn't like their eyes, the way they would leer at her, thinking she didn't understand or couldn't read their minds. Or their mouths, the way 'can I take you to dinner' meant 'and then can I fuck you', Or their hands when they touched her arms or her shoulders, thinking she didn't mind when she did, or their voices, always affected and never real.

Women, she knew, could never hurt her that way. Yet she could hurt them with her lies and deceptions, and often she did. For that she hated herself the most, rolling onto her side, her breasts bare and smooth, her nipples pink little crowns smudged with blue bruises put there by the one who invited her to dinner the evening before because she looked younger than she was and she was beautiful. His wife wasn't, not any longer, and he missed his daughter who was. His name was Charles Cooper, Chuck, Chuckie, and he lay quietly in the bed across from her staring at the ceiling and not saying a word.

She met him the day before, though their paths had crossed many times over the past year. He was American and gauche, en route to Paris, away from his wife, wanting what he could never attain in his dreams, and she said yes. He was a passenger, persistent from L.A. to the City of Lights and in town for a week. She was in Paris for the night, and she said yes on a whim. She would change from her uniform and meet him for drinks because she wanted to know that she was right, knowing full well that she had never been wrong. The worst part was her terrible lie when she spoke on the phone.

At her hotel she showered and changed into a chic and sheer summer slip dress that danced across her thighs as she sauntered towards him in open-toed stilettos, her deep red hair combed to one side across a bare shoulder and covered with a wide-brimmed chapeau. She wore no jewellery at all, not even a watch, which, to her, was a tool required for work much like a pen or a computer.

She studied his eyes, closing the distance between them. He was focused on her near-naked thighs backlit by the late-day sun. While other men were giving her due attention, other women no less appreciative, this guy was the real thing: a total pig, hoping and praying her thong was as sheer as her dress. As she sat the swell of her breasts became his focal point, his eyes fondling them with eager anticipation. He was unabashed in his attention and she wanted to tell him a secret. She didn't though, not then. She would wait. He didn't deserve to know right away. She didn't think so.

She knew his real name. All First-Class passengers were addressed by name onboard TGA. Hers was Collette, which wasn't her secret. He simply didn't have to know what he would forget in a day or two, the name he hadn't seen on her tag while crossing over a continent and an ocean. To him she was simply Collette. She was always simply Collette to men she despised.

Together they enjoyed an apéritif, Collette ordering for him, waiting a while before suggesting another. She wanted to remain outside as long as she could talking about the weather, each one casually glancing at women strolling by their sidewalk table, each one thinking similar thoughts.

Deciding the time had come for dinner Collette went inside to the ladies' room. She paid the bill as well, asking the petite and pretty serveuse de bar to advise the gentleman at her table, once she was seated, that the drinks were compliments of the manager. The barmaid agreed with a smile, her obvious curiosity clear in her eyes. Why was such a sophisticated young woman the companion of such an ordinary man?

Dinner was at a nightclub that Collette knew well, the second best cabaret in all of France. The premier club, where she was a frequent visitor, Les Filles du Ciel, was her private domain, her retreat, a place where women like her could spend an evening alone or together without pretence, whose clientele and staff would never think to gape at or deride one woman holding hands with another. No. Les Filles du Ciel was not for the likes of Chuck Cooper.

This cabaret, however, she chose not to be seen. The wine alone was 190€, 250 USD which she could easily afford, which wasn't her secret either. The meal was exquisite, each sumptuous course ordered and explained by her, and with their dessert she ordered two forty-year cognacs, all the while quietly witnessing a man on the verge of a cerebral hemorrhage, a man she watched swallow thirty-five Euros in a single gulp. She chuckled from within. Imagine, had they gone to the other?

He was middle management at best, or possibly a low-level bureaucrat, she knew, flying First-Class to Paris on points he'd accumulated over the past several years in Coach. Few people could fake their way through First-Class; the same way his demographic didn't fit into a cabaret whose female performers on stage wore G-strings for showy glitter, not modesty sake, whose waitresses were seductive, not wearing much more than the performers. Nor would he have thought to spend that much in an entire year of dining out with his wife. He stood out.

He was getting a divorce, he told her, which he wasn't because he was wearing his ring. His daughter was fifteen, which she thought put him around forty, older if he was a late bloomer, younger if he was a child molester who married instead of going to jail. He no longer loved his wife and wanted once more to be seen with an attractive young woman whose company he truly enjoyed. That's what he said. She was attractive. He might as well have called her handsome.

When the waitress came by Collette halted her with an open palm, giving the girl six one-hundred Euros. Cooper objected vehemently, of course, claiming his chivalrous right as a gentleman. She ignored him, telling the waitress sincerely in French how cute she was, though with a purpose, rewarded with a kiss on her cheek. He didn't understand a word.

At the hotel his room was standard, not remotely elegant, with twin narrow beds that in the US would be better suited to a kid's room in a basement. Her suite for that evening only, a few blocks away, was elegant with a view of the Eiffel Tower, turndown service and complimentary champagne and chocolates for discerning guests, the motif not much different from the home that she owned not many miles away.

"So, you actually came back here with me. I can't believe I lucked out this way. You know, I knew there was a thing happening between us, some sort of synergy going on."

"Did you like the place, Chuck, the cabaret?"

"What's not to like? I'm a healthy guy. You go there often?"

She nodded. "I like to see the women. I like sexy women." She smiled, coquettishly. "And they like me. You know, I could have taken the waitress back to my hotel with me."

"She seemed to know you."

"She does. She knows me very well," she lied.

"That was some dress she was wearing, not much left to the imagination."

"I don't have to imagine, I remember. So, yeah, you lucked

out, which means shower time because I have an early flight tomorrow."

"No kidding. You've been with her, like on a date."

She nodded. "She has a thing for redheads."

"And you, what's your thing?"

"Most times, Chuck, the pungent scent of a woman. I have a thing for little French girls. It's why I learned the language, though I do enjoy the taste for something more traditional every so often."

He blew loud air through his lips, puffing his cheeks. "So you swing both ways. That's hot."

"That's very hot, something to talk about after our showers." She removed her chapeau. "You first, while I call down for a few drinks. Even in Paris mini bars are stocked for general purpose drinking, Chuck, not for the end of a delightful evening. So please do not come out in your pyjamas. She never does. And please pass me a couple of towels."

When he disappeared into the impossibly small bathroom Collette called room service ordering two bottles of Dom Pérignon. While Chuck was showering, or doing whatever else she imagined, the bellhop knocked discreetly, announcing himself in a low voice from the corridor. She unlatched the door and let him in; allowing the door to close behind her as he set the bottles nestled in ice and the fluted glasses on the table, the back of her body perfectly framed by the mirror on the door. He was young and most other women would have thought him good-looking. Collette did not. To her he was young, which suited her purpose.

Her hair was tucked into a turban, her head lowered, waiting for him to face her with the chit. Reaching to take the leather folder from his hands, the towel that she'd wrapped around her body from her breasts to her upper thighs somehow slipped from fingertips straining to pinch the open edges together, unexpectedly filling the mirrored canvas behind her with a beautiful full-length nude.

She didn't smile and didn't look up, letting him hold the folder while she scrawled Cooper's name with her left hand, adding fifty Euros while barely managing to keep the towel across her breasts with her right. That he saw her in the mirror was more important. He wouldn't remember her face. When he left, thanking her profusely, she closed the door and pulled the towel from her head. She poured two glasses, snorting a terse laugh, thinking old Chuckie might yet die of a heart attack or stroke if he asked to see the bill.

When he came out his hair was blow-dried, his body was laced with cologne and his towel was knotted at the waist like an ancient and shapeless Greek in a bathhouse. He looked ridiculous. Collette was once again wearing her flimsy dress, her panties tucked into her handbag, and she asked for a few minutes to do her toilette. The towels she'd tossed onto the worn carpet by the wastepaper basket. She couldn't remember if she'd ever felt anything so thin and rough against her skin. Perhaps the kid had seen more of her than she had intended. Good for him, she thought. Good for her.

She went into the bathroom with her purse and her glass. She didn't need Chuckie ruining her evening. She ran the water, working the archaic brass knobs with a facecloth in her hand. She patted moisture onto the length of her body and her face, patting herself dry. She dipped a finger into a vial of scented oil, coating the delicate tissue between her lips before stepping into a clean pair of silk tap pants she'd brought for the occasion. She knew what Chuckie wanted. What she didn't want was the pain.

With her shower finished she shut off the water and swept her towel across the tub to dampen the thin fabric in case Chuckie had to pee first. She emptied her champagne into the sink and stepped out draping her breasts with a dry towel that was larger and fleecier, laying her dress and her thong at the edge of the bed she thought was the cleanest.

"So, am I getting this right? You're really into girls?"

"Yes, I am into girls, big time. Isn't everyone? Aren't you?" She filled her glass, sipping her champagne, enjoying that he was so obviously ogling her. "Chuckie, how old do you think I am?" She giggled. "Don't worry. I won't leave you if you guess wrong. I want as much out of this evening as you do."

He shrugged. "Don't know, maybe twenty-four, twenty-five, because of your job. Anywhere else I'd say straight out of college."

"Thank you. I did go to college, though I didn't have to. I'm rich and I earn more in a year from flying than any lawyer my age. You're right, though, I can pass for a college kid, and I do…with college girls. I think that's the reason I did stay in school. College girls like to have fun. So let me ask you something. When you're back in the US, if, if, and if, would you be interested? Do you ever see your daughter and wonder, especially now that you're getting a divorce? Do ever wonder what it would be like with a girl almost that young? Or do you remember what tight actually feels like?"

"You hit that nail on the head. The kid's a real looker, the way her mother used to be. Thinks her old man can't get it up, strutting around in her bra and her panties like I'm a frigging eunuch and the wife lets her do it. I'm talking real sexy stuff. Her drawers are filled with them, believe me. I've rummaged through a few times when I'm alone. And tight, I haven't had tight for years."

"You will this evening, Chuck."

She reached for hers on the bed, twirling them on her finger. "Like these, or the little thong my friend was wearing under her dress at the club?"

He chortled. "Shit, I wish. If I were that lucky I'd never leave the house. The kid's three years from legal."

"It's normal. Girls are attracted to their fathers. It's difficult to be sexy with a pimple-faced boy. She wants to be sexy for you, the real man in her life. And, believe me, if or when you catch a little naughty glimpse of her, she won't mind. She'll feel ten years older. She'll feel like a mature woman."

"Yeah, like you. You're ten years older."

"Yes, I am, and I look five years younger than I am, more like a teenager. Imagine a real college girl." Collette put down her purse with one hand, reaching for the bottle with the other, refilling his glass. "I think the girls I'm talking about will like you. I know they will. So what do you think… a little threesome once in a while?" She sipped her wine. "Until your daughter starts college, of course, that could be a little awkward."

She let her towel drop to the floor without the slightest unease and went to the bed, throwing back the covers with a single effort. She went to her purse, searching inside with her fingers for a condom, staring at him, placing both on the night table with her glass, kneeling seductively onto the bed and waiting.

She wanted to laugh, seeing his towel drop to the floor. She wanted to say that she was sorry, that she'd bought Extra Large because she was accustomed to fucking real men. Instead she watched him cross over the bed on his knees. He was ready. He was grinning, reaching for the foil, fumbling, stretching the latex over what she thought resembled a stale hors d'oeuvre more than any erect penis she'd ever seen.

She crawled over his knees. He was anxious, desperate, clumsy, watching her, his eyes dancing between her breasts and the flared legs of her panties that she pulled to one side to show him her lips that were completely naked and smooth, glistening and pink. She ordered him to lay back and relax. She was accustomed to being on top. She was laughing, wiggling away from his knees to frame his head from behind with her thighs. No way was Chuckie up to an all-nighter with any woman, especially her. He probably hadn't been in years.

"Chuck, I have this fantasy. I like fucking guys through my panties first. I find that totally sexy."

"I can't believe I'm fucking my flight attendant."

"You guys, you always think of yourself first. Do you like my breasts, Chuckie? You do, don't you?"

"Yes, I do."

"So do I. Pinch my nipples, Chuck. Pinch them hard."

He reached up, squeezing his fingertips close together, feeling her nipples resist, feeling them come alive and grow hard. "Shit, the wife never wanted this. This is amazing."

"And I bet she was never this clean. This is how college girls look, Chuck. It's all the rage and I know a lot of them. So I hope you're into little plaid skirts and not much else. Believe me, from now on, you'll never see your daughter the same way again."

She crawled forward, deliberately, taunting him, not giving him time, turning, straddling his legs.

She was perfect, the most beautiful woman he'd ever seen. He couldn't see a single flaw. And her pussy, he thought his chest would explode.

He was ready, on the verge of eruption. There was no better time. She leaned forward, bracing her arms on the bed, not wanting to touch him more than was necessary, shifting a little to help him, letting him guide himself into her. She didn't want to touch it with her hands. She never did. Nor did they ever see her bum. They never saw all of her. They never touched all of her.

He was barely at full depth before he began grunting like the pig that he was, bucking, craning his neck to see as much as he could of her.

"That's good, Chuck. I like it rough. So will the girls." He was struggling to be good. She could tell. He probably never lasted more than a minute with his wife, fantasizing, imagining his daughter prancing around without her panties and bra. "Do you remember your first time, how good she was, how good she felt?"

"The first few times were good, though never like this. Not once," he groaned. "Shit, you are gorgeous. Anyway, I married her...had to."

"Oh, this is so good." She reached for her purse. "But she gave you a beautiful daughter who runs around in her little panties teasing her daddy." Collette sat straight, watching him strain under her weight. "You think about her, don't you, Chuck? You must. I mean, who wouldn't?"

"Yeah, I think about her. I do. And I don't see it as a problem. It's not like I'm dead. Shit, no one cares when I see her in a swimsuit. So what's wrong with a little innocent T and A in the home? You know what? You're right. She must be doing it on purpose, for her old man to see."

"Do me harder, Chuck, and deeper. As hard as you can and I want you to pretend. You know what I mean."

He was suffering; his eyes squeezed shut, his hands grabbing at her waist, Collette pushing them away. They were weak hands, slippery, a memory she didn't need.

"I think I've got enough going on at the moment. If you don't mind I'll leave her until I'm at home bagging her mother. I don't see that I need the kid right now."

"I remember my first time. Harder please, Chuck. Hmmm, yes, like that. I remember the pain, the way he pinched my nipples, the way he made me ready with his spit. I remember wondering why he was doing that to me and why he came into my bed without his clothes when he never did before." She was leaning forward, over him, reaching. "I remember when he left me in the dark. I remember wondering the same thing your daughter would wonder the first time you fuck her. Because I think you will, Chuck. I know you want to fuck her young, tight body in the dark."

"Oh shit, don't get me started, I'm dying here."

"Yes, you are, except now your daughter won't have to wonder why her daddy hurt her that way. She won't have to lie in her room each night waiting for the shadows to disappear into the dark, waiting for the pain. Or wonder why they took her mommy away. Your daughter will never be afraid of the dark."

Chuck was at the edge, confusion etched into his face, ecstasy and fear melding; Collette pulling away from him, slamming the long blade deep into the centre of his heaving chest.

Collette eased away from him. She sat by his side awhile and waited, sipping her wine. He hadn't lasted very long, four or five seconds before dying. Perhaps he heard her last words, perhaps not. Whether he did or whether he didn't, didn't matter. He understood. He was dead and his daughter was safe.

She never left a man's room when a date was over. She preferred the hustle and bustle of early morning pedestrian traffic through the corridors and lobbies of hotels. And she never took showers, not before and not after. Instead she pulled back the covers from the other bed and went to sleep. Morning would come quickly and she had much to accomplish before her eleven o'clock flight time. She would have no time to go home, safe from another lie.

When she did wake Chuck hadn't stirred, staring at the ceiling with unanswered questions etched into wide-open eyes. The bruises would soon fade from her breasts and her vagina had expunged any and all sensations of him as she slept.

She first took his suitcase and briefcase from the closet, discovering nothing of value other than his phone and computer. The man travelled light with one suit, one tie, and a carry-on half full with a week's worth of shirts, socks and boxers. She'd been right about low-level something or other, if not a bureaucrat.

Waiting to dress she stood over him, her feet balanced on either side, yanking the blade from his discoloured chest, careful not to spill a drop on the floor, letting the blade rinse in the sink with the hot water running. She stripped both beds and pillows, his without the slightest difficulty, tugging the folds easily under his dead weight. When she was done she folded the linen into manageable squares and placed them neatly onto the corner of the bed she slept in.

Minutes later the towels were squared and placed with them. Then she emptied his suitcase neatly into a corner, filling the vacant space with the linen, the towels and the facecloth she'd used, the glasses, one empty bottle and one empty foil. The other bottle she placed in his briefcase. She left his watch, his ring, his passport and his wallet, minus a thousand plus US dollars for her trouble and her sundry expenses at the café-terrasse and cabaret.

She threw in her spare panties. She no longer went on a date with a list.

Once dressed, as careful as the night before not to touch more than what she needed in her hands, she went for his phone. His daughter's name was Candice; his password into his computer was MyLittleCandice. No shit, she thought. She'd been right about him. She hadn't misconstrued what she'd seen from over his shoulders while serving other passengers.

The media centre contained not one photo of an older woman, his wife. Candice, though, was the main attraction, either a naïve little girl or in competition with her mother for her father's love and attention. Either way, she no longer had to worry about past or future pain. The bikinis were tiny, tied with strings, father and daughter alone at a lake or with a mother who didn't know or didn't care that many of the other photos were taken at home.

His wife's name was Sybil, Sybil without a face, Sybil at Sybil dot homemaker. How quaint, she mused, twisting his ring from his finger, removing her prints with the hem of her dress before centring the gold symbol on the tip of Chuckie's nose, stepping back for a longshot and in for a close-up. Chuckie was no longer a big man in anyone's eyes. He was a childish clown. Apart from the wound in his chest, the brownish blood against a backdrop of greyish skin, the condom was no longer in place. The shrivelled latex was plastered to his leg because little Chuckie had a bad dream and peed the bed: His wife's last and lasting memory of him.

She forwarded the photos from the phone to the laptop and sat by his feet to compose a concise letter explaining that Sybil might want to talk with her daughter, that her husband hadn't died hours earlier cheating with a whore in his hotel room, but with young Candice naked in his diseased mind, calling her name. She added the photo library of the girl as an attachment and prepared to leave.

She washed the computer, the cell, the hotel phone and doorknobs with a soapy cloth, retrieving the knife, adding the cloth with the knife to the suitcase and pressing SEND, flushing the limp condom on her way out.

Collette left room 412 with her purse, his suitcase and briefcase amidst a hectic crowd of disinterested rush-hour workers, her distinctive red hair twisted into a tight braid and covered by her wide-brimmed hat. She went unnoticed despite her appeal and walked a kilometre before hailing a taxi after first dropping the kitchen knife into a sewer.

In her hotel room she showered him from her body and changed into her uniform. Her panties, dress, shoes and her hat from the night before went into a separate bags. The soiled linen from Cooper's room she added to a maid's trolley as she went for breakfast and by eleven AM she'd forgotten about him, Sybil and Candice. She'd done her part. The papers in the briefcase she'd shredded in the crew's lounge, the generic briefcase she tossed along with her prints where something of questionable quality belonged. Her four-piece ensemble from the night before she discarded where eyes never search: four airport washrooms.

The Dom Pérignon she took with her.

Gilligan Rose arrived at her Long Beach home from

Paris fourteen hours later, five PM local time, to an empty upscale apartment. She no longer cried. Her eyes were empty. She hadn't cried in years, not since all her reasons had gone away. She stood naked in front of her mirror longing for soft and tender hands to love her and caress her, for a breath so sweet to whisper gentle words in her ears, to forgive her for such terrible lies. But who could she trust not to betray her when the one person she could trust and did trust she would never betray.

She wasn't working the next day. She went out onto her wrap-around balcony in the nude and reclined, as she did whenever she could, to infuse her body with the late-day warmth of the sun and not discolour the unblemished hue of her body…this time with a glass of the finest champagne.

The next day she would wake late and alone. She would eat alone and shower alone, dress alone and look out across the vast ocean alone.

She was anxious to talk on the phone.

Ten
This Year: June 30th

Gilligan Rose didn't have very many friends. She didn't need friends. Her busy life didn't allow, but she did love the few friends she did have. What she loved most of all was her job, travelling, seeing the world and eating. She loved eating, especially hot Latin dishes. She spoke fluent Spanish because she loved Latin women the most. She also loved her time in Miami the most where she spent two weeks each year in a collection of thongs with her breasts bare and smothered in SPF 50. Or covered in billowy muslin dresses with panties too small to see when she didn't want her near-naked body photographed, imagined or dreamed about by men who could never afford to touch her or by women too shy to ask her. Her wrist devoid of time, her fingers devoid of commitment, she appealed equally to men as she did to women. Although she didn't mind the casual company of men, she could and she did live without them. Not once had one ever made it into her bed or into her home or into any of the temporary homes away from home.

That was Gilligan Rose when she wasn't circling the globe.

She loved the Latin beat and she loved dancing ever since she was a little girl. Dancing let her forget, let her be someone else: happy and carefree. She loved laughing and being happy. She was educated with a Master's in psychology because she wanted to understand. She needed to know. And now that she did know, now that he was dead, no longer haunting her mind or her dreams, she didn't care. Yet she hated the dark. She hated closed doors that would open to the light. She hated shadows, shadows standing in the doorway, shadows whispering that she shouldn't be afraid when she was.

She never did like her other name, the one they gave her when she was fifteen when she was taken away, the day Gilligan waited on the stoop while, in her mind, she knew Gilligan was hiding in the attic, huddled in a corner and afraid.

She never did like her new parents, especially the man who never stopped looking at her, the same way all the boys at school looked at her, constantly ogling her in her bikinis, doing his best whenever he could to see under her short skirts, always taking pictures and his wife was no better, the woman often not waiting until her bedroom door was closed before undressing in the living room to entice her husband onto the couch. The woman never loved her and Gilligan soon began to understand that she'd been adopted for a reason.

The woman was forever walking around in her underwear and often times intentionally to be seen naked either to excite her husband with another woman so near or to prove she was still young because her new daughter was a beautiful girl who looked and acted more like a young woman because her childhood had never existed. Gilligan had never known how to live as a child. Either way, Gilligan didn't care. She wanted out.

When she was not far from eighteen, one night she saw the man naked at her window, erect, taking pictures, and not for the first time. Not many weeks before he'd walked into the bathroom naked while she was taking a shower, dropping his robe onto the floor, feigning shock when he was actually smiling. The woman came running at hearing the shouts, wearing only her panties, furious at what Gilligan was suggesting. But Gilligan knew and the party was over.

She knew that eventually the man would rape her, with or without the woman watching. She locked her bedroom door that last night and remained awake till morning when she left early without saying goodbye. She never saw them again and within a week she took back her name.

She didn't need them or want them. She was days from eighteen with a trust fund established on the day she was born. She was wealthy. What she wanted, what she wished for every day, was to see her real mother, to say she was sorry for what she had done. But that never happened because she never once looked in spite of her greatest temptations. She'd been warned by the doctor that to find Emma Rose would be their undoing and that was never to happen. She remembered the tears, the second time she'd seen her mother cry, the day they took her away. Instead she went in search of her essence to make herself whole.

On her own and determined, Gilligan put herself through college; the top five percentile of her graduating class, downplaying her scholastic smarts to get the job she'd dreamed of for so many years, a job where well-shaped breasts trumped brains and well-toned legs protruding from form-fitting skirts got you farther than any letter of reference from the dean. The fact that she had a killer ass on the beach or on a plane was a plus. She thought so.

She didn't date men and not many asked her. She was too disarming and those who did were either married or transparent, wanting her for a night, to see her naked and to touch her, to hurt her and to leave her alone in the dark. Men were strictly a matter of business. She dated women, never taking them home to her bed. The risk was too great. What if she fell in love and was hurt? Everything she loved about women she hated about men. Women didn't lie with their eyes, not with other women. She loved their smooth bodies, their long silky hair and the warmth of their sweet breaths tracing whispers onto her skin. She loved their soft voices, their soft lips and tender kisses, their gentle love-making and their scents. Most of all, she loved not being hurt.

Yet she would hurt them, saying goodbye after a week or a month and not telling them why, pushing their wet eyes and sad lips from her mind. But Xara was different. She couldn't let Xara go. They'd been good friends and lovers for close to a year, since the flight from Madrid where Xara Mendiga had spent the week on business, since asking her flight attendant for a glass of champagne, since telling Gilligan Rose she believed she'd just fallen in love.

The airline knew, their friends knew, and no one cared because everyone loved Gilligan Rose. Seeing the women together was any healthy man's dream, though they never flaunted who or what they were. Not even at the Christmas party months earlier when the men left their good-natured wives to stand in line under the mistletoe for a double dose of exotic Christmas cheer.

The sand was hot, her body coated with a sheen of oil and sweat. Her breasts were bare, who she was cloaked by dark glasses and a wide-brimmed straw hat, oblivious to the leers of old men and the envy of young women dressed in thick one-piece suits or hiding their child-bearing flaws with polka dot skirts. She wasn't naked for them, her thong a narrow strip of glittering yellow. She didn't like flaws, her body covered in a patchwork of sun-deprived straplines, triangles and squares to make her appear unsightly any other time of the year.

Xara was in the water dressed in a white thong, red Serengetis and a white satin turban. She was waving. She was beautiful and happy despite living in Long Beach and not once having seen Gilligan's high-rise home, never once having seen the sun set or the early morning glow of golden light sprinkled across the ocean. She loved dancing and she loved singing. She loved Gilligan and wanted to live with her, to be a real couple the way everyone agreed they should be.

But then what of the half-truths and dark secrets? Xara, she knew, would not understand. Gilligan took up her camera, zooming in to petite Latina perfection. Xara had no scars, whereas Gilligan had so many invisible to the eye. Xara had no secrets; Gilligan had so many haunting memories to keep hidden. Xara loved life, whereas Gilligan had killed a man over and over again in her mind until at last she understood that what she had done wasn't her fault.

Only once, the first night together in her home, the first time Gilligan lay in her bed, did Xara wonder aloud at the light: a lie. Only once did she wonder as Gilligan spoke on the phone, not the least bit jealous: a lie. There would always be so many lies, so many reasons not to tell a secret. Xara was frozen in time at several frames per second, her hands waving through the heated air, her legs kicking at a cool and turquoise sea. That's how she would forever remember her Xara.

She was three years younger than Gilligan whose name she wore on a small silver heart at her neck: a lover's first and uncertain gift. She was Mexican, sexy and smart, tiny and vivacious, and soon she would hurt. That evening, before flying home alone, Xara would hurt. Gilligan would not be going with her. But this time was different. This time Gilligan would have tears in her eyes as well.

She remembered the pain, the first blood between her legs. She remembered the shadows and the fear, her heart thumping loudly, then not at all, never again. He'd stolen her heart. She remembered the blood, the black shiny handle sticking out from his chest, her hand shaking, covered with blood, her body trembling, Gilligan crying. She remembered each vivid detail each time she closed her eyes to the light.

Xara was skipping from the water, beaming. Click. Click. Click. She fell onto her knees, breathing hard, patting herself dry with a towel.

"Te amo," she panted, her black eyes heated with passion.

She always said 'te amo'. Why did she have to say the words now?

"I love you too, Xara. I believe in my heart that I will forever."

"I know that you will, chica."

Gilligan wanted to call her cariño, resisting the temptation. Not then, not ever again. Darling had no place in tearful goodbyes. She stood, slipping her feet into her muslin sheath, Xara snatching the flimsy fabric away. Xara stood with her, taking her hand. The walk along the beach to the time-share luxury condo was twenty-minutes and Xara loved walking hand in hand, or with her arm around Gilligan's waist, or tapping her bum with an open hand, or rubbing away invisible specks of sand when she knew that transparent men slowing their pace as they walked past wanted to be in her place or inside her thong. She was a tease, a beautiful tease, not expecting that Gilligan would take back her dress.

Xara feigned a practiced pout, creasing her brow. Her white-skinned girlfriend never stayed long in the sun, she knew. She could wait. The rest of the day was for strolling, sipping chilled wine, shopping and loving before their flight home.

They showered and savoured white wine on the balcony, letting their damp bodies dry in the cooling shade. Gilligan wore low heels; Xara wore high, though both skirts were short making both sets of legs appear eye-catchingly long. Their toned midriffs were bare, their white and black bras intended for show under loose-fitting gauze tops, their hair combed into straight tails and tied with silk scarves.

They sat for an early dinner in the shade and in the quiet, as far as they could from the hustle and bustle. They didn't shop and they hadn't made love. They sat face to face, not side by side, and didn't hold hands. Xara left the table first, leaving her meal untouched, her wine barely tasted. The worst part was walking away.

Gilligan left one hour later. She had never seen Xara as sad, her face drained of colour, her unblinking eyes tormented with grief. She thought Xara had stopped breathing and that she might die, wishing herself dead instead and that she had died such a long time ago in her body and not in her mind.

At the hotel Xara Mendiga and her luggage were gone. All that remained were her scent and her bright red lipstick on the mirror. "Te amaré, chica, para siempre." Xara always wanted the last word, often blurred in excited Spanish, often with her soft lips curved into an impish smile.

Gilligan Rose didn't see the letter till morning when her head had never pounded as much a day in her life, knowing that this time Xara was wrong. They would never be with each other again unless in their dreams or by chance in the sky. Xara would not love her forever. How could she possibly?

Eleven
Twenty-seven Years Ago

Tommy Dune was not doing well. When Emma Rose gave birth he believed he'd been sentenced to death. What he'd wanted was a good life with young and good-looking women on his arm, in his bed, and money in his pockets. He had never wanted a wife and not once in his life had he contemplated becoming a father. That wasn't what women were for, not the pretty ones anyway, the ones who wanted their bellies flat, their legs slim, their breasts full and firm, their asses tight and unmarked.

Emma was twenty-five, still all of those things, as yet unscarred by nature's inherent cruelty. She was desirable, though seldom was she there for him when he wanted her. If he was lucky, which he rarely was, he'd have her three or four times a month, on her back with her knees in the air, her eyes closed, never anything different, never anything special. She was a different woman in the dark, not like before when taking her bath she would contentedly hum, her face calm, her body relaxed, enjoying the warm water, the feel of his body behind hers, his hands at her hips and at her back. Or the times on her foam bed, when again she would hum in his ears while her eyes searched for fairies in a room as empty as her mind.

He had always been so careful except for that one night he would forever regret, when innocently massaging her bare skin under her sheet, her mind sedated, he left late to turn out the lights.

Now the bath at home was too shallow and small. The humming had stopped, her curious eyes closed in the dark. And when she wasn't at school, mocking him, making him inferior in everyone's eyes, she was cooking or spending her waking hours with her red-headed spawn.

She had her high school certificate and now she owned a car, her car bought by Phillips that was newer and better than his, and she was attending college to learn how to draw. She wanted to become an artist when he scarcely had a penny in the bank. She was taking all his money each week, every week, spending every dime on little dresses and shoes, dolls and doll houses, a wading pool, tricycles and bicycles and nothing for him while she wore fancy clothes to school.

And what right did Phillips have telling her how to dress? Telling her empty head that she should dress like an attractive and successful young woman if she ever wanted to become one, her dresser drawers filled with expensive silk that she wore at home more for the neighbours than for him. She thought nothing of taking the garbage to the curb in her short slips, her legs and her feet bare, dancing and prancing her way, waving at them and blowing them kisses, cutting the grass in her baby dolls and slippers, singing, stopping to chirp with the birds or talk with the squirrels, or washing her car in bikinis that would look like pulled-up panties to anyone with a brain larger than hers.

This while he wore cotton briefs and a singlet under a white cotton uniform, the same uniform that he now wore home every night because the stitching of one suit had rotted apart and the other had shrunk when he tried to launder the jacket and slacks at home thinking to save the twenty dollars to spend on himself later. And each rainy day, whenever the rain came, she would run outside and dance or wash her hair in the yard, in a tee-shirt and panties, not caring, the neighbours gawking at her and laughing at him from behind their curtained windows.

His life was humiliating.

That was Phillips' fault, as was Tommy's worsening poverty. He hadn't been given a bonus better than anyone else since his promotion. Nor were his increases any better since the first. The one good thing was that Phillips' visits had dwindled to less than monthly occasions since making his workdays and weeks longer, spending more time with his airheads and zombies. Not that Emma could properly manage the home as a good wife while going to school. The place was a constant mess, littered with toys, her paints and her easels. She was terrible at being a wife, and for that and what people saw of her and the kid no one ever came to their home.

What he wasn't aware of was that Emma's classes did not end at eleven twice each week or that she met with Zeke Phillips for a coffee before returning home. Seeing Zeke alone was much less stressful for both of them irrespective of the pain in Phillips' back that hadn't left him after the accident, or his leg that was as stiff as the day they encased him from his foot to his hip in plaster. He didn't mind. The discomfort was nothing compared to what he owed Emma for the way he and so many others had wronged her for so long.

They had no friends because of her, because of her antics, because of his job and because the neighbours were troubled by the girl, not wanting their little girls to chase after the wind, or talk with invisible friends, or chirp while talking with birds. He didn't matter. What mattered was Gilligan and her mother's macabre canvases of half faces she never explained, not that he cared: one side twisted and dark, the texture of stone, a distorted dead eye staring, the other side left blank save for an eye emitting bright light, a half mouth painted in greens and yellows and reds curved into a smile.

He didn't exist in her world, her mind too polluted by Phillips.

He wanted to run. He wanted to leave his job and run. He wasn't afraid of hard work. He could hide in the north or far to the east on a fishing trawler out to sea for months at a time, returning to port with pockets filled to overflowing and young women, married or single, ready to whore for a bit of attention, a free meal and a few drinks. That's what he wanted, still not convinced that Phillips wasn't the father.

He was tired of watching the near-dead push rancid shit from their bowels, tired of flushing toilets or washing fetid backsides and thighs, stripping piss and feces-stained sheets from beds, helping them to eat or wiping drool from their chins and loose snot from their noses. His life wasn't about helping the weak or caring for frail bodies; his life was all about the shit they could never keep inside.

All that was good, his single reprieve, was that the constant wailing was over, the sleepless nights, and Gilligan was a month from the first day of school.

He didn't love Emma, he never had. She was the lesser of two evils forced upon him by Phillips. Nor was he a father to Gilligan, nor would he ever be. Why would he be? Too bad the doctor hadn't died in the ditch that night instead breaking a leg and cracking his skull.

He knew then how bad his life had become, that he couldn't survive, pleading with Emma to agree to adoption. However Emma was resolute without knowing why. She had no concept of poverty or good living, the privations of motherhood or being a real woman with a real man. How would she know? For her, days followed days and weeks followed weeks. She was insane despite what the doctor had said. And everyone knew, including the neighbours, the men who eagerly waited for each new summer when her car might be dirty or the grass too long, or to see what they could of her in the rain.

He needed more money. The home was too small, filled with toys and childish etchings on the walls, with nowhere for him to escape. His single relief were the photos hidden from sight, brought out when she was at class, when Gilligan was asleep in her room. He could handle his wife. What he could not manage was Phillips. He needed to make his life better or somehow get rid of the doctor.

But Phillips was firm. Tommy's salary was not a topic for discussion. He had already reached the peak of his pay scale, which was unfortunate and the next day he called in sick.

He arrived home that night in a new shirt and tie. He had a new job. An abattoir on the other side of town was hiring unskilled entry-level workers. The pay was the same as what Phillips was giving him, which isn't what he told her. He would begin in the Kill Room slitting gullets, working his way to eviscerating and packaging, which is what he hoped for but was never guaranteed. He didn't tell her that either and he began the next week, spending his days dressed in blood-stained white and wearing black rubber boots, his skin and his hair tainted with death, his nostrils never clear, standing eight hours a day over a sluice that was a torrent of blood. More importantly he was free of Phillips and the stenches of old men and women.

He didn't take Emma to see her new home, not at first, the one he had chosen for her. Instead he took her to a place where he wanted her to belong, where he wanted her to stay with another man, any other man, a place with very small rooms, bare walls and no light, no space to run, no birds or beautiful butterflies to chase. The strange men in the hall, he told her, would never go away. They had a right to live where they could.

For the first time in years Emma wept while Gilligan held her hands wanting to know why daddy was making her mommy cry, though Tommy was no less distraught, unable to cope with seeing his family in tears. Yet what could he do? He needed more money to make everything well. Even with his better paying job, their home and their life, her college and Gilligan were taking a toll he went on in a way he knew she would understand.

She had one year remaining before her diploma would come. Then what would she do? She was unknown, he told her. Her paintings wouldn't sell for a year or two or longer, if they sold at all. She wouldn't bring money into the home, helping him the way any good wife would want to do. However he did understand. He did. He didn't blame her at all. Things would get better. In fact he did have a plan because he loved her and he wanted to see her happy. He hadn't meant to scare her. He simply needed her to know what might happen if she didn't agree.

Tommy saw the day coming, he had for five years, from the very first night, which was his sole reason for leaving the institute. He would never be more than he was, not then, not ever because of Phillips. If Phillips hadn't gotten in the way his life would have been fine. He liked his job once, before his fall from grace because of what Emma had caused him to do without thinking, teasing him, stripping and folding her gown before going to bed, lying naked and ready under her sheet. So he'd planned for the future which was now the present and took her to her new home, hers unless she could understand what she must do.

She'd never been to that part of Solaceville, but her new home was bigger with grass and trees and was no farther from her school, better for raising a family and for those reasons she signed away the home that she loved.

Gilligan Rose began school on time in a new dress and shoes. She was happy and eager to learn from the very first day. She wanted to be like her mommy. She wasn't always afraid, nervous or scared, not now that mommy would always be by her side to play with her, to sing and to dance. Though often, without knowing why, Gilligan was sad. She wanted to cry and not tell her mommy why. More and more she began to tell Gilligan when they were alone because Gilligan knew how she felt and why.

From that point on a disconsolate Zeke Phillips saw his

favourite girls a few times less often each year, the next time with a gift for the home a few weeks after the move, ignoring Tommy as best he could. No love was lost between the men, the threat of prison still fresh in their minds.

Phillips did sense that something was wrong, though Emma couldn't imagine what that might be as hard as she tried. She didn't think so.

For a year the couple continued their life without friends. Tommy didn't want friends. He was ashamed of his work and his wife. Emma would never change her demented ways, though he doubted very much that the new neighbourhood men would want her to change. They were no less obvious when seeing her the way that she was, which they did often, the neighbourhood women no less appalled, no less protective of their daughters and boys. And then there was Gilligan whom he now wanted no one to see. She was growing to become like her mother.

Tommy rarely went outside himself. He believed the more everyone saw of Emma's oddities, the more they would stay away. He wanted to avoid friendly questions and he knew that going out would eventually mean inviting somebody in, which he didn't want to do. His two concessions were shovelling snow which he did in the dark when his neighbours were in for the night and putting Gilligan to bed when Emma was at school or in her studio hard at work.

Emma did everything else. She didn't think not to.

And so his life went, one year following the next, Emma's diploma lost in a drawer, her paintings unsold and littering the house.

Twelve
Nineteen Years Ago

Emma sold her first painting when Gilligan was nine. She'd never stopped painting. By the time Gilligan was eleven all two hundred were sold and by the time Gilligan reached her teens the one-sided faces of Miss Emma Rose were in high demand.

She loved to paint by the window where she could see the trees, the grass and the snow and Gilligan began painting with her. She painted all day and late into the night when she wasn't at galleries explaining her work or sipping wine with Zeke Phillips after the unveilings that Tommy never attended. That part of his life he hated the most, left alone with the kid and her moods except when he put her to bed.

He was tired of cutting animals' throats, the blood and the thick smell, too proud to ask Phillips to forgive what he now knew was his third worst mistake. His second, her fault as well, as much as the first and the third, was a punishable crime that no one must ever discover. He'd gone too far, waited too long.

Instead he quit his job and stayed home. Emma made more from one painting than he earned in a month. When, at a time, he didn't love her, now he despised her. She wore designer clothes, her skirts too short and her blouses too sheer, and she drove a Mercedes sedan that she paid for herself. She mowed the lawn every Saturday, well able to afford a service, and the neighbours knew at what time to watch. She washed her car every Sunday in patches and strings she called her bikinis and her hair in the rain whenever she could, so that he could hate her with all the more lust, though he knew if he touched her that Phillips would send him to prison.

They rarely had sex, which he resented, when legally Emma was his for whatever his need. Nor did he see her naked most days. Yet she would hang out their wet clothes on the line in her thongs and her bras, flaunting her bare ass, thinking nothing about what she was doing, enticing the neighbours, being a whore in everyone's eyes while he was a laughing stock they all believed was a fool. That much he knew.

She never complained about him not working. She liked that he no longer smelled the way that he had, though Phillips was less understanding. The men seldom met and when they did neither one had much to say.

All through her days and into the late evenings she hummed and she sang without any words, amusing her daughter who was no longer a baby, painting her lips red, dusting her cheeks a pale shade of pink, her eyes a light shade of green, turning thirteen into thirty in eyes that couldn't stop looking.

That summer they rented a villa by the ocean, leaving the house, Zeke Phillips and the neighbours behind. Gilligan came home less of a child, still loving her mommy who was now mother and wanting her daddy who was now father who never once that she could remember let her fall asleep alone in the dark after her mommy had kissed her goodnight.

But the nighties had gone in favour of baby dolls and tap pants with camisoles when Emma should have remembered her own first years in the dark. Pigtails became ponytails, skirts and sweaters replaced school tunics and bedtime stories were a thing of the past. For the first time in years Tommy Dune was anxious to know the dates of his wife's upcoming unveilings, the next of which was three weeks away and with her growing success she wasn't wrong to expect many more.

Gilligan was constantly on his mind, his crime never forgotten, his fear never quite tamed. Yet how could he stop? How could he confess to the world the wrong he was doing without going to prison?

The night three weeks later Tommy sat by Gilligan's bed, gently squeezing her knee through the duvet, saying he loved her and that her mother was sorry. She wouldn't be home to kiss her beautiful daughter goodnight. Gilligan smiled and turned over. She liked turning over so that when she awoke in the night she would see Gilligan a mirror away and talk in a whisper about all that was in her head. She was always so happy, yet in her mind she was always so sad. Or was she forever sad and in her mind she sought to be happy? She had so much to say and Gilligan loved to hear every word.

He watched her in silence, slipping a hand under the weight of her cover the way he'd done since her first day of school, since Emma's increasing neglect, her smooth skin warm to the touch of his trembling hand, the smell of bourbon staining his breath, the sting of its taste burning his tongue. That she was one day so happy and one day so sad wasn't his fault. He could never undo the damage Emma had done by refusing to accept what was the right thing to do that fateful night at Solaceville General. He moved his hand higher to the small of her back, rubbing in circles the way he knew that she liked since she was small. Now she was as tall as her mother.

He brought his hand down, letting his palm rest where she now felt more like a woman, wanting more than the feel of her silk at his fingertips, remembering all the young girls in his bed before he met Phillips. He whispered her name, repeating how much he loved her and, when he was certain she was flying with fairies in a faraway place, he took a deep breath. Draining his bourbon he pulled back the cover. He hadn't touched her that way since before the summer vacation, easing his hand under her panties. He waited as long as he dared, hating to leave her and went to the basement where he laid out her pictures.

The next evening Emma was home in her studio while he sat on Gilligan's bed without very much to say, listening as she spoke quietly about her day at school and her day with her mother. Thinking that she did, or thinking that she didn't want to do this or want to do that. Tommy sat and listened with nothing to add. He had begun to feel stupid that at forty he knew nothing at all beyond his four walls.

Again his daughter turned over. He knew that she would. He listened for footsteps and heard not a sound. Emma was painting, her studio well-lit and the window wide open. He knew the neighbour was watching and waiting

Again he pulled down the covers, controlling his breathing, taking her in, recalling his past. From her waist to her shoulders she was so soft and smooth, her skin warm under his touch, his eyes fixated on the fullness under her panties that was enticing. Unable to wait, first easing his hand under one side of the loose-fitting silk to linger, then the other, lingering as long as he dared, absorbing her warmth and once again he hated to leave her. That night, however, Emma wouldn't say no. He wouldn't allow her. Not this time when all the pictures he'd taken at the beach and the cottage would do him no good at all. He needed a woman and took Emma early to bed to make love with his daughter.

The next morning Gilligan went to school dressed much like her mother when other teenage girls wore sneakers, tight jeans, tee-shirts and hoodies. She loved all that she learned most days. Though often, no longer surprised by her moods, her teachers were at a loss to understand what the girl understood and what she did not, what subjects she liked and the ones she did not. They didn't know what they should think. They had once met her mother and thought Emma was more of a child than the girl in so many ways and not a good mother in so many more. They were aware of the rain, the car and the grass, the despair and delight that she created on canvas and the scandalous way in which she hung her wash out to dry.

But Emma had flair, and they certainly did not. Emma had money, a European car, which they certainly did not. And Emma had looks which she's passed on to her daughter and dressed in fine clothes. They certainly did not and kept their mouths shut.

Nor did Tommy have anything to say.

Thirteen
Last Year: July 31st

The southeastern bureau of The Federal Task Force on Major Crime was as close to luxury as any cop could expect, situated on the fourteenth floor of a steel and mirrored-glass tower with a view reaching out over the Atlantic Ocean. Not that Captain Gayle Brannigan could see the ocean from her corner office perch that was more comfortable and better appointed than the finest boutique hotel lobby and intentionally comfortable to the point of distraction.

What she could see through her reflection dripping with rain was the parking lot and a stunning Deena Archer slouched in her car, waiting alone with the wipers standing at attention on a windshield coated with thick rivulets of water, the engine switched off. She was waiting for Johnnie Fennell, speaking into her cell.

She always waited for Fennell, the two arriving separately and coming in together, first meeting side by side in reserved parking spots, and often Brannigan would wonder from where and from after what. Then she would admonish herself for entertaining such a ludicrous thought. The time was eight PM. Other times she thought: what a waste. However what Archer did or did not do on her own time wasn't her business unless they did have something going on under the covers, which was impossible, almost impossible, in which case Archer would be terminated immediately and without discussion from the squad. Fennell was practically untouchable.

That wasn't the reason, she knew. When they weren't flying to another state or city they arrived separately because Fennell refused to park an agency black and shiny SUV on the street outside his humble apartment. He didn't need the publicity, he insisted. Neither was he willing to be a rich girl's chauffeur, dropping her off in the evening and waiting for her like a lapdog on a leash in the morning. That's what he said. What Brannigan knew was that he could simply piss off more people with his private parking and an SUV that no one else could drive, not even Archer unless he was dead or bleeding in the backseat.

Archer was purely business, likeable, proud to be the second best agent in her view, and if his bleeding in the backseat was what she needed in order to drive the SUV that was fine with her. No one liked Johnnie Fennell. He was one big, independent, self-satisfied pain in the ass and her ass was no exception.

Archer was poised, a pampered prep school teenager who chose criminology over catwalks at thousands of dollars an hour. She didn't need the money. She was filthy rich and lived in an ocean view penthouse. Conversely, Fennell was not a diamond in the rough. He was what he was. He was Fennell. He was rough around the edges and didn't care about too many people, if anyone. Because really, truth told, how many were actually worth the trouble. Not many in his view, an opinion that Brannigan discovered early on was pointless to argue.

They were love-hate, water and oil. Archer wore designer, Fennell wore the same thing every day: black shoes and black socks, a black suit and a black tie. Though Brannigan was fairly certain, or at least she suspected, that he owned seven white shirts. Whether they were pressed was another matter entirely.

At restaurants Archer knew her wines. She had expensive taste and never drank from one-litre jugs disguised as carafes. She knew the difference between filet mignon and steak tartare. Whereas Fennell believed one was overpriced, the first time he'd paid for her meal, not believing her for a moment that anyone would pay to eat the same meat raw, chopped into pieces, mixed with raw egg and served cold. Not at any price. Nor did he believe the price of the wine or the grin on her face when he continued insisting that he would pay.

He preferred most of his meals in a bun served with a beer. That was Fennell and Archer.

Most times Fennell would exit his vintage Malibu Classic, lean against the quarter-panel and wait with his back to his partner, letting Archer come to him, but not that last night in July. He never once opened her door and Archer never once expected that he would. He was rude and arrogant and often Brannigan found herself regretting that she had never learned to read lips, not that she couldn't read Archer's eyes.

Fennell stood six-foot, Archer inches shorter in heels, Fennell predictably a few steps ahead, Archer predictably arriving a little out of breath, not once thinking to hold him back, never once asking him to slow. She wouldn't give him the satisfaction: Fire and water.

Fennell arrived late. The man never hurried. He didn't care and Brannigan had given up years earlier threatening him. All she ever got for her effort was a silent and very infuriating grin. She shook her head. The duo exited, Fennell several feet ahead, not waiting, walking briskly, he seldom ran, Archer running, her purse on her head, her designer shoes splashing rainwater to her designer-clad knees.

Brannigan didn't have to see their faces to know she would have that scotch before going home, though she seldom got away from Fennell without two.

Fennell walked in first. He was dripping, his black hair matted to his head. He took off his jacket, shaking a shower of beads across the captain's carpet. She wasn't impressed. He didn't care and she knew he didn't care. Archer strode in a moment later, her long dark hair hanging in thick strands stuck to the sides of her face, framing a rich palette of black and aubergine at her eyes, a deep prune pursed between her tight lips. The deep rose at her cheeks was real. Her Armani suit was soaked through. She was shivering and Fennell seemed not to care because, in fact, he did not.

She swept the rain from her face, combing her hair to the back of her head with open palms, their expressions telling her instantly that she'd done something wrong. God! She wanted to wipe the smirk from his face.

"You are a complete and inconsiderate fool, Fennell. You knew very well I was calling you and why and you didn't answer me."

"Why would I answer you? We spoke an hour ago and, besides, we were late. You know boss lady here doesn't like us coming in late."

"A gentleman would have offered me his jacket."

"Even if I did, your pants would still be soaked. Besides you are wearing a jacket, which you should take off, by the way, before you catch a chill. And the pants, don't forget the pants. We don't want you catching a cold. So, you see, I am considerate"

"Thank you, I'm fine the way I am."

Fennell turned to Brannigan. "A dime to a dollar she isn't wearing a bra, boss lady. Not that she has to, I suppose."

"Archer, you look like a drowned rat. If you are wearing a bra I'm sure he's seen better. So get that jacket off. If you're not, do us all a favour and suffer. Do not, however, even think to call in sick."

She didn't answer.

"I was right, boss lady, no bra. Isn't that something a lady would do, you know, wearing a bra? And let's not forget her slacks. She's drenched. Unless, of course…"

"Yeah, right, Fennell. Good luck with that sick dream. You're such an obvious pig."

"Fennell, shut up. You called this meeting, so get to it. And don't either one of you even think to sit on my fine furniture."

Johnnie Fennell was an old-time cop in a young man's body. His father and grandfather were cops. He knew what they knew with his personal savvy to boot. He was thirty-five and believed that perhaps one person out of every hundred he passed on the street was good, or could be good. The rest in varying degrees were not. And some angry broad out there was decidedly not. Give Joe or Jane Blow a chance, a good chance of getting away, and they'll do something illegal, bad, wrong or indifferent. The world was increasingly not a good place and some pissed-off female was lurking the streets of the world killing two-faced American businessmen.

Fennell loved the rain, mostly because he saw fewer people that he could look at and distrust on the spot. This night the gods were pissing down big time. Not satisfied with drowning his city they had to ignite the skyline with elongated and twisted white flashes and threaten every pane of glass within the city limits with deafening thunder.

Gayle Brannigan said, "Repeat that, Fennell."

"I said he's the tenth corpse sent home with a hole in his chest in ten years. So why are we dragging our asses?"

Archer disagreed. Agreeing with him didn't seem natural. "From what I know these guys aren't worth the effort, Captain. They're perps in their own right. Each one died with a wet dick. Remember, Fennell? Each one got what they wanted...royally screwed. That's a wife's problem, not ours. We're not here to solve marital issues. My guess is the women are better off without them. I can't see that dead or divorced would make much difference after they're gone."

The captain added: "Archer could be right. I've been

with the same man for twenty-five years and he hasn't once thought of another woman and, be with one, he would be better off dead."

"With all due respect, boss lady, he's either a liar or not anatomically correct."

She leered over the rims of her glasses, her eyes white, her skin ebony black. She had the stern façade of a calypso dancer and the tight, pulled-back hairstyle to match. She was sturdy, not slim, most of her cloaked most days in her signature two-piece suits.

"Is that so, Agent?"

"Yeah, that's so. Us guys, we all look and we all imagine. Take little Deena here. She's a perfect example. Every cop in the building's been to bed with her dozens of times while doing their own dog-faced women." He smirked at her. She wanted to kick the side of his head. "Besides me, that is. I'm more of girl-next-door kind of guy. And I'm pretty sure you've had your time in more than a few fanciful scenarios, boss lady. You know, back in the day."

"My time… back in the day."

He nodded. "You're a fine example of womanhood, boss lady. You know what they say, black is beautiful, though let's face reality," he grimaced, "fifteen, twenty years with the same woman."

He yawned.

"I said twenty-five years, Fennell, and my husband's just fine where he has to be. Thank you for your concern."

Johnnie Fennell shrugged.

Archer was miffed. "Captain, creeps like that never change… like this one here will never change." She glared at her partner. "Dog-faced, what does that even mean? And by the way Fennell, the ones who have to imagine won't ever be good enough to see me in my bed all naked and sweaty. The others don't have to imagine. They've got the memories, very good memories, hot memories, hot like in steaming hot…you sanctimonious, self-centred idiot."

The captain crossed her legs at the ankles, leaning against the front edge of her desk, crossing her arms. She was going to have that drink. The cops in her squad knew better than to ever to sit in her office. People who sat too long, she believed, were less likely to do what they were paid to do: think, solve crimes and stay alive.

"We get the picture, Archer. You're hot," the captain allowed, raising her eyebrows at Fennell. "And, Fennell, you're left out in the cold, which is exactly where I want you. If either of you even hints at playing touchy-touchy together you're out of here. I mean it. I don't need my cops seeing each other naked and sweaty and getting sloppy on the job."

"Captain, that is so revolting. I mean, look at him. God! I cannot believe you said that."

Brannigan was a good-looking woman Fennell thought, in anyone's day past or present. She was a head-turner. Hubby was a lucky man. "Not to worry, boss lady. It'll never happen. No freezer burn from the ice queen on this boy. Besides, women who wear pants all the time, it's either penis envy or they've got something not quite right going on in the lower half. You know, like veins, or knobby knees." He hunched his shoulders. He didn't know. He couldn't be certain. "Or it could be the back half is a little, you know, dented."

Archer scrunched her face, wanting to smack the grin from his face or shoot him. She was cold. She wasn't wearing a bra and all she wanted was to go home, soak in a hot bath with soft music and candles.

The captain shook her head, thinking she should make them each stand in a corner, different corners. Put them in the same corner and she couldn't imagine. She didn't want to imagine. Deena was not an ice queen, not by any stretch of the imagination and Johnnie wasn't self-centred, just a pain in the ass most times. In fact she was surprised that nothing had happened between them.

"So what do we do? Convince me. We've got ten dead guys in five or six foreign cities. Are we talking copycat, coincidence or trend, a wife's problem or ours? You tell me."

Archer went first. "Whoever she is she's not our problem, Captain. She's got a burr in her panties. Okay, that's not good, and she'll probably kill again. That said; she isn't domestic. She isn't our problem. Guys wake up all the time in foreign cities, in places they shouldn't be, without their organs. What makes these guys any different? At least they never had to explain to their wives that they were killed by a whore," she snickered, "because they didn't perform up to par."

"Spoken like a prim and prissy female on both counts, Archer. First off, the broad's not a whore," Fennell argued. "Or, if she is, she's making enough money with her feet in the air to fly around the world and broads like that they don't come cheap like the others. We're talking five to a grand or more depending what's being served from the menu. Fact number two: pay the fee and come up short or wear them out. They don't care either way once they're paid; not much different from a dinner date for the rest of us who can't come up with the finances. So we find what we can where we can and after they're well-fed we take them home then put them in a taxi before we have to cook them up a breakfast." He brushed his hands together. "Adios, au revoir and sayonara. I'll call you sometime."

The women exchanged glances. Fennell had a way of reducing most arguments to an elemental truth.

"Like the ones you know, I suppose."

"My guy's cultured, and very selective. He prefers not to swim in public pools or dip into sewers."

"You mean the thing hasn't already fallen off in some alley?"

He   shook   his   head.   "He's   clean   as   a whistle...figuratively speaking."

"You're disgusting."

Fennell eyed her up and down. Deena Archer was 5'6",
slim with auburn hair and wore her pants like a second skin
with never a tell-tale line. In her shoes, strapped at the
ankles, she was still a couple of inches shorter than Fennell
and he never stopped hoping that one day she would wear a
dress or a skirt. Her blouses were sheer, open at the neck,
which he liked very much, with a jacket to match her slacks,
which he didn't like at all. She was also the reason he
worked most weekends. He didn't have a life, she did, and
he didn't like that very much either.

During the week, any day of the week, he would take a
bullet for her without hesitation, a fact he kept to himself,
thinking that perhaps once, or possibly twice, he wouldn't
mind having her in his home eating pizza and drinking wine
without Berettas clamped to the their belts, laughing and
seeing if, yeah, they could work. If not, at least he would
have tried and maybe see her naked. That wouldn't be a bad
thing. Naked was good. In that way he wasn't so different
from the other guys in the building.

The reality being that they ate lunch when they could,
every so often a fast dinner in a restaurant where she would
do the ordering instead of take-out. She didn't like street
corner diners. They weren't street cops who needed to rub
elbows with squealers or pimps or dealers. Then they went
home late each night or to hotel rooms to separate lives,
dreams and empty beds, at least he did, never speaking on
the phone unless someone worth their time was found dead
in another city or had less fun than expected in Miami's
nightlife. She was thirty and way out of his league. Her
father was a senator, her mother a DA, and she might even
be richer than him by a few million. His suit for work was
off the rack. Hers were designer. His shirts for work cost
19.95 on sale, her blouses cost 500 and she didn't wait for
bargains.

"I'm not the one talking about my hot, sweaty body and all sorts of memories." He paused. "So, Archer, how many are we talking here, ten, twenty? You know, most guys, they don't like too much history."

"You just have to know about one, Fennell, the one who doesn't stand a chance."

The captain interrupted the banter. Her workday was about over and she wanted to get home.

"When you teenagers are finished with your dirty talk, perhaps we can open or close this file before I die of starvation."

Archer opened her mouth, ready to speak first. Fennell cut her off.

"Listen, ladies, ten dead guys is sort of a no-brainer. Don't you think? And while Archer here is out doing the town and writing notes in her diary so she doesn't confuse the names of the guys who want seconds, I've done some checking. These guys were all businessmen, all in their thirties and early forties, all of them married with kids, all of them dysfunctional, some with marriages on the rocks, some getting divorced. In all cases the women were either getting or taking the kids. So yeah, they were looking to get laid with something younger and prettier. Go figure. Who doesn't want young and pretty? All these guys were killed on July 15th, all of them on the night they arrived, all of them with some sort of knife in the chest. And something else, she's never left a trace. She even takes the sheets and the condoms, glasses and bottles. She has this thing about ordering expensive cognac or champagne on their tab. I suppose when they're in the can getting ready for the big bang."

Gayle Brannigan asked, "What about security cameras? Nobody's seen this woman?"

"Big hats each time, and classy, with little dresses, the kind Archer wears to her fancy parties and those big floppy shoulder bags she needs for clean underwear in case of a sleepover or, in this case, a knife. And this broad, she leaves her dead dates each time in the morning, in the middle of the big rush. And get this; she uses their frigging luggage to carry out the evidence. She never stays at the same hotel or, if she does, she goes somewhere else to change. This broad is smart…and cold. After she kills them she sticks around to tidy up or catnap."

"Could be that she goes to another hotel, changes in the ladies' room," Archer tried.

"No. Like I said, she's smart. Some of these cities have cameras on every corner. No, this broad's on a mission. She's not doing this to get caught. She doesn't want to stop. She's doing her thing, like some sort of a vendetta. The question is why. Who pissed her off?"

"Bad husbands," Archer tried again. "Maybe she has one herself."

"Then he would probably already be dead. And all these wives, they had perfect alibis. They were all at home doing dishes and watching TV like good women. Not a one showed up on a passenger list. But that's not it, not about bad husbands. We're talking bad fathers here, ladies. The last guy, Cooper, she did him in Paris. He had his computer and phone loaded with photos of his daughter in her swimsuits and underwear. She's barely touching fifteen." He snorted. "After he was dead the broad emailed everything to the wife with a note. The wife must have barfed. He didn't have one photo of her, just the kid. I spoke with her. She's glad he's dead. Good thing for her that he was killed 7000 miles away or she'd be a prime target for us."

Johnnie Fennell went to the window, one instant seeing the city, another moment his vision blurred by herculean raindrops smashing at the glass, highlighting Brannigan and Archer in the plush setting behind him.

The captain waited, exchanging curious glances with Archer. Fennell often went into another dimension, another place and time. He was also an excellent cop and Deena Archer wouldn't think to work with anyone else. She'd been with him for seven months, taken from Robbery, introduced to her mentor by Gayle Brannigan without any preamble at the department's New Year's luncheon. She was a favour pulled in, one that her boss had not yet regretted.

Yes, he was a complete asshole and anyone who didn't think so didn't know him. Archer felt sorry for the lady in his life, putting up with him 24/7, but that part of his life was private. Johnnie never spoke about his personal life, his weekends or his vacations. All she knew about him was that he was single, which didn't surprise her, and that he certainly wasn't gay. No way could he be gay, apart from the fact that he dressed like an indigent street dweller and shaved once a week.

"Care to share what's whizzing through that scary head of yours, Agent Fennell?"

"We need to do this, boss lady. This broad's young. She has a lot of years ahead of her. Stop her now or we could easily see another twenty or thirty July 15ths. She won't stop anytime soon."

"Fennell," Archer broke in, "no one's seen the woman except for her arms and legs, yet you know she's young. Get real and stop fantasizing. What if she's simply in good shape? Maybe she works out, or maybe she's an athlete."

"She is in good shape, very good shape." He grinned. "She probably doesn't wear a bra either. Too bad she'll have to spend her life in prison for multiple homicides. And she is young. These guys were all in their thirties, very early forties. No guy that age wants to bag a broad in her forties or fifties, not unless she frigging wealthy."

"Thank you for that, Agent Fennell."

"Not you, boss lady. Not too many females look as good as you at your age." He beamed. "You got married at what, fifteen, sixteen, tops?"

"I forget. Why don't you ask my cheating husband?"

"Fennell," Archer barked, "did you even have parents...ever? Or did you just grow out of the ground?"

"That hurt."

Deena Archer rolled her eyes. Nothing hurt Fennell.

"So where are we going with this?" Brannigan asked.

"Ladies, she's thirty-something and she started very young. Here's something else. She's not a passenger. She could be a pilot, though I doubt it. For my money she's a flight attendant in First-Class for Trans-Global Airlines."

"Fennell you don't have any money. Can you even remember the last time you bought a new suit? No wonder you're still a bachelor. And what would you possibly know about First-Class?"

Archer could feel her skin growing clammier.

"Hey, I make more than you do."

"Oh, that makes all the difference. In case you haven't noticed, that car, the one parked beside your Chevy Clunker, that's a hand-painted Aston Martin."

Gayle Brannigan moved from her desk. She was getting a headache. She sat in her chair, opened her drawer and brought out a bottle of malt scotch with three old-fashioned. She filled each one two-fingers deep, thinking three wouldn't be enough.

"Sit, both of you, and drink." She led with the first sip. "Tell me why she's not a passenger. And you, Archer, drink and shut up."

"All these guys flew First-Class with double rows port and starboard, comfy seats with high backs in 747s and 380s. Not your usual five or six deep, impossible to see what or who is behind or up front...unless you're standing. And what guy doesn't dream of doing these broads? They're all drop-dead gorgeous, travelled, lonely or bored, and most can use words with more than one syllable. They're the cream de la cream."

Brannigan waved an instant warning finger at Deena. "I

said drink."

"And something else, most of these passengers don't dig deep into their pockets to fly that way, their companies do, and entertaining that brand of female takes serious cash. These guys didn't have it to spend. They were a hundred percent expensed. That's why the booze doesn't make sense. The broad ordered it and she paid for dinner, so no paper trail, no restaurant and no possible identification. We're talking a few hundred dollars for a bottle or two, supposedly ordered by guys who wouldn't know good booze if they drowned in it…and Dom Perignon. Give me a break."

"Dom Pérignon! It's pronounced dom-pear-een-yo." Archer looked to Brannigan. "God, he's so incredibly annoying."

He ignored her, on purpose. The captain chortled, making a mental note.

"So what I believe, boss lady, this broad's after guys who have a thing for their daughters. Each one of them had a stack of pictures and videos hidden somewhere in the house. After the last guy, this Charles Cooper guy, I called them. I've spoken with each one. They've agreed to meet with me and Archer, all of them, and all of them out of state." He glanced at Archer. "So pack a Gucci and, you know, a bra and some sexy panties in case we get a few rainy days."

She camouflaged her snarl with her glass.

"So you meet with them, then what's the next step?" Brannigan wanted to know.

"I don't know."

Archer coughed scotch through her nose. "Finally, something he doesn't know. Call NBC."

"Archer, say one more word and I'm giving Johnnie here permission to spank little Deena over his knee, right here, right now. I mean what I say and I will disavow that he did." She tilted her head. "So unless you want him to paddle your skinny tanned ass, and I'm beginning to believe that you do, shut up." She turned her attention to a satisfied Fennell. "Talk to me. Say something good so I can go home."

"Somehow she knows. I mean, she has to. She's never been wrong. So I'm thinking these guys talked a bit too much. Or they spent time checking out child porn in-flight, their own kids, while a flight attendant with a knife looked over their shoulders and made her own plans. She has to be a flight attendant. Remember, these flights were all over water at night when most passengers are sleeping, dead to the world. What if these ten guys weren't as tired as everyone else?"

"She could be another passenger, another one not sleeping, sitting beside them pretending to sleep."

"What are the odds that on the fifteenth, for ten years running, Jane Doe would be sitting beside some guy with a thing for his daughter? No. This broad's an attendant with fifty weeks to go and counting."

"I don't like where this is going. Uh-uh. I do not. This is not our jurisdiction. They were all killed offshore while doing the dirty with a killer which, to my mind, is far better than what else they were doing, which you're suggesting is what got them killed in the first place. At least now we don't have to deal with messed up kids."

"Or are we?" he countered. "Me and Archer, we interview the wives, get a better sense of things, after which we spend fifty weeks one step ahead of her before closing the file. We set her up."

"What you're saying is one year to solve one case, maybe."

"One month each including the next guy who might think he's worth our time."

Archer cut in. "This is how I see things happening, Captain. We interview, and we find out what Fennell already knows. Then on the fifteenth, because we know who this woman is, or will, Fennell volunteers to get himself laid by a killer and he gets stabbed in the chest. Is that about right, Fennell?"

"That's it, in a nutshell, with a few tweaks to work out in the meantime."

"Then I'm in, Captain. I say let's go for it."

Gayle Brannigan refilled her glass. She slid the bottle across her desk telling Fennell to fill Archer's first, if he could manage that. He knew when to say nothing, when a warm smile went much farther.

"May the good Lord have mercy on me! How did I ever think to make you two partners?"

"Well, she was young, still is, inexperienced, getting a little better, insecure, and she needed guidance. That's why you're the boss lady."

"Fennell, shut up."

He did. Brannigan sipped her scotch, deep in thought. So did Archer with both hands, feeling cold and miserable. She hated him.

After a few minutes the captain inhaled a deep breath. "I want this woman caught on the fifteenth…and I want your 'guy' to stay dry. Do you understand me? I do not want you interacting with a perp. I don't care how good-looking she is. You get your jollies somewhere else and you get her on American soil. We're not working for the French or anyone else. Whatever you do, you do here and you do whatever standing up. I'll have enough trouble explaining this to the money people downstairs. I don't need the State Department on my ass."

"That's why they're downstairs and you're up here, boss lady. No sweat and nothing from the honey jar, scouts honour."

"Captain, I want to be reassigned," Archer interjected.

"You are, Archer, to wherever he takes you. And before you do you're taking him somewhere with a thousand dollars. He can't be seen like this in First-Class."

Deena Archer scanned her partner from head to toe. "You want me to repair this with a thousand dollars? You can't be serious. Look at him. All he's missing is a tin cup."

"My man dresses very well, thank you very much, for half that. And he is a fine-looking man."

"Your husband isn't a social mongrel. I mean, look at the man. I'm sorry; I mean him, it, the thing slouched in your seat like he doesn't have a backbone."

"One thousand, that's all, and not on a workday. So work things out."

Archer sipped her drink. "How much do I get, the same?"

Brannigan chortled. "You must be joking, little rich girl. You get him, all to yourself for fifty weeks... and in separate hotel rooms or I don't want to hear anything about the sordid details".

Archer's mouth dropped open, her jaw frozen in a grimace. "That you could even think that, Captain, is revolting."

Brannigan ignored her. "Ten years and we know the cities. We're talking ten specific flights. We know the airline and we'll get a warrant to obtain the recorded duty rosters. This isn't rocket science. Some woman, a woman, was on each of those flights. Could be a few times she's been on vacation. Find out. And when you do, you track her. That's your job, Archer. You find out everything about her. You," she looked at Fennell, "you keep a low profile. You fly with her on or near the fifteenth of each month. You've got the better part of a year to work this woman. So don't mess up. Fly anywhere else, you do so on another carrier."

Archer slouched and sighed. "I should have been a meter maid."

Gayle Brannigan was sympathetic. "Oh, you're just saying that because Miss Armani is all wrinkly and damp, you poor little darling. You call me in the morning, sweet thing, if you still feel that way. We can have you outfitted in rubber-soled boots, striped pants and a neon nylon jacket by noon on Monday." She sipped her scotch. "Did I mention button-down cotton shirts and your very own scooter with an orange flashing light and a space for your little Gucci lunch bag?"

"It's the scotch talking, Captain. Sorry."

"I thought as much and we're done here, boys and girls. I want weekly reports and monthly in-house one-on-ones. And Fennell, don't do anything to make this girl kill you. And, you," she turned her attention to Archer, "the next time you come into my office from the pouring rain you make certain you're wearing a bra or a raincoat instead of leaving water marks on my furniture."

Archer's brow creased. "Fennell is too."

"Don't pout when you're wearing a weapon. It's unbecoming. Fennell has an excuse. He's Fennell. I expect a much higher standard from you. And Archer, if you are going to shoot him anytime this year, you do so on your own time, in another city, and claim insanity. I'll back you up. Now get out of my office and take him with you."

They stood and left quietly without formality. Gayle Brannigan wasn't a boss given to 'good luck' or 'call me 24/7'. She brought the best into her squad and expected the best. She phoned her husband, waited five minutes and went from her office to a restricted elevator that led to secure indoor parking.

Though moments before, in the corridor and in another elevator, Archer was fuming. Finally: "We're a team, Fennell, so stop thinking you're so much better than me."

Then she went quiet, hating that he was standing so close to her without saying anything.

In the lobby: "Do you even have a thousand upfront dollars?"

"Well, I do have a credit card, but things are pretty expensive these days and…"

"...okay, you don't, surprise, surprise. You'll owe me. Or better yet I'll expense it myself. At least that way I know I'll be reimbursed."

The rain had stopped, not the rumbling. The parking lot was empty except for two cars and a black SUV, a thin carpeting of vapour hung over the pavement. His car was metallic baby blue, hers was high-gloss prune: a five k option that she opted for to match her favourite nail polish and lipstick.

"So, what's the plan, Agent Archer, ten AM, eleven? If that's good for you I'll come for you, naturally. That should give you enough time to rinse out and dry your clothes."

"Me, go shopping in this thing? No. I don't think so. That doesn't work for me. I'll come for you at ten. I know that you're accustomed to leaving a store with your new suit in a paper bag, Fennell, whenever that might have been, but this should take a week or two with one or two fittings. Just so you know."

They parted, Johnnie Fennell calling her name as she opened the door of the Aston Martin. She turned, expecting something off-colour, something he'd waited for the perfect time to say. He was such a prick.

"Just so we're clear, Archer, you are a good cop, practically the best. And if you haven't figured things out yet, you're assigned to me so that one day you will be the best, at least as good as me." He opened his door. "Also, so you know, you look terrific tonight. Not many women can wear a thunderstorm that well. I love what you've done with your make-up and your hair, very chic, very avant-garde. I have to say, I was pretty tempted to follow through with that spanking." His grin was wide. "Let's do lunch tomorrow, somewhere nice that doesn't serve raw meat, my treat. Oh, and by the way, one question before I go. Is what Brannigan said true?"

"Is what true?"

"Your ass, is it tanned?"

He climbed in behind the wheel. His restored 350-four barrel Malibu Classic purred. He didn't hear her or see her lips curl.

At home in her bath, submerged to her neck under a film of designer oil, Deena Archer rummaged through her mind for Saturday's wardrobe. If she looked terrific drenched in rainwater, and she did, he wouldn't believe how great she could look. Wait, jerk. She wasn't just pretty or beautiful, she was drop-dead gorgeous. She faced into the mirror by the side of tub, her intake of air loud. She looked frightful; her face plastered with two seamless smudges the colour of dark mud, her hair clumped with unwanted knots.

She sank beneath the surface thinking okay, maybe not right at that moment, but she would be gorgeous in the morning. And she wouldn't be wearing her primary weapon because she wouldn't have anywhere to conceal a gun, not even a small one. She burst into the air gasping for breath. Veins my tanned ass! Screw you, Fennell.

At home Johnnie Fennel stripped to his straight-backs and tee-shirt. He hung his pants from the top edge of his bedroom door, his jacket from another and his tie on a doorknob. His shirt found its way to the floor with his socks.

He went to the fridge for a beer, found CNN on the remote and fell asleep on the sofa.

Fourteen
Last Year: August 01st

Saturday morning was clear and warm in South Beach, not hot or oppressive, a perfect day for the beach. Deena Archer's ocean playground wardrobe was varied, a mixture of one-pieces, two-pieces, bikinis and thongs. The first three she would wear often to the beach where she would sit alone. The thongs she wore at home in her top floor penthouse garden and spa, alone. She was tired of being alone, fending off one-night stands.

She seldom dated because she was rarely asked out. Men didn't like the thought of dating a girl who wore two guns, or one that could break an arm or a leg with no effort at all. Getting into her pants, that was something else. Some could get past her good looks, though never her guns or what she did for a living. Cops had no chance at all. She didn't date cops and no one had to ask why. She worked in an elite squad and lived an elite life, albeit alone most of the time.

She sipped her morning coffee, peering out over the ocean from the edge of her private pool, searching for answers, answers that would explain why she was with him: the beauty and the beast. Saturday morning and, instead of sunning at the beach with a friend or a lover, she would be spending the day with Agent Johnnie Fennell. Not John or Jonathon, Johnnie like some little boy who never matured. That she didn't have a lover didn't matter, or that she didn't have many friends. What mattered was that he ruined her entire weekend and he was an absolute jerk. She knew very well she would spend all day Sunday cursing his absolute lack of finesse and decorum.

He thought he was so superior and smart, so all-knowing and better than anyone else. So what if he never said that he was; that's what he thought which was no better. In fact that made his conceit so much worse. He was always so smug. His parents, she thought, must be very much like him, or so disappointed by how he turned out. So what if he was good? Okay, so he was, she conceded. That didn't give him the right to be right all the time.

She stepped inside to refill her cup. The day would be hers. Screw him. She would make certain of that, if she hadn't already.

She looked at her watch: 8:55 and she wasn't yet dressed. She wanted to wait for her arms and her legs to appear naturally smooth, soft and silky to the touch, not pampered with creams as she was an hour before. She wanted her perfume to make her alluring, not cheap or trashy like the women he would be accustomed to sniffing like a barnyard dog. Not that he would think to touch her or stand near enough to inhale her discreetly feminine aura. She was happy enough to know that everyone seeing them together would believe she was doing charitable work with the homeless.

She exhaled. What was she doing? She was following strict orders. That's all that she was doing. She went to her bedroom and dressed in her latest purchases. One hour and five minutes later she was outside his address in upscale Boca Raton.

But this wasn't his home. She'd screwed up. She never thought of Fennell having a home. A cave, yes, or a hole in the ground with a lid for the days when it rained, never a home with a door and a garage, a driveway, green grass and everything was so well maintained. She hadn't thought to question the address. She should have known better. She had to stop being flustered around him, aggravated.

She phoned him to apologize, to explain that she would be late, that somehow she'd noted the wrong address. Somehow she'd gone to the wrong house, which wasn't good for a cop. He told her that he'd be out in a minute and while she waited she wondered who would have taken him in, given him a room in the basement or at the back of the house. No one in that neighbourhood needed to take in lodgers. Who was that hard up for an extra few dollars a month? Certainly no one with a midnight blue, late-model Jag parked in the driveway.

She climbed from her car and stood inside the gate to make the biggest impact possible in her four-inch, open-toed stilettos, bare and tanned legs, a skirt whose pleated hem was closer to her bum than her knees and a matching two-button bolero that left no doubt whatsoever that she was wearing a bra that didn't come six to a box.

When Fennell came out he stopped dead in his tracks, spoiling her moment, his arms stretched out with genuine surprise, his jaw wide apart, slowly closing, a sly grin forming.

Archer was no better, her haughty façade vanishing. Her eyes might well have popped out if not for her Versace sunglasses. Johnnie Fennell was coming at her in oxblood dress boots that glistened, blue kid leather jeans and a bright yellow V-neck sweater trimmed at the collar with a white tee-shirt that seemed too white, too pure. His blazer was Mediterranean blue; the buttons were brass, the pocket hanky was a deep yellow silk. He was clean-shaven and his hair was combed into a style. This wasn't real. Agent Johnnie Fennell never combed his hair. She doubted that he even owned a comb, let alone knowing how to use one. She wanted to see his eyes, to see him laughing at her. She couldn't, annoyed. They were covered with bright gold-rimmed silver Ray Bans.

She was totally screwed with nothing to say. The

bastard, she thought, the absolute bastard. He'd dressed that way on purpose to make her angry. She was angry. He'd probably borrowed the clothes from whoever owned the house. She needed something to say. She needed to say something.

"Good morning, Deena."

He opened the gate, letting her pass through ahead of him, lightly grasping her elbow as she stepped from the sidewalk. At the car he opened her door, smiling, making her hate him. She couldn't see his eyes to see what he was seeing or thinking. She wanted to smack him.

She followed his every long stride from her door to his. God, he was handsome. He wasn't supposed to be handsome. He was Fennell, a fennell: a creature she believed lived in a gutter where he had somehow learned to breathe on his own and develop a language that scarcely resembled English. And now he was sitting beside her, like a human, not slouching, adjusting his seat as though he'd been in a luxury car at least once before. And what! Cologne! No way was he wearing cologne, not after all the time and the effort she'd taken to make herself perfect.

"Deena, thank you, I appreciate what you're doing, giving up Saturday for me this way. It's really above and beyond and I hope I haven't infringed on other plans." He leaned to one side, his side. "I see that you're not carrying a weapon. That being the case I feel secure in commenting that you are absolutely stunning." He flashed a smile. "No veins and nice knees. No wonder you occupy so many fanciful dreams. So, Deena, where have you decided to take me to dress me up for my First-Class adventure?"

"Is this a joke?" She twisted in her contoured leather seat, painting the air around him erratically with her hands. "This, is this a joke?"

"This? No, this is me." He examined himself. "My suit was still wet from last night. Guess I shouldn't have hung it on the line."

"What, you mean after you finished cleaning their pool?"

"Actually I did clean my pool this morning."

"Your pool," she snapped. "And I suppose that's your Jag? You're so pathetic."

She pulled her glasses away. Without them her brown eyes sparkled in the sun. He didn't have to follow her glare.

"Yes. Do you like the colour? I wasn't sure about the tan seats."

"Yeah, right, like I believe that."

"It's true. I'm not very good with colours and I do have to say that you should wear your hair combed out more often ...very appealing."

"Shit, Fennell. Who are you? And whose home is that?"

He shrugged, checking the time. "Mine, though I don't have much of a green thumb. That's the work of my gardener."

"I'm beginning to think dirty cop here. This isn't your address, Fennell. You're a federal cop. There's no way you could afford this place."

He didn't answer, checking out the interior of the car, nodding his approval. He made himself comfortable, breathing in the warm air.

God! She wanted to scream. He was wearing a Rolex! Instead she straightened her skirt, the little she had to straighten, and putting the car in gear she sped away wanting to choke him. She knew she looked stunning. Was that all he could say? Seven months of seeing her hidden in tight-fitting slacks and all he could say was 'no veins and nice knees'...frigging asshole.

At the haberdasher, after a silent ride, she parked in No Parking by the front door. She lowered the ragtop and put her gold-blue shield on the dash. Rank had its privileges.

She knew the exclusive men's' store because of her father, her uncle and her brother, though she had never thought to ask how much they paid for their tailor-made suits. She hoped she might get away with something for under a grand from their less popular fabrics with enough left over for a shirt and tie in a department store. His shoes he would have to polish for once. She looked at his boots, so well-polished that he could probably see under her skirt if he stood close enough. Good luck with that, she thought. So what did he think he was doing? What was he trying to prove?

She went to the manager who knew the family name at once. She didn't know where to begin. How could she? Why would she? Mommy had never taken little Johnnie shopping before. She wanted dark blue; he was not to have black no matter what. Nor was he able to afford the finest, she explained. He was a cop. She wanted a four-season blend and he had to be fitted for a weapon.

With that over she sat in the corner, fuming, leaving the manager somewhat perplexed. He would do his best. However his establishment was not very often visited by public service people of the gentleman's particular level of achievement, he wanted her to know. She understood.

The manager removed Fennell's jacket, suddenly somewhat more impressed, not to mention somewhat confused between what he was hearing and what he was seeing, asking that the gentleman remove his sweater, not quite certain how to react to the 92FS chrome-plated Berretta that Fennell rested on a cluster of dark-coloured bolts.

All Deena Archer could think was that he'd better not be gay. She was not doing all this for some gay guy, the micro-fibre tee-shirt defining every rippled inch of a physique she had never thought possible under wrinkled black polyester.

"And to what side does the gentleman dress?" the manager queried.

"The gentleman dresses to the right," Fennell responded with a smirk, "and very well-dressed at that, the gentleman might add, particularly in those imported wool blends I see in the corner."

Deena Archer wanted to stop breathing, at least long enough to die. Until without much warning the morning was gone and Fennell was considering shoes and shirts and ties. The bastard, he knew she wouldn't say anything to embarrass herself and her family. He'd chosen one of the most expensive blends. If he wanted to make a fool of himself, let him. She wasn't getting involved.

Not one shirt or two, no, four, with four ties, a belt, a dozen pairs of socks and two pairs of Italian handcrafted shoes. Thirty-five hundred plus tax was the best the manager could do and the first fitting was scheduled for the following week.

Deena was experiencing a stroke, her brain threatening to burst, at the cash reaching into her purse, hating herself for being sucked in by a creep that a millennia ago she thought she could respect. Now he'd become a big disappointment. She turned to stone. She couldn't laugh, cry or smile, grin or grimace when the fennell produced his own platinum card and signed as though he had not a care in the world.

Outside on the sidewalk he looked up at the sky. The day was clear and pleasantly warm.

"So Deena, now that you know on what side of the tracks my guy hangs out, are we on for lunch? I'm thinking boardwalk, fish and chips and a glass or two of four-dollar wine. I'll even hold your shoes. Or, do I see you on Monday? I would certainly understand if a woman as beautiful as you is busy. I didn't think last night to ask whether you had other commitments."

"Fennell, are you insane? You're out four grand."

"Thirty-seven-fifty, plus another twenty, that is if we're having lunch."

"No we are not having lunch. The boardwalk and holding shoes sounds a bit too much like a date and you're creeping me out."

"So hold your own shoes."

"Sorry. I'll see you Monday. I need to go somewhere and breathe."

He twirled her around, holding her shoulders, giving her the once over.

"Nope, don't see it."

She tried to twist free. "Okay, what now? What don't you see?"

She hated herself. She hated him more.

"Well, your skirt is so short, you know, the one you wore so I couldn't help seeing most of your legs, I thought I could see the stick."

"What stick? And let me go."

He let go. "The stick you've got up your ass."

"Screw you. In fact screw yourself with the one you've got stuck in your brain, the one you wear on the right."

She stomped to her car, climbing in behind the wheel, counting each second until the top was raised and concealed. Turning over the ignition she glared at him once and sped off. When she braked, searching into the rear-view mirror, he was gone. Shit! He was gone.

An hour later she found him at the boardwalk gazing out to sea, which he didn't know for another thirty minutes.

She wanted to drive her heels into his brain; instead she tapped his shoulder with one.

"I'm being the bigger man."

"With those legs, and other things, who are you kidding? Anyway, apology accepted. I thought you might show up."

She glanced behind her, then to the horizon. She was there, her mistake. She couldn't, wouldn't be the one to leave first again. She controlled her breathing and sat with her shoes between them. They had nothing in common except a woman thousands of miles or a few feet away. She could be any woman they were seeing. Or could they be seeing the wife of a man she would kill in less than a year if they didn't find her first.

Lunch was 21.50, wine included. And why was she wearing his jacket because of a gentle offshore breeze when the night before she was soaked to the skin and he couldn't have cared less? Why were they sitting in the sand and why did she still not know anything about him? What kind of cop was she?

"Thank you for joining me for lunch, Deena. I enjoyed your company. Unfortunately I do have to go. I'll walk you to your car." He helped her to stand, avoiding her legs in spite of his better judgement. "Think maybe you can drop me at the florist? I'm a little short on time and my lady loves pink carnations."

"I've never taken a guy to buy flowers for another woman. What would your mother say about that indiscretion, Fennell?"

"She'd probably say thank you. They're for my grandmother. She took me in when I was ten, after my parents were killed in a freak accident. I lived with her until I left for college. Now she's eighty-six and needs more care than I can give her at home."

Deena remembered the night before. "You've just made me feel like shit. Thanks, Fennell."

"Don't. You didn't know. No one does. I like my life private. So let's maintain status quo. Today didn't happen. Not that I'll forget those legs anytime soon and before I become remiss once again, the embroidery on the bra…very chic. You were delightful company."

"Remiss, you're saying remiss." She bit her upper lip, snorting a laugh. "Does this mean we'll have more to talk about in the company car while you're wolfing back doughnuts and hotdogs?"

"No, however I could do with a ride right now."

She tossed him the keys. "This isn't a date; I get that, which doesn't mean that everyone here can't think that I've got one. You drive."

At the very posh residence he climbed out, reaching for the flowers, placing a single stem on the now empty seat beside her. He had nothing to say. Their day had been sufficiently weird. Deena stayed as she was, adding kind wishes for his grandmother. Two hours later she was sitting on 5000-dollar paint wrapped in a shawl with her legs crossed, making tight circles with her toes, her fingertips stroking the petals of her flower.

Not a hint of shock was visible on his face. Nothing ever shocked Fennell.

"Deena, beg all you want. I am not taking you home, undressing you and making you all hot and sweaty. You're not my type. Besides, I know your ass is a little on the skinny side and I'm more of a meaty kind of guy."

"Get over yourself. I had nowhere else to go because you've already spoiled my day. Anyway, I stayed to hear how your grandmother is doing."

"She kicked me out. She has plans. I arrived too close to her mealtime and Saturday night is Dance Night. She needed time to primp herself, to make herself viable. The old girl said viable. She's on the prowl."

"I like to dance. And we are nicely dressed."

"If you want to damage a hundred pacemakers and go home with goo on your shoulder, you go ahead. Enjoy yourself. This time I'll wait for you."

She tossed him the keys. "Drive."

Parked at his gate he didn't know what to say or do. Neither did Deena. They'd driven themselves into a corner under an early evening sky that was still bright. He climbed out. She should have driven, she knew. Now she had to climb out with him, manoeuvre around him; slide in behind the wheel and leave.

"Thank you again, Deena, for a very different day. I'll see you Monday."

"Don't thank me. You're the one going to debtor's

prison. What were you thinking?"

"Actually I was thinking how good we're going to look in Paris or Madrid or wherever else we end up." He beamed a toothy smile. "You raised the bar. Now my ladies have to reach a ten instead of eights or nines."

"So now we're ladies, not broads, skanks or females?"

"It's a job, Deena. Keeping it separate keeps me sane, and don't worry about the money. I'm not."

"So you actually want me to believe this is your home and that's your car and that you're not a crooked cop?"

"My parents were well off. They were topnotch trial lawyers with decent investment portfolios and, with the insurance policies, everything compounding pretty quickly with the help of a good accountant, I'm pretty comfortable."

"Comfortable. That's more than comfortable, Fennell. That's a two-floor hacienda with a pool in the centre of Snotsville. We're talking nine, ten million."

He glanced at his home. "I paid cash to avoid interest payments on a mortgage, so I do have enough left in my pocket to spot for a pizza. What I don't have are any wines in the house more than fifty a bottle. I don't see the need. Expensive wines are pretentious, don't you think?"

"Wait!" She was flustered. "Are you inviting me in?"

"Yes, I am, for a pizza. That's it. I don't dance, not very well, and I'm not talking sleepover. If you want something more you'll have to leave early to find some. I won't be insulted."

"Well, that's a relief."

"What is?"

"To know that in spite of the nice clothes, the watch, the phony gentleman act and the clean mouth that you're still a pig."

"Is that a yes?"

"Yes, that is a yes, on the condition that my car goes inside and your clunker comes out. I don't want a squad car passing by and seeing that I'm here and I'm leaving after we eat. Comprende that, amigo?"

He chortled. "Sì, Señorita Archer, claro. Comprendo perfectemente lo que digas."

Instead of her eyes and her mouth opening wide, her entire face drooped in concert with her shoulders. She wasn't as jaded as Johnnie Fennell. Her face did show unexpected emotion.

Fifteen
Last Year: August 02nd

Deena spent the evening in shock. Suddenly the cave-dweller cop was a sophisticated man of the world. He'd travelled to most of Europe and throughout the Americas, never to Asia or Africa because he didn't like overcrowded populations or food prepared from household pets. He knew a little about wine, not as much as her, and he was fluent in Spanish. Something she didn't know despite living in Miami and working with the man for seven months.

She was stunned by the tour of his home, insisting after her first glass of cheap fifty-dollar wine that she see his wardrobe. She couldn't wait. She had to see his wardrobe. She wouldn't take no for an answer. When she did she thought she might pass out and spent the next hour experiencing sporadic bouts of laugher. He had more clothes than her.

After the pizza, which they ate sitting side by side on the kitchen counter, he suggested a swim. He had nothing for her to wear, but if she wanted a dip in her panties and bra he suggested a head start and promised not to peek. She had a better idea. She promised not to swim in his pool. Instead they spent what was left of the evening talking about everything except killers, bad people and dead bodies.

Deena was surprised by the passage of time, the good time she was having, leaving much later than she'd expected. She left the next morning, with him.

Saturday night she stayed over, alone in his guestroom,

in a silk shirt he'd never worn to work or anywhere else, waking Sunday morning to a breakfast he'd prepared for her by the pool: freshly squeezed juice, a platter of fruits, and toast with imported jams and rich Colombian coffee.

She came down in the shirt that for her was a robe. He was in silk boxers, a three-quarter robe and bare feet.

"Sleep well, Agent Archer?"

"Yes, and if Brannigan ever finds out I'm dead."

"Then don't tell her." He filled her cup. "This is sort of neat; Archer and Fennell eating breakfast the morning after in their jammies by the pool. By the way, here's a hundred."

He slid the bill across the table.

"Don't you usually pay more for your female company?"

"Hey, this isn't Monday. Talk nice."

"You're right. I'm sorry. What's it for?"

"For throwing you into the pool after breakfast, as I assume you didn't come down... you know, commando style. You didn't, did you?"

"Sorry, all wrapped up like a nun."

"Then, is a hundred enough?"

"You must be joking, closer to two hundred."

"Can I write you a cheque?"

"Write one first, and if it doesn't bounce I might let you throw me in when you're dreaming. I'll be easy to see amongst all your bimbos. I'll be the one with a brain." She scanned the deck and the yard. "I still can't believe we're not invading someone's home. I'm thinking I should call DMV and run a check on you."

"They're closed. It's Sunday and I can't believe beautiful Deena Archer is having breakfast with me in my shirt."

She slid back the hundred. "For my shirt, that I just bought, and I want change."

"That was my hundred."

"You gave it to me."

Fennell stood, slipping one hand under her knees, the other around her back and under her arm.

"That's my money. So either return my shirt or drop the cup."

"No… and no…and don't you dare, Fennell!"

He swept her up, carried her to the twelve-foot end and dumped her before continuing on to finish his coffee and toast. Deena stayed in the pool, bathed in blue silk, wishing Saturday hadn't come and gone so quickly making Monday all that much closer. She was actually enjoying herself and she knew Monday would ruin the memory.

Of one thing she was certain: she was leaving by noon and had a lot to say before she left.

She couldn't believe what she was seeing. He was carrying a tray to the shallow end, placing their breakfast at the edge and easing his feet into the water. He was pouring coffee as though having her in his pool and in his shirt wasn't the freakiest thing in the world. He was watching her, smiling nicely, warmly, not like a smart-ass, sipping his coffee, slipping off his robe, sliding in, swimming past her and back, climbing out and sipping his coffee.

"Spend the day with me."

"No, I will not spend the day with you." Then: "Why?"

"Because you're treading water wondering what the hell's going on, what the next twelve months will be like, whether we're going to sleep together, which one of us will get transferred or tossed from the squad, whether you should take off my shirt because you're getting ready to drown. Because it's been so long since I've had a beautiful girl to myself that I want to be greedy for a day before Monday comes and I have to wake up to remember a wonderful dream."

Shit! This was not going her way. "I would take off… my shirt. I'm not a prude. I've been to Europe, and places, and for your information I've got tons of thongs for the beach. I've also got a skinny ass. Remember?"

"Good point. Guess I'll have to remember you that way, you know, with a skinny ass."

"I'll stay for lunch, Fennell, not a moment longer, and because I have to dry first. I can't exactly drive home in wet underwear."

"You're so sexy when you talk dirty."

She swam to where she could touch the bottom. She unbuttoned her new shirt matter-of-factly, tossing the wet mass onto the deck. "You tell anyone about this, Fennell, and I swear that before I quit the force I'll tell everyone you couldn't do me because you've got a penis the size of my pinkie."

He watched her pull herself onto the edge, the tray between them.

"That's why I'm sitting here and not in the water. Besides, what would I tell them, that I'm with a naked goddess? Think they'd believe me? I don't believe this myself. However, so you know, I've seen you this way before and I'm giving myself a perfect score for imagining perfection."

"Okay, Johnnie, lunch. That's it. After that we're back to Fennell and Archer, Dickhead and Miss Prissy. And I am not naked."

"And what are we now?"

"We're eating breakfast at a home I still don't believe is yours. Cops can be arrested too, you know."

"Can I take pictures"?

"No you cannot."

"Can I get some SPF? The sun's getting pretty strong."

"No you cannot."

"Can I invite you for lunch by the ocean?"

She sighed. "Yes, because we have a few things to discuss that I might as well get off my chest. I'd hate to see you throwing a tantrum at the beach."

"Like what, your bra? You need another hundred, or you want me to hold it?"

"No I don't and my bra is fine where it is. I mean that you won't ever again wear that black suit or those horrible white shirts. You've got a dozen imported loafers in your wardrobe and I want you to wear them. And your ties, you're going to wear them and not use the knot just to keep the two ends together. Now that I've seen your closet there is no way you're getting out of this one. I've had my fill of people glancing sideways at me because I'm partnered with a matted mongrel. Now it's my turn to laugh at them and make as many snide remarks as I want. Do you understand me?"

"So, Agent Archer, does this mean that you're completely oblivious to the fact that you're sitting with me in your little panties and bra? I have to tell you, if that's what nuns wear I'm joining a choir."

"We're partners. I'm a cop. Think of me as another guy, Fennell. That's how you should be thinking of me. This is just a body to get me from one place to another. It's not my fault that I'm beautiful and you're a pig." She sipped her coffee. "So, are we still on for lunch or do I go home now to change into something dry?"

"Lunch sounds good, after we go to your place to get you into something dry. Fair is fair. You've seen my place."

She stood, reaching to the tray for a piece of fruit, sauntering lazily to the deep end, staring at him, devouring the orange sliver by sliver, studying him, watching him study her, diving in.

Johnnie Fennell bit into his fruit. She wasn't wearing panties. He'd seen bigger patches on men who couldn't afford a glass eye and her ass was Grade A. She was right, though. The big problem was Brannigan. He and the boss lady had history. If he followed through with what Archer wanted the shock would be cataclysmic. He didn't get the job because of who he knew; he got the job because he was the best in his class throughout college and at the academy, the best on each successive rung of the ladder that had brought him to Major Crime where he was the best. Brannigan didn't know any other Johnnie Fennell.

She came up by his feet. "I think I'd like that SPF now…in a self-serve bottle if you don't mind. I think your dreams are fine the way they are."

*

When Fennell came back Deena was stretched out onto a chaise-longue on her front. She wasn't ashamed of her body and what she had said was true. She did wear thongs when on vacation, alone. So what was wrong with someone she trusted with her life seeing her bare ass and most everything else? He wasn't like other cops. Or she would simply kill him: justifiable homicide

She felt a drop of cream at her shoulders, threatening with a curious smile to kick his 'guy' from the right to the left side of his pants if she felt even one more splatter. He stopped, reclined into the chaise-longue beside her and watched the show. They barely spoke for the rest of the morning. They each had too much to consider. Not the least of which was a woman who, if everything went well, would soon want to ram a blade into his chest.

Close to noon they drove in separate cars to Deena's condo. She'd decided against lunch at the ocean. She wanted a picnic by the sea. If Johnnie Fennell was screwing with her brain the way that he seemed to enjoy without the slightest remorse, the least he could do was take her to the beach and let her pretend for an afternoon that she did have a life.

He agreed to everything, all her previous demands, submitting three of his own conditions: She would help him explain the new and improved Fennell to Brannigan in a month's time, she would wear a thong and he could photograph the most glamorous girl on the beach just once or a hundred times. She acquiesced; not having to pretend that the weekend wasn't going the way she'd expected.

Neither was his regularly updated mandate. He was still

barred from her back, her legs or anywhere else, though she did agree to hold his camera out of the sand while he greased himself. She was so near yet so far. He was being tortured. She didn't care, unduly insensitive to his agony. Since first meeting her months earlier he'd imagined her in his bed each night: an unattainable dream no different from all other private collections of exquisite objets d'art in the world. Now to have her so close and not be able to touch her was painful.

He had never expected this and by day's end she was glowing, accentuating his misery, Fennell enthralled by the girl thing she did that let her go home with her bikini top in her bag without the slightest concession to her sense of propriety.

At her condo, the sun in hiding well beyond the horizon for yet another night, the sky sprinkled with silver, she was making him hamburgers and hotdogs with a twenty-year grand cru from the cellars of the Canyon Estates.

"You live here alone. That's incredible."

She nodded. "I'm wealthy," she said matter-of-factly without the slightest pretention, "but most guys in my league are shallow. I don't want a shallow guy. The only other guys I know are cops, macho and full of themselves if not so full of shit they can't keep their shirts buttoned. I want a guy who's full of me and doesn't care about all this."

"So the calendar's blank quite often."

"The calendar is always empty, thanks for reminding me I can't get a date, and the other night I wanted to smack you for what you said, Fennell." She flipped a burger. "I do not sleep around."

"I didn't say anything. That was the guy in a black suit, the wet guy."

"You just make sure he stays dry from now on." She punched him. "You know what I mean, because the next time I see him and he says something stupid I will smack him." She ordered him to the table for the plates. "So where do we go with this? I mean, I spent a night in your home, you've seen me virtually naked all day and now were tossing burgers in the moonlight in…well I look good, you look like a beach bum."

She was wearing flared satin shorts with cuffs and a cami-top, à la 50s. He was wearing sweats and sneakers.

"Like you said, tomorrow we're Fennell and Archer. I'll have memories of a wonderful weekend, a beautiful and funny woman with a to-die-for body that I would love to make sweaty, and a partner who's going to help me catch a serial killer. I was teasing you the other night, saying ten or twenty when I was hoping for none at all. Now that I've seen you this way, bringing my dreams to life and, of course, what's in your pretty head, I don't want to think of anyone spreading SPF over you while I'm still alive. But I am a cop, remember, albeit not a very poor one. Where do we go with this? We go to LAX tomorrow. We find out who she is and we make damn certain we're not wrong Then we go wherever she goes and possibly one night we'll get drunk and wake up looking for new partners because we'll feel like shit about what we've done. I don't want that. Just don't tell me when you bag a rich guy who isn't shallow. I think I'd have to get drunk on my own. I haven't had a weekend like this in years. I'll need time to adjust. This has to last me awhile."

She lowered the flame. "You're not shallow, Johnnie. You were an asshole until yesterday, yes, though I never believed you were shallow." She dressed their buns. "So Fennell, at least you know I don't have a skinny ass …tight and tanned, but not skinny." She paused, "Right?"

His grin was real, and wide. "Archer, I'm kind of a tactile guy. We can't always trust what we see. You should know that as a cop."

"This is your fault, you know. You should never have let Brannigan assign me to you when you knew I was so hot."

They sat by the edge of the pool to eat, discovering more about each other. Little things that didn't mean much alone until strung together to complete a fuller picture.

When they were done she asked Fennell to take in the dishes and find another grand cru, unless he was in a hurry to get home. He wasn't. She was happy. The air was still and warm without a sound, lit by the moon, her garden, her pool and her spa an idyllic setting. She wanted him to stay a while longer. He wasn't the only one with a weekend to forget because remembering would make life so much more difficult.

When he came through the patio doors through the garden to the spa, her clothes were placed neatly on a padded bench, a bright white triangle that she intended him to see slightly off to one side. The jets were swirling agitated water around Deena's shoulders, diffused light illuminating her abstract contours below the aqua-blue waterline.

"Johnnie, when you said tactile a few moments ago, what did you mean exactly?"

He didn't hesitate, neither was he smiling. "I meant this isn't going to happen, Deena. Me getting in there with you now, it'll change our whole dynamic."

"Will change? No, has changed, and what don't you understand about a naked woman in a hot tub?"

"You're caught up in the moment with too much grand cru in your blood."

"And you're not."

"Someone has to think straight. What happens tomorrow when you wake up, Archer? I'll be gone and we'll have to face each other all day. You'd hate yourself. Believe me. You'd want to be sick just thinking about what's in your head right now. I won't do that to you."

She stopped the jets, her abstract nude transitioning into precise lines.

"I would not be sick. Would you?"

"I wish you hadn't done that. No, I wouldn't be sick."

"So what you're saying is that it's okay for me to feel stupid standing in here naked while you gawk at me. I don't see you running anywhere or gagging."

He chortled. "You're right. Move over."

She stayed as she was, watching him kick off his sneakers and drop his top by his feet, push his pants to his ankles and fling them helter-skelter into the air.

"Aren't you forgetting something, like the fact that I'm naked? The only one naked," she added.

"Believe me. I will never forget seeing you naked, Archer. Do you have any idea how perfect you are?"

"Yes. I do"

He eased himself over the edge in his micro-fibre straight-backs, easily sweeping her over his shoulder. He brought her to the side, stepped from a moulded seat to the edge and onto the deck as though she was weightless and carried her to the deep end of her pool ignoring her yelps, her kicking and flailing arms. He eased her to her feet. He wanted to kiss her, clearing his mind, filling his hands instead with the firm flesh of her ass, bringing her in closer, lifting her to his waist, etching her expression into his mind, her warm flesh into each fingertip, watching her mouth scream open, watching her fly backward into the cool water.

"Okay, Archer, your ass isn't skinny; it's perfection, like every inch of you, and now I won't sleep for a year without thinking of you very naked and very soft and I'm not leaving until you're out of there. I need to know you're safe and won't drown. So you've got ten seconds."

"You're a complete fucking shithead."

"Yes, I know." Towelled as dry as he could be, he pulled on his pants. "Time's up. Get out, right now, unless you want me to come get you, put you into a cold shower and throw you into bed." He pulled on his top, zipping in the warmth to his neck. "And wrap yourself in a towel. My brain's already short-circuited."

Deena clambered out, dripping, ignoring the ladder, muttering. She didn't care. She couldn't be more embarrassed than she was. She wrapped her body in one fleecy towel, wrapping her head in another.

"If she doesn't kill you, I will."

"Believe me, I feel worse than you."

"Spare me. You aren't the one feeling like a cheap slut. At least we both know that I'm anatomically correct."

"I do feel worse than you, which is why I'm leaving right now." He turned to walk out, stopping, smiling. "By the way, partner, I've never seen anything more beautiful than for the few seconds you were airborne. Now that's a moment to remember. I'll see you in the morning."

He couldn't have said anything more humiliating.

She searched for something she could hurl at his head, nothing, deciding not to waste good wine. Instead she followed him quietly to the door, seething, leaning against the inside when he was gone without saying goodbye. Her mind was a whirlwind of emotions. She wanted to cry. He'd seen her naked body, more than naked, sprawled in midair, suspended forever in his mind, her legs opened wide, crashing onto her back. Oh, God! What hadn't he seen? What she had chanced to give him in a warm, tender way, he'd made seem ridiculous and crude. She wanted to die. How could she face him in the morning?

Right then she knew that she wouldn't. She never would again. Being a federal cop wasn't everything.

A moment later she felt as much heard the knock, her heart skipping a beat, her face heated in a deep flush.

"It's me again."

She stood still, not breathing, her heart threatening to explode. He tapped once more.

"I know you're there, Archer."

She opened the door. "What? Think you're going to get another picture for your girlie file?" She held out her hand. "I want the memory card, Fennell. Then you can get lost."

He put a fingertip to her lips. "I suppose, given that we've had a few meals and some wine, on a weekend, without our guns or cells, and that we had a sleepover last night and what was essentially a great piece of ass for me a few minutes ago, that we were sort of on a first date."

"Yeah, a blind date. Give me the card and go home, Fennell."

"No, not blind, far from blind, and we were ordered by Brannigan to do this. We were, pretty much. We both heard her. We were under direct orders."

"So what?"

"Well I was thinking on the way to your elevator. If you don't manage to find a guy that's full of you by Christmas, perhaps we could attend the office party together. You know, like buds."

"Do I look like someone's bud to you?"

Danger!

"In the meantime we could have a few meals outside of work."

"You mean more gluttonous crap in those greasy diners you like. No thanks, Fennell, and Christmas is five months away. I could be married by then. So why don't you go home and leave me alone? You don't appear to have a problem doing that."

"Good, so we each have impossible dreams. However I was thinking more of whatever you want, what you would like to do," he looked at his watch, "dinner, dancing, the occasional movie and popcorn at home, yours or mine, museums, whatever. And on the QT, at least until we catch this woman because I don't want another partner. It's taken me long enough to break you in. I was also thinking that I left you too early this evening because I saw where this was headed. I was wrong. I'm sorry. I should have at least stayed to tuck you in and kiss you goodnight."

"I can tuck myself in. I've had lots of practice and you can kiss yourself goodnight. You're more your type. Now leave me alone. Go home."

"But it is still early and, with all the stress you put on my heart this weekend by flaunting yourself, I could use a good soak, you know, for curative purposes."

She wasn't smiling. "You have a pool, Fennell. Go home and drown yourself. I don't want you near me."

"Okay, listen up. I left because I want to catch this woman. I want her stopped and you're the one person in sync with me...most times, the one person I trust, and I know the reason you were a little petty and argumentative on Friday was that you were wet and cold. I get that."

"Yeah, and I'm still wet and cold."

"I thought staying longer would screw things up, break us up as a team. Or believe me, I would have stayed. Not jumping into the pool after you was a major effort. And anatomically correct, don't worry about it. I mean, hello, naked woman, naked you. Believe me, I am anatomically correct big time and I did not want to leave you."

"So what's different now?"

"I have a law degree."

"You have a law degree. Good for you. The mongrel cop has a law degree, from what box of dog food? You expect me to believe that?"

He expelled an exasperated breath. "You're not making this easy." He eased her gently into her foyer with his hands at her shoulders. He stooped, sweeping her feet from the floor, securing her to his shoulder with a hand firmly affixed to her ass, rethinking his tactic and sliding his hand under her towel, pressing her closer as a means of added precaution. He didn't want her to slip away, he told her. If she was going to kill him, better to find out before she heard more. He closed the door. She pounded his back once, twice, and relaxed, giving up. In the garden he reached for the bottle and managed the glasses, bouncing her to the pool, enjoying her grunts as much as his side view, setting her down. "Yeah, I have a law degree. My full name is John

Francis Templeton Fennell. My mother was Wendy Templeton."

Her shock was real. "Wendy Templeton, no way, as in Stuart and Victoria Templeton, the who's who of society. I studied her legal arguments at university. Everyone had to read her. My mother often talks about her and Victoria."

He nodded. "And I wasn't exempted because of familial proximity. Victoria is my grandmother, the one who likes carnations. Perhaps your mother would like to meet her one day, perhaps you would. She kept the firm going until I graduated, not long after Stuart passed away. Now I'm the sole legal owner of the The Summit Group, though I'm not currently active due to certain conflicts of interest. I have been for fourteen years. That's why I want this woman so badly, Deena, because I want you so badly. I have since the first day I saw you. She's my last case file. I'm quitting the task force. Something I was going to tell you later on, in a few months, in a restaurant with candles and wine, either before or after I told you that I love you. After we get her I'm JFT Fennell, Attorney at Law. That's why Brannigan can't find out about this. I want that woman and we're going to get her, me and you. Then I want you, all to myself."

The loudest sound was the moonlight.

"Fennell, you just said that you love me, that you want me. Are you insane?"

"Yes, I do. Yes, I am, because of you."

"That's why you practically let me drown and die of pneumonia the other night...you prick!"

"That was business, part of your field training, you know, trying to make you a better agent."

"God, I should have smacked you so hard."

"Or you could drop your towel and invite me in for a nightcap, though I'll understand if you have other commitments."

She scrunched her face. "You're such a total idiot,

Fennell. You're already in."

"So can I stay? You know, for that nightcap?"

"You know who she is, don't you? That's why you went to Brannigan. You know more than you told her."

"I don't, not yet, though I don't believe a year will be too long to find her and track her. This woman's good and I don't doubt for a moment that she'll enjoy putting a blade through my heart when we meet."

"Yeah, right, that would be over my dead body, John Francis Idiot Fennell. She does not get to kill you before I do. That's if you're any good. If you're not she can have you. I'll even give her the knife."

Deena shoved him backward into the calm water. She would die before letting anything happen to the fennell she'd begun to hate loving several months earlier.

The next morning her towel was still in the pool and John Francis Templeton Fennell began his day much later than usual. Agent Deena Archer began her day with him. Before catching a killer she'd gone to his home to first kill his black suit along with the white shirts, tie and scuffed shoes.

Sixteen
Eighteen Years Ago

In grade nine Gilligan Rose began going to school dances, though she danced mostly rock 'n roll with the girls because she knew all the boys wanted was to slow dance so they could touch her and tell other boys how she felt, hoping she was like her mother and might come across in the boy's lavatory or locker room before going home.

That's what her father told her. He told her the boys just wanted to feel her breasts and touch her between her legs, especially the boys in grade eleven and twelve who looked like men, the ones who constantly invited her to parties after the dances. Though she never said yes, she never could. Her father wanted her home by eleven and waited outside to drive her home.

Gilligan knew they all talked about her because of her clothes, clothes that girls out of school might wear, and because of her mother who many boys had seen washing her car, though none of their parents could ever afford what her mother did for a living. Emma was now thirty-four and known from New York to L.A., from Seattle to Miami while other mothers answered phones or cross-filed invoices by name and number before scurrying home to prepare dinners.

Her unveilings were now much sought after social soirées with champagne and hors d'oeuvres, black tie and gowns, swarms of aficionados and suitors vying for her attention. Everyone wanted the whimsical and engaging

Miss Emma Rose, everybody except Tommy Dune who hadn't stopped wanting his daughter.

At school the staff let Gilligan be. Everyone believed the girl would end badly. She was flighty and capricious, or sombre and morose. No one knew from one day to the next what to expect or what to think. One day she would eat with the other girls in the cafeteria, the next day alone by a grove of tall trees with a girl who had bright golden hair the colour of wheat in the prairies and a face speckled with freckles, a girl no one else liked because she was foreign from somewhere in Britain. However the other girls would usually forgive Gilligan that particular eccentricity because Gilligan Rose was the prettiest girl in the school and with her they were all assured more attention from the boys. On those days the golden-haired girl ate alone in the grove wondering why.

Over the winter months, or the days when rain made going outside impossible, the girl sat in a corner, watching her one friend sitting with others and laughing, wishing she was living the next day and not the day after. She missed Gilligan when Gilligan seemed not to know or to care who she was. She didn't mind. She knew Gilligan was never the same from one day to the next, different like her, not always happy, needing her company when she was sad, when she was quiet and didn't want to talk. She liked Gilligan more than the boys who never seemed to know she existed.

On career day, when everyone brought their fathers to class, Gilligan Rose brought her mother. The accountants, lawyers, plumbers and dentists didn't matter. They all wanted to see Miss Emma Rose and her one-sided faces that now sold for over ten thousand dollars apiece.

She knew the boys laughed at her daughter along with a few of the girls. Gilligan told her often how that made her feel, the days they spent together when they would dance and they would sing in her studio and Emma thought to make things better. She suggested an impromptu auction for all the fathers who were so eager to see her: Her most recent canvas beginning at four thousand dollars, less than half the value she would expect from a gallery. Not a doctor or lawyer, teacher or banker thought to raise their hand, not even to ask a simple question.

That, Emma told the class with an affectionate smile, was what was meant by success, when they could each do for a living what they loved without the help of bankers or lawyers, teachers or friends.

With that the school day was over. The next week the papers would report that the painting had sold in Manhattan for 12,000 dollars.

The girl with the bright golden hair sat at the back of the class, forgotten, wondering why Gilligan hadn't thought to introduce her to Miss Emma Rose. She wasn't surprised, though she was disappointed. That was the day they didn't eat lunch, the day Gilligan was once again cheerful and gay.

She'd never been to Gilligan's home. Gilligan wasn't allowed to have friends in her home, and neither was she. Her mother and father had heard of the strange teenage girl and her outrageous mother.

Later that night an Emma unchanged by what she'd achieved tucked her young daughter into her bed, her new bed in her new room. She kissed her daughter's forehead, her cheeks and her lips. She loved her daughter so deeply, and Gilligan loved her mother that much and more. She loved their long days alone, their painting and dancing, their singing and talking and playing pretend.

Gilligan no longer had a mirror by her bed to talk with. She no longer had Gilligan to whisper with in the dark as soon as the door closed. Now the door remained ajar as she fell asleep. She wanted the door to stay open, the light in the hall, to see shadows crossing her ceiling, her walls and her floor, long shadows and short shadows, shadows she loved that made her feel good, and shadows she began to feel should make her feel bad. She thought so, and Gilligan thought so too. She needed to believe she could speak with Gilligan whenever she wanted.

When her mother was gone she laid still, warm under the covers, and listened, waiting for shadows to pass by her door and the footsteps to fade. She no longer fell asleep right away, or possibly she did. How would she know? And she thought to one day ask her mother who seemed to know everything, whereas her father seemed not to care about anything except when he would come to her room to kiss her goodnight and stay with her a while.

Emma was gone early the next morning, arriving at Zeke Phillips's home one hour later. They were driving together to the Big Apple. Zeke, now seventy-two, wouldn't think of declining her invitation to accompany her to the once-a-year exhibition, the largest art show in the world. Her fame was spreading to Europe. Nor did he ever forego an unveiling. To say the least he was proud to call her his daughter, never forgiving himself for what he no longer believed was his most appropriate course of action years earlier.

Tommy Dune had proven himself a profound disappointment, a layabout, a ne'er-do-well living off the avails of his wife. Sadly, Emma was content with her life which consisted of her upstairs studio and Gilligan who continued to be his greatest concern. The varied moods he'd witnessed over the years were troublesome to his professional mind, though Emma was steadfast in her resolve that young minds should be left unspoiled, free to create and imagine. That she was once and for a long time hidden away in a dark room for no other reason that chasing butterflies and talking with birds was never forgotten.

Zeke understood, not wanting any ill-feeling or fear to taint their infrequent and brief times together. For that reason he worried quietly. As for Tommy, Emma still liked Tommy though she never thought of him as a good or poor lover, despite having no way of telling. He rarely touched her and she rarely cared.

That night and for a week Tommy was left alone to manage the house. He promised videos and pizza if Gilligan could be ready for bed by the time he returned. He came home with an extra-large and a movie for each night.

Gilligan was no longer a girl, despite the big teddy bear by the bed in her new room. She was accustomed to dressing much like her mother. She liked her feminine peignoirs and her smooth satin slips, her baby dolls and satin camisoles, though often she liked her flannel pyjamas and fleecy bathrobe as much.

Tommy Dune no longer saw her as child, rather as two separate women. One was flighty and capricious, the other quiet and pensive. Each one the same in the way that he felt, still believing after so many years that Phillips might indeed be the father.

He loved her smooth skin, her warmth and her breathing, the way she writhed under his weight when he culminated those feelings with Emma less frequently than he wanted or needed, never thinking for a moment that her closed eyes and inert body might be his fault, not once thinking to ask why she was afraid of dark.

He no longer joined Gilligan during her bath, a difficult and abrupt transition, her body now much more private as she metamorphosed into a woman. All he could hope for were a few precious moments with her most evenings as Emma remained in her studio to paint and the neighbour peered through his window.

Emma drank wine on occasion, with Zeke Phillips and clients, though rarely at home and she never drank bourbon. She saw no need to stock a cellar because they never entertained and spent less and less time together as man and wife. Only after her thirteenth birthday did Emma allow Gilligan an occasional glass of fine wine, but Emma was gone and Tommy saw nothing wrong with a glass or two more with the pizza. He spent a few minutes in the kitchen preparing, burying the blister packs and empty capsules deep into the garbage. His heart was excited, his mind usurping one image after another, one imagined sensation after another.

By ten o'clock with the lighting subdued, the movie half over, Gilligan lay asleep on the couch; her head nestled into a cushion. Her breathing was shallow, her face infused with pink from the wine. The pizza box was empty. She was a cherub, imbued with sensual innocence. He slipped her satin robe from her shoulders, untying her belt. Then he left her and went to her room. He made up her bed and made her teddy bear ready to see Gilligan safely through the night.

He stepped lightly onto each stair, eager to see her sleeping. What he was thinking wasn't his fault. Nor was he wrong in what he expected. She was practically a woman, certain at that moment that she wasn't his daughter. She looked so much like her mother, nothing like him.

Easing her into his arms she was as light as a feather, on her bed she was peaceful and inviting, her camisole dark against her white skin, her tap pants loose and compelling. He coated her lips once with the powder, left her and went to the main floor where he cleaned what little mess they'd made together, Tommy and Gilligan. He turned out the lights and carried her once again to her room, retracing each precious moment, each thought and emotion, the warmth of her skin and her breath. What he was feeling wasn't his fault. If only the wife had been more of a woman.

In her room Gilligan lay dreaming, the way she often did in school, with her eyes closed. This time he turned on the light. He wanted to see her, easing a hand under each side of her body, pulling gently until the satiny fabric lay by her feet.

One hand went under her top, first cupping one side, then the other, his fingertips tracing her youthful curves, neither daughter nor father seeming to breathe, though in his ears was a cacophony of eager emotion. She was nubile and soft, her scent young and pure. He eased himself between her, making his body ready, kissing her lips once, not a trace of the powder remaining. He told her he loved her and that she shouldn't worry. He was her father and her friend and would never think to hurt her. He would never think to hurt her after waiting so long to love her.

She was all that he wanted and more, willing himself to be tender and not wake her, struggling to master his will when he wanted to push deeper, touching their lips together as he neared the precipice of what he'd longed for, sharing their ecstasy together .

He remained with her a while longer, drinking in her youthful beauty, savouring the scent of her moist body. He kissed her again and eased from her bed, placing her satin pants by her hands, bringing the duvet to her chin and kissing her lips for as long as he dared before at last leaving the bear to protect her as he stepped into the light of the hallway, his shadow reluctantly disappearing.

The next night Tommy Dune cooked supper, finishing what he said was the rest of the wine when, in fact, he'd opened another bottle and, once again, by the same hour, the movie far from over, Gilligan was asleep on the couch.

From where he sat he explored her, his fingertips probing lightly under her slip. She was ready for her bed, he determined, tiptoeing to her room to dim the light and make everything ready.

Easing her from the couch they went up the stairs together, father telling daughter how warm and inviting she felt in his arms. He laid her down gently, easing her slip from her thighs to her breasts, easing her panties past and away from her feet.

In his room he stood by his dresser, his heart on the verge of eruption, coating a fingertip heavily with white powder. Again with his daughter, his long-awaited lover, he coated her lips and went for his camera. He wanted to see her that way forever, for one day, he knew, she would leave him.

Kneeling between her he lost track of time. She was perfection, her deep red hair disguising her pillow, her flawless white skin accented with the pink tips of her breasts, her essence, as yet untouched, heated and fragrant beneath a bed of lustrous and sensuous soft curls.

He breathed her in deeply, inhaling the scent of her innocence, easing his body cautiously forward. He whispered his love, pressing his lips to hers, their bodies melding as one, the weakening strength of his mind urging his resolute body not to awaken her, not to ruin what remained of their week, not to undo what father and daughter had at last found together.

The next morning Tommy called the school. Gilligan had woken with a fever and he felt that keeping her home for the week was for the best. He'd spoken with his doctor who agreed, he assured them. Then Monday and Tuesday were no different from Wednesday and Thursday.

Friday night Gilligan sat on the couch with her legs crossed. She liked to copy her mother. She wanted Gilligan to know that somehow she felt different, but Gilligan hadn't come to her room or into her mind since her mother had gone. She missed their nighttime alone, their quiet time to whisper without ever being heard.

For three days that she could remember, and didn't know why, she woke from her sleep not wearing her tap pants or panties. Two other days, without knowing why, she woke to the light of late morning with her pyjamas bottoms on the floor by the side of her bed and once with her slip by her pillow. She thought that she must now be a woman because often her mother would leave her own bed naked on her way to the toilet or shower.

When her father was gone into the kitchen she pressed her hand against what her mother called her secret place of wonder and good feeling. However that night she didn't feel good, yet she knew why she was bleeding. Her mother had told her the reason a long while ago: because she was a young and beautiful woman. So, yes, she was now truly a woman.

She missed her mother terribly, the same way she missed Gilligan, their time alone in the dark, not able to remember when the last time was that they did speak together in the quiet and the dark. She missed Gilligan so much.

When her father returned with her soda and his bourbon to watch the last movie, Gilligan took her hand away from her secret place of wonder that her mother once told her was for her to enjoy by herself whenever she wanted to smile until a man would one day come into her life that she knew she could love. And she knew that she must love her father.

That Friday night there was no white powder on the tips of Tommy's Dune's fingers. Instead Tommy lay sleeping in his room. He wanted Gilligan to feel better so that her mother would not overly worry the next day upon her return.

Gilligan locked the house and turned out the lights, save for the upstairs hallway. In her room she crawled into bed and waited to sleep.

She once asked her mother how she could be certain that she was living, and not dreaming that she was alive in her dreams. Emma replied that living inside a fanciful dream was no different from making her life a dream in her mind by being whatever or whomever she wanted to be whenever she wanted to be who she wasn't. Despite which Gilligan often didn't know who she was or who she wasn't.

When Emma came home later than expected Saturday night, after a coffee with Zeke in his home, she went to her daughter's room and kissed her goodnight on the forehead, her cheeks and her lips. Stepping out into the hall, thinking of how much she had missed, she stole into the room on her toes and kissed her daughter once more.

The Hunt for Gilligan Rose

Emma loved Gilligan more than her one-sided faces. Tommy was asleep in her bed. She could smell him from where she stood.

Seventeen
This Year: July 01st

Xara Mendiga returned to Long Beach from Miami alone. She wasn't merely distraught, she was beyond devastation. Sunday night she paced her home in a daze, not believing her new reality, not believing the time they'd spent together in Miami loving and laughing was destroyed for no reason over a glass of wine and a dinner she hadn't tasted.

Monday night she called Gilligan a dozen or more times. Not once did Gilligan answer. Whatever dark secret her best friend and lover might have was not enough reason to give up what she knew in her heart was the right thing for both of them: to have one another and not care about anything else. She called once more and left in a message what she felt in her heart. What right did Gilligan have to ruin their lives?

"What right do you have to do this terrible thing to me and to us, Gilligan? You have no right at all to pretend not to love me when I know in my heart that you do. Call me. Please call soon, because I want to forgive you for the cruel way that you have crushed my heart and my soul."
*

Gilligan arrived home on the Monday, staunching her tears until she was once again free from the world in her high-rise asylum.

She heard all the messages, one by one, over and over again. She did love her Xara, though she had nothing to say, nothing to add to a shattered heart. All she had left were her tears.

Her phone chimed again, and again at ten minutes past midnight as she lay awake in her bed.

"Querida," she heard. "I know that you are in your bed by the phone. Please let me hear your sweet voice. Please do not send me away once more."

Gilligan Rose reached for the phone. "Soy yo, Xarita. Forgive me for what I have done. I have spent my time in tears since you left me, since I sent you away."

"You must tell me what secret you carry that weighs so heavily on your heart that you believe you no longer have room inside your warm and loving soul for me."

"This I cannot do, not today or tomorrow, not ever. I am not who I seem to be. Yet I am what I am. That is my secret, cariño. I am not who you want me to be."

"Gilligan, no hables en clave. This is not a time for us to speak in riddles. I am coming to your home. I will wait in the lobby if you do not let me in and tomorrow I will stand in front of your car. I will do tomorrow what was mine to do on Sunday, when instead I walked away from you. I will do this until you understand that you are wrong."

Gilligan filled her lungs. She stopped breathing until she felt dizzy, heedless of the tears flooding her face or how fiercely she was biting into her lips.

"Pues bien, ven aquì, Xara. Come to me if that is what you wish. And I will tell you my secret, if that is what you want. Then you will know to despise me, to find me repugnant, and I will understand. So come to me, if that is what you truly want."

The phones disconnected.

The sound of Gilligan's unexpectedly calm voice chilled Xara's blood. She arrived at Gilligan's high-rise retreat at moments past 1:30 AM. The night air was still, the ocean dark, the gentle waves silent.

"You do not look yourself, mi querida. In fact you look terrible, and for no reason."

"Do not call me that until you have heard what I will tell you, what you wrongly believe you must hear. But I will tell you. The time has come for me to tell someone." She eyed Xara's suitcase. "Leave your luggage by the door; you will not stay long once you have heard what I will say. What we once had is now in our past, Xara: a short and sweet memory for me, a horrible regret for you."

"Chica, I am Xara not a flighty child. Do not think to implant thoughts in my mind. I know what I see. I know what I believe and what I know is true. Tell me, and I will decide for myself what is sweet and what is not."

She trailed her suitcase into the living room, ordering Gilligan to a hot shower and to change into something cozy and warm while she made strong coffee to keep them awake. When Gilligan came out in satin and silk, because she had nothing else that she might wear, Xara was sitting by the patio doors staring westward across the 33rd parallel to Asia and Europe.

"Querida, do you remember the many times we have spoken of the home where one day we will live together somewhere on the south coast of Spain?"

"Sì, claro. Recuerdo. But Xara that was a dream we must dissolve from our minds, a fantasy best forgotten."

"We dream when we sleep, my darling. We never once spoke of our villa in Spain as we slept, your sweet breath so close to mine, our hearts so anxious for one more day together. Are we sleeping now as I gaze through this black sky toward our new home?"

"No, we are not, though the dark you see beyond my window is my life, Xara. That is my secret, though much darker to me than the night."

"When I first saw you I thought how wonderful my life would be to live with such a happy and beautiful woman, sad in my heart that your life was not similar to my own. Then, when I discovered your love, I thought I might live forever, or that I might soon die without you." Xara tipped a bottle of cognac over her cup, diluting the rich flavour with heated strength despite the humid night air. "I am too young to die, Gilligan. I want us to live forever together. So tell me now of this secret that darkens your heart."

Gilligan fortified her coffee, stepping onto the patio. Xara went with her letting long minutes pass in silence, quietly watching tears trickle from the corners of her lover's green eyes, commanding herself not to intervene with the strength of her arms or the soft warmth of her lips.

Then Gilligan turned, touching her cheek: "I murdered my father." She smiled without humour, the burden of so many years lifted from her heart and her mind, suddenly freed from the memory of her blackest night, the one memory of her youth that ruined all others. "With a knife from the kitchen, Xarita, on the fifteenth of July at ten in the morning, I murdered my father." She glanced over her shoulder at the clock on the wall. "Seventeen years, two weeks and eight hours from this very moment, I murdered my father."

*

Deena Archer was pommelling his back, struggling to put her feet on the ground, again, threatening to kill him, again, this time with her new diamond ring if he didn't stop pestering and annoying her. After eleven months Fennell was still a huge pain in her ass. He never stopped buying her flowers, cooking her dinners, or throwing her into his or her pool. At the moment she was headed into the deep end of their pool.

They began as usual in the spa where Fennell was adamant. They would have five kids and she would stay at home as a good mother should to raise and nurture his family. That's what women did best, he assured her. That's how she would best serve the nation, by raising decent children and spending her days discovering the joy and comfort that comes with paying obeisance to her benevolent lord and adoring master.

Deena thought to run to their bedroom for her gun, splashing the water around her to make him disappear. This time she was going to kill him, she shrieked, but later. In the meantime she punched his lordship in the stomach as hard as she could and smacked her master's face with adoration, purring in his ear that if he wanted five kids he could grow a vagina with which she would be more than happy to assist him. All he need do was step into the kitchen.

For that, he admonished, she was going into the pool and Deena knew to surrender, not to struggle. She was going into the pool, again. She raised her arms and let her body fall limp over his shoulder, waiting, once on the deck pounding his back with soft open palms. His instant retaliation was of course expected.

The water was warm.

"I love you, sweetcheeks."

"I love you, Johnnie. I want our new home to be special for both of us."

"It is, every time you walk through the door."

"And the kid thing… you don't mind, really? This world is too sick."

"We're not mommy and daddy material, apart from the fact that I see no reason to widen and possibly damage a perfectly good one-lane expressway." He swam back a few strokes, diving to her feet, emerging slowly, stopping at her hips to kiss her belly, expelling his breath. "No reason at all."

"You're a pig."

"I'm your pig, at least for another two weeks."

Deena slapped his face with more force than she intended and swam away, climbing to the deck by the ladder, wrapping herself in a warm, fleecy robe. The evening air was unseasonably cool. He was inches behind her. Sometimes he still stepped over the line, remnants of the old Johnnie Fennell.

"That wasn't funny, sweetheart. That wasn't funny at all. We're too close to her now to make silly jokes. That woman is going to try to kill you. I know her. There's something deep and dark in her head, the way that she sees the world. I've seen into her eyes. Behind the deep green they're black with despair. Her voice, somehow always happy when I don't believe she's been happy a day in her life. How can she be? She's sick, Johnnie. She needs help, pretending all is well with the world while each year planning a kill. And if this stupid plan of yours does work, in two weeks she will try to kill you."

"Try to kill me, sweetcheeks. I think she'll be a little disappointed. Besides, you'll be in the next room with a perfect three-sixty view."

"And a laser-guided 92FS, Fennell, and after I shoot her I'll shoot you if you even think of stripping past your little pansy panties. And I'll aim to inflict the most damage," she glanced downward, "to your ego."

"I wear Italian straight-backs. So please let's not be nasty until there's a reason, you know, beyond a reasonable doubt." He grinned. "Besides, now that we know when, we have fourteen days to rehearse every possible scenario. She'll be winging it. All she knows is that she's going to kill someone, not yet where or exactly when. We do. We do know when, right here in the US of A. She's not expecting that. We hope. We also know how. Let's not forget the how."

"Let's not forget you've got zero tolerance before I put a 10 millimetre round in her head. I'll kill that bitch in a blink, Johnnie. She is not going to make me a widow before I'm even married. That's my job after we're married."

Johnnie Fennell checked his watch. "Can I stay the night?"

"Don't be an idiot."

Deena Archer scrunched her face, pushing him

backward into water, waiting for him to surface to see her victorious smile before she sauntered into their South Beach condo to change into loungewear for dinner. The closer they came to the fifteenth the more she knew how much she loved him.

*

Three thousand miles to the west Gilligan Rose stood alone on her patio gazing at the stars and across the black sea. She had no lover to playfully smack, to stay over or to prepare a fine dinner for in sexy lingerie.

She had not for a moment in her life regretted raising her young arms into the air, taking a deep breath, closing her eyes and plunging the carving knife deep into her father's chest. She hadn't thought of anything else at the time, not the noise he would make, or whether a lot of blood would gush from the hole, whether he would awaken and ask what the trouble was or whether he would be angry with her for finally saying goodbye.

He hadn't made any noise at all, not that she heard. She didn't think so. She couldn't really remember. She did remember the blood and the black handle protruding from his chest, not like the movies or TV. And for a while she stood waiting for his wide-open eyes to close, wanting to run to tell Gilligan what she had done, waiting. Yet he never once attempted to say he was sorry for the pain where she hurt or to tell her goodbye. So she did, speaking quietly to explain a simple truth. She didn't like him anymore.

She stood on the patio naked, alone in the rain. The rain made her feel pure. She liked being naked in the rain, alone, remembering those days with her mother, in the rain, dancing and singing, washing her hair, wanting to talk alone in her bed with Gilligan later each night. She lathered her hair with shampoo and stood in the rain, watching the white foam drape her breasts and her belly, flowing like white lava to her legs, slipping away from her feet through the tiled floor into the drain and into the air. Gone forever, like her mother and Zeke.

She remembered her mother that last morning, the day she was taken away because of what she had done, what she knew was the right thing to do to save Gilligan from more pain. She remembered her mother's smile, her last warm and loving embrace, the tear her mother stopped on her cheek with a kiss. She remembered Zeke Phillips, the pain in his eyes, the strength of his hand at her shoulder, the grief scrawled into his beleaguered and ancient face.

At least uncle Zeke was now dead, dead for a while, free from the pain of what she had done not for herself but for Gilligan who, from that day on, and for such a long while, had never again come to her bed to whisper kind words and make her feel good. Most of all she remembered wanting to hide from them in the dark attic with Gilligan.

Eighteen
Last Year: August 03rd

Deena Archer didn't conceal her disgust that he would have so many beautiful clothes, yet dress for the job like a hobo in a bad black and white movie. She stepped onto his jacket, tugging once, tearing off a sleeve, stepping onto one leg of his pants, yanking hard, dropping the tattered halves into a garbage bag along with his scuffed black shoes, his collection of white shirts and the tie that had taken on the look of an unusable garrotte.

She was not crossing the country with any man dressed as though he couldn't afford her.

The day couldn't be more spectacular for new lovers. The air was calm; the midmorning sun bright and warm, the water in his pool was clear, glistening and inviting.

"You seemed to enjoy that."

"I did enjoy that. I can't tell you how much and Brannigan's going to kill you, Fennell."

"Why will she kill me and not you?"

"Because I'm young and I'm beautiful and because you took advantage of me when I was weak."

"I can't believe this."

"What… your first day on the job as a human?"

"No, that I watched you dressing. I wondered for the longest time how you could possibly wear anything under those pants. Or that I made Deena Archer all hot and sweaty."

"Get over yourself. You took as many showers as me."

He twirled her in a tight circle. "Sultry and sexy Deena Archer is my girlfriend. Can you believe that?"

"No, I can't. It's too weird."

"So, you're keeping me."

"I haven't decided." She examined her reflection in the garden doors, "though I do see how easily all those lovey-dovey words must come to you when something this good-looking and hot is naked and vulnerable underneath you."

"Vulnerable? You were on top more than me. I was the vulnerable one." He kissed her. "So am I a keeper."

"Yes, you're a keeper, which is even weirder. And Brannigan is going to kill you because she likes me more than she likes you. Nobody likes you, and I'm very new to the idea, so don't do anything to piss me off anytime soon." She kissed him, hanging her arms from his neck. "When you left me, I thought I would die. I really thought I would die."

"The worst decision of my life, choosing a door that might have stayed closed over you, your bed, us. I'll spend my life saying I'm sorry, proving to you how much I love you."

She punched him. "You already have, I think about six times, until I lost consciousness, or passed out or collapsed." She wriggled. "I don't need anymore 'I'm sorry, sweetcheeks' until tonight," she punched him again "when I expect the same breathtaking performance."

"Thank you."

"Thank you for what? I meant my performance, and you will never ever call me that in the squad room."

"We can't tell her, sweetcheeks. I want you in on putting this woman down, a hole in her chest instead of mine or twenty-five to life. Either way, she's going down."

"We can work at home, save LAX for next week or the week after. Besides, I don't feel like flying this week. I need to figure out where exactly to file you in my head, Fennell. Fennell, shit, I don't even know what to call you…John

Francis."

"Nothing you called me in your bed, or in the tub or in the pool."

"God, what am I going to tell my mom?" Deena sipped her coffee. "We are a thing, aren't we, Fennell? I'm not going to tell my mom that I finally have a guy in my life, get us both all excited and watch you walk out again?"

He feigned a moment of doubt, reaching for her cell by her Gucci. Keeping her at arm's length, an open palm at her forehead, standing firm against her flailing arms and feet, he pressed Speed Dial, waiting, teasing her with his smile. All of a sudden making a face that was real. He was expecting the message centre.

"Yeah, hi, Mrs. Archer, this is Agent Johnnie Fennell. I work with your daughter. What? No, she's fine. I'm calling because I thought you should know that I love Deena. We had sex last night, hot, steamy sex which is okay because we're getting married, you know, after she tells you herself. By the way, you and your husband are invited to my home this Saturday but I only have fifty-dollar wine so you might want to bring a couple of bottles of the good stuff. Pardon me? Yes, of course, she's right here getting ready to skinny dip in my pool. She really is quite insatiable, can't keep her hands off me, which is, you know, entirely understandable. However you might want to give her a moment to catch her breath."

He waited for Deena to blink and close her mouth, passing her the phone while he moved to the far side of the pool. Fifteen minutes later she snapped her cell closed. She didn't seem angry. He knew angry. He'd seen angry often enough. He waited, uncertain. She was undressing where she stood. Right there, off came her jacket and blouse, her slacks and her bra, placed neatly beside her purse, her phone and her 92FS chrome-plated Berretta.

They traded step for step, Deena inching her way toward him, Johnnie Fennell sidestepping his way by the same increments to maintain a safe distance. At the dive board she ignored him, reaching for a towel, taking each of the two rungs deliberately, pausing on each one, making him crazy, walking to the edge, laying out her towel, kneeling, stretching out on her front, laying her head onto crossed arms and closing her eyes.

Ten minutes later, the hot sun caressing her legs, her back and what wasn't covered by intersecting strings; his head appeared at the front edge of the board, his fingertips white with exertion.

"What, Fennell?"

"Well we're sort of late for work, Agent Archer."

"I'm not working today. I'm taking the day off. I need a personal day." She turned her head to see him. "My mother thinks you're charming, mildly offensive and somewhat forward, though charming. She wants to know if you're serious, or whether my father should call a few of his more covert buddies." She moaned. "I told her to wait until Saturday. Mother knows best." She searched his eyes, stretching to kiss him. "So, we're a couple? This happened pretty fast, Fennell. Are we sure about this?"

He fingered his way along a side edge, pushing her over. When she surfaced he was on the board, stretched out.

"Would you take a bullet for me, Archer?"

"Yes, darling, you know I would," she sputtered.

"Out of 212, now 215, how many nights have you dreamed about me, thought of me in your bed?"

Her tanned arms fanned the water. "Two that I can remember, lover-boy. Sorry."

"You're lying."

"Yes, I am, babe. Friday night I dreamed of killing you while I was in bed, alone, shivering from hyperthermia."

"What kind of wine are they bringing?"

"Champagne, my love," she tried, her chin closer to the water.

"Are you drowning?"

"I think so, sweetheart."

Fennell propped himself onto an elbow, lazily watching her arms sweep through the clear water, her legs opening and closing. "I think I prefer sweetheart. Sort of goes with sweetcheeks. Don't you think?"

"Yes, sweetheart, I do."

"Then it's settled. I love you, you love me and we're getting married as soon as the job's done and you tell Brannigan. This is girl stuff, better done one female to another."

He arched himself to his feet, stretched, and went into the hacienda. Deena drew herself onto the deck, pranced to her phone and speed-dialled her mother.

August 10th

The week passed quickly, the duo and new couple working between condo and hacienda.

Saturday's dinner went well. Mrs. Archer took an immediate liking to John Francis; Senator Archer was somewhat less disposed from the door to the living room to forgive the man for stealing his daughter without the proper advance notice and the decorum of courtship. That until he was introduced to a very gracious and regal Victoria Templeton who believed the young couple had fallen in love as they should without any help from old fogies who'd forgotten what love was all about. The way she fell in love with her Stuart one spring day in her parents' garden. Their first bed a freshly mowed lawn, their only cover a gentle and warm breeze caressing moist skin, love's ardent nectar the fragrance of lilacs by the pond and lilies floating in the low water, gardenias and prize-winning daffodils conspiring to secrete the passion of newfound amour from unforgiving eyes.

She was happy for Deena and John Francis whose blood and passion was as heated as her Stuart's. She patted Deena's knee. The romance, she told the young woman, was just beginning. John Francis was, after all, a Templeton.

That was enough for the senator who went to the kitchen with Johnnie for something stronger than champagne and more pragmatic conversation. When the evening ended, the senator and his wife drove Miss Victoria to her home. The old girl wasn't tired and invited them to join her in the lounge for a sherry.

Sunday Deena and Fennell went to the beach to recap the day before. Deena was floating, Fennell was proud. Even on South Beach crammed with the glamour of European women, his woman stood out.

Monday, the 10th, Fennell phoned Brannigan with an update. They were flying to upstate New York by way of La Guardia. She knew Archer strictly flew First-Class, for the space, not the status, and that she paid the difference willingly. Fennell was Fennell. He didn't care either way, though Deena did care and his days in Coach were over.

"What did she say?"

"She asked about you. I told her you were over your tantrum." She pinched him. "She wants separate receipts for the hotel, and she wants to see room numbers on different floors."

"This is so weird. A week ago I was shivering in her office and you were as Fennell as ever. Now I love you and we'll be working a case from the same hotel bed."

"You loved me since day one."

"No, sweetheart, I didn't. I hated you since day one."

"Love and hate are the same. You hated not having me. You were jealous, misdirecting your frustration towards me instead of yourself for not doing what you knew was right when we first met. You were too shy to express your true feelings, that you were inexplicably hungry for me, famished." He reached for his juice, studying the brilliance of Miami beneath them, the turquoise sea, a necklace of white waves crashing to delineate white crystal sand. Deena preferred aisle seating. "You have to admit, sweetcheeks. Since you confessed your love and, by the way, your incredible appetite, you feel so much better, so much more complete as a woman."

"You thought I was pretty complete our first night, and last night, and the six nights in-between." She curled into him. "We'll talk more about this tonight, sweetheart, when I call you from my room."

She patted his arm, closing her eyes. She'd never driven the meandering back roads along the Hudson; pathways her mother had told her were so romantic in the summer and the autumn.

Her mother was half right. Half the drive along the I-87, once out of the melee of bumper-to-bumper traffic, bad manners, third fingers and a few 'fuck-you' followed by red-faced apologies when Fennell flashed his shield, was in the passing lane, once again federal agents trumping state troopers.

Deena was quiet, Fennell was pensive. She was thinking of him, he was thinking of her along the second half of their 200-mile road trip, lovers holding hands, polished 10mm Berettas on their hips.

Their meeting at the facility wasn't until the next morning, three days of tours and research planned. They passed a corner store and liquor outlet that wasn't on any corner. They also had plenty of time, Deena knew, pouting, her sad eyes guiding him into the parking lot.

She bought cheese, surprised by the selection, two bottles of good wine, an opener, a knife, a French baguette and cold cuts. At the cash, her gun and her shield visible, she asked for directions to the nearest lake. Thirty minutes later the lovers were enjoying a mid-afternoon diversion. They were alone, the wine delicious, the lake water perfect for a dip, Johnnie's face smeared with invisible smacks, his mouth numb with deep prune-coloured kisses. He loved her.

That night she called him on her cell from her bed,

maintaining appearances for Captain Brannigan. He answered from his. When they disconnected she turned out the light and snuggled into him. Neither one spoke of the next morning, or anything else, though the morning came early. The morning always came early with Fennell.

The state-run teaching institute had no name they could see as they drove through the gate and along the winding driveway. The grounds appeared well-maintained, though the flowers and trees, manicured lawn and hedges didn't camouflage what the place was, didn't dispel the stigma. The building was old, the interior making Agent Archer cold with, she didn't know what, sympathy, her imagination running wild, soon discovering what was worse than any prison she'd walked through.

At Reception the male guard asked matter-of-factly and without a smile for their weapons, producing a steel box with a combination lock loosely attached. Fennell accepted the box, locked it, spun the wheel and pushed it toward the guard, empty, explaining to the man the difference between his federal warrant and the state facility's wish list. The man had no opinion either way. He was more interested in Deena's ass as she stood at the steel door with her partner, waiting for him to enter the access code. He took his time.

The first day they toured the facility: the offices, the gardens meant for the staff, no longer for Phillips' patients who hadn't yet died or newer patients who replaced those who had. The bathrooms, the toilets and the open area intended for meals and the recreation of staring at walls and each other were so white and bleak. Where others might not, they saw lenses and restraints concealed. They saw the nine-to-five eyes the staff couldn't disguise. They saw depression and fear and loneliness. They saw frail bodies and empty souls, faces with one eye peering through wire-reinforced glass portholes, minds without memories of love or compassion. They saw what Emma Rose once knew and remembered. They saw where she might have spent endless nights in the dark.

Deena wanted to leave. She wanted to get out. She'd seen the painted faces of Miss Emma Rose in galleries and on the web and now she understood. She understood and told Johnnie Fennell: "I want to get out. Please, get me out of here."

That night she cried until she fell asleep in his arms, waking the next morning.

Again at the institute they went through every file covering the previous seventeen years, finding not a trace, not a single word about Emma Rose. Yet seventeen years earlier the world-famous artist was sentenced to an undetermined incarceration, which meant, everyone knew at the time, that Emma Rose would never leave. Yet she did. Not only did she leave. She apparently never arrived. So what did happen to Emma Rose?

Deena Archer stood firm. She was not setting foot into that hell once more to see those grim faces. They were going to New York City, to the Gattelsburg Gallery, to see Emma Rose through her work. Johnnie Fennell agreed, as the senior agent. He made that very clear and he wasn't glib either in the way he spoke or in the way that she saw him.

He waited until they arrived at the hotel to console her in loving arms, keeping to himself the way that he felt.

Thursday Fennell insisted on buying lunch. He knew a great place on the corner of Fifth Avenue and 49th Street. He knew she enjoyed haute cuisine and this, he promised her, was the best. She would never taste anything better. Deena stood back in shock, witnessing her well-dressed man regress into a fennell. She would wait for dinner, told him. She was not walking and eating at the same time. Standing with him in one of his greasy and smelly diners was one thing; she shook her head, trying not to regurgitate something that should have eyes and was buried under a heap of soggy sauerkraut as they strolled along Broadway was quite another matter.

They walked together quietly; Fennell more infatuated with each savory bite, preoccupied, Deena guiding him through a green light from one corner to the other, her face contorted with real pain as she studied his love affair with the offal wrapped in a bun. She was almost jealous, believing throughout the spectacle that he loved his lunch more than he loved her.

When he finished he thought to kiss her, she thought perhaps not, not until he washed his mouth, though at the gallery he did redeem himself. This time he was the one to take a step back in awe. To see eye-straining thumbnails enlarged on a computer screen did not in any way compare with the three by four-foot oils assaulting his senses with the sombre and macabre textures of her canvases.

Miss Emma Rose's paintings were not for sale. They were on loan to the gallery unless, of course, the interested party had deep pockets. The asking price was 150,000. Asking meaning, if one had to ask, then one couldn't afford her. Could one? Deena asked. Even in New York Archer meant something.

Fennell and Archer flew home early. She wanted time alone, she said, she insisted, which he didn't think was such a good idea. So he went with her, cooked dinner, put her to bed and waited until Friday to talk business. Thursday night wasn't a time for shoptalk, rather for keeping her warm and safe from haunting and dark thoughts. When she woke his hands were damp with her tears and she kissed him. She turned onto her side, propping herself onto an elbow.

"Fennell, sweetheart, something's not right. Those faces in the gallery, one side dreadful and dark, the other side blank, white, with bright light shining through the eye."

"They scared you."

"Yes, they scared me. I'm a little girl afraid of the dark. Don't be stupid." She sat straight. "Can you listen to me for once?" He nodded. "Emma Rose sold her first painting, what, twenty, twenty-two years ago?"

"Yes, about, I suppose."

"Sweetheart, she was only sentenced seventeen years ago. Yet we couldn't find a frigging word about her in the files. She didn't exist." She touched his cheek. "Did you even look at those doors, the glass plates, the faces, the eyes, Johnnie, those poor, desperate eyes searching ours? No one captures that much sorrow in a day."

Johnnie Fennell bolted. "Shit!"

"Yeah, that's right, Fennell, very big shit. Emma Rose was in that nightmarish place long before she killed her husband. I'm thinking for a very long time. Sweetheart, she painted those terrible faces from memory."

"That's where she met Dune, or could be she was Phillips' play thing first, with privileges. Maybe he let her inside to paint the dark side in return for certain favours. You know, give some get some."

"No, sweetheart, that's not it. Emma Rose lived there. She was imprisoned there. No artist can capture such desolate grief the way she did without living it. And somehow she got out. I think if Phillips were still alive he'd be in prison right now for aiding and abetting an escape after his assessment put her there a second time. He got himself appointed as the psychiatrist, got her put under his care, then he set her free and went along for the ride."

"Hard to believe that all these years no one knew she was missing."

Deena hunched her shoulders, hugging herself, rubbing warmth into her arms. "Harder to believe that no one knew she was supposedly there, or cared."

"They still don't. We don't need a bunch of New York State puritans screwing our chances of shutting down Gilligan Rose."

"I can't imagine the horror Emma felt at being sent back. She mustn't have known. I don't think he would have risked telling her. Those are her faces that she painted, Johnnie, Emma's faces that she saw every day. Those are her imploring eyes searching for someone to understand. Emma Rose is the key to all this, Johnnie, not her daughter. Gilligan Rose is the killer, Emma Rose is the reason."

August 17th

Monday morning Johnnie Fennel checked in with Brannigan as ordered, as senior agent. Deena Archer stood beside him, wondering what she would tell the captain when her time came to report in.

He was too good at being a cop. She wasn't certain how good a lawyer Fennell would be, or how good a cop she would be without him. They were Archer and Fennell: Beauty and the Beast. How would she go home at night and tell him about her day with somebody else, somebody she wouldn't care about? How would she call her mother each night to vent that he was a total jerk and the absolute best, pig-headed, constantly and infuriatingly right, obnoxious and how much she hated him, or that she couldn't wait for Monday to learn from him, or just once if he thought to invite her to dinner at a restaurant whose menu didn't include beef jerky?

Then they were together twelve hours a day, five days a week. Now they lived and breathed each other twenty-four-seven. How would she explain all that to Brannigan?

They drove to Miami International, boarding American Airlines flight 203 en route to LAX where they would put a face in real time to Rose, Gilligan: Flight Attendant and Killer Extraordinaire

The deal was he wouldn't wear jeans and boots if she wore a short skirt and sweater. Lots of guys wanted to hide their girls from the leering world; John Francis Templeton Fennell wasn't one of them. He was proud. However the gate guy needed proof, half wondering where she could conceal a weapon even if she were a cop. He'd never seen cops walking up to the gate arm in arm.

Onboard they sat side by side, holding hands. On TGA

flight 1814 from LAX to JFK and on to London, they would not.

Over the previous eleven years Gilligan Rose was the only female TGA flight attendant to work the six cities each year at the time of the murders and five weeks earlier she'd spent the night between flights a few blocks from Cooper's hotel. She was thirty-two and attractive, attractive enough for any executive type to want a chance to cheat on his wife with her and not feel bad about it.

The woman was college-educated, spoke three languages and was allegedly adept at killing with not too much effort. She was the key to two mysteries: Why she was killing, and possibly where her mother was hiding. Her father was dead and buried, forgotten. He wasn't an issue. What they knew about him was sufficient. He was murdered in cold blood by his wife after working a few years at the asylum, before political correctness made the place a therapeutic and teaching facility, and a few more as a cutter in a slaughterhouse. Then he disappeared off the chart until they took him away in a bag. Not a man to envy, his scholastic standing a joke in today's world. Nor was anything known of Emma Rose since her disappearance from the institute where she was sentenced to live out her life, judged by the court, once assessed by Phillips, to be of unsound mind and not responsible for what she had done.

That's what they knew.

"She was famous, sweetheart, and successful. Everyone wanted her paintings. Why would she kill her husband? Why wouldn't she simply leave with her daughter? She didn't need him. Why would she give up her daughter for a loser when she had the entire world in her hands?"

"The court thought she was nuts. Could be she was and that the girl was better off without her."

"Yeah, right, adopted by a couple she ran from after two years and a couple of months, a few months before her eighteenth birthday, taking back her real name. What's up with that?"

"Who knows? Maybe her new daddy liked her more than he liked her new mommy. Or, neither one liked her. It's not like she needed their money. She's worth millions, Deena. The big question is: Why is she working?"

"We're wealthy and we're working. What's your point?"

"She works to kill. How else could she get away with this? She couldn't, not without TGA. So the question becomes: What pissed her off, and when? Something did before the system screwed with her life. That's her anniversary, sweetcheeks, the fifteenth, the day they took her away."

"She was abused, Johnnie, by her father, and quite possibly by the other guy. Who knows? That's why her mother killed him. Now she's going around looking for abusive fathers. She's giving back in her own way, trying to make the world a better place."

"Yeah, she is, by keeping up the family tradition, by making the planet worse each time."

"And you have a problem with that, you, Johnnie Fennell, the guy who believes everyone is a criminal?"

"As a cop, yes, I do. Everyone is potentially corrupt. As a newly reconditioned human being, albeit somewhat against my better judgement, no I don't."

"And as a lawyer?" she asked.

"I'll answer that when this is over."

"Do you think Emma Rose is dead?"

"She could be, if she's still Emma Rose, or if she's lazing on a beach somewhere in paradise and she's not Emma Rose. We'll probably never know. She wouldn't be old and she's well-off. The day before she was sentenced her accounts were closed, the money probably transferred into Phillips' briefcase. His accounts were closed a month later, pulling a pretty spectacular stunt for the day. Give the old guy credit. He had cojones to do what he did. That money went somewhere. My guess is into a few different banks over time. He also died penniless with not a cent left to disburse from his will, another dead-end. He was protecting her, sweetcheeks. How else do you figure a guy from old money dies broke? Anyway, she's ancient history. So is he. Maybe they did have a thing. Kudos, he was more than twice her age." Fennell chuckled, reaching for his drink. "Perhaps he was long in the leg."

Deena scrunched her face. "Or maybe he was fatherly towards her. He might have known something about her that no one else did. He was, after all, the court-appointed psychiatrist."

"Imagine all the art she left behind, selling at auction for ten times the value simply because she murdered her husband, all the money going to a daughter she hasn't seen in years and she can't tell anyone who she is."

"The daughter could know where she is and if Phillips did give her his money before his time to avoid a paper trail you might be right. Maybe they were an item. Emma Rose didn't spend a day at the institute. What if this was all planned ahead of time? What if, after this Dune guy was killed, mother, daughter and Phillips worked together?"

"They had no contact. Emma never knew about Collette Salazar, neither did Phillips. The art money was held in trust until she was eighteen when she became Gilligan Rose again, terminating Collette Salazar." Fennell paused for a moment. "She started killing four years later, a year after she began flying. So what got her started, why the delay? What happened over those four years?

"That's why she could know, Johnnie. She was Colette until something happened to make her leave what should have been a comfortable life. Otherwise why would she want to re-establish a link to such a horrible past?" Deena raised the armrest between them, nestling against him. "This is still so weird, you and me. I'll feel very strange sitting beside you, watching you without touching you."

She sighed. "You're very handsome in your new suit, sweetheart, please don't make me think to put a hole in it. I'll have enough to explain to Brannigan when this is over without explaining why I shot you."

August 18th

Archer and Fennell had no choice but to leave their weapons at home. Flight attendants knew when cops or marshals were onboard. They knew who had guns and who didn't. Mr. John Francis Templeton Fennell did not. He was an executive who eyed every young girl boarding TGA flight 1814 en route to London via New York as they stood waiting with their parents who were too preoccupied forging their way inch by inch into Coach to notice.

When he wasn't ogling them he was fixated on his laptop, every so often lowering the screen. The woman seated beside seemed not to notice or care, nor did he pay much attention to her despite her chic appearance, her hair tucked under her beret, her silk blouse open indiscreetly enough to show delicate lace, her legs covered in sheer nylons from the cuffs of her short designer shorts to her four-inch stilettos.

The take-off was smooth, Fennell working on his first mimosa. It was noon in New York.

"Good morning, Mr. Fennell. Would you like another before we serve breakfast?"

Her eyes were green, disappointed, he thought. She'd come from behind without warning. She'd seen what he was doing, what he was seeing on his computer screen: his young daughter.

"Thank you, yes," was all he could manage. He was embarrassed, glad she was speaking to the passenger by the window.

The weekend before John Fennell had taken countless shots of his daughter in her ruffled pink panties, and in her bed, his hand tugging at her bottoms as she slept. Over the past weekend he'd begun taking pictures of his daughter by his pool, from his bedroom window, capturing her body scantily cloaked in a thong, the strings of her triangle top dangling over her chaise-longue, and from the same window as the young girl showered in the patio stall.

Once again he was slow to react as she returned with her tray, taking a deep breath, his face flushed, snapping his laptop shut.

Gilligan Rose was something to look at and he wondered who did apart from every man on the plane. She was beautiful. Not Archer beautiful, he reminded himself, though stunning nonetheless.

He eyed her nametag, "Thank you, miss."

"Miss Archer, since you're not eating breakfast I thought you might enjoy an extra mimosa. We prepare them ourselves in the galley, not the food service. And I must tell you that you're a complete knockout in that outfit. You must tell me where you shop before we land. I'm so sorry you won't be continuing on with us. We could have done some shopping together in London."

"Thank you, Gilligan. I buy most of my outfits in Miami or Tampa. I live in Miami, not L.A. where I was in town on business. New York's a two day stopover before heading home."

"I vacation twice a year in Miami for a week. Perhaps I can give you a call when I do. Do a girl's day."

"Are you based in L.A.?" Deena asked. "I get there quite often. Are you in the book?"

Gilligan Rose nodded. "I am, but I live in Long Beach." Her lips curved into a toothy smile, not the usual in-flight smile, her eyes confirming that she was sincerely pleased. "I'll look forward to a surprise call."

When she was gone Fennell stooped forward to stow his computer, whispering. "Just to let you know, Archer, I am not destroying those photos. If she knew they were of you, I think you would have had a pretty steamy date by now."

She crossed her arms, pinching and twisting his. He was being a fennell.

When lunch was served Mr. Fennell was once again surprised from behind, though not before Gilligan Rose saw images of his daughter standing on the rung of a ladder in front of a wall of books wearing knee-highs and a short pleated skirt.

Landing in New York she stopped by to wish Miss Archer a pleasant flight on her trip home to Miami.

"Mr. Fennell, thank you for flying with us. I'm sorry you won't be travelling on to London."

"I will at some point, miss. My base is L.A. However my firm's recently performed some necessary surgical procedures on the sales staff and management's filling the gap for the next year or so." He shrugged, grinning. "So, yes, at the very least I'll be doing monthly trips to various cities in Europe, London and Paris included. And TGA's got my business."

"Thank you. We look forward to seeing you again."

She left him, reaching for the mike. When she faced the passengers she caught him with his eyes glued to her ass.

Disembarking, Deena promised to look her up during her next trip to L.A., surprised by the warmth of Gilligan Rose's hands clasping hers. With Mr. Fennell she exchanged courteous nods.

Later that night they were at home, Deena's home.

"She's beautiful, sweetheart."

"That's an understatement, and no ring. Did you notice her skin? Do you think she could be any whiter?"

"Gee, I don't know, sweetheart. Why don't you stick a colour chart to her cute little ass and find out? You seemed to like looking at that particular attribute enough."

"Who wouldn't? Besides, I was on the job, gathering Intel."

"I bet you were."

"Really though, who wouldn't want something like that

in their bed for a lifetime?"

"You, Fennell. You wouldn't want something like that in your bed anytime, apart from the fact she's bad for your health."

"Sweetcheeks, she's dog-faced beside you. I was talking from the average male perspective. Thanks for being jealous."

"Don't be an idiot. The woman's gorgeous, Fennell. Being jealous is easy."

"Yeah, she is gorgeous. Looks like I'm in for a difficult year. A dirty job, but someone's got to do it."

His lips curved into his annoying smirk.

Her lips curved into a snarl.

"This is one of those times I don't like my job. When we were speaking I found myself thinking we could be friends if things were different. I simply can't imagine her killing anyone. Quite frankly I thought she was adorable."

"I'm sure the judge will take that into consideration"

"What I meant was she seemed so bright and full of life, so likeable." She read his mind. "Okay, so now you're being a fennell. Get your mind out of the gutter. Don't make me think all my hard work over the past eighteen days was for nothing. Repairing something as badly damaged as you hasn't been easy, and I'm not finished. I am far from finished. To begin with, you are not eating anymore of those disgusting hotdogs, not if you want anywhere near my sweet and soft lips. You got that? And we're not eating anymore meals in those disgusting dung piles you call restaurants. I need you around for a long time, John Francis, until I kill you. Not some beautiful redhead."

"Uh-oh, John Francis, that doesn't sound good."

She ignored him.

"C'mon, sweetcheeks, I'm arresting her and marrying you." He stroked her cheek. "Besides, from where I was sitting, she was far more interested in you than me, which could be the reason she doesn't have a ring. Let's face it,

Deena. She is gorgeous, picture-perfect and she's never married. We also believe she was abused as a girl. So maybe we're overlooking something here. Perhaps we jumped the gun on that girlie shopping day." He peered out over her patio at a cloudless sky painted deep amber with wispy strokes of deep red. "Perhaps, Deena, I should be the one who's jealous. Not that I'm not every time we step out the door."

Nineteen
Seventeen Years Ago

Gilligan lay in her bed early one Saturday morning in June, the door slightly ajar, taking her time to make herself feel good. Her mother wouldn't be home until late the next evening. She enjoyed making herself feel good. She enjoyed telling Gilligan in the dark, whenever she could, when the light in the hall was turned out, how she felt as she made herself feel good. Some mornings, though, she felt groggy and her stomach was upset.

She couldn't be certain that her father had touched her there in her dreams, or that she liked that he did, with his hands, making her feel good. She didn't think so. And then she did think so. In her dream, she remembered, she saw his head between her legs. He was smiling and she felt good. Then he was kneeling between her. She knew her father loved her. She remembered how he told her in her dream, the same dream. She thought so. How he told her to close her eyes, to sleep and to dream. She remembered seeing him naked, walking through her door. She thought so. She'd seen her father naked before, and her mother. Perhaps she remembered him in her dream from another time.

The hallway was dark. The sky outside her window was dismal and sad, she thought, the pane clouded with mist, the rain tap-tap-tapping at the glass. Her father never woke early the days her mother was gone. She went to the bathroom to pee, leaving her panties by her pillow. Often she would wake early to pee, her panties or her bottoms by her pillow or by her feet. She peed most times that she awoke from a dream that made her feel good. And sometimes, back in her bed, she would cover her head with her blankets to speak with Gilligan alone in whispers.

Gilligan knew when to come to her room, when she wanted to talk, the same way she knew when to find Gilligan. Together they shared secrets with nothing to hide. What one young girl's mind thought, the other one knew.

"Gilligan I saw father again in my dream. I think so."

"I've seen him before too when I'm supposed to be sleeping."

"But I don't open my eyes because I'm supposed to be sleeping."

"In my last dream he hurt me and I did open my eyes. I don't think he should hurt me."

"He hurt me once too and he told me he loves me. He doesn't mean to hurt me. I don't think so."

"He told me he loves me and that I should sleep."

"When I was sleeping he made me feel good and the pain went away."

"I know father loves me the way he loves mother. I think so."

"I saw father love mother when mother was dreaming. I think he hurt mother too. She made funny noises. I wanted him to stop hurting mother."

"I know father loves me."

"I know father loves you the way he loves me. But I don't want to dream anymore."

"I want to feel good by myself. I don't like when he hurts me that way."

"Then I promise I won't let him hurt you the way he hurt mother."

"Gilligan, I know a secret."

"You can't know a secret."

"I do know a secret. I think I like girls more than I like

boys. I think so."

"No. Don't say you like girls. How can you like girls when we're supposed to like boys?"

"I do. I know that I do. I don't think I ever liked boys."

"I don't think our mother likes father. Not anymore. I don't think so. Not since I saw mother cry.

But I know I like girls. Not the way I like you, Gilligan. I love you more than I love anyone else."

"How can you know you like girls? You don't have a girlfriend."

"I do have a girlfriend. I kiss her at school in the yard behind the trees. She kisses me too and I like her. I want to kiss her again on Monday behind the trees. You can kiss her too when you see her, if you want to."

"Will she make you feel good?"

"I think that she wants to."

"And do you? Do you want to make her feel good?"

"I think that we both do. I'm not afraid."

"I don't think that I want to."

"You can come if you want to. I know she would like you and you can kiss her after I do."

"I might like to kiss her, if you do."

"I have to pee."

"I have to pee too. We should put on our panties. Father might see us."

"Father's still sleeping. I think so.

Gilligan slipped from her bed once more and tiptoed to the bathroom.

Saturday night she watched another movie, this time with popcorn and Coke, with nothing but the taste of salt on her lips. Falling asleep, alone in her bed, she thought of the blonde girl at school and was anxious for Monday when she would kiss Wendy again.

On Tuesday they spent time by trees under the sun reading their books until all the teachers had gone. Wendy was so happy that Gilligan was with her both days at recess and lunch and again after school, ignoring the other prettier girls who seemed very put off by the snub. Wednesday was rainy and cold without kisses. On Thursday she went home with her lips and her fingertips tingling, her heart beating wildly. On Friday Wendy took her home for the first time while her parents were gone and she knew then that she liked the girl as much as Gilligan did.

Gilligan never again heard her mother cry.

Twenty
Last Year: Last Week of August

By breakfast the next morning Johnnie Fennell was forgiven for his fennell lapse and Deena was holding her breath, poised in his arms at the edge of the pool.

All that day and the next they worked from her home. Friday he called Brannigan. She stood by his side and when the inquisition was over they drove to his home. The weekend was theirs. Since Archer he no longer worked seven-day weeks. Weekends were for the beach, the pool, museums and dinners at sidewalk cafés where he could show her off.

Sunday they went shopping. She didn't need Brannigan's money. They had agreed that Deena should meet Gilligan Rose twice: once in the fall, once in the spring and possibly once in January by coincidence somewhere on the beach. They'd confirmed that she was there in June with a woman called Xara Mendiga who worked out of L.A. for a Mexican firm.

She didn't think that Gilligan would dress in anything less than the finest and she would not be outdone.

Through to the following June Fennell would see Gilligan Rose once each month on or near the fifteenth without Deena. On his final excursion, to wherever she might lead him on the fifteenth of July, she was expected to kill him. In the meantime they would study ten previous murders, her adoptive parents, her school records, her banking and Xara Mendiga. Gilligan Rose had four weeks of vacation time coming, Fennell had four. Deena had three, Fennell deciding that one of his four weeks would be in Long Beach, California with her.

Throughout the last week of August they studied her flight schedules out of L.A. to Europe and Asia over the coming three months. She'd already told them, or told Deena with him in-between overhearing, that she liked South Beach in January and June and the Spanish Mediterranean in May. And why would she want to hook up with Deena who was obviously not lesbian when she'd spent all her time in May and June in a hotel room with Mendiga?

On the last Friday of the month Deena Archer pulled into her parking spot near 8:20 PM. Johnnie Fennell arrived ten minutes later for an eight-thirty face-to-face with Gayle Brannigan.

This time the captain could see the ocean well beyond the horizon that beachcombers could see as they sifted through a day's worth of littered sand, or lovers strolling off a meal hand in hand. What else she saw she didn't believe. Why was Fennell waiting by his car, facing her, smiling? And whose car was he driving? And why was Archer smiling? Archer never smiled around Fennell. No one smiled around Fennell. If they weren't envious of his success as a cop, wishing they were as good as him, they hated what came from his mouth. And what in the hell was Fennell wearing? And since when did Archer have legs to her neck?

They came in ten minutes late, side by side, Fennell opening the door. Why the hell was Fennell holding the door for her? Suddenly she was not having a good day.

"Good evening, Captain," Archer began. "Sorry we're late."

"Hey, boss lady, ditto that...engine trouble. You are looking exceptionally spectacular this evening."

"Engine trouble, in a Jaguar, that's what you had? Who

the hell are you, and what have you done with my bad-mouthed crumpled agent?" She stared down Archer. "Agent Archer, who is this white boy all tanned and spiffy and how did he get through security without a pass?"

"Captain, you said to make him ready for First-Class travel." Deena sighed just a bit too dreamily, her eyes a little too bright and happy. "What else can I say? I'm good." Fennell was wearing a dark blue blazer and a deep red silk shirt, a darker shade than his pocket hanky. His pants were cream-coloured with single front pleats. His shoes were dark blue loafers with tassels.

"I told you one thousand, Archer, not a hundred and one. Fennell whose car is that? Who on God's green earth would be that stupid to trust you with a Jaguar? And why are you wearing my new clothes on a Friday night, clothes that I paid for?"

"The car's mine, boss lady, and I've got a date. The woman doesn't like antique rides. She's a little snooty that way."

"Yours… and snooty, and you got what for the trade-in?"

He straightened his collar. "Your suit's at home hanging, boss lady, still in the bag."

She strode towards Fennell, standing behind him. First she checked under his jacket collar, at the tongue of his belt, she massaged his pant leg between her thumb and her forefinger and ordered a shoe from his foot. He obliged. When she was finished the inspection she stood.

"Not on a cop's salary, Agent Fennell, not unless these are the clothes you'll be wearing for the next ten years. So start talking and do not tell me anything I do not want to hear. You're a smart man, too smart to be so obvious without a reason. Talk to me."

"Boss lady," he paused, "the thing is my life has sort of taken an unexpected turn and, well, I'm sort of affluent. The car is mine. The Malibu's a hobby, something to do on my free time. I don't have much of a life. Or I didn't."

"You're sort of affluent," she repeated. "What? You're an eccentric millionaire cop who dresses like a homeless body and drives a fancy car in fancy clothes with a snooty woman when nobody's looking." She made a humph sound through her nose. "Is that what you're telling me, Fennell?"

"Yeah, pretty much. The black suit kept me level, gave me balance, inner strength, until Archer here used what was my essence, my soul, to get rid of her frustrations and she was pretty frustrated at the time, boss lady."

"Your essence... and your soul?" He nodded. "You're serious?"

"Yeah, she was pretty brutal. The black suit's gone, beyond repair, unsalvageable and the only one I had. A part of me is gone forever, boss lady."

"How sad, and now I'm thinking that, out the blue, call me crazy, that you don't live in a stuffy one room apartment with a Jaguar parked on the street."

He shook his head. "Boca Raton. I let some poor guy I know live in my apartment as long as he doesn't get me in trouble with the landlord. He did me a favour once, sort of saved my ass. He took a bullet for me that somehow wasn't detailed in my report...whenever that was. I owe him."

Deena's face showed real horror.

Brannigan's face showed real displeasure mixed with belated worry.

"You're such a good boy. Who else would think to make such a sacrifice? Is this a joke?"

He chuckled. "Archer asked me that same question a month ago. This is between us, boss lady, especially the car and the home. I've got enough issues with some of the people around here, the ones with the kids and the homes they can't afford. This would either freak them out or piss them off. I don't need the grief."

"And you care?"

"No. I do not care. And while we're on the subject, boss lady, there is a little something else you might be interested in knowing which, heretofore, I never thought to mention. I never thought the information was relevant. You know, I'm kind of a private guy."

"Dear Lord, I can't imagine."

She waited. Gayle Brannigan knew Fennell. She trusted him. He was all cop, honest to a fault which didn't mean he didn't cross the line when needed, when he believed crossing the line was needed. That was his problem, often shared by her, too often shared by her. What she did know was that he would never to anything to blindside her.

"I own The Summit Group. I suppose you could call the firm a family heirloom. It's a paying hobby. I don't get involved. Most of them don't have a clue that I'm a cop or even who I am. The truth is, when I joined the squad, I very much by accident omitted some information on my full disclosure about hobbies and interests."

She chuckled. That was funny.

"Fennell, I know people at Summit, the who's who, the top dogs and I never once heard your name."

"And you won't. I'm buried deep. Only the most senior partners know who I am and they very much like their paycheques. Beyond that I don't get involved. The others know me as John Francis Templeton Fennell. So I am sort of wealthy, boss lady, like Archer here who, by the way, owes me a suit."

Gayle Brannigan took a moment. She believed him. She didn't want to, but she did. She turned her attention to Deena. "Archer, you knew about this?"

"No, Captain, not until…well, the first weekend."

"I know, a month ago. And you did this? So you've known for a month. You made rich boy Fennell into a something approaching a functioning android."

No response was necessary. Deena was proud of her work, the way she was eyeing him. No, she wasn't. Gayle

The Hunt for Gilligan Rose

Brannigan's epiphany struck her like a white-hot bolt. She was proud of him. Worse, she was wearing a skirt, a short skirt that would auto-activate anyone's imagination, with stilettos when she usually wore sensible low-heeled pumps. And she was wearing a bra. She was definitely wearing a bra and standing very close to him. She never stood close to him. No one stood close the fennell.

"Archer you're at work in a federal office building, not one of your fancy downtown nightclubs. What's with the outfit?"

"I have a date after our meeting as well, Captain. I wouldn't have had time to go home to change."

"And you have a date, Agent Fennell, all decked out and looking so fine."

"Thanks, boss lady. I'm a new man, you know, thanks to Archer. I guess you could say she's my mentor."

She wasn't amused. She studied Deena and scrutinized Fennell.

"Archer your outfit is delightful. You're a beautiful young woman, charming and sweet, and I'm sure that Fennell here is delighted to see that you don't have veiny legs. I'm sure that every man you've passed this evening is delighted to see your legs, and probably a few women. So where exactly is Agent Fennell taking you after our meeting to celebrate your final day on the job, Miss Snooty?"

Brannigan wasn't smiling, nor was she leaning against the edge of her desk. She was standing straight, her arms by her side, expecting an immediate answer.

Deena's mouth dropped open. She might have heard the ocean from inside the hermetically sealed building if not for the sound of her heart erupting in her ears.

Deena went to speak.

Brannigan changed her mind.

"You, shut up. Don't say another word." She pointed. "Sit yourself in that seat and don't say a word... and there had better be something between your pretty white ass and my fine chair, Agent Archer." She pointed to Fennell. "You, you sit over there, and not a word until I've finished my first drink." Gayle Brannigan went to her drawer. She filled three glasses, giving a silent command to Fennell with a flustered hand. He took one glass, gave the other to Deena. When Brannigan wanted quiet, accommodating her was generally regarded by the members of her squad as a wise choice.

She was at the window gazing at two cars she could only dream about. She knew Archer struggled with certain others of the squad who believed she was a spoiled little rich girl with a gun mocking them from high above the clouds with not a care in the world when what she wanted was to earn respect as she struggled with the resentment. That's why she teamed them together. Now Fennell drops this bombshell: a duo of rich and, she had to admit, good-looking cops...and The Summit Group. Lord Jesus!

"I knew this would happen. Lord, I knew this would happen." She faced them. "I hope a few episodes of hot and sweaty were worth your future, Agent Archer. The good news is that perhaps now you can apply as a private detective at The Summit Group. Now that we know Fennell likes long legs and short skirts...yours in particular."

Fennell corrected her. "That would be a few episodes each night of really hot and really sweaty, boss lady. You know, for the record. And if anyone goes to Summit, I do, though I don't really have an office right now. That could be a problem."

"Fennell, why are you talking? Nobody wants to hear your stupid talk. You're going nowhere unless I tell you."

Deena broke her silence, worried; Fennell didn't seem worried at all.

"He's right, Captain. I love him. I know that sounds sick and perverted, but I really do."

"Isn't that the sweetest thing I've ever heard?" She drained her glass. "Four weeks ago you wanted to kill him.

Or was someone else I don't remember screeching at him all drippy wet from that seat you're sitting in?"

"I still do, Captain, sometimes," Deena glared at him, "like right now. He hasn't changed that much. He can still be a fennell at times. He has to be closely monitored and managed. But I do love him, Captain. We're getting married." She turned to Fennell. "I'm sorry, sweetheart. She would have found out sooner or later."

"I'm standing here listening to Archer call Fennell sweetheart." Brannigan put her empty glass on her desk, ordering Fennell with her eyes to correct the deficiency. "I have either died, reincarnating into some bizarre world, or I didn't wake up this morning and you two are in my worst nightmare." She turned to Archer. "Please tell me I didn't wake up. And when exactly do you plan to marry this man?"

"We're a good team, Captain. This won't get in the way."

"Uh-uh, you were a good team, once, until a month ago, because this is in the way. How do I possibly explain to the director two very privileged cops in my squad doing the dirty while flying around the world in First-Class seats and that one of them owns The Summit Group? Deena you are glowing, girl. I saw the difference the moment you walked through my door. Everyone will see the change in you. And Fennell here, who isn't Fennell, how do we explain that to the human race? You did too good a job." She sipped her scotch. "I'm sorry. I truly am. However I don't see that this will work. We're all cops here. We're trained to see through smoke and mirrors. And that, neither of you has done well."

Fennell cut in. "We're different, boss lady. So look at us differently. We're well-off. What's the big deal? Archer gives a hundred percent to the job. She also gives more to charity each year than she earns here. She's got nothing to apologize for and my record is exemplary, beyond reproach. I'm the best you've got. You know that, everyone knows that." His frustrating smirk began forming. "And now I'm the best dressed best cop...a total picture. And since when does Gayle Brannigan give a good shit about who thinks what? Or am I missing something here?" He savoured his scotch. "One more thing, no other agent in this building is better equipped than Archer to help me get this Gilligan Rose woman. They're both young and they're beautiful, worldly and rich. They talk the same talk, walk the walk. You should know that as a young and beautiful woman of the world yourself. Anyone else here you think matches up? And, to answer your last question, she plans to marry me very soon after we do get her...if I don't regress too much."

"Archer, I should fire you this very instant for what you've done to him."

"Think of what I feel each morning, Captain, knowing what I've done." Deena sipped her drink, the faintest glimmer of a smile forming. "You think you've got issues?"

"The last thing I want to think about is what you feel in the morning." She leaned against her desk. "Fennell, now that Archer here is no longer part of the squad, do you stay or do I lose you to Summit because you'll go all pouty on me? Is that what this is all about, big, brave Fennell protecting little Deena?"

"No. It's about getting Gilligan Rose. That said; I've never known you to make a bad decision because of popular opinion, boss lady. She's a good cop. Don't ruin her career simply because she's waited this long to find the perfect man."

She ignored him.

"Deena, this is for real...the wedding, not just temporary insanity? You're sure about this? Lovers working together are one thing, jilted ex-lovers, for whatever reason they're jilted, that's something else."

"Captain, I still might kill him. However I know now that living without him will never happen. I also know that I won't work in another squad. I work with my fennell or no one. After all my hard work repairing him, teaching him to breathe air and walk straight amongst us humans, I deserve him."

"You will work where I tell you to work, Archer. But tell me one thing, woman to woman, or I know I won't sleep tonight. What does your debonair sweetheart call you to make you all warm and fuzzy while you go about solving the crime of the century?"

"He calls me sweetcheeks."

Brannigan closed her eyes, tilting her head towards the ceiling. "Dear Lord! Come down and carry me away!" She began laughing. "It's hard at times to believe we all carry guns. My William calls me sweet cocoa." Her face went stern. "But you didn't hear that, did you?"

"No, Captain."

Fennell remained non-committal.

"Archer, you will not for any reason get pregnant. And you, Fennell, you will not let her get pregnant. Do you understand me? You will come in separately when you do come in and, Fennell, you're going to leave that blue thing that's parked downstairs at home. Until this is over you stay away from Dispatch. Drive one of your own pretty cars. Archer, this is the very last time I will see you looking this stunning. No more skirts and no more," she pointed to Deena's blouse, "of that. And Fennell, the next time I see you, do something to make yourself look more like the fennell we all love to hate, just not too much. Archer, you make sure that he does. And Fennell, you get this girl a diamond. What kind of man doesn't give his girl a ring? She should have killed you already, you sad and pathetic excuse for a man."

"Captain…"

"That's right, Archer…Captain. You and Fennell are on special assignment. That's what I wanted to tell you before you came in here all bright-eyed and pretty to ruin my weekend. From now on you come in here when you're called, not until. This mess stays between us till I figure out what to do with you because I am not losing my best agents. Now get out of my seat."

Deena stood.

"Thanks, boss lady."

"Fennell, shut up."

Brannigan went to her second best agent, wrapping her arms around and squeezing a shocked Agent Archer.

"Congratulations, Deena. I suppose someone had to marry it sooner or later. Now sit and tell me what more I need to know about Gilligan Rose. Tell me what you're doing about her. And, Fennell, you clean that smirk off your face."

*

Brannigan's last words before the agents walked out were to thank Deena for killing the suit.

Twenty-One
This Year: July 09th

Special Agent Deena Archer sat by her pool, Johnnie's pool, alone Saturday morning. She was finalizing her wedding plans, not really concentrating, missing him, dreaming of her honeymoon in Rio. He no longer had a home of his own. Her home was their home. They had months earlier decided that high-rise living suited their way of life more than luxury living in Boca Raton.

August 01st was less than four weeks away. She wanted to marry him on the anniversary of the day she discovered the real John Francis, the day she discovered he wasn't a fennell all the time. She wanted a quaint wedding on their private rooftop deck with thirty invited guests whose names and faces they actually knew. From nowhere in Miami could anyone appreciate a more spectacular view and only Gayle Brannigan and her William were invited from the office.

The day was one of the few she hadn't spent with him since the fateful Friday Brannigan had commissioned a new Agent Fennell and had made Deena responsible for the near impossible task. She missed being dropped into the pool. She missed him and she missed not having him in their bed. She wouldn't see him for seven more days and six nights, days Brannigan had approved as personal time without being asked. A bride whose husband might be killed wasn't any use to her squad. Words she didn't speak. She didn't have to.

The following Thursday Deena would fly to New York onboard American flight 1510. She would spend the afternoon and next morning in Gilligan Rose's room at the Excalibur Boutique Hotel with techies from the Miami office, making sure that Rose's one-night stop over was far from private while Fennell was in France alone after sending home someone's young and impressionable French daughter.

He would spend the first part of his week at La Marquise with a new and eager member of the squad, a young woman recently graduated from university who was beginning her crime-fighting career as Brannigan's office gopher. She was in the right place at the right time. She was a twenty-year-old who could pass disturbingly for a shy little fourteen-year-old with very little trouble. She spoke fluent French because she was French and had trained with Fennell for the past several weeks. She knew what to do, how to act and what to say. Her name was Marie Anisette. She would be John Francis Templeton Fennell's underage companion for an evening at Gilligan Rose's favourite cabaret and had spent an hour on the phone with her parents and brother in Chicago the day before departing Miami on American to meet with Fennell in Paris. She couldn't tell them very much, except that The Task Force needed her to help solve a case. She told them how Johnnie Fennell was the absolute best, now that she liked him because she didn't at first. He wouldn't let anything happen to her. He was the best and so was Deena who would join them. She would learn so much from them.

Deena stared into her watch.

Johnnie was at LAX boarding his flight, greeting a green-eyed killer, probably studying his new risqué thumbnails of her and of Marie who had agreed to pose once Brannigan assured her that Deena would be with them and that Fennell would not post them on the internet or show anyone at the office. That's why she didn't like him, because of what she'd heard in the office and when he told her with a wink and sly grin that she would have to pose in a thong and go topless for the best results. That's when Deena stepped in and by the end of their first week together she sort of liked him, though she liked Deena more. Now she liked him a lot.

He was to remain in Paris on business for his firm through to the fifteenth when his return flight to New York would depart Orly at 1700, descending into JFK at the same hour local time. Both he and the crew of TGA flight 1811 would stay over in the Big Apple. He knew the TGA crew would stay at the Excalibur Boutique Hotel. He was confirmed at The Franklin. He also knew that other agents would be in the room adjoining his with Deena and Anisette.

Brannigan wasn't taking any chances, nor did she want her best agent's pretty 'sweetcheeks' and bride killing a perp two weeks before her wedding. Gilligan Rose had been approved as a case file by the director. They'd spent a year tracking her, studying her. They wanted her badly and she wasn't getting away, whether snatched from France because she changed her MO or in New York. Either way, Gilligan Rose was not going to her home in Long Beach anytime soon. Not to mention that Captain Gayle Brannigan had already bought her dress for the wedding.
*

Gilligan woke early. She'd spoken on the phone most of the evening before and went to bed early. Thursday and Friday were her days off that week. Thursday she'd gone shopping for a new outfit. Buying a special new outfit near the middle of July was her tradition and Paris in July was warm and sultry, the women captivating with their inherently seductive bodies if not inviting with their eyes like Elixia de Montfort.
*

She'd gone shopping with Deena one day in late October.

They did lunch and dinner and went to the theatre. They kissed each other goodnight on the cheeks and Deena was gone.

In January Gilligan sat in a chaise-longue planted in the sand by her South Beach beachfront time-share, waiting and wondering when, wondering if. She'd already waited three days. On the fourth, clad in a thong, a triangle top, glasses and wide-brimmed hat, as aware as any other near-naked to-die-for female on the beach of freaks with cameras and cells, Deena Archer casually strolled to where she lay.

Gilligan Rose beamed, wriggling from her seat, hugging Deena and kissing her cheek.

She wanted to say 'I couldn't stop thinking of you', thoughts of Xara who couldn't be with her flooding her mind. She didn't. Instead they sat for a while and went for lunch. Deena had just come home from New York and was leaving early the next day for Biloxi. Her company was having a convention. She'd just come home to repack her suitcase. Bad timing, but one day was better than nothing.

So once again they went for lunch, shopping, dinner and sat until late in the evening at a sidewalk café sipping Pernod. Johnnie Fennell as usual was not far away, thinking what a shame, needing to remind himself that she was a killer until once again the women said goodbye, Deena promising a trip to the west coast in April.

As it happened Deena was onboard TGA 1814 during the last week of April en route to London through Newark with a crew change. From the US to London they sat together when Gilligan Rose had free time. In London, each woman regretting the other for different reasons, they walked along the Thames and enjoyed dinner.

"Deena, I suppose you've guessed by now that I like girls."

Deena nodded. "No ring, pretty, with everything going for you, single. Yes, the thought has crossed my mind. But I'm not Gilligan. I did kiss a girl in college once, on a dare, and copped a quick feel of her breasts."

"Did you like the feeling?"

"I liked her. She was sexy. Now she's a mom somewhere in Idaho. The last time I saw her at a reunion she was two-fifty with a double chin and three fat kids."

"My first girl was in high school. I was fourteen. We were a secret item until the middle of July the next year. The last time I saw her she was with the love her life: one year younger than me, blonde like her, and beautiful. They've been together since the summer I left her, since she knew I wouldn't see her again. Go figure."

"So, men were never part of the equation, not even on a dare?"

Deena forced a convincing smile. She knew the answer.

Gilligan smiled. "Not even a double dare."

"I once dreamed of having a man like my father. I date once in a while, but they invariably come up short. I suppose I'm reaching too high." Deena paused, sipping her Pernod. "What Gilligan? What did I say?"

"Deena, between us, you and me, you're one of the three prettiest girls I've ever been attracted to. However we are what we are, so let's not each of us hyperventilate over what won't happen. That said; I would like to spend time with you when we cross paths. Pretty girl number one won't mind. Her name is Xara. We're pretty much in love. Cancel that. We are very much in love."

"Life's too short to judge, Gilligan. And I'm sure our paths will cross. I'm thinking possibly over the summer. I'm curious though. Your parents, did they judge you for your choice. Were they supportive?"

"My mother never knew. I was just discovering myself. The girl's name was Wendy. I suppose I would have told my mother sooner than later. She would have understood. She was a bit of a free thinker. Did you ever hear of Emma Rose, the artist?"

"No, I'm not much into names."

"I haven't seen her in years, not since they took me away. And my father, I dream of killing him each night that I sleep long enough to dream. My mother killed him when I was fifteen, the morning after he raped me for the last time."

"Your father raped you?"

"Yes, he did, many times."

"And now your mother's in prison for protecting you?"

"No, she's gone…somewhere."

Deena put down her glass. "And you don't know where?"

"That's a story for another day; though I do remember the day the police arrested her and took me away. I wanted to run and hide in the attic, in the dark when, strangely, I was always afraid of the dark. That's when he would come for me, when the light was out. My mother was afraid of the dark. She was a bit of an airhead. I mean that in a nice way. Anyway, I was put in a foster home and adopted almost right away. I thought maybe my life would be better. So I went along with it until things went bad, at least for me. I was almost sixteen," she smiled, "and cute. And suddenly the man had another woman in the house, not a baby or a girl. You tend to grow up quickly after your father rapes you and your mother's sent to an institution. Anyway the next guy was always walking around in his underwear, leaving doors open, at first not very often. Gradually as I got older he got more into wanting me to see him. I think they had more sex in the living room than in the bedroom. One evening I remember I caught him peeking at me through my bedroom window taking pictures of me while I was undressing. He was naked and ready. I can't imagine how he managed to take pictures. He looked ridiculous. He said he was simply passing by, going for a nighttime dip, which he wasn't. He wasn't embarrassed at all. I left the next day later after destroying the film to stay with a friend. One sick father is enough. Not long after I changed my name back to who I really am."

"You were left without any family."

"I didn't want one or need one. I had a different view of family from other kids. Family for me wasn't a good thing. I had money. I didn't need to work and I don't need to work now, Deena. I knew who and what I was. I had Gilligan. Somewhere deep in my mind I had Gilligan. All I had to do was find her. She's the one part of me that keeps me sane."

"And did you, find Gilligan?"

"Yes."

"She lives in Long Beach, working at living a happier life. She's there to make me smile when I need her. We speak often. She's my best friend. We tell each other things we can't tell anyone else. She's so much a part of me. We help each other forget. She was no better off than me at the time. In fact her life was worse. I try so hard to help her block out her pain, but she still hurts." Gilligan took a deep breath as though wondering what to say next. "They were French and Spanish, her parents. They lived in New York and vacationed in Europe a few months each year. Her name was Collette Salazar." Gilligan sighed. "Can I hold your hand, Deena? Girl stuff, I promise, nothing kinky. I won't propose or smother you with kisses."

Deena held out her hand. "I think I need something to hold on to. I can't believe what I'm hearing. You seem so well-adjusted."

"I have my moments. The man couldn't get enough of her, always trying to see her in her underwear or in the bathroom, taking pictures of her in her bikinis, always trying to pull her strings, always insisting that he should rub SPF on her. His hands were always slimy and the woman, she just sat and took everything in. I think she got off on watching. I know she did. Then one day Gilligan was with this girl. She was so cute. Her name's Elixia. Gilligan thought she'd died and gone to heaven until he found them in bed together. They were about as one on one as it gets when he came into the room to sit leering at them, scaring them, taking everything in as though he would never see another naked woman in his lifetime, watching the girls hurrying to dress. He wouldn't leave. He wanted to join the fun. They left instead."

"I'm so unhappy for you."

"Don't be. I have friends, not many. But who needs a lot? And I have Xara. There's a definite attraction."

"But she's not committed the way you want."

"Actually I'm the problem. It's complicated." Gilligan Rose drew a deep breath through her straw. "So now you know pretty much everything about Gilligan Rose at TGA. I hope this doesn't make you change airlines. We're not all psychotic lesbians. By the way, in Miami in January…well, I don't think you'll be alone very long. I have to admit, I did my fair share of admiring." She forced a chuckle. "Why is it that the prettiest ones are most often hetero?"

"Perhaps you have met the prettiest one and you aren't giving her a chance. Perhaps you're risking losing the one you really do love. That's what you said, that you love her."

"Like I said, it's complicated. I'd have a better chance of finding Emma Rose painting faces on a beach than expecting her to understand my life when I don't. I think so."

*

Deena Archer remembered the evening perfectly, as though reliving her time with Gilligan Rose in real time. That was bad enough. She knew Gilligan Rose needed help, not a lifetime behind bars or a few thousand volts of current searing her brain for two minutes. She would not let that happen. And Johnnie was right. How would she face Xara after the time they'd spent together in June? She hated herself. This wasn't supposed to happen.

She laid her fountain pen on the patio table and dived into the pool to free her mind. She had wanted to tell him for weeks, every night, every morning, stopped by his

constant 'I love you, sweetcheeks. Soon this will all be over', too afraid of what he would say, too afraid he was doing the wrong thing and that she was doing the wrong thing. She couldn't help believing that Johnnie would hate her for what she had done without telling him.
*

Deena's cell phone chimed.

"You'd better be dressed and all alone, Fennell."

"I love you. That's why I called, to tell you how much I love you."

"I love you too, sweetheart. I miss you. I think Brannigan's still having nightmares about us."

"Listen, I just want to say, if something goes wrong, if..."

"Don't be an idiot. Nothing will go wrong. I'll shoot the bitch, I swear. If she even breathes wrong I'll be through that door."

"That's not what I meant." He was serious. She could tell when he was. "I mean, if, just if, I have to sleep with her, you know, sleep with her, well that's all part of the job, nothing serious. I'll hate every moment, you know, like when you and Mendiga were all oily at the beach."

"Sweetheart, darling..."

"Yes, I'm here."

"When you're in bed with her, when you're working so hard to save the nation, tell her I'd love to do Xara again. Tell her that I haven't forgotten her lover's hot kiss, her warm sensual hands caressing every inch of my eager body...every inch, sweetheart." She chuckled. "Oh, I'm sorry, you can't tell her. I forgot, because I've killed you."

"You keep that thought. I'm at the gate. I love you. I'll see you Friday in New York."

"And you'll call me each night and morning."

"Yeah, I will if, you know, I'm not too busy."

"You're being a fennell, Fennell."

"I've never loved anyone more than I love you, not even

myself." He paused, she waited. "I never loved anyone until I saw you and trained you to be the second best."

"Excuse me. I trained you. I also put you on your butt. How second best is that, smart guy? Oh, sweetheart, I'm sorry. I really have to go, I'm naked and the milkman's at the door. Call me whenever...or not."

"I miss you already. I can't wait to see you in white."

She gulped a breath. "I won't be wearing white and," her voiced failed her, "I won't be wearing black after all my hard work to make you a passable human. You don't do anything stupid until I'm with you. Do you understand me, Agent Fennell?"

"See you Friday, Mrs. Archer-Fennell. And, please, wear something sexy for a change. These silky baby dolls, sheer teddies and thongs, you know, they're getting a little drab. Don't you think?"

She would have smacked him. He adored the way she dressed for him.

He pressed END. He never said goodbye, not since the first day she met him.

She would wear something sexy, a chrome-plated 92FS. That she wanted to help Gilligan Rose didn't mean that she wouldn't put a round in the woman's head for hurting her man.

*

Gilligan constantly thought of Deena, though not that morning watching passenger Fennell board, wondering what he would think of her new white summer dress and sandals, hoping Fennell wouldn't change his travel plans at some point during the week. Most business types travelling across the ocean did not. The penalty fees were too exorbitant. Staying put and working from their hotel rooms was the cheaper alternative. She didn't have to think. She knew.

She didn't doubt for a moment that he would drool over white on white: a belted white satin shirtdress with flimsy white faux-pockets that would give the impression of concealing her breasts, open at the neck to attract, unbuttoned to within mere inches of white satin high-cut panties showing through. Her white hat was satin as well, and her sandals.

She wouldn't wear earrings or a necklace, they were too easy to grab or lose and, of course, she had a penchant for large shoulder bags, this time white leather, and a fourteen-inch blade. She wouldn't wear gloves. She knew in her mind what to touch and what not to, what she must make clean with hotel soap and what she must take with her in the luggage he would no longer need.

"Good morning, Mr. Fennell. We are so glad to see you again. May I bring you a morning pick-me-up?"

Fennell shut his laptop. "Thank you, miss."

"I see by our passenger manifest that you're retuning on Friday. So we'll see each other twice this week. I'm stopped over in Paris tonight and again on Thursday. You must be exhausted with all these trips. Do you ever get to spend time with your family?"

"Divorced actually, though I do get to see my little girls every second weekend. They're real dolls, both of them."

"How old are they?"

"Fourteen and fifteen…going on nineteen and twenty."

"I'm sure they miss you as much as you miss them." She patted his shoulder. "I'll bring your mimosa."

In the galley Gilligan Rose wanted to spit in his glass. He was like all the others, the other sick bastards who drooled over their teenage daughters or up-skirt photos off the web, or porno trailers on overnight flights because they didn't want a credit card trail to jail for getting off on child porn. Miss, not Miss Rose, or Miss Gilligan like some of the Southern ladies would call her. He was scum, an asshole like all the others. However he would buy her dinner Friday night.

They always bought her dinner first. Not a prerequisite,

more of a prelude to a memorable evening.

*

Johnnie Fennell slouched into his seat. He was tired of the travelling, sitting in hotels twiddling his thumbs. He was tired of banal conversation, of passengers seated beside him wanting to tell their fabricated life stories. He was tired of Gilligan Rose, of waiting to play her game her way. She was every man's hypocrisy: a gorgeous lesbian. Every cop's nightmare: a practiced and intelligent killer. Most of all he was tired of drinking mimosas or vodka with orange juice because drinking that many scotches would put him on his ass prior to landing.

He finished his orange juice-champagne mix: a girl's drink no matter how well concocted with TGA's TLC. He wanted to sleep. He wanted to dream of Deena in his arms, throwing her into the pool, diving in after her, kissing her and generally pissing her off. He loved being a pain in her beautiful ass. He had wanted to tell her for weeks, at breakfast by the pool, at dinner under the stars. Yet somehow he couldn't. Instead he told her what she wanted to hear. How could he tell her when she loved him so much? How could he tell her that what he was doing was wrong?

Her photo was tucked into his inside jacket pocket. He closed his eyes with his hand pressed against her.

Twenty-Two
Seventeen Years Ago: First Week of July

Zeke Phillips was in his early seventies with two aspects of his life remaining that he cared for deeply. One was his institute, newly recreated in his mind. The other was Emma Rose. He continued thinking of Emma as his daughter. Whatever her request, he never refused her. Nor had he ever travelled as much, most times for a day or two, never for an entire week.

In Gilligan he continued to see divergent personalities that were increasingly a concern to him. Due in large part, he believed, to Tommy Dune's despicably selfish nature. He was certain something was amiss, unable to define his misgivings. Yet Tommy Dune for some time had lived a privileged life he didn't deserve and had barricaded himself beyond the good doctor's influence as Emma was increasingly called upon to attend social functions decidedly outside Dune's scope, this one in London for Emma's first showing at La Galerie Royale. By Christmas she would see Paris and Luxemburg, Madrid and Rome in the spring. The world wanted more of Miss Emma Rose and so did Zeke Phillips. He would insist that for once that she listen to reason. She had to understand that Dune had served his purpose and should be considered defunct, a means to an end achieved long ago. He was no longer required by her in the least imaginable way.

Phillips was getting old, feeling older than his years. He wanted to transfer responsibility for the institute to the state, procrastinating, each day of the week producing a different reason not to proceed. Above all he feared what might happen.

He'd released five more of his younger patients over the previous year, the ones he deemed ready and able to exist in an imperfect world. He feared that his more liberal approach to their well-being would abruptly cease, that the institute would revert to its previous preoccupation with finance and a spurious culture of caring and compassion. Emma Rose had changed all that. However neither did he want to one day be found dead at his desk and retirement would mean more time with Emma who deserved more than Dune in conjunction with her flourishing career.

This time he would make Emma listen to reason, make her recognize and face what she must do. He studied her from across the room. How she had metamorphosed into such a sophisticated woman with girlish qualities still inherent in her eyes and each word she spoke. With butterflies and one-side faces mixed in her mind she stood chatting with the cream of society, completely at ease amongst the who's who of the well-heeled.

He snorted. There was no greater irony in his life or hers than witless Tommy Dune.

*

Gilligan was glad school was finally over. She was fifteen with two more years of learning before she could leave home and study to work as an airline attendant. She'd known ever since her mother flew with her to Chicago, when she didn't stop asking questions of the good-looking women in chic uniforms who travelled all over the world.

Gilligan wanted to fly also. She thought so, though other times she didn't think so as much. Yet she knew in her mind that Gilligan did and she would never do anything to make Gilligan unhappy. She was already unhappy that her mother had just gone away.

She waited for the dull glow from the hallway to turn

dark, waiting for the shadow to cross over the light, holding her breath. He never came in when the light was on in the hall, not once he was gone.

Next time, she promised, she would ask her mother whether her friend Wendy was telling the truth. This time when she opened her eyes she didn't see her father at all. She felt him behind her. He wasn't hurting her. She didn't think so. She was no longer certain that he might be. He was rocking her with one hand on her breast and his other at her shoulder. His hands were warm. He was telling her to close her eyes and to sleep, that he wanted to comfort her. She closed her eyes and waited, blinking them open when his body jerked once and then twice. He was stroking her hair, telling her how much he loved her; how she was such a lovely young woman and so mature.

When he left she felt between her legs. She was curious. She was wet like the last time or the time before that. She felt a strange soreness that didn't hurt, though neither did she feel good. She fell asleep soon after the hallway was dark. She thought so, when in the morning she woke cuddling her bear with tears wetting her cheek and her pillow.

"He hurt me last night, and the time before that. I think so."

"He hurt me too. I don't feel good anymore. He made me cry and made me promise not to tell mother. Mother wouldn't like that he made me cry. He told me that mother would hate him if she knew that he made me cry. I told him he can't hurt me anymore because of what my friend Wendy told me."

"Now she's my friend too. I like her more than the other girls."

"I knew you wanted to kiss her."

"She likes kissing me. She told me."

"Last week we took off all our clothes when her parents were gone and she let me touch her."

"Did she touch you too?"

"She touched me like father, but I didn't cry. You can touch her that way too if you want to. I know she won't mind. I don't think so."

"Last night I wanted to cry. He made me sore between my legs."

"Wendy touched me there, too. I didn't feel sore either. Then I was anxious to touch her."

"I want to go with you next time you touch her. And I want to tell mother."

"I don't want you to tell mother. Then mother would hate father."

"I think we should tell mother. I think so. My friend Wendy told me it isn't right for fathers to touch their daughters."

"Did you tell my friend Wendy everything?"

"No, I didn't tell her anything."

"We should get up, Gilligan, and go outside close to the fence where no one will see us and before he wakes up. Mother will be home tomorrow."

*

Tommy Dune knew he was out of control. Yet what could he do. His crime had worsened over the years. They would never understand the blind fear that ravaged his mind the day she was born.

He'd always liked young girls, from the crowded bed of his youth to the warm baths with Emma or in her sanitized room as he did with the others. But Emma was thirty-five, Gilligan and her art more important than him. She rarely made time for him, whereas Gilligan was always there for him, during the day and at night. She was a woman, no longer a child, young with a beautiful body he couldn't resist, not awkward like other girls her age.

He missed the times they once shared during her bath. He knew she would soon understand and cry out his name in the dark. Each time he loved her she moved with more passion under his weight, soft groans in her throat making him more ardent, her warm tears numbing any thought of restraint. Yet he knew that he would soon lose her.

He had so little time left to enjoy her and what scant time they did have they would share.

Two nights before Emma returned home Tommy Dune went for pizza and wine. By ten, her lips coated with a dusting of fine white powder, he carried her to her room and put her to bed, returning downstairs to lock the front door, turn out the lights and fill his glass with bourbon.

He stood in her doorway watching her sleep. He was the shadow watching her chest rise and fall, her lustrous hair spread across her pillow. He went to his room to undress. With the wine and the drug he was sure she would sleep until noon. She would know in her dreams how much he truly did love her, what he would do to make her feel loved. He had no need for her to hear the words.

Gently he drew back the covers, pulling her slip to her shoulders, her panties past her feet, not hurrying to make her naked, not hurrying to ease himself between her. He spent long minutes absorbing her body, kissing her breasts, making her ready before raising her legs at her knees. She made not a sound other than purring.

When he was done, his chest heaving with pleasure, he eased himself onto his knees to sit watching her body glisten with his sweat, her bare breasts taunting. Her red mound was damp to his touch, her scent pungent on his fingertips, the curve of her buttocks compelling him to lay by her side a while longer, to caress her and soothe her. He knew that soon all he would have was his fond memories of her and his collection of photos.

He tugged at the hem of her slip, draping her body in pink satin. Her panties he put by her pillow, not wanting to wake her from peaceful slumber.

In the bathroom he stared into the mirror, satisfied that at forty-three he was still a young man, healthy and virile.

He flushed away her flimsy protection that he noticed quite clearly was stained and he showered. He often showered after their love when his wife was away. Though once in bed sleep wouldn't come, her lingering scent invading his senses. He threw back the covers and went to her room. She would still be asleep for hours.

*

"Father hurt me last night. He made me cry. Why didn't you hear me? When he came in my room there was no light in the hall. There was no shadow to see and I opened my eyes when he hurt me."

"He hurt me too. I think so. Because when I woke up I was bleeding when I shouldn't be bleeding. I called you. Why didn't you hear me?"

"I'm telling mother tomorrow. He hurt me and made me feel bad and this time he kissed me the way we kiss Wendy. I like kissing Wendy. I made myself believe I was kissing her, not father. Her mouth is much softer and she doesn't taste like father. And after he kissed me like Wendy he kissed me all over and he bit me. Why would father kiss me all over and bite me?"

"I don't know. I don't think father should bite you or want me to bleed. We should ask Wendy?"

"And after we do I'm going to ask mother why father would hurt us when he first tells us he loves us."

*

Emma Rose arrived home on time. She had listened to Zeke the night before, throughout the six-hour flight and the two-hour drive they shared along the Hudson. At his home she gave him a hug. She would do what he wanted. She couldn't remember when Zeke Phillips had ever been wrong. She would get rid of Tommy Dune.

Emma walked through the door in shorts and a V-neck sweater, high heels and her ponytail tied with a silk scarf, all from exclusive boutiques. Her husband greeted her from his chair in a silk shirt, linen slacks and slippers. The drink in his hand was neither his first nor his last of the day.

Gilligan, she thought, seemed tired and drawn, yet happy to see her. They hugged and kissed. Upstairs in her room, the evening sun much brighter at the back of her home, Gilligan seemed much paler and blue, her cheeks brightening a little from her mother's soft touch.

With her luggage unpacked Emma went straight to her husband. Her mind focused, her painting could wait until morning.

"I'm divorcing you, Tommy. I don't like you very much anymore. I don't think I have for a very long while. You're lazy most days and you smell of that drink more than you should. I think so. I never see you and none of the neighbours here like you. So why should you be here when none of us like you? You don't make me feel good the way that you used to and now with my art I really don't need you. Not that I ever did except to keep you from prison. I expect you to leave very soon."

He sputtered a laugh "You're talking stupid, but I did see this coming. This is Phillips' doing, filling your head with shit. I'm fine where I am and I'm staying. So get used to it. There's nothing wrong with us that your open legs won't make better. When was the last time I saw you naked? Don't blame me for not getting any. You give more to the neighbours who, by the way, think you're crazy. And you are, Emma. You are as crazy as you ever were."

"I expect you to leave very soon and to sleep in the spare room until you do."

"You went to London with Phillips. This is his bullshit idea. You won't do that ever again. Do you understand me? I do not want you to see him anymore. I know what you do with him and he's not welcome in my house."

"This is not your house and the car that you drive is mine also. Zeke is my friend. He doesn't like you because you are lazy. He told me about you, the bad things you did with the other girls during their baths and on their beds. I thought then that you liked me, that I was special."

"What I liked was fucking you, the way Phillips enjoyed fucking you and still does. How can you fuck anyone as old as that?"

Her expression changed from relaxed determination to confusion.

"Zeke never touched me that way. He never thought to make me feel good."

"Make you feel good. I'm so tired of that bullshit lunatic talk." He paused, draining his glass. "He was fucking a nutcase and to cover his ass he made me believe I was the father. I'm right. I know I am. I've known for a long time that she's not mine."

"I'll give you enough money to live for a while. You are leaving. So you get used to that."

He stood, reaching for the bottle. "I am not leaving. Gilligan needs me and so do you. She believes I'm her father. I won't hurt her that way. We'll talk about this in the morning after you show the neighbours your tight ass in the yard or the driveway. What does old Phillips say about that? Or doesn't he know that his precious Emma Rose prances around outside practically naked to entertain the neighbours? And what does that guy next door see when you're in your studio painting and I'm down here on my own? What keeps him coming back?"

"I know that he's peeking. He sees me smiling and talking, painting my faces. I know that he likes me. That's what he sees. I'll write you a cheque in the morning, when I expect you to leave for the day. I don't want you here at all during the day. You have to find a place to work and a new place to live. And you cannot take the car."

Tommy Dune finished the glass he was holding, reaching again for the bottle. He knew Phillips hadn't stopped with simply getting him out of the house. More was coming. He'd lived well for too long. He had no intention of reliving the stench of slaughter or living on the street while begging for nickels and dimes during the day and fucking diseased whores at night in an alley.

"What do you think for a moment you could do without me? Without me you would still be fucking in bathtubs, sitting on floors and staring at windows with nothing to cover your bare ass."

"I can paint faces trapped in my head and become famous. I can go to London and Paris with Zeke. I can make people smile and be happy like the young man next door. I can dance in the rain and be who I am."

The phone chimed. She answered and told Zeke that she was fine, that she was telling Tommy to leave. She insisted that she was fine. She said goodnight and goodbye and calmly rested the phone in the cradle.

"Too much of a coward to come here in person, letting a crazy woman do his dirty work?"

"Zeke is a good friend who is old and concerned; who wants you to know you can still go to prison."

"Not after all these years. Do you think I don't know that? Unless, that is, I get sent up for murder. That might work. That might definitely work. So keep your mouth shut until the morning," he screamed, "and get out of my sight. I am not leaving my home."

He guzzled his bourbon and refilled his glass. In the morning she found him asleep in the same chair, curious eyes at her side watching from the corner.

When he woke he had a breakfast of what little remained the bottle. He left with a cheque for ten thousand dollars and spent the day in the park, his twelve-ounce lunch disguised in a brown paper bag. That night he didn't go home. He went to a downtown hotel for a few hours of much needed sleep, then to a club where the girls were young and appealing. He found a few that were willing to dance and drink with him as long as he paid. He was the man of the hour. When he left two of the least attractive girls went with him. He gave each one a few hundred dollars, though he woke the next morning alone. The girls were gone and with them several hundred more that he'd left in his wallet.

When he returned in a taxi to what was once his home, his face shadowed and haggard, asking Emma to pay the fare for him, she suggested instead that he go to the bank in the taxi.

Twenty-Three
Seventeen Years Ago: July 14th

After a week of hopelessly searching Tommy Dune hadn't found a place to live or to work. He was single, he told them. He had his fill of working odd jobs in cities all over the country. He wanted a real job in place he could call home. He was ready to work hard, to prove himself, to become a good neighbour and tenant.

No one believed him. How could he tell them that he once worked for Phillips, wiping the soiled asses of lunatics before sinking to a low of decapitating steers? How could he tell them whose husband he was or that his wife drove a Mercedes while he arrived for his interview on a bus? Who in Solaceville had not heard of the one-sided faces of the eccentric Miss Emma Rose?

She wanted him out before the end of the month and each day she spoke with Zeke Phillips about him.

Gilligan didn't know what to think or believe. She first wanted to talk with Wendy who seemed to know so much, however her friend was at the lake on vacation. So she stayed with her mother each day and night until she slept alone in her bed waiting for her mother's shadow to cross over the light and make the hallway dark. As much as she missed Wendy she was happy that her mother was home, sad that her father had yelled at her mother the way that he did. She was certain now that her mother did hate her father, happy that Gilligan really believed her.

When she asked her mother what she should think,

258

Emma told her that all children should want to love their fathers, but that some fathers could never love their families the way that they should. And Gilligan wanted so much for her friend Wendy to come home.

On the thirteenth Tommy Dune returned from his day of job hunting with a pizza and wine, although this time Gilligan didn't want pizza and a small glass of wine. She wanted what her mother was cooking and Dune ate his pizza alone with his bottles of wine and bourbon on the back deck.

On the fourteenth, still unemployed, he cooked them hamburgers on the grill adding spices he'd decided upon while drinking his bourbon in the park. To each of their sodas he added a little more and by eight that evening he wished them all a goodnight. At nine he went to look in on Emma whom he found sleeping soundly. He coated her lips and left her to dream once he saw Emma suck her lips from a dusty white to a shade of bright red.

Gilligan slept soundly as well. He knew from past nights that she would lick her lips clean of the powder. He'd watched her so many times before. He knew the affect and how much she needed.

He went to the basement, not certain what to do with his photos and video footage, deciding that the next day he would buy a briefcase. In the meantime, afraid she might find them; he put them into a suitcase that he would take with him in the morning. To the album and VHS he added a bottle of bourbon.

Satisfied with his locked luggage by the door, once more he coated Emma's lips with twice as much powder, waiting to see them licked clean as he stood in the doorway with his glass. When she obliged him he went to see Gilligan, kissing and coating her lips, cupping and kissing her breasts. Compelled by her faint silhouette he kissed her and fondled her once more, tapping more powder into the shallow crevice between her soft lips.

When he came from the bathroom undressed he filled his glass two-thirds full. This would be his last time to have her, to lie with her naked and caress her with loving attention. He pulled her tap pants from under the matching silk chemise her mother had brought her from London, undoing each button intently, watching her body unfold teasingly inch by inch. She was lovely, laid out before him on a carpet of rich midnight blue.

He was eager. This night he would remember forever. He would remember her lips, her taste, her scent and her warm breath. He would remember the hue of her delicate skin, her vibrant red hair. This time he would be the best of any who might one day be her lover.

Between her he made Gilligan ready, his fingers exploring, his eyes photographing what his camera could no longer see. He leaned forward, his arms taut, kissing her breasts, first one, then the other, kissing her chin and her mouth, feeling her heat and his sudden arousal.

He put his ear close to her mouth, her purring and short bursts of air through her nose urging him deeper. She was moving with him, gently rocking. After a while, wanting more, he leaned to one side, taking her with him, free to explore the curves of her back and her buttocks, free to kiss her breasts and excite her nipples.

He lost track of time, her body not glistening, soaked with his sweat. Pulling himself free he eased from the bed to drink his bourbon, her body too tempting to ignore. So he didn't. He crawled once again gently between her long and white legs to make himself ready, her purrs this time more guttural, more exotic and intoxicating, more demanding of his strength, his arms aching under the strain.

He left her sometime later feeling exhausted and empty. He already missed her. He would miss her for a very long time, worried that he would never again be with anyone like her.

For an hour he roamed through the house distracted,

checking on Emma, dusting her lips to be certain, thinking that he might one last time teach her a lesson, teach her that he was a man and that without him she was nothing. She was nothing. She was Zeke Phillips' whore. And why would he fuck a whore when he could be with a young and pretty girl who would one day soon be taken from him against his will. He might never see her again.

He eased the door open, standing with his legs apart, balanced with one foot in the hallway and one foot in her room. He had to be certain and coated Gilligan's lips, wanting not to wake her or to scare her. Then he went to the kitchen to fill his glass. When he returned she lay still. She appeared as a waif tired with this life, an angel ready for heaven. She was an angel: sweet and soft and tender.

He eased her chemise to under the small of her back and away from her shoulders. Her panties he put on her chair. He whispered his love, crawling gingerly between her, surprised by the suddenness and strength of his arousal.

He kissed her and smelled her. He fondled her breasts and inched himself closer. He wanted each moment preserved in his mind forever.

He couldn't imagine a more perfect lover, her body moulding to his, moving with his, a thin layer of moisture between them, each movement measured until he let passion rule. He'd never felt her so responsive, wishing that just for a moment he would see her green eyes adore him.

He wanted to gasp, instead he held his breath. He wanted to push as deeply as he could one last time, to see her mouth open, to see her green eyes, instead he pulled away, reaching the floor first with one foot then with the other, reaching at last for his near-empty old-fashioned.

He went to the kitchen for more bourbon. The time was 3:32.

He was raw and chafed, too aroused to feel any real pain. The condom he threw into the toilet as he'd done with the others.

Emma was sleeping, dead to the world. He had no reason to worry and went again to his daughter's room to see her so perfect and nude for as long as he dared. She turned onto her side, her hands tucked under her pillow. How many years had passed since he'd seen her hands tucked under her pillow? He couldn't remember. He couldn't think beyond the contours of her body, the lines of her back, the cleft between her buttocks, the perfectly straight seam between her legs, the way one delicate foot hung over the other.

He gulped the last few ounces, put down the glass and reached for the foil. The protection went on easily; she was that enticing as darkness began to fade into the early morning. What power she must have, he thought, to be so disarming.

He knelt by the bed kissing her shoulders, her back, her buttocks and her legs. He slipped in behind her, stroking her hair, pushing himself gently between her legs. He was ecstatic. She was moaning, not purring in sleep or whimpering through a bad dream. She was moaning for him. She wanted him as badly. He knew what she liked. He grabbed breasts firmly, from one to the other, and bit into her shoulder.

*

Gilligan woke with her head pounding, facing the wall. She felt the bruises on her breasts before she saw them and the pain at her shoulder. The pain between her legs was foreign, not like before, and she knew instinctively that her father had come to be with her.

But something was different. She could smell him. She could smell his bad breath and his body. Her father was still in the room. She knew then that what Wendy had told her was true. She tried to turn over. She couldn't. His body was blocking her way. She manoeuvred herself close to the wall, wanting to sit, wanting to see what could hurt her so much. That's when she saw him, naked and gruesome, his hair tangled and wet, his mouth wide open, his member shrivelled and wrapped in a loose-fitting sleeve. Seeing him that way made her feel sick, his scrotum loose and purple, his bloated stomach rising and falling.

She scrambled away as quickly as he could, not wanting to wake him, wanting to scream out for Gilligan to come to her and to help her not be alone. She looked into her mirror and wept. She didn't recognize the girl staring back, her wet eyes imploring, her body convulsing. She was naked. The tops of her thighs were tinted with blood, her labia swollen, sore to her uncertain probe. They felt as though burning with fire. Behind her she saw her father, her body trembling with pain as much as with fear.

She went to the kitchen in a hurry. She never woke so late in the morning. By ten she was usually dressed, painting and laughing with her mother. Why did her father hurt her so badly? Her white breasts were turning yellow. Her pubic hair was matted and smelled; she could feel the deep ridge his teeth had chiselled into her shoulder. She wanted to throw up. She wanted her head to stop pounding. If she felt this way she knew that Gilligan must feel this way too. He would never hurt Gilligan again, not one more time.

She sank into a corner, convulsing, whispering Gilligan's name, promising, her eyes fixed on the wooden block, the black hilts protruding like miniature soldiers standing at attention. She'd never known the sensation of her eyes flooded with tears, her body convulsing, her lungs gasping for breath. She'd always been sad, though never gripped by fear, stricken with grief or tortured with searing pain. The sun was so bright, the sky was so blue, the knife in her hand so heavy and gleaming.

She thought of Gilligan, her mind filled with Gilligan. In her room she stood over him wanting to ask him why. Why he would want to hurt his young daughter? He was snoring and she wanted to think of Wendy. Yet she couldn't no matter how much she tried. She choked. She wanted to vomit for the way that she smelled, the way that she looked in the mirror. At that moment she was certain. She didn't like her father for what she knew in her heart he had done to Gilligan.

She didn't say goodbye. She just wanted him to leave her alone, to go from her room and never again come through her door. Her mother would understand. Mother no longer loved father. She raised her slender arms into air, waited a moment, poised, and drove the thick blade into his chest.

Tommy Dune's blurred eyes opened wide with real shock, from what he wasn't certain, his mind clouded. He saw her one last time, for a fleeting moment, aware of the sharp pain in his chest, craning his neck, his expression quizzical, not quite understanding that he was murdered.

She said, "I killed you father, for being a bad man. I don't like you anymore."

With that Tommy Dune died the way he was born: unloved and unwanted.

*

Gilligan stepped into the hallway and closed her door. She was naked and wanted the smell coating her body to go away. She wasn't afraid. She was quietly sobbing until very soon Gilligan came to see what the matter was. Gilligan always knew when she was unhappy.

I killed father."

"I don't believe that you killed father."

"Yes, I did. I did kill father because he hurt me. You can see that he hurt me. I'm telling the truth."

"He hurt me too, this time much worse than the last time. He put bruises on me and made me bleed. See, I was bleeding and I'm swollen where he hurt me the most."

"I should have killed him before he could hurt you. I promised myself he would not hurt you again."

"You didn't kill him, Gilligan, I killed father."

"No. I killed father. I swear that I did. I can show you the body."

Gilligan went to her room and opened the door. He was there on the bed the way that she'd promised. He was grotesque with a handle in his chest for someone to carry him away. She closed the door and went to the kitchen to find the next biggest knife. With it she went directly to Gilligan's bedroom, unafraid. She would make certain that he would never hurt Gilligan again. Killing him must be easy. She opened and closed the door. She went to the man who was once her father. She raised her slender arms into the air and crashed the blade through his chest not far from the other.

Gilligan stepped into the hallway, closed the door and went to the shower, the hot water scalding her delicate skin. She shampooed her hair and sat on the floor of the stall letting the water course between her legs where she hurt the most.

When she was dry she went outside in the nude to sit where no one could see her, where the warm morning sun could begin to soothe her tender wounds.

"I told you I killed father. Sometimes you don't believe me."

"I killed father too."

"Are you glad that he's dead?"

"Yes. I am glad that he's dead. I think so. Do you think I will always be afraid of the dark?"

"No. I don't think so. Do you?"

"I don't think so either."

"I love you. I also love Wendy. I think so."

"I love you, too. I will love you forever. I don't mind if you love Wendy more than me."

"When he hurt me I know that he hurt you too. I will never let anyone hurt you again."

"I suppose now I'll go to jail for killing father."

"I'll go to jail with you. And when we get out we can fly

wherever we want…like the women on the plane."

"Will you miss Wendy, when you're in jail?"

"I think so. I think I'll miss Wendy."

Gilligan gazed into the sky. "I won't ever again dance with mother."

"I don't think so. I don't think you will dance or sing with mother again."

"Our hair is dry. We should go in and tell mother. I think she should know that I killed father."

"We'll go in and tell mother together. Mother will know what to do."

Inside Gilligan went to her room. She dressed in a tee-shirt and panties, most of her body too tender to struggle with clothes. When she saw her father on her bed she felt nothing at all.

*

Gilligan waited as long as she could. He mother wasn't waking and she wanted to talk. In the bathroom she made the water as cold as she could, soaking and wringing the facecloth until her fingers ached and the cloth was cold but not very wet.

Emma stirred from the abrupt shock. She felt terrible. Her mouth was dry and caked, her eyes clouded over. She never felt that way in the morning. She always awoke bright and alert.

"Good morning, my darling."

"Good morning, mother. Mother, I killed father."

Emma's brow creased. She wanted to sit, her head whirring, her temples throbbing.

She wanted to smile. "Who did you kill? You shouldn't want to kill anyone, my darling. That's not very nice to say."

"I killed him too, mother. I killed father with a knife because he hurt me and I wanted him to stop."

"You were dreaming, my darling. How did you dream that he hurt you?"

Gilligan showed her mother her breasts.

"He did this to you?"

Then Gilligan pushed her panties to her thighs. There was never a moment of shame between mother and daughter. "He hurt me here, too."

Emma sprang from her bed and ran from the room. Gilligan's door was open. Tommy Dune was on the bed naked with two handles protruding from his chest. His eyes and his mouth were wide open. Seeing the condom she closed her eyes, clasping her hands tightly together. At least he'd done one right thing in his life.

She saw very little blood, surprised, taking each hilt in her hands to make the wounds worse causing more blood to seep covering her hands with the irrefutable proof she would need.

She didn't cry, nor would she. She didn't miss him then, nor would she later. Instead she called Zeke Phillips at the institute and told him of the overdue murder she'd committed.

Twenty-Four
Seventeen Years Ago: July 15th

Zeke Phillips stood by the corpse speechless. He felt not the slightest empathy for Tommy Dune. He slumped against the wall. What he did feel was abruptly and violently sucked into a whirlwind of shit. He ordered Gilligan into the yard and Emma into the shower where she stayed for fifteen minutes. When she was clean, her hair dried, he went with her into her bedroom and stayed with h er facing away, talking as she dressed into jeans and a sweater.

They spoke for an hour, her hands in his; Phillips poised between sheer disbelief and utter amazement at what he was hearing. Though not once since he'd known the real Emma Rose had he raised his voice in anger or disparagement, nor would he then. What he was hearing was not real.

"Gilligan killed him, Emma, not you. You know the truth, as do I. And, quite frankly, she's guiltless, which doesn't imply that she's not in for an unpleasant few years. She killed him first, and she killed him again so that one mind would not bear the guilt of the other. Gilligan is two girls who can never be apart, two minds that can never be separated. She can only exist together, never apart. You know that. They share a single mind divided, my lovely and sweet girl. For that reason you cannot proceed with what you are contemplating."

"No, Zeke. I killed him. I did. I would never lie to you. I saw him in Gilligan's bed. I saw the terrible damage he did to her young body and I killed him while he was sleeping."

"Emma, do you remember the day so many years ago, when you were a year younger than Gilligan, when you came to me?"

"I was afraid, Zeke, because then you were not Zeke to me. You were Doctor Phillips. What I remember, what I remember more than anything is not seeing my mother when I turned to see her for the last time. I remember Tommy and I remember how frightened I was of you. You were so tall and scary." She smiled for the first time since London. "I can't imagine now that I would ever be afraid of you. I love you so much, Zeke, and Gilligan loves you so much. I am Miss Emma Rose because of you, not him. You made me Miss Emma Rose; you gave me my faces to paint."

"Faces I'm not proud about, Emma. I would prefer that you don't remind me. Seeing your work, for me, is often a penance of significant discomfort."

"Zeke, when I dance in the rain, I know that is what I should do."

"Because you are Emma Rose, vivacious and capricious, and you are not telling me the truth, my girl, which I understand completely. I also understand that you are wrong in what you are thinking."

"And I know this is what I should do. Please do not stop me. I know the feeling of being taken away, of being locked in a room twenty hours a day. I don't want Gilligan to know that feeling for a single day. I want her to dance in the rain. I want her to always be happy. Locked in a room she will never forget what he did and she will always be sad. Then which Gilligan would survive: a Gilligan so delightful and happy or a Gilligan so serious and sad most of her days?" She took him by the arm and led him downstairs. "You will find them a nice home while I'm gone. That is what you must do for me."

"Emma you're not thinking this out. You're talking as though this is a common occurrence. He was a terrible man and he is deservedly dead. However you will spend most of the rest of your life in prison if you wrongly confess, whereas Gilligan will not. She'll be tried as a minor. She was raped several times and over several months, if not years. At worst she will spend time where they can help her forget, to deal with the pain, quite possibly under my personal care to heal. My reputation is somewhat well-established, my girl, my list of acquaintances somewhat impressive. However such will not be the case for you, Emma. Not since this revelation. They will want to know why you acted so eccentrically and with complete disregard for convention. Nor will Gilligan be spared their zeal in establishing that as a mother you were unfit. They will talk with the school and ask questions of your neighbours, neither of whom are likely to portray you in a very good light. Some might well consider the initial wrongdoing no less deliberate and heinous than Dune's vile and persistent obscenity." He squeezed her hand. "You must absolve yourself of the murder, Emma. Either way, Gilligan will be taken from you for a very long time."

"This is what I want...with you by my side. Is what I did worse than committing a young girl to an asylum because she was raped by her father? I don't think so. Gilligan is the prettiest and the brightest girl at school. The teachers don't like her because she's so different...so much like me. She asks questions they don't know how to answer. So which is worse, a child's bright and curious mind or a teacher whose mind is dulled by routine and has stopped learning?"

"I will always stand by your side." He patted her knee and stood. "We will do this together."

Emma Rose smiled. She was calm. "Tell them I'm nuts, Doctor Phillips. How many people do you think will believe that I'm not? I would have killed him, Zeke. That I did not doesn't matter. I would have." She kissed his cheek. "Please give me time in the yard to say goodbye before you call the

police."
*

Zeke Phillips phoned a friend who then phoned another, explaining that Emma had called him because she remembered him from her time at the institute and she trusted him to do what was right. Emma Rose was taken into custody midafternoon moments after Tommy Dune left his home zippered into a polyvinyl bag as the neighbours stood gawking with nothing to say though anxious to talk. She was given the time she needed to kiss tears from Gilligan's eyes.

Gilligan stood crying watching her mother stand at the squad car with her hands cuffed, her bright red lips smiling, her green eyes sparkling without the slightest regret. Gilligan hid her face into the side of Zeke's jacket searching her mind for a dark place to hide and from where she would never leave. She was afraid of the dark. She put herself into the attic to be afraid for her mother.

At the end of the day a black car arrived with a man and a woman to take Gilligan away with clinical detachment. She would never see Wendy again. Zeke stood hunched over staring at the neighbours staring at him from their doorways and windows. He would have gladly killed Tommy Dune had he once thought for a moment that Dune had been so despicably hurtful and cruel.

Neither was the worst over. He couldn't bear to think of Emma living each day in a cellblock crowded with hardened criminals, those who would most certainly do her harm. That evening he returned Emma's previous history to his private office, certain the DA would want substantive proof of her pre-existing insanity.

By the end of the week all Emma's money was placed in trust while she sat in a room no different from the one she once loved. By the end of the month her home and her cars were sold by appointment. Everyone wanted something belonging to Miss Emma Rose, save for her neighbours who could never afford her paintings that soon after were selling at auction for ten times the price she expected.

Gilligan Rose from the age of eighteen would not have to work a day in her life.

Emma spent two days in jail and what remained of the summer she spent at the Phillips Institute, remanded into the care of the good doctor until her trial date in the fall and until which time she would undergo a battery of tests preparatory to the expert opinion he would deliver to the DA's office and her defence counsel.

His staff didn't know and didn't care about her because she wasn't there. She was in Zeke Phillips' home, in her room that hadn't changed in fifteen years. She was transferred from the county facility to the institute by sheriffs who were just as happy to leave after dropping her off at the main doors, Doctor Phillips greeting them personally. As much as the place had changed for the better over the years because of Emma Rose, public opinion had not.

Behind the wrought iron fence and gate still lurked the demented, unsleeping bodies devoid of souls and the criminally insane like Miss Emma Rose.

From then until October Emma was coached by Zeke Phillips day and night. She knew what to say and when, how act and appear to a judge. There was no jury of her peers because, counsel argued, Emma Rose had no peers. She was unique. She lived in a world of her own. She did have neighbours though, neighbours who knew beyond any reasonable doubt that she was bewildered, crazy. She was troubled, counsel argued, mystified, her view of the world distorted and therefore not responsible for her interpretation of what was right and what was wrong. She needed help, not punishment. Emma Rose would not benefit from prison; rehabilitation was not an issue. Her paintings were not art, counsel asserted. Her one-sided faces were her plaintive cry for help. The faces were her face. The eyes were her eyes.

The respected Doctor Zeke Phillips emphatically concurred.

When the trial judge asked Emma why she killed Tommy Dune twice when the first wound was indeed fatal, Emma replied with a smirk that she killed him first because no one else would. She killed him twice because she wanted more faces to paint.

The judge agreed at the end of a two-week trial. Emma Rose should have more faces to paint. Emma Rose was charged with second degree murder, for the DA had proven that Emma had taken sufficient time to think of what she could do and to consider the consequences. She killed a man while he slept when she could well have left or called the police. Sent to prison she would likely be paroled from an overcrowded system at some point after ten years for good behaviour and such leniency did not sit well with the judge when her aberrant behaviour was the greater question and not the crime of murder which she did not understand.

She would not receive the help she needed in prison. In fact she would worsen. The expert witness agreed, his face expressing real concern, his heart on verge of eruption. Emma Rose was that day sentenced and transferred forthwith to his facility where she would live out her life and paint faces, the judge adding that, had Miss Rose been a better mother or not a mother at all, she might have been on her way to the Seine and not to the Hudson.

That Emma Rose would never see Gilligan again was her single regret. She could not. At first she insisted that her daughter would never see the real one-sided faces and when she discovered what Zeke Phillips had done she was too late. Though, despite the passage of time, mother never forgot daughter and daughter never stopped thinking of where her mother might be.

Gilligan, at the age of eighteen, would be content to know where her mother was not and that her life was now finally her own.

Doctor Zeke Phillips had important connections. He had influence which he exploited at County Child Care Services. Gilligan Rose was to enjoy the finest life, the best education and not incur the slightest difficulty to which end he deposited into a trust in her name an amount that would ensure a life without hardship.

Sitting with Gilligan for the last time he told her in part of her eventual wealth. He told her how much he and her mother loved her. He told her that she must never think to search for Miss Emma Rose for to do so would cause great pain and sorrow for her mother.

Child Care promised Zeke Phillips that Gilligan Rose would enjoy a wonderful and carefree new life, free of worry and fear with adoring new parents. What they gave her once he was gone was Tommy Dune with two different faces and a life from which she more than once believed that killing might again be her only escape.

Twenty-Five
This Year: South Beach, May 01st

Johnnie Fennell sat in the warm late-day sand facing the
sea, Deena Archer framed between his knees, locked in
place with his arms.

Two young and tanned women in thongs passed in front
of them holding hands, neither one talking, glancing
sideways and exchanging smiles with Deena. When they
were gone Fennell moaned a deep guttural lament. She
twisted free and jabbed him with her elbow.

"Just because girls hold hands doesn't mean they're
lesbians, sweetheart. They could be sisters or cousins or just
very close friends."

"Yeah, they are... kissing cousins, close kissing cousins.
Guys can tell. Besides they smiled at you, not me."

"I wonder why."

"Still, you've got to admit they're hot together."

"I wouldn't know. I'm a girl."

"What's your point?"

"So you think seeing a couple of guys together is
something hot, two guys with their oily biceps and short
shorts holding hands? That's a turn-on for you? Now you
tell me."

"Not the same thing. Women are women. I mean, really,
check them out. Tell me you don't think that is sexy."

She did think so, choosing not to encourage him. Instead
Deena pointed to another female couple in the distance

275

struggling on their hands and knees to spread out a blanket. "But add a hundred or so pounds, a few dents and moles and it's not so hot. Is that about right?"

"That's disgusting and what I'm seeing is more like two hundred."

She wriggled into him and sighed. "Life's too short, sweetheart. That's what I told her."

"Told who, sweetcheeks?"

"Gilligan, that's what I told her last week when I was with her."

"Gilligan Rose, not Gilligan, Deena. You have to start understanding that it's not a good idea to be on a first name basis with a killer."

"Because I'm arresting her doesn't mean I can't feel compassion for her. You don't know her the way I do. You've seen her from a distance through binoculars. I've held her hands. You've seen her when she's working. I've spoken with her. Besides, sweetheart, remember that she believes you're a child molester."

"Believing what I might be is one thing, knowing she's a killer is another, Agent Archer."

"Sometimes it's difficult to believe she's a killer."

"She's also a nutcase, sweetcheeks, one hundred percent certifiable."

"She's a different case. I'll give you that."

"Different? I guess she's different. She's a lesbian who's attracted to you, which I don't have a problem with speaking as a male of the specie because she is, you know, hot. Yet she's dating this woman called Xara, which she has for a while, and she's got a thing going with the one in France. Once a year she kills some guy she doesn't know, yet she's smart, very smart, university educated and she's wealthy. Yet she works a pretty thankless job she enjoys one day and not the other. I've seen her on flights where she buddies-up, yet I can tell she'd just as soon rip off my manhood. Yet on a couple of other trips, like our first, she barely gives me the time of day and walks around the cabin all cheerful and flashing her big white teeth and green eyes."

"Sometimes I'd like to rip off your manhood, sweetheart. That doesn't make me crazy. It makes you insensitive."

"I'm thinking it's too bad you're not lesbian or curious. Think of what she's told you over a few dinners. Imagine if you stayed for breakfast. However she was right about one thing. In January, you two did have the hottest asses on the beach."

She wanted to smile; he knew she wanted to smile.

"Pardon me."

"What I meant to say was that you had the cutest butt: tanned, firm and perfectly shaped. Her, she was a tad too white for me and, really, a little flat along the back half."

"You're an idiot. The woman's gorgeous." Deena's lips curved into a smirk. "And what makes you think I'm not curious, sweetheart? I never told you I'm not curious. You never asked me, which sort of surprises me now. Besides, I wouldn't be the first girl to dump her good-looking man for something a little softer, a little smoother and more sensitive...another girl."

"We'll finish this conversation in bed, or the spa or in the pool. But, Deena, I'm half serious. If this was a normal case we could hook up with her somehow, see what goes on in her red head behind those green eyes. Instead we see her for a few days once a month to maintain a low and believable profile, track her when she's at home and then nothing."

"I wouldn't have had much trouble last week staying for breakfast despite her thing with Xara and the cabaret woman. It's so strange. The women are so loving and gorgeous, yet Gilligan is so lonely and she's very sad. She is pretty and she is smart. I've seen her in fitting rooms, sweetheart, and you've seen her on the beach. I can see where those women would be and should be jealous if one knew about the other. Still, I know I could have slept with her. What's up with that? How confused can she be?"

"I never have understood that particular euphemism. So she's sexy and smart and she's horny. She's cheating on two women and who wouldn't want you in her bed, the pretty ones anyway. She can't keep her fingers away from the honey jar." He chortled. "Think about it, sweetcheeks. In seventy-five days and counting she'll have all the honey she can handle. I don't doubt that for a minute. Short, tall, fat, thin, or something in-between, we're sending her to paradise."

"Don't talk like that. It's unbecoming."

"She's a killer, Deena, and in a couple of months when she's in my room I won't be thinking of her ass. I'll be thinking of yours and I will kill her when and if she gives me a reason. The morgue or prison is her choice."

"What she needs is help, sweetheart. She's not well. I know this girl. I've held hands with her. We hug and kiss when we see each other. As much as I want her off the street I can't think of her in prison and I certainly don't want her hurt."

"Or dead. Somehow I don't see her hugging and kissing you in July. She's way over the top. She's schizophrenic. She lives in another world and she's dangerous. She is not your buddy. Remember that"

"I can't help wondering how she would have turned out if her mother hadn't escaped. If she'd done her time she'd probably be out by now. She could have a family."

"The mother is out, somewhere. We know her name isn't Rose or Phillips. The whole thing was a setup. Old man Phillips convinces the judge she was nuts, gets her sent to his clinic, he waits a while, removes her files, he retires, removes her and they're gone. The best part, no one knew a frigging thing about the collusion until we came along. All these years and no one's been the wiser."

"So much for a caring system. She's been missing seventeen years,"

"Shouldn't we be thinking so much for a caring mother? I can't wait to find out what's in her head before the courts order an evaluation. She's got to know where momma is and I'd love to know what the old guy got out of it. He was too old for her to be his play thing."

"She could by lying about not knowing where the mother is. She told me she went to the institute and played dumb when she discovered that Emma and Phillips were gone. Getting Emma would be the icing on the cake. Perhaps I'll ask her in June when I happen across her somewhere here on the beach and she'll be with Xara this time."

"Forget Emma Rose. She's gone. She's history. So is he. They don't exist anywhere." He squeezed her. "Tell me about this new kid. She got a French stick up her ass, too much Botox or what"?

"Don't be so mean. I like her. She's sweet and she's nervous when you're around because she thinks you don't like her."

"She's seen me twice and she's taking sides."

"No, she isn't. She wants you to like her but she hears about you every day and you've never spoken with her. She knows you call her the French kid. You should stop that."

"She is French, and stays late to suck up to the boss lady."

"You really are terrible, sweetheart. She's applied to the academy. She wants to be an agent and the reason she stays late is to study the case files of Brannigan's pet agent because somehow, and not from me, she heard you're the best. Brannigan gave her permission." She jabbed him. "Starting to feel a little contrite about now?"

"No. How old is she?"

"Twenty. Originally from Paris she moved to Chicago with her mom, dad and brother. That's where she got her degree and now she's here on her own. So be nice to her. We should take her to lunch one day."

"She has a nice little body...from what I've seen of her."

"Yes, she does, and in a sick world you could be her father. So what's your point?"

"Gilligan Rose is my point. This is a sick world. And, yes, I could be her father...if only in a few photographs. Voluntarily speaking, of course, and we know where Rose will be the week of the fifteenth. I'm thinking maybe a little French tart, so to speak, for a middle-aged American pervert in Paris."

Deena twisted free, facing him. "You're serious."

"Think she would mind a day at the beach, a day away from the squad room, and a free ride to her motherland. It wouldn't hurt to have a few more photos in my laptop. As young as you look, Deena, the French kid could pass for thirteen or fourteen with a bit of help."

"Let's do it. I don't see Brannigan as a problem."

"You get her permission for this one first. I don't want her to think I'm getting soft. Then approach the kid. Take her shopping for some bikinis one step racier than she's comfortable with. Also set her up with some little girl outfits, knee socks, that sort of thing, and something for Paris that a fourteen-year-old shouldn't be wearing for another ten years. Make her real and when you're done we'll take her to lunch and I'll say something nice to make you both happy."

Twenty-Six
Seventeen Years Ago: October

Emma Rose spent the last two weeks of her incarceration at the county facility across the road from the law courts, driven to and from one complex to the other once each day to hear her counsel and the ADA argue her future.

The trial was by judge. Solaceville was too small and opinionated to sit in judgement.

When nothing was left to be said or heard Doctor Zeke Phillips won out. Emma was not going to prison, though the ADA didn't care. Of greater importance to him, as with the judge, was that the accused would spend more time at the institute than she would in prison which scored better on his conviction record.

Zeke Phillips left the courthouse alone without once acknowledging Emma Rose who was once again delivered to his institute that afternoon by county sheriffs, greeted by Phillips who'd generously given his hardworking administrator the afternoon off and the nurse was never involved with new arrivals.

Once the sheriffs were gone she changed into the clothes he'd placed by a cluster of trees near the side garden, walked to his car and went home.

For the next fifteen months that was Emma's prison. She didn't undergo therapy or see a single one-sided face inside the institute, nor did Phillips submit a single report. None was requested at trial and once her original documents were returned from the DA Emma was forgotten in favour of current cases.

The institute and stately manor were sold to a university whose administration wished to add psychiatry to its core curriculum and the Phillips Institute met their criteria as a fine teaching hospital on the condition that they not retain any of the current staff. Phillips readily agreed. The turnover rate was still high and his administrator who wasn't far from her own retirement was content to leave with a bonus. He couldn't have wished for more.

During that time, though closer to the end, Emma Rose systematically disappeared.

Of the many influential contacts Phillips enjoyed, most were righteous and upstanding. Others were somewhat less enviable and they had contacts with whom he met directly on two occasions. He didn't know them, he didn't want to know them, and once the mutually gainful transaction was finalized they forgot one another.

Phillips removed both sets of Emma's records, verifying several times that he hadn't passed over the minutest indication that she had twice been his patient. He transferred his assets to the Swiss banking system, auctioned his worldly goods and walked out from his empty home on February 28th without the slightest remorse. What he had left to carry fit into a single large suitcase.

He went first to the outskirts of London where he had months earlier purchased a modest yet inviting cottage, visiting the couple renting the cottage to see that they were content. They were. He then bought a car and drove to the south of France where he would live a pleasant walk's distance from the home of Mademoiselle Emmanuelle Lerosier who had now lived and painted in Nice for a month.

*

Gilligan Rose didn't spend much time in the system. She was swept up by new parents in early September. In time for the new school year Collette Salazar was living in a

Manhattan condo with a couple who, until they saw her, had everything in life except a lovely young woman as a child.

Madame Salazar had never wanted children. Her body was too finely crafted to consider even the slightest marring. She was also too successful in business to devote a quarter of her lifetime to a project that would never show a return on investment. Señor Salazar shared his wife's point of view. He could never imagine his wife's breasts discoloured with white streaks, her flawless and toned abdomen swollen to disfiguration for the better part of a year or her marvellously sculpted hips, thighs and buttocks abruptly misshapen for the sake of social approbation. Then what of their yachting, the all-inclusive resorts proposing an adult flair and their frequent appeal to other like-minded couples? Not to mention the financial burden required to properly sustain another human being throughout such an unthinkable span of time.

They were on the young side of mid-thirties. They wanted a girl who would appear believable as their daughter, not an infant or one so young that she would require constant attention. They were in the market for a teenager, fifteen or sixteen, tall, mature, beautiful and bright with clear skin and enviable features. A girl suited to private schooling at the best academy, a friend as well as a daughter, though adept at self-sufficiency when left alone. That was their wish list. What they told Child Services was that they wanted to adopt an older girl whose previous life lacked the love and attention they had to give, a good life they could easily afford.

They'd waited a very long time for the right girl until they were called to visit with Gilligan Rose whom they saw right away was their dream daughter and Gilligan was at that moment twice torn away. They seemed not to care about her tears, or her fear of letting go.

The paperwork took less than a day. The couple was preapproved. They were upstanding with established careers, respected, affluent and well-educated. One day later mother and father took their new daughter shopping. Although her current wardrobe was adequate, she would learn to dress and comport herself as a young woman of style, good taste and good breeding.

Collette's new room was twice the size of her old room. Her drawers and closets weren't stocked with pyjamas, baby dolls and fleecy robes; they were brimming with silk and satin lingerie and peignoirs, thongs to wear under the short dresses and tiny bikinis to wear on the yacht or on the south coast of Spain and the French Riviera. She liked her new wardrobe, the way her real mother had taught her to dress. She didn't have to be told, though she didn't see anything wrong with the clothes that she'd brought with her which she wasn't allowed to keep.

From her window high above Central Park she saw the full expanse of green grass and trees and thought of her real mother, how they would sit together on the grass and talk for hours. She wanted to believe that she would see her mother again, one day soon, when she was old enough to live on her own. She had to believe that Zeke was wrong to say she would not, that she could not, and that she must also change her name so that she would never once in the future stir memories of Miss Emma Rose. For that reason she was Collette Salazar, despite which she did not and would never regret killing her father.

She knew where her mother was and that she was well, that she would never to go jail and that she was with Zeke who would take care of her and love her. She knew her mother was in the house of one-sided faces.

The woman at the agency had even prevented her from keeping precious photos of her mother, destroying them, telling her that memories of such a terrible mother would not be healthy. She remembered crying and began to worry that one day she would forget how beautiful her mother was.

Her new parents insisted that she become fluent in their languages as quickly as possible, for what good was a daughter who could not converse with their many friends. And by June the next year she'd made remarkable progress, gifted in a way she had never thought to consider.

The year passed quickly, though she didn't make any friends at school. There weren't any girls like Wendy; they were all stuffy and arrogant, full of themselves. All they could do was talk about what their parents did for a living. She missed Wendy terribly, wondering if she had found another girl to kiss and be friends with. She didn't think so. And each night before she fell asleep, her eyes closed to the dark, she whispered to Gilligan what she was thinking.

She didn't dislike her new parents. They were different, not like her mother. She didn't love them, the same way she knew they would never love her. She was however anxious to see Spain and France and to spend her summer on a big yacht. She had read everything she could about the Mediterranean and the people, despite which she wasn't prepared.

Listening to her mother and father speak slowly with her in their foreign tongues was one thing. Trying to understand lightning fast Castilian and the blurred French of France were quite another. Nor was she prepared to see thousands of women strewn or strolling along beaches in thongs with their breasts bare, coated in oil to enhance what she saw and believed were already flawless bodies, including Madame Salazar and her friends onboard the yacht or by the sea. Nor was she prepared for the custom of drinking wine with each lunch and dinner or during the afternoon for no reason at all.

She spent her first month sailing between Marbella and Majorca, her second between Marseille and Monaco. Alone on the beaches she tested her new freedom, enjoying the feeling, wishing that Wendy was with her and whispering to Gilligan as she strolled or lay in the privacy of her cabana how good she felt with the heat of the sun and the coolness of the water all over her body. Onboard the yacht however she wore arguably more modest Rio bottoms and tops despite her father's persistent urges that in Europe wearing the least possible when at the beach or onboard was not merely appropriate but preferred by all women of a particular beauty.

By the time they sailed into Marseille. Madame Salazar often stood at the helm as her husband sat on the foredeck with their daughter massaging SPF into her skin to protect what he knew was flawless, often tugging apart the strings of her top so that he wouldn't soil the expensive material, often lifting the edges of her bottoms to make certain that no part of her would burn.

At night in her cabin, when the guests were gone to their own yachts or homes, she heard them in bed, sometimes giggling and laughing, other times groaning and shrieking. One night, the first of many that summer, hearing a series splashes, she tiptoed to the afterdeck and peered into the surrounding night that was pitch black, muted lighting, enough for her to see clearly, coming from deck lamps to illuminate the stark white fibreglass.

Her mother was kneeling, looking across a black sea speckled white with anchor lights. Her father stood behind her, bent over, his hands at her hips. Her mother and father, which she thought was no worse or better than using their names, were naked and dripping with water, visible under the stars.

She stood watching, wondering who else might be watching, wondering why they hadn't turned out the lights first. She waited until they were finished, curious. She remembered the feeling, the hurt, curious to see what her mother might do. She saw nothing, the man helping the woman to stand. She saw the two kiss and the couple disappear onto the transom. When she heard the two splashes seconds apart she returned to her cabin and bolted the door.

At the end of summer the yacht was returned to Marbella for storage. Collette was more fluent in French and Spanish and slightly tanned with her decidedly more feminine features darker than ever before. She enjoyed that part of her trip without telling either her mother or her father. They wouldn't know. Since seeing them that night on the afterdeck and once when they had forgotten to close their cabin door, her door remained locked each night which she didn't neglect to do once home in Manhattan when she began locking the bathroom door as well.

They wanted her to attend university the following year and remain at home with them until her graduation and eventual employment. She didn't think so. She wanted to train as a flight attendant, though she didn't tell them that. She said she would think about whether or not she should, and where. They agreed to wait until the following summer when she would be seventeen. In the meantime, however, they would submit applications to select universities which they believed were the best.

Her seventeenth came and went with a Carolina Herrera handbag complete with ten 100-dollar bills and a few dinners in Miami for a midwinter break from a cold and colourless season.

She loved Miami and she thought the Latin women were as beautiful as the French or the Spaniards she'd met, telling her father that she would like to attend college in Miami. He laughed at the thought and said no.

In the spring, while the other girls continued hiking the skirts of their uniforms outside of school, dropping them inside, Collette kept hers well above her knees. At home she wore the clothes they bought her: short dresses and skirts, silk blouses and scoop-neck sweaters. Sweatpants and shirts were forbidden, as were jeans and sneakers. Madame and Señor Salazar entertained regularly and expected their daughter to present herself as a viable and elegant young woman.

She never once sat by him on the sofa, though often she saw him at the bottom of the curved stairway as she climbed to her room on the second floor. He would often touch her knees, rubbing her legs with an open palm at dinner or as she ate breakfast, the same way he would press his hands into the back of her skirt whenever he had an occasion to hug her. As did her mother, Madame Salazar was constantly touching her affectionately, sometimes kissing her lips and not her cheeks or stepping into change rooms with her each time they went shopping.

On the first day of summer, winter and spring behind them, Collette Salazar graduated from the girls' academy in the top ten percentile, Madame and Señor Salazar having decided for the best that she would attend Columbia. Collette decided as well that she would, until such time as she decided she wouldn't.

On the third day she was in Marbella helping her parents load the yacht with new summer fashions and a supply of wine and liquor sufficient to see them through to Marseille.

Collette still would not wear a thong on the boat as her parents suggested, or bask in the sun on the foredeck with her breasts bare the way her mother did alone or with friends. She waited for the privacy of crowded and long sandy beaches. She did the same in Marseille where they docked for a week at a private seaside villa they rented as a concession to their daughter who enjoyed the sea yet wanted to spend time sightseeing on her own rather than seeing Europe from ten miles offshore unless from inside a restaurant.

She had not the slightest idea that a pleasant drive by car to the east would lead her to Mademoiselle Emmanuelle Lerosier in a studio perched high upon a hill and looking out over the sea while she painted a young girl in a mirror

She'd needed a reprieve from hearing their voices each night in their bed, and often midday as they lay on the foredeck kissing and fondling, pretending to tease when she knew they weren't teasing at all.

She wanted to lie on her back and gaze at the stars, to tell Gilligan in her mind and in her heart that she was alright, that she wasn't sorry for killing her real father. She was sorry she didn't have her mother to talk with, that because of her they'd taken her mother away. Instead she was locked in her cabin, hearing their splashes, afraid to step out, afraid of what she knew they wanted her to see. She needed time to herself. She felt trapped. They weren't the parents she wanted.

The day was warm, though not too warm, and cloudless with a gentle sea breeze making the day delightful and ideal for shopping.

She was less than six months from her eighteenth birthday, though to anyone seeing her she appeared at once more mature yet strangely much younger. Her outfit was sandals, a short and billowy summer dress that tempted all eyes passing her by as well as imaginations, a wide-brimmed hat and tinted glasses. She loved that she was becoming a woman, hating that she didn't have one of her own to hold hands with and talk with, or to say nothing with, repeatedly refusing dates hoped for by the eager sons of her parents' oldest and newest friends. Although she knew in her heart that neither mother nor father Salazar was very disappointed, wanting not to share her with too many.

She saw the girl first. She didn't know, in the fifth or sixth boutique she'd browsed through. She was very pretty, Collette thought, cute, eighteen or nineteen, in the company of a young man who, no one could deny, openly adored her.

She saw the girl again in the next boutique she visited, again with the young man. She saw them kiss and him walk away. She saw the girl again in the next boutique, smiled at her, and went for a light salad and Perrier sprinkled with lemon. She put the girl out of her mind. She knew one day Wendy would find her again, in another body and with a different name. She knew. So why didn't her new father or mother?

"Pardonnez-moi, mademoiselle, my name is Elixia de Montfort."

Collette's head jerked involuntarily skyward. The girl was breathtakingly good-looking.

"Bonjour, je m'appelle Collette Salazar."

"I do know this already. I did ask the clerk in the last store. Your French that I heard you speak is good, however you are not French and you do not look at all like a Spanish girl."

"I'm American."

"And I am French." She paused, not hesitating. "I would like to join you for your lunch, if you do not mind. When we did smile at each other before, I did see in your eyes that perhaps we could be friends or enjoy one meal together."

"I would like that, Elixia. I don't have any friends. C'est la vie." Collette let her eyes scan the nearby sidewalk. "Won't your boyfriend mind? Won't he come looking for you...the young man in the store?"

"He is my much older brother. He treats me like I am a child, I know, but I do love him so much. I visit with him each summer from Paris where I do live with my parents. He is the one who suggested for me to meet you. Et me voici! Here I am. He did so because I did tell him that you are so pretty, that I would like to know you, and he did see in your eyes also that we should meet." She sat. "How can I believe that a girl as lovely as you are has not a single friend?"

"I'm here for a week on vacation with my parents." She beamed. "Thank you for joining me. My lunch will be much more fun now. I think so."

The girls sat and talked through salads and a carafe of fine cabernet. Elixia knew the couple who managed the bistro. A lunch without wine was not lunch, merely fast food. When they were finished the man and woman came out dressed in black berets and spotless white aprons to hug and kiss the girls, shooing them and their money away, making them promise to visit once more before the week was over.

They spent what was left of the afternoon shopping and went to dinner, their sidewalk table surrounded with bags of every description and colour.

Elixia was on vacation with her brother who doted over her. She was Parisienne, nineteen, in her third year of college. Her dream was to one day own the finest cabaret in France. Collette loved her immediately and Elixia was no less taken with the beauty, red hair and strange accent of the girl she discovered would one day soon be Gilligan Rose once again. Collette was not attending Columbia or any other university, not after her eighteenth birthday. She had other plans.

When they parted the girls kissed, their first touch demure, promising to meet the next morning for breakfast, their second kiss making them more than unexpected good friends.

The next day they strolled the beach hand in hand, swinging their tops with the other. That evening they dined with her brother who later drove her to the villa where her mother and father wanted to hear of her day. She told them everything except the truth.

On the third morning the girls went shopping. The afternoon they spent in Elixia's room talking about Wendy and the girl Elixia had known for a short while, though long enough to discover who she was. That evening they had dinner together, alone at a quaint café-terrasse where they held hands and talked as though they'd been each other's best friend for years.

The Salazars wanted to meet her, inviting Elixia for dinner the next evening, Collette explaining that her friend had plans all that week with her family, which included wanting to show off her American friend, suggesting instead that they invite her for a day of sailing on their way from Monaco to Marbella. As much as she wanted to invite Elixia onboard, she would not. She was afraid of what might happen. She didn't want her mother or father making Elixia ill at ease or nervous with their self-indulgent behavior.

The next day the girls toured the city, held tightly together by each other's arms, Collette amazed at how not a single passer-by seemed shocked or disgusted each time they kissed. Elixia's brother invited them that evening to dinner at a small cabaret. So happy was he that his sister had found such a wonderful friend. He'd seen Elixia so unhappy and alone for so long.

Then too quickly came a fifth day to share.

"Collette, I do know very well that I will miss you so much when you are gone from me."

"I made them promise to bring me back in three weeks. So I will see you again, and next year maybe you can visit me in New York or meet me in Miami. You would like Miami. The women don't wear very much and they're all beautiful like you."

"I cannot. I will have my classes." She sipped her espresso. "Collette, since five days I want to tell you something. I like very much that you kiss me so nicely…"

"And now you want to kiss me in bed."

"Since I saw your red hair and then your green eyes I have wanted to kiss you in my bed, yes, which of course I do know will make me much more unhappy when you do go from here." She paused. "My brother has gone for the day. Even so, he knows very much how I feel in my heart."

"I'm nervous. I want to see you in bed also and to kiss you all day. I think you're so hot."

Elixia held out her hand. "And you are so hot." Her lips curled into a curious smirk. "So why are we not starting our fire?"

By the end of the day the girls were sitting on the

veranda, exhausted. Collette could not have imagined that her lips could be as numb as they were or that she could love a girl with such eager abandon. Elixia was nothing like Wendy who was more tentative and shy, her body beginning to blossom and afraid someone might see them and run to tell the entire school. She was beautiful and sexy, her breasts soft and smooth, her body exquisitely formed with every curve perfect and firm.

"You can tell me, you know, that you do love me."

"I wanted to, Elixia. I thought you would laugh."

"So how will you know this if you do not tell me?"

She did. "Je t'aime. Je pense que oui. I think so."

"I know that you do. And do you see? I am not laughing."

"They'll be on the yacht all day tomorrow and my room has a view of the ocean. Or we can make love on the patio by the pool."

"I do not believe that I will sleep very well tonight in my bed alone. I wish that you could stay here with me until you must leave."

"They won't let me. I told you why I don't want you to see them. They're strange. But we have all day tomorrow and the next day together."

"I regret in my heart that you are not older. Then you could stay here in France and go with me to my classes. These people are your parents for two years, not more, which is nothing. This is not very long or difficult to forget."

"From now until this time next year is long. I've seen a lot of pretty girls here, Elixia. I'm feeling myself getting jealous. I think so."

"Yes. However we are the prettiest of all these girls, you and I. N'est pas?"

"Yes we are the prettiest, bien sûr."

"And tomorrow I will come to your villa to plan something special for our last day and to damage our lips once more. We will exchange our numbers and speak many times from now until next summer when you will come to see me again."

That night, her eyes closed to the dark, Collette told Gilligan all that she could. She was in love. She thought so. And she knew Elixia felt the same way.

The next morning the parents were miffed, not pleased that their daughter had planned not to join them onboard. The yacht inched away from the dock at nine. She went to meet Elixia at the gate at five after the hour. She was anxious to make love, to swim in the pool's heated water and to bask in the sun, luxuriant cream massaged into her body by Elixia's attentive hands in long, sensual strokes.

The pool came first once Collette could no longer see the yacht cruising along the coast, each girl taking a turn at carrying, pulling or pushing the other nude body through the warm water.

They ate a lunch of croissants and cheese with a bottle of chilled Bordeaux and talked of the coming year. They agreed not to make foolish promises, though Elixia would be far too busy at school and in a month's time Collette would enter her first and last year at Columbia.

They hadn't noticed or hadn't cared that the clear blue sky was turning grey or that the deep blue of the Mediterranean had darkened to black. When they did, the patio spotted with raindrops, they went inside to shower away the pool and rich cream from their bodies.

Collette stepped from the ceramic stall wrapped in a towel. She had so much to tell Gilligan in a few hours' time. She would whisper how beautiful Elixia was, how she tasted and smelled, how warm she was, sweet and gentle. How her eyes were as black and iridescent as coal, her straight hair obsidian black and lustrous, her skin slightly darker than her own with summer's pale glow. She realized then that she hadn't been sad for a week. She couldn't remember not being sad except for the days she'd once spent with her real mother sitting in the grass or dancing in the rain, or the few times she was alone in the grass by the trees with Wendy.

"I know now, Elixia, that I will always love you. I don't want to meet anyone else. I am coming back to you."

"And you do see that once again I am not laughing. My brother, he does see this also. He does believe that very soon you should come here to France to live. Here we are not like Americans. We do not laugh at girls who hold hands or go blind behind dark glasses when we do see women whose breasts are bare. Yes, my brother is right. You must soon live in France and together we will make your French much better. You will be a French girl."

"Once I turn eighteen, you will see me often. I can spend the whole summer, and see you at Christmas and Easter. That won't be so bad for a while. And then my French will be perfect."

"I do believe you and I will come when I can to America because I do want to see New York and to see Miami. Anyway we can talk of this when we are dressed. Now we are naked and you did promise me to show me your bed."

The sky was sufficiently dark to simulate nighttime which made their lovemaking all the more ardent with no sense of time. Everything was new and exciting, each touch and kiss, each probe a gentle caress. Neither girl had ever felt as intense or aroused to where they did not hear the yacht easing into its slip or the bare feet on the tiled floor padding closer. Nor did the girls see his eyes straining to see more through the door they'd left slightly ajar so that they might hear. He might have stood there five minutes or sixty until the door creaked as he wanted to move closer.

Elixia and Collette were at opposite ends of each other's body, exploring, lost in unexpected and tender romance. He was caught. They saw him and he stepped in, switching the room from darkness to bright light.

The girls jolted apart, their shock dissipating instantly,

passion and desire usurped by anger and rage amidst a flurry of English and French as he calmly sat by the door to watch them hurry to dress.

"What a fine sight, a very fine sight" he began, his voice mocking, "your faces shining and wet. I can smell them from here. Your mother would want to see you like this, Collette, doing something sexy for once. Yes, she would enjoy this very much. Come. Kiss your father. Let me taste your girlfriend's juices."

Elixia spit, "Va te faire enculer." She'd thought to reach first for her dress. Then she ripped the cover from the bed and stood between him and Collette with her arms raised.

"Like she said," Collette yelled, "fuck off!"

"Teenage sluts, that's what you are, all this time pretending that you're so prim and proper, innocent and pure. And what do I come home to see, thirsty kittens licking their milk from their bowls. And what nice bowls you both have. Your mother won't be pleased to learn that she missed this entertainment. I should join you in bed, Collette, both of you. I feel myself very ready for you." He stood. "Stop dressing. We can have some fun, the three of us."

She screamed, "I told you to fuck off."

"You are the worst kind of whores, you two. You're dykes and Mademoiselle de Montfort you will not see my daughter again. I have a good mind to spank you later, Collette, for being such a bad little girl when all the while you wouldn't even show your tits on the beach or the yacht. Or would you prefer your mother to spank you while I watch? "

Collette was dressed. She took the blanket, holding her hands high for Elixia to finish dressing.

"I did show my tits at the beach, asshole, and my bare ass, just not to you or your sick bitch of a wife. You know who I am, Eduardo. I'm Gilligan Rose and I have a secret you will not like to hear, a secret that will stop you from sleeping at night. So get the fuck out of my room and do not ever think to touch me again. As for tomorrow I will see my friend again and for the rest of the month. I'll meet you and your nauseating wife in Marbella. Have fun explaining that one to her."

He watched her pack a bag and leave, through the villa and out onto the pool deck where Elixia calmly smashed the empty wine bottle and crystal goblets into the pool, smiling.

His screech was real, his reaction frozen by a caustic threat he believed.

On the way to her brother's home she asked, "Collette, what secret do you know that would keep him from sleeping?"

"I knew you would ask me." Collette took a deep breath. "I'll tell you if you promise not to hate me until you understand why."

"I will never hate you."

"My name is Gilligan Rose."

"I do know this already."

"My mother killed my father while he was sleeping because he raped me. She's in an institution for the mentally ill. She would kill any man who hurts me."

They sat at the first bench they came to where Collette spoke for an hour as Elixia held her hands, neither amazed nor worried. When she was finished Elixia hugged her and kissed her.

"I would have killed him also for what he did to you. This does not change who you are to me and I do like your real name much better than the one they gave to you. And one day I do know that you will see your mother. This I do know in my heart." She gurgled a laugh. "I do think so. And, Collette, this is now my secret also. No one will know of this from me, not even my brother."

That evening before dinner, enraged at hearing what had taken place, young de Montfort went on his own to the villa where he introduced himself as a prelude to happily and thoroughly making Señor Salazar wish he hadn't come home to the villa as early as he did. He paid his respects to a stunned and terrified Madame Salazar and bid them goodnight.

The next day Salazar paid for the damages, including the pool, and set a course not for Monaco rather for Marbella where they waited for the last day of August.

Over the next few weeks Collette Salazar lived with Elixia and her brother, a young man experienced in international travel. He knew a thing or two about airlines, listening intently to Gilligan speak of her dream. He understood. He followed his dream of becoming a consultant in international trade and was successful. He was also educated with a Master's. Elixia also had a dream, to which end she was now midway through her commerce education. The difference, he told her, of becoming a flight attendant or becoming the best flight attendant, would be four more years of school. By which time she would be twenty-one. No reputable airline would hire anyone younger. So what would she do to pass her time until then, work in a coffee shop when she was so bright, to become less than she could be? To do so would be an unconscionable waste.

He had an idea and on the 30th he drove with his sister and Collette across the border to Marbella.

Twenty-Seven
The Four Years after Marseille

Salazar and his wife agreed with young de Montfort. What choice did either one have? The Salazars flew home through Málaga and Madrid without seeing Collette who flew to the States by way of Marseille and Paris a week later, spending more precious time with Elixia.

Once in the US, taking a week to sort out the never-expected events flooding her mind, she attended Columbia until the last week of May at their expense, visiting Paris between Christmas and New Year's at their expense as Collette Salazar and again at Easter as Gilligan Rose without the couple once crossing her mind.

Three months earlier on her eighteenth birthday she filed a petition with the court to dissolve her adoption. She cited her adoptive parents as lewd and lascivious, deviant by nature, proving beyond a doubt that she'd seen them on more than one occasion in the nude, having sex where they expected or hoped that she might happen by or on their bed with the door wide open. The couple was openly provocative with other couples, the man and woman touching her where she didn't want to be touched and she explained in detail how the man had humiliated her five months earlier on the French Riviera. She had affidavits signed by the French Court to support all that she claimed.

She wanted her natural name and birth certificate restored. The court agreed, recommending that she press charges against them. She declined. She wanted no further contact with them. She needed to forget that such people existed. The court understood and took action of their own, making certain the Salazars would never again adopt and abuse. What the court didn't know was that she hadn't lived with them since Marseille.

On June 01st Gilligan lay in her bed for the last time in her private room near the campus with her bags packed and the door locked, whispering to Gilligan what she would do. Gilligan agreeing that what she intended was the right thing to do. When the phone rang she sprang to the floor beaming. She was most happy when she spoke on the phone with so much to say.

She rented a car and drove north 200 miles. She'd never driven as far on her own. She drove to where she once lived, where she once sat in the grass with her mother, where her mother once washed her car singing and laughing without a care in the world. She remained in the car remembering how the neighbours would watch, especially the men, trimming their lawns at the very same time as though on cue. So much time had gone by, yet so little. They would still remember Gilligan Rose, the way she remembered her promise to Zeke never to search for her mother.

She drove across town to the institute she'd never seen, not once in her life, expecting tall gates and wrought iron fences and that's what she found. The pine trees and maples remained, the walkways meandering through Zeke Phillips' short-lived luscious gardens and vivacious fountains gurgling. The flowers were in full bloom, silver water still gurgling under the sun, picnic tables scattered across the front lawn. All that was missing were people.

She went through the doors unafraid, not knowing what she might expect, remembering how she would watch as her mother painted each of her one-sided faces. At the desk she asked to speak with Doctor Zeke Phillips. Surprised by the response she asked if he might have passed away. No, the orderly replied. He went away, to England he believed.

She then asked if she might visit with Miss Emma Rose, the artist, the man replying without hesitation that the name was not remotely familiar. He'd worked at the hospital since the takeover sixteen months earlier and was acquainted with each patient personally. He knew of no Emma Rose. The name was not familiar at all.

Gilligan thanked the man and left smiling. She now understood Zeke's words of caution, the prudently worded letter he'd written to remind her. She waited until she reached the car to laugh. Zeke Phillips would never take her mother to England. Miss Emma Rose was too full of life and far too carefree to ever live in such a pompous and sterile place. What a ridiculous notion.

She booked a room at the airport hotel and spent the night in her room talking and crying with Gilligan before her early morning flight. Their mother was safe somewhere in the world, she told her, tears blurring her eyes, and one day, not right away, one day, yes, they would dance together again in the rain. She knew this, she told Gilligan, because Elixia had told her so.

*

Gilligan had to know. That's why she studied so hard to excel, to be the best in her class. She wanted to understand the human condition, why a man would repeatedly drug and rape his young daughter when in his bed each night laid a beautiful wife not much older. No one in her class ever suspected why her papers were written with such depth, her presentations so eloquent and emotive.

She had no expectation that she would one day become a psychiatric specialist. She had no intention of curing the world of its inherently deviant nature. Such aspirations were far from her dreams. She first wanted to cure herself. She wanted to understand how one half of who she was could at once be cheerful and smiling while wishing for the darkness of anguish and sorrow, or wishing for joy and elation when overcome with foreboding and the misery of despair. That's what she wanted: to understand who she was or who she was not and to circle the globe from one city to another. That was her dream.

At eighteen she was wealthy. The lawyer who knew how to find her, who knew all along where and how she lived, called her one day to his office. He also had a sealed letter to deliver from Doctor Zeke Phillips explaining that her mother was well, that she would remain well without question unless she might one day be found, that Gilligan should weigh her love for her mother with utmost selflessness lest she rob Emma once again of her much deserved freedom. That Emma was forced to live without her daughter was a sufficiently harsh sentence. How then could he ask less of a daughter whose mother's love was once and forever abundantly proven?

She asked the lawyer where she might locate Doctor Zeke Phillips, or whether he might have died. He declined to answer. He'd been retained until his obligation to his client was terminated and such was the case in part. He was instructed to give her no further information. Doctor Phillips, whether alive or deceased, had his reasons to believe that Miss Gilligan Rose should make her way through life alone, to follow her dream to fly and be of one sound mind.

She knew what the letter meant. She was intended never to live a complete life, never to exist as a whole person. She was being punished by Doctor Phillips for what she'd done to her mother. By destroying her father she had destroyed herself, Gilligan and her mother in the time she took to bury fourteen inches of steel into his chest.

Before she left the lawyer's office she engaged him to file a petition with the court to regain what she owned of her past: her name and her memories without the dilution of recent and less happy years. She wanted her life her way, not one bought and paid for, expected to conform who she'd become to fit the lifestyle of strangers, not abruptly dragged into one existence as though she hadn't lived fifteen years and six months in another before being taken away.

She was Gilligan Rose, not someone else. Her mother had taught her that. What her most recent parents, deceased in her mind since Marseille, thought or believed didn't matter. She needed to know that Gilligan would never leave her, that she would always be there in her mind and in her thoughts no matter what. That's what truly mattered. She would never let Gilligan go, as much as she knew in her heart and in her mind that Gilligan would never leave her alone. Their minds were inseparable, indivisible.

She moved to Long Beach, far away, to continue her studies, leaving her past and her temptation behind. She purchased a high-rise luxury condo by the ocean with a private patio when other girls squeezed two or three bodies into a single dorm room, though she told them that she lived in a rented sub-basement not far from the campus. Her clothes she could also explain. She was the best dressed girl in her classes, telling them they should buy classic designs and dress for the job they wanted, not for free drinks on Pub Night for guys who one day wouldn't afford them, if they were even remembered.

That word got around. To the girls that meant she had a sugar daddy somewhere paying her way, a professor or the dean, whereas to the male contingent, frustrated at not getting into her panties to claim their reward, she was a stuck-up dyke bitch.

She became very clear in her mind that she preferred the company of girls, no longer curious as she was the first time Gilligan let her kiss Wendy and touch her breasts when they were alone just the two of them one day after school. She remembered Wendy, though didn't miss her at all. Wendy wasn't hers to miss, not any longer; she had always belonged to Gilligan.

She hadn't dated once throughout her years of adoption, content at first, after a while, in a world where she could sleep with her eyes closed to the dark in a room closed to the shadows. She knew she would never date a man, not ever. She would never again in her life awaken to the horror of that morning, her breasts stained blue and hurting with bruises, the tops of her thighs caked with sticky blood that was hers and foul sweat that was his.

That's what she remembered of Wendy, that she was soft and warm, that she could one day find someone to love without pain.

Her second and third years passed quickly, her weekends spent at the beach when other girls worked to make ends meet and soon the men who thought themselves perfect for such a perfect young woman learned not to bother. She'd adopted the fashion of tiny and colourful thongs for her not for them and most days she lay appealingly on her front to avoid strap lines on her back, her glistening body saturated with SPF.

She told them straight out that she was a lesbian, even though she'd only been one once or twice for a few hours each time, which didn't stop them from gaping or clicking off a few frames to inscribe perfection in perpetuity. They didn't matter, faceless bodies, there one day and gone the next. Whether any of them woke the next morning disappointed or with someone else, she woke safe and sound. That's what she cared about. And the women were no better. She'd seen too many couples break up: a quirk, a college flirtation they could use to excite future husbands or one-night stands.

She went to the beach to study, not to be seen or to see. She could make the pastel hue of her tan seamless at home whenever she wanted. Let them ogle and stare, she was saving herself for another. She wasn't in a hurry. She had a year left to study before living her dream and perhaps one day soon becoming complete.

*

In Paris Elixia graduated the previous year, working to save as much as she could in a small yet popular cabaret for the experience which she lacked to manage a club of her own. She didn't perform, nor would she ever. Her waitress uniform was low-heeled pumps strapped at her ankles, sheer stockings with dark seams running the length of her legs, a black décolleté dress with a short stiff skirt over white ruffled panties. She didn't mind. She was French and as many women were drawn to her inherent charm as men. She was doing very well for herself being a cliché.

In her club, though, her girls would wear black sequined dresses, short and décolleté dresses with a hint of black panties and bras, a beret, high-heeled sandals and clear stockings without seams. Her club would be the finest and most elegant in all of France and her girls would dress the part, not like quintessential French maids.

Gilligan had one year of study remaining before graduation. She'd been anxious to spend what would be the last of her long summer days with her friend and her lover, anxious to spend her nights on a barstool adoring the most beautiful girl in the whole of Paris. Now she would not, anxious, yet nervous, to tell her friend the reason. She never did tell Elixia about Gilligan, afraid, or confess that she had killed her own father, or that Emma Rose, wherever she was, was a famous artiste. She saw no purpose in speaking of someone Elixia would never comprehend or imagine. No one would ever understand Gilligan, their closeness or how they felt about each other, or how they missed each other, or why they even existed. And how would she explain Miss Emma Rose without confessing?

She wanted Elixia to have her cabaret and not waste precious time working in another. That morning she wrote a cheque for the difference between what Elixia had saved and what her parents and brother had insisted she accept, the one stipulation being that, once Elixia opened for business, they would deserve the best seats in the house.

Elixia coughed the air from her lungs. The amount was unthinkable. She refused, igniting their first lover's quarrel. Elixia hadn't once looked at her that evening despite knowing that her Gilligan was the most delicate rose in all of gay Paris.

The difficult time came when the cabaret closed. The girls had to do something, say something. They couldn't simply walk home together, side by side, wanting to hold hands, not holding hands, wanting to kiss and not kissing. Each girl stopped as though gripped by invisible hands, Elixia taking the high road, Gilligan taking the high road.

"You did not tell me that you are a rich girl."

"I am a rich girl, a very rich girl." Gilligan paused. "The story's complicated, chérie. The man who helped my mother escape, he was rich, very rich. Each year for my birthday he put a large sum of money in trust for me because my father was no good and my mother seldom gave thought to anything beyond what she was doing at the moment. The thing is, I didn't know. Not until the last time I saw him and even then I didn't know how much. He told me I could live a very comfortable life, do and become whatever I wanted, though I never imagined how comfortable. There wasn't anything he wouldn't do for my mother; he was like an uncle to me. I loved him very much. I still do. I miss him, Elixia, and I miss my mother. When they left they put even more money in trust for me, lots of money, money I did not know about, too much money for me to ever spend in my life, which was his way and hers of saying they love me too. They know I can never search for them. The money was their way of saying that they're okay, they're fine. I didn't work for this money. I'm rich because I am loved by them. Now do you understand chérie? I want you to have what I have for that very same reason. Please let me do something good. That's what they want. That's what my mother would want. Please let me be like my mother."

"The money is too much. I want the cabaret to be mine. With this I will owe you too much."

"So you don't understand." Gilligan pursed her lips into a tight grin. She was learning to smile on occasion, when she was Elixia. "Rich, okay, I'm more like frigging wealthy for a girl my age. Just remember that I loved you before I was told about all the money. So what's the big deal? Mi dinero es tu dinero, chica."

"Do not talk with me this way. This is not amusing to me. This is my dream the way that you wish one day to fly."

"I can fly, chérie, next year. TGA has accepted me for training. That's the other surprise I had for you until you got all girlie on me. But I have to do more and you know I don't want to work as your partner at the cabaret. I just want free drinks." She pressed a warm palm to Elixia's cheek. "You know I'm not good with people most times, but with this you can open in two years instead of ten and work where you are until the construction is finished and you're ready to open with the most talented staff and performers. With this you can afford the finest in France. You have no reason to wait. Best of all, you get to tell the bank you don't need them. You are all that I need or want. So, yes, you are letting me do this."

Elixia breathed in deeply, her shoulders slumped. "I do need you also. I am sorry, mon coeur. Je t'aime."

"Is that a yes?"

"This is a yes." She kissed Gilligan's cheek. "Yes, I do think so. And you do get the best seat in my cabaret as well, with house wine only. Or I will not make money with you or my brother. Merci mon coeur. Tomorrow we will meet with my attorney and after we will celebrate together in the second best cabaret in France. I do believe that one day soon madame will not like me at all."
*

The deal was made legal the next morning. Gilligan owned a ten percent share she didn't want in a Parisian cabaret. Elixia had insisted that she accept twenty. Gilligan, though, stood firm. She would accept ten or nothing at all.

A year later construction was midway through its on-time schedule, designers and decorators taking up most of Elixia's time when she wasn't working as a waitress, eager job applicants stealing what little was left of her days. The one breath of freedom she allowed herself was a week set aside from her schedule to attend Gilligan's graduation and share in her gift which was extravagant though she couldn't resist the temptation of a fleeting seven days in a Miami she'd heard so much about.

With the week over, Elixia more tanned than her lover, she flew home to Paris. Gilligan Rose flew to Los Angeles to begin her training as a flight attendant with Trans-Global Airlines. She was exhausted. As much as her heart ached to be with Elixia she felt she could sleep for a week.

She hated sleeping on planes, sometimes waking to discover that what she hated didn't matter. She hated feeling the seating fabric on her bare bum; she knew what people did on planes: things most or many would never think to do at home. However Elixia loved seeing her in short skirts, thongs and sexy blouses, which was much more important.

She could scarcely believe they'd been together four years or that she had a degree from one of the world's finest universities or that she would begin her training a week later, exhausted at the end of each day. She would speak on the phone each weekend afternoon, hearing the news from France, hearing sobs and tears wiped away, kisses, regrets and hopes, dreams and aspirations, hearing what Elixia was hearing, each night drifting into a dimly lit slumber, weeping, her last night 220 feet above the sand, her private patio 500 feet from the shore. She had a new home. So what? Without Elixia her home was empty.

At Christmas she flew to France, returning after New Year's and celebrating a birthday somewhat early to begin her career. Her gift was a diamond ring. She'd never seen one as clear.

Neither girl was into gauche public displays, neither girl thought of herself as a lesbian. They went to regular clubs and restaurants with nothing to prove, young women drawn inextricably together and that was nobody's business. That la famille de Montfort embraced Gilligan with open arms and hearts was enough. She had family, yet quietly they wondered when seeing her gift why she cried tears they each knew were unhappy.

Deep in her heart Elixia knew that one day she would hear the truth when Gilligan was ready. She knew Gilligan hadn't told her the entire truth, if any. And she knew why. Gilligan was so foolish to think she would not understand.

The flights from Paris to New York and on to LAX were arduously boring; sleep her eventual escape from excruciating monotony. She switched on the overhead light, curling into her seat to nap, alone in the row, her dreams her sole freedom from darkness. Though when would her dream become real, when would Gilligan stop slipping away with the morning sun?

She arrived home depleted to a half-furnished condo. She hadn't much time for shopping. She froze where she stood in the doorway. There on her couch was Gilligan Rose, standing, running towards her, her hands outstretched, her wide eyes sparkling like deep green jewels, her lustrous red hair bouncing at her shoulders. She wanted to cry, resisting the urge. She wanted to speak, unable to. She wanted to awaken from such a horribly cruel dream, trapped in inescapable slumber. She felt Gilligan's warm lips pressing on hers, her wet tears mixing with hers, her sweet breath whispering into her ears as though she'd never gone away.

"I've waited so very long to see you, darling. Do you

remember how mother would call you darling?"

"I remember each night. She called you darling too. I miss her terribly and I've missed you terribly. You cannot be real. I'm having another bad dream."

"Yes, I am real. The man in the office thought I was you. He gave me a key. I knew I would find you. I knew that I would. I never stopped searching once I was free."

"I never stopped searching for you because my name was Collette Salazar."

"I didn't know your name was Collette Salazar."

"Did you bring mother. Is mother here with you? Did you find mother also?"

"No, I did not. I found you."

"Is mother dead, Gilligan? Do you think so?"

"No. I don't think so. Mother is alive."

"I should never have killed father, though I'm glad that I did. Then mother would be here with you. I miss mother's faces. Do you know I've begun painting too?"

"You must remember that I killed him also. I'm as guilty as you."

"Yes, when he was already dead. That's when you killed him. I was the one who killed father first. That's what I remember and you are not as guilty as me. I don't think so."

"I never did like mother's faces. They made me afraid. Do you think I was wrong not to tell her? Please tell me you don't paint faces like hers."

"No. I paint nude women. Nudes make me feel good. Nudes somehow are innocent and free. They like how I paint them and they like being nude when they're with me. I think so, innocent and free."

"Where have you been? I never stopped looking."

"I've been all over the world. I now speak Spanish and French. Did you know?"

"I speak Spanish and French also and now I know about father. It's good that he's dead. I know that now and you should know too. We were right to kill him. We did the right thing."

"I know that we did."

"Are you in love with someone I know?"

Gilligan kissed her ring. "Yes, I am in love, with a beautiful girl who lives in Paris. She's the girl I paint most. So, are you in love too?"

"No. I have no one to love but you. I talk with you each night. I thought you would know. I never stopped searching and I'm glad you're in love, that you're no longer sad. When can I meet her?"

Gilligan shook her head. "How can you meet her? No. I don't think that you can. What would I tell her? How would I explain you after so many years?"

"She doesn't know…about mother or about father? She doesn't know about me?"

"She doesn't know. I told her a lie. I told her that mother killed father and how could I tell her about you. Who would believe me? Who would ever believe what father did?"

"Do you remember, Gilligan, when we whispered in bed with our noses touching?"

"Yes, I do, when we had fun, when we danced in the rain with mother. Not after he hurt us. I try not to think of his smell or the way that he hurt us."

"That's why you were always so sad. Are you ever that sad now?"

"I will never really be happy, not happy like you. I don't think so. I should never have killed father, or lied about mother, though I should have killed the others, the couple who bought me, who wanted only to hurt me."

"You're wrong about father. We were right to kill him the way that we did and one day we will see mother again. I think so. I know we will see mother again. One day when Zeke Phillips is dead and no one can hurt mother."

"Did you ever see Wendy once you were free?"

"I saw her when Zeke's lawyer refused to help me. I suppose you're very wealthy too."

Gilligan nodded. "Yes, I am. I don't have to work a day in my life though I still want to fly the way that we said and I do."

"I begin flying the day after tomorrow, though not all the time. I want to help people with my money."

"And I want to paint when I'm not flying. I'm really quite good. Perhaps I can paint you."

"Then I would have you to see when you're not with me." Cheeks were still wet, eyes glistening with tears. "Then we should fly together and never be lost again."

"We can fly together. I think so, and whisper each night in our bed when I'm not with Elixia. I don't see why not. Do you remember our times with Wendy? We can fly together. I know that we can and are you still afraid of the dark?"

Gilligan nodded again. "I sleep with a light in my room. I am still afraid of the dark and will be until I die because of what father did. I think so."

"Tell me about Wendy."

"I went to see Wendy when I was searching for you. I thought you might still love her and that I might find you with her. She's very pretty and in love with another, a pretty young girl, though I believe she loves you as much as before. I think so. She was sorry I lost you. She hopes that I find you and now that I have we can see her together."

"I'm glad she's in love and, yes, we can see her together."

"Why are you smiling?"

"If I hadn't killed father I would never have met my Elixia. Perhaps you should kill someone too, someone like father. I want you to love someone soon."

"I will one day soon. Do you know I like Latinas because of you, because you let me kiss Wendy and touch her all over? You should. I've told you so often."

"Do you think we love girls for the same reason I killed father?"

"I killed him because I love you."

"That was my reason too."

"Can I stay for the night? Can I sleep in your bed and whisper all that I want to say? I have so much to tell you."

"Yes, you can stay for the night. Of course you can stay for the night. How else will I keep you? I never forgot how you look."

Gilligan giggled. "How can you forget how I look? I look just like you when I look in the mirror. We are each other."

"I'm so tired, Gilligan. I could sleep for a week."

"Then how will you hear me?"

"I will hear you, the same way that each night I find you, in my dreams. I won't ever let you go, not ever again. And one day we will find mother together and one day you will help me tell Elixia that I really killed father. Then I can be happy like you. I think so. But for now let's go to bed. I have so much to tell you."

When Gilligan woke she lay quietly, her eyes closed, her mind puzzled, wondering why she'd slept at all, her pillow wet from a nighttime of tears, her ears straining for sound, her nose testing the air. She wasn't onboard a 747 whirring its way through a black sky above a continent too far below to see, curled into her seat. She was at home in her bed crying.

She wanted badly to call Elixia to worsen one lie and confess to another, lies that each day would grow more difficult to explain.

She whispered into her pillow, "I love you so much, Gilligan. I have never stopped loving you."

"I love you so much too. I've told you each night with my eyes closed to the dark and hoped you could hear so that one day you might find me. Instead I found you. We will do this again, talk under the covers."

Twenty-Eight
This Year: South Beach, June 23rd

The air was stifling, heat hovering over the sand in visible ripples. The turquoise sea was calm save for white splashes around youthful and half-naked bodies. Old men stood waist-deep in the warm water gawking, old women gasping with the shame of it all: a veritable feast of nubile flesh for the eyes.

Her top was clenched in his fist.

"I won't tell you again, Fennell."

"You're in the ocean, sweetcheeks. Who can see?"

"We're on assignment. This isn't funny."

He sighed, disappointed. She was right, of course. He set her onto the ocean floor, Deena's mouth and brown eyes opening wide. She pushed him away, thrashing and sputtering, intent on clasping her thong in place with one hand while the other flailed blindly in search of four strings that seconds earlier were holding the minuscule triangle together. She wanted to punch him and she would, later.

"I always draw the tough assignments."

She held out her hand. "Give me, unless you miss your dirty-minded bachelor life and want to live on the street."

He handed over the triangles. "That hurt."

She made a face and left him, not waiting long before glancing over her shoulder, pointing and snapping her fingers. "You...right here, right now. Move it."

He pushed through the water to join her. He adored her, sweeping her into his arms, carrying her towards their lounge chairs. She was squirming, a little.

"Sorry, water in the ears. What was that?"

"Why don't you put my bare butt on a platter and pass me around for a midday snack?"

"Okay." He shrugged, flipping her like a burger. "Sorry, sweetcheeks."

"Put me down." Struggle was futile. "Sorry for what now?"

"Nobody's looking, which isn't surprising. You are a year older after all, which doesn't mean I still don't love you despite, you know, the flaws inherent with aging, which," he hastened to add, "really are not that noticeable to the casual observer."

People were watching and smiling, envious, half the men wishing they could lift their knees as high, most of the women having long forgotten any such feeling of weightlessness.

She snorted. "You find a single flaw on this divine body and I will tell my father he's wrong about you, and my mother that she doesn't need glasses."

"Yeah, she thinks I'm handsome and charming."

"No. No. She said 'reasonably handsome for a cop' and 'charmingly rude' Get it straight. Now put me down."

He flipped her again, easing her to her feet.

"Your ass is beautiful, divine and mouth-watering like a well-done filet mignon: round, juicy and tender. Sort of makes a guy hungry."

She smacked him, taking his hand. "Save your appetite. I've got lunch plans."

At their chairs Fennell ordered Coronas, nursing them for an hour. They were on the job and Gilligan Rose never ate lunch before two, pretty much ending her day in the sun.

"So what's your guess, happy or sad, perky or glum? What's the Gilligan Rose du jour?"

"She was having girl problems, sweetheart. Xara wants them to live together and Gilligan doesn't feel ready. Give her a break. Even killers have love lives."

"Two girls are a problem...really? Since when would that be?"

"Gee, I don't know, darling, possibly since whenever you're stupid enough to let me find you with one who's not called Deena."

"Good answer."

"I thought so."

Their beers finished, they walked quietly for a while, stopping at a shower where he commandeered her body to remove all but the most stubborn specks of sand.

"I won't be far. And Deena," he was serious, "don't let her give me a reason."

"Don't be silly."

"That's right. I'm silly. So humour me."

He patted the side pocket of his bag.

She hugged him tightly anyway. He never wore cargos, hence nowhere to conceal a weapon. He wore Italian and French micro-fibre straight-backs, claiming that with the exceptions of South Beach, Venice Beach, Québec and Mexico, North American men wore cargos to camouflage certain and distinct anatomical deficiencies despite how ridiculous they looked weighted down by three-quarter and lined, belted and zipper-laden pants in the frigging ocean.

"This is weird, sweetheart. We're three weeks away. I was never trained for this at the academy."

"You're doing what no one else can. Don't tell me you're not thinking of the expressions in the squad room when this breaks."

"I'm thinking of my wedding, of my groom standing beside me...alive."

"Your handsome groom, remember." He stopped her. "You're on your own." He patted her bum. "Go."

"I love you."

He made a stupid face. "Duh."

She smacked him and walked southward meandering

aimlessly to a specific spot not far from the gate of Gilligan Rose's time-share.

To passers-by Johnnie Fennell was a creep, a voyeur, a sicko. No one knew he'd previously taken a thousand shots of her thong-bare butt, a thousand more without her thong claiming he couldn't decide on which were the best, which he should keep. He was a creep, one of hundreds, one of them.

One team of cops approached from behind, a male-female combo, thinking what everyone else was thinking, unaccustomed to someone not stopping for them, not intimidated, eyeing the gold-blue shield as Fennell maintained his pace. The woman was visibly disappointed. She was young, a newbie upset that she couldn't crash her knee into a pervert's neck. The cop with her, not much older, looked straight ahead to an almost naked Agent Deena Archer who was strutting her stuff, Fennell reading his mind. He was thinking that he might like to join The Federal Task Force. Yeah, good luck with that. He told them to go play in the sand or he'd arrest them for interfering with a federal investigation.

Under a baseball cap and glasses Johnnie Fennell left them behind, slowing lazily to a stop some twenty minutes later. She said 'I love you, sweetheart' into her pendant and he sank onto a lounge chair leaving a few hundred feet between them. He could hear every word; see every kiss on the cheek and friendly embrace, or anything that would make him shoot Gilligan Rose where she sat.

"Hey, hi, remember me."

Gilligan Rose glanced up from her Kindle, shading her eyes.

"Deena, hi, and yes I remember you. I'm sorry. I should have called."

"Don't be." She giggled. "It's not like we're dating."

Gilligan stood, hugging her, kissing her cheeks. "That's your fault, not mine."

"Sitting alone today?"

"No. I'm with Xara. You remember, I told you about her. She's in the water. The better question is: why you're alone when you're looking...well, so incredibly fantastic?"

"I don't know. It's like I've got a price tag showing somewhere that's a little too pricey...or a wart somewhere I can't see."

"Price isn't an issue, not here, and I think if you had a wart I would have seen it by now. So I'm thinking either blind or stupid men." She sat, making room for Deena. "I do know a few girls who aren't blind or stupid."

Deena sat. "If things don't improve I may have to start rethinking that alternative." She glanced towards the ocean. "Your girlfriend won't mind. I can leave if I'm going to cause girl waves."

"Xara won't mind. She's the one in the green bikini. Well, her thong's green anyway. She acts like a little girl whenever she's in the Atlantic. The water's different at home."

"I don't see green anywhere."

Gilligan waved towards the ocean for Xara to notice, smiling as the woman pranced through the water to the sand. "That green. That's Xara."

"Wow! She's gorgeous. You're a lucky girl. How did you meet?"

"Join us for lunch and we'll tell you all the dirty details."

"Ooh. My condo's being renovated. I recently decided to make a few changes; otherwise I would love to have you and Xara for lunch and a dip. Next time, I promise. Let's fix a place to meet after we've changed." She was following Xara's saunter. "What a darling. Is she so cheerful all the time?"

"At times she's too cheerful, which you're about to discover."

Xara stopped at the foot of the side-by-side chaises-longues.

"Do not tell me, you are Deena."

"I am Deena. Hi. Wow, I'm surprised you know about me."

Xara stooped lower, pressing her lips into each of Deena's cheeks, Deena wanting to tell her pendant to grow up. So what if the girl was wet, naked except for a single eye patch, tanned and stunning.

Xara towelled herself, pulled away her kerchief and combed out her hair before reaching for her top.

"Yes, I know about you, that you like white wine and shopping. Gilligan's friends are my friends as well. We talk about you once in a while. We think it is unfortunate that we cannot see more of each other, the three of us." She looked to Gilligan. "I suppose we are doing lunch and shopping. ¿Es verdad, chica?"

"Sí, claro, with Deena."

Deena, she couldn't help thinking, felt like shit. Undercover work to build a case, to get into someone's head, that was one thing. This was off the chart. Nothing was ever written in the code book about liking the perp.

She said, "Sometimes I really don't like what I have to do, happily lunch and shopping aren't two of them. I was telling Gilligan how lovely you are," she smiled, "from a hetero perspective."

Xara squeezed her again. "We do not mind at all that you are one of them. Besides, chica, the way you are dressed you could easily pass for one of us."

"I think I'm getting jealous, Xarita," Gilligan added.

"It is good to be jealous, chica."

"I'm anxious to know how you met." Deena raised her wrist. "Can I have an hour to make sure I'm not the ugly sister in the group?"

The three agreed on a time, a place and what to wear, Deena surviving more hugs and kisses, Johnnie Fennell barely surviving.

The women slipped into sarongs and muslin beach dresses before parting, Deena choosing the stone walkway shaded with palm leaves over the beach, the others disappearing onto the pool deck of their gated time-share complex. Deena told him through her pendant where to meet her. At the second watch tower she came to she stepped onto the sand, Johnnie Fennell watching her as the lifeguard called the Beach Patrol. They were in a hurry and needed a lift pronto, and the kid didn't argue with his leather bound credentials.

They arrived home five minutes later to a newly decorated and refurnished penthouse. The contractors had finished their work weeks earlier.

"So that's the famous Xara. Little Miss Gilligan Rose did okay for herself. That's one tasty burrito"

"She's adorable, sweetheart. This is going to devastate her." Deena stripped away her dress and bikini, stepping into the shower. "You know, really, sweetheart. Why did we ever start this? I mean, really. Why?"

"First off, you keep that question between us and get a little balance. We didn't start this. She did. We're stopping her. Killing ten deviants is one thing. Okay, I agree, the world's a better place without them. That's fine. That's understood and not the main reason she's going down. She committed ten perfect murders. She just didn't know when to stop. The reason she's going to prison to stop her from killing fifteen or twenty more and possibly by the time she gets out she'll have forgotten how to kill. And tell me this, Deena. How would you sleep before and after July 15th for the next twenty years if we don't stop her? She's not stopping anytime soon without us."

"Still, I feel like a total shit. I can't imagine when she sees me in New York."

"Don't imagine, and don't care. Okay, so she's killed a few freaks. She's done good work, I agree with that between us. But tell me what happens when she comes across some lonely guy, divorced or separated, some guy who can't get a girl because he can't get it up, some guy just doing innocent stuff on the web that she doesn't agree with. Those CDs in our bedroom aren't instructional videos from the ladies' temperance league, sweetcheeks." He smirked. "They're more like instructional videos for those two. I wonder what Gilligan Rose and Mendiga would think of that? And don't think for a moment that they don't have their own collection. This is classic Jekyll and Hyde."

She reached out for a towel. "Sometimes I don't like you, sweetheart."

He understood. She was going through a woman thing. "When, exactly?"

"When you're right and I don't want you to be."

He pondered a moment, watching her pat herself dry. "Yeah, I suppose that can be annoying from another's perspective, like when I helped you fall in love with me because you were too shy to come out and say that you were."

She threw her towel at him. "No, like right now when you're being annoying."

He watched her blow-dry her hair. "There aren't enough adjectives for how phenomenal you look."

"Don't suck up. In fact, go away. Lay out my new linen slacks and blouse with something white to wear underneath and don't be a pig. Please. And put my weapon in the safe."

She watched him walk out, smiling.

He came in five minutes later. "Your wardrobe awaits, Majesty. And might this most humble of servants praise your Majesty for the excellence of her royal nakedness and her most divine aspects?"

"Sweetheart, I feel like a sneak. I'm going to spend my afternoon doing lunch and shopping with these ladies like we're best friends. I don't think I'm cut out for this. This isn't in the job description."

"Correction: one lady, a cute one by the way with

certain pleasant characteristics, and one killer with one not so pleasant characteristic. In addition to which you are not a sneak. You're a spy. We've never been this close to the homey Gilligan Rose, the cozy lesbian with her pants down or her skirt up, so to speak."

Her mouth dropped open. "That is so totally male."

"No, it's not, and I've got the CDs to prove it." He sat on the bed. He loved watching her dress, though he enjoyed the inverse much more. "Deena, seriously, try to get some alone time with Mendiga. She'll have a different perspective on the redhead."

"I think I've got that figured out, sweetheart."

He nodded. He didn't have to ask. He stood, clasping the pendant at the nape of her neck.

"I won't be far."

"If I know anything, sweetheart, I know that." She cinched her belt. "By the way, I like you again, until the next time you're a fennell. I do have to admit you've made remarkable progress in eleven months."

He checked his weapon. "Thank you."

"I didn't say complete. I said remarkable. Now kiss me," she smiled, "or I'll be late for work."

She had a way of smiling: full glossy lips, ever so slightly pinched at one corner and framed by shallow dimples, her brown, liquid eyes always in agreement.

The evening passed slowly for him, his ears plugged with distant girl talk. He would never say so. He couldn't. However Deena was right. Imagining Gilligan Rose as a killer was difficult. She was the envy of most models, let alone Miss or Mrs. Average. There was nothing average about her. He could well imagine Mendiga's world exploding apart or imploding, crushing her heart. She wasn't involved. They knew that. She was an innocent bystander waiting without knowing for her catastrophic and inescapable tsunami.

Girl talk became chatter when lunch was over and

shopping began. He shook his head. He had to chuckle at a couple of millionaires arguing over a luncheon bill of a hundred dollars, snorting when he heard, without seeing, Mendiga grabbing for the chit.

After shopping, and more shopping, Fennell thinking he would have to move his clothes into another room, Gilligan invited Deena to dinner. Unfortunately she simply couldn't. She had a family commitment, until Johnnie Fennell thought he heard wrong.

"I will join you for just one glass of wine, though, if you ladies don't mind."

"You will upset us, chica, if you do not. We would believe that you do not like us after such a fantastic afternoon."

Fennell didn't like the pause, not at all, his face twisted with the worry of what he would hear next. He didn't have to imagine the three women standing at the outside lectern. He could see them.

Gilligan Rose added, "You do like us, don't you, Deena?"

He watched as Gilligan Rose wrapped an arm around the love of his life, his future wife, a federal agent, squeezing, Mendiga with her head tilted waiting for an answer. He could imagine Gayle Brannigan convulsing her way into a coma.

"I'll stay for one glass. I'd love to hear more about you ladies. And, yes, you're both very disarming."

Okay, not a bad response, he agreed.

"And we will drink slowly, chica, to keep you with us longer," Mendiga went on.

Shit! No! She was getting in over her head.

Xara Mendiga, apparently frustrated with waiting for the hostess, led the herd to a table the three agreed upon, first looking this way and that, repeating the process.

He thought what the hell; just sit your pretty asses down. The one glass lasted an hour. How was that even possible, Fennell wondered? He'd gone through three. Then, as Deena pushed her seat from the table, standing to leave, stooping to hug and kiss their cheeks, which was bad enough, he thought, Fennell's head exploded. He was experiencing an aneurysm.

"Chica, we are only halfway through our vacation. Spend the rest of our time with us at the beach. We promise. We will not try to convert you. ¿No es verdad, querida?"

He could see Mendiga smirking.

Gilligan Rose said, "That's a great idea, Deena. It'll be fun. Please spend more time with us."

Deena was thinking. He knew the look, he knew her eyes. She had something in her head that wasn't good.

"Ladies, I can't, as much as I would love to. Duty calls. I don't work a normal schedule." She hesitated. "But I am free most of tomorrow, just not for dinner."

Xara Mendiga squeezed Deena's hand. "Then we will make the day seems like three. Gracias, chica."

"Tell me what time, ladies."

Gilligan Rose answered. "Let's say ten or any time after that's good for you. We'll make the most of the day. I'll reserve our lounge chairs. I suppose you'll want to get away from your contractors as early as possible."

"You suppose right. I'll see you at ten. You ladies enjoy your evening. I have a distinct feeling you will more than me."

You're damned right about that one, Agent Archer, Fennell muttered. People nearby turning to stare.

The three kissed and hugged again. Deena walked beyond their line of sight, hailed a cab and climbed out a few blocks later waiting for the storm to approach, which he did.

"I know you think I messed up, but…"

"Messed up? No. You fucked up, big time, and this doesn't go away with a little toss in the pool and a few kisses, Deena. You shouldn't even be on this case. This is serious shit. Brannigan put her nuts in a grinder over this because of us. Now you do this stupid thing after having the gall to wonder what Rose will think of you in three weeks. Walk, and don't say a single word, not one word. I don't give a shit what she thinks of you, me, or anyone else. The broad's a fucking killer and she's going down. I'm putting her ass in prison. The one thing that'll keep her from death row is her satanic head and you want a day at the beach with her. Shit!"

"Sweetheart..."

"Sweetheart, yeah, that's what I am. I'm your sweetheart and that's the real problem. I'm not Fennell, or the prick, or the asshole, or any of the other endearments you once used when talking about me with your fellow female agents." He looked straight ahead. "Yeah, I knew. I also knew you had my ass covered. Now I'm your sweetheart. What the hell was I thinking?"

Deena's heart constricted. "Don't say that. Don't ever say that. Can I explain?"

"Explain what? I heard every word. I heard every time you swallowed your food or drank your wine. Explain what?"

"Nothing."

"That's about right."

Not during their first six months together was he ever that upset with her. He never raised his voice, not once.

She blurted, "I love you, sweetheart."

"I love you, Deena. So what? That's us. This is her. You're off the case. So let's not say anything more until we get home. I'm working real hard here at not having a stroke."

That wasn't good enough for her. She grabbed his hand, closing her eyes and breathing deeply when he squeezed hers and didn't let go.

*

At the penthouse Johnnie Fennell changed into a pair of

micro-fibre straight-backs. He poured a glass of wine and went onto the deck, taking the bottle with him. He eased into the spa, groaning away the day, thankful for the curative heat.

He knew he overreacted, watching her pad across the deck in a teddy, her glass empty.

"I used to relax in here at night whenever I was pissed with you, which was quite often, Fennell. Does that make us sort of even?"

"No, it does not."

"Then I've decided that I'm phoning Brannigan tomorrow, taking myself off the case."

"No, you are not. I overreacted. What you're going to do is get in here, let me fill your glass, and talk with me. Tell me why you did what you did."

She hesitated, her expression serious, not coy or demure. "Then are you going to toss me into the pool?"

He thought about it, reaching for her glass. "Yes. I'm tossing you into the pool and I'm marrying you in five weeks."

"Thank you. I was sort of hoping you would."

"You're welcome."

"I love you, sweetheart."

"Don't push your luck. What you did was wrong. Just get in here and talk. Tell me why and please don't say anything to cause my cardiac arrest."
*

Deena was tossed into the pool, despite the fact that he disagreed with her.

Crazy or sane, schizophrenic or balanced made no difference to him. He was quite certain the dead guys would agree. Deena thought differently. Something about Gilligan Rose didn't sit right with her. A wealthy woman with a stunning partner, a luxury condo, a good job that she didn't need, simply wouldn't go around killing men once a year. Not for a moment the previous day did she appear remotely as though she had a dark side, a split personality? Not then.

He was willing to let her do her thing. What he did differently was to book a hotel room directly behind where Deena would spend her day. She really didn't need him. She was equally good without her weapon as with one, which he'd discovered the hard way at the gym during their first week together when he wanted to know personally how good she was. He wasn't accepting some senator's baby girl who'd get him killed one day because she drew her compact instead of her weapon. He changed his mind quickly enough while sitting on the floor in a daze, feeling the sting where her foot made contact with his jockstrap, stunned where her other foot made contact with his padded head. She was no less conciliatory when, a nanosecond later, she kicked his feet from the floor into the air. She didn't bother helping him to stand because he was the man, which was why he specifically forbade her from going topless. If he couldn't see her perky twins, no one else would.

She agreed.

He scoped them from eighteen floors and a room-service meal of sandwiches and soft drinks. The beer he brought from home, twisting the first cap at 10:30, listening. Rose and Mendiga understood listening to Deena explain that topless wasn't such a good idea because she lived there. Not that she wouldn't like to, she added, if she were in Europe or the islands. The women agreed and kept theirs on so she wouldn't feel out of place

He had to admit, there wasn't anything better on the beach that he could see up close and personal for a half-mile in either direction.

Mendiga dragged them both into the water. He shook his head imagining Brannigan transferring him to the mailroom after reading his report of June 24th. Subject: Special Agent Deena Archer played beach ball with lesbian killer and lesbian killer's girlfriend in thongs. He was thinking he would write something different.

They frolicked for an hour, prancing from the water holding hands, chasing the ball with their feet. He thought, okay, the day was a third over. They would have a relaxing lunch, take some sun, take more time in the water, and then part company. Not quite, in fact far from not quite he discovered.

He stepped from the scope to the tripod-mounted 500mm Nikkor attached to a Nikon D3X that was his Christmas gift.

Deena was reaching into her beach bag. Rose was easing onto her front, adjusting her hat. Mendiga was kneeling over her with a leg on either side.

"Don't bother creaming, Deena. Xarita's a fabulous masseuse. If you ever wanted to blow a few minds this is the time."

Deena tapped her pendant. "This is weird. I'm sitting watching one lesbian giving another lesbian a massage and waiting for my turn. You've got to know you're in some guy's viewfinder."

"So are you, Deena, but when you're floating in heaven you don't care who's watching." Gilligan Rose moaned. "You'll see."

"I don't know. For some reason I had the impression that lesbians were super jealous, especially beautiful lesbians."

Xara giggled. "We are like you people, chica. We can look if we do not touch."

"Then how do I get my massage."

"Until you leave us you are an honorary member. We can do that in these special cases. We are allowed, and we think you are special. We talked about you last night at dinner. We missed you."

"Thank you. I'm honoured." She watched, intrigued. "I feel sorry for anyone working."

Xara patted Gilligan's buttocks. "Wake up, querida, and turn over."

Xara began at Gilligan's feet working her way to her breasts, massaging discreetly around her triangles to her neck, shifting her weight onto the sand to finish with her cheeks, forehead and temples.

Johnnie Fennell figured she was a size four.

"She is sleeping. She always sleeps during a rub. Flip over, chica," she said to Deena, waiting to position herself.

She drew lines of white cream from Deena's hips to her ankles and began with the soles of her feet. With the back of her legs done Deena was in a dream state. She'd never been touched as intimately by a woman. What she'd told Gilligan earlier was a lie. There was never a curious girl who moved to Idaho.

Xara's hands were kneading her buttocks, Deena hiding her disappointed when she was finished.

"Hmm, I know what Gilligan meant by floating in heaven."

Xara spanked her. "Cállate, chica. Speaking is not permitted."

Fennell was thinking he'd resign over the phone and hurry down to pull up another lounge chair. He was forcing himself not to be angry. Another blowout would be difficult for them to recover from and he couldn't deny that seeing Mendiga's bare ass planted on Deena's bare ass wasn't hard to take.

With her hands at Deena's shoulders, Xara shifted her weight into the sand. "Flip over, chica."

She did, moaning into her pendant. She knew Fennell was watching, zoomed in, virtually with them, which isn't why she moaned.

Xara did her toes one by one, her calves and her thighs, working her way to her hips and her belly. She'd never felt a bare woman sitting on her, let alone there. Xara didn't ask, scarcely touching her triangles while massaging around her breasts. Deena missed her weight instantly, feeling herself drift to another place, a place of calm and quiet as

Xara worked her chin, cheeks and temples.

Johnnie Fennell watched Mendiga squirm between her chair and Deena's.

"Hmm, I have to say that was very sexy. I'm thinking I should take out a full membership."

"I do this for Gilligan all the time. Her job is very demanding. First-Class does not always imply classy. Her life is very stressful working with jerks. And, yes, doing this with her is very sexy."

"That's why I'm so surprised Gilligan didn't mind. I mean, wow!"

"We want you to visit us in Long Beach, to stay with us. We each have a big place with a guest room. Come for a week."

"You don't live together. I'm so surprised. Why not, Xara? I don't think you could breathe without each other."

"My querida has a few hang-ups. She has a history that is very personal that we are working through. We love each other deeply, yet I continue to leave in the morning. She does too when she stays over. For that reason morning is my worst time of day." She reached over, patting Gilligan's leg. "She sleeps so peacefully once her eyes are closed. She is afraid of the dark, Deena."

"She told me not too long ago about her father and her mother. I couldn't stop thinking about her for the longest time."

"She was hurt very badly, and still she is not fully recovered. And yes, her mother was very brave to do what she did to protect her." Xara pulled her feet onto the lounge chair. The midday sun was beginning to burn her. "Everyone likes her so much, yet she has no real friends apart from the few that we share. So will you come, perhaps in the fall or the spring, perhaps for a week?"

"I can't tell you, Xara, how much I truly want to be able to do that." She looked at Gilligan sleeping peacefully, reaching out for Xara's hand. "I really do wish I could help her. I would do anything to help her. I want you to believe that. It's very important to me that you do."

"She told me a few times how nice you are. Now I see for myself, though I knew yesterday as soon as I saw you, chica."

"Just believe me."

"I do."

"You're beginning to turn pink." She took the SPF bottle from Xara's hand. "Lie down, chica, and be quiet."

Xara's mouth opened wide with playful amazement "You want to lotion me, chica, really?"

"I am going to lotion you. I'll tell you when I'm done if I really wanted to."

Fennell didn't believe a 16GB would be enough capture the mood.

Twenty-minutes later:

"So, chica, did you want to? Should we sign you up for full membership?"

"I'm thinking I could be convinced."

*

He watched them say goodbye. He watched Rose feign disgust as Mendiga went about brushing sand from every part of Deena that wasn't covered. He watched them hug and kiss, listening to Mendiga tell Deena that she was still honorary until their time together was over, kissing her shocked mouth as well as he ever did, waving a final goodbye.

Thirty minutes later Deena was at home. Johnnie Fennell walked in ten minutes behind her.

"Did you get what you wanted?"

"I believe I did, and I suppose a little more than I expected. And you?"

"Yeah, I'd say about three hundred. So how did you feel being fondled by a lesbian from head to toe, twice, and reciprocating? I have to say I was pretty lonesome up here when I saw you spanking each other."

"Don't be a pig. She gave me a massage, I gave her one, and we weren't spanking. We were patting. There's a difference so don't get all horny on me. However, if you must know, yes, I felt sexy both ways…very sexy"

"I know, I heard."

"In Rio I am definitely getting massages." Deena stepped into the shower. "I am right, sweetheart. The woman's troubled."

"Yeah, I heard that too. She's afraid of the boogeyman when, really, he should be afraid of her."

"That was insensitive." She stepped out. "So were you turned on?"

"I still am."

"Good because I'm having a headache for a few days."

"You're as horny as I am and think about this. In three weeks your friend is going to try to murder me. Maybe you can have my funeral in Long Beach, you know, after your massage.

"I didn't hear that because when she's arrested we're going to do what we can to help her, you and me. The Gilligan Rose at the beach today isn't the one you know."

"That's right. She's never kissed me. Is she a good kisser?"

"You're being a pig again. She didn't kiss me like that; Xara did, and yes she is a very good kisser…pig."

"You put a truckload of shit in the wind today, sweetcheeks, just to find out what we already know. Because of you Mendiga's going to fall apart when she hears about all this, if she doesn't already know. And if she doesn't, imagine finding out that your girlfriend's a serial killer and that she massaged the arresting officer's sweet ass."

"She doesn't know. She might know that Emma Rose murdered her husband, not about Gilligan. No way she's an accomplice."

"Still, the next time you meet, I'd suggest a Kevlar vest.

Don't imagine for a moment that she'll believe or remember how much you want to help. Nice touch, Deena, albeit way out of line. And another thing, you're writing this report since you now have such a more intimate perspective. I'm your partner in this, I just don't agree with what you did. No kidding. And let me remind you that is the job, not us."

"I meant what I said."

"Yeah, I know, and ditto for me, sweetcheeks. As hot as you are, and you are, you stepped over the line…with my full support. That doesn't mean we're not drowning in shit creek."

Twenty-Nine
Ten Years Ago: July 15th

For a year or more she thought the worst: that she would fly short-haul for years on twin-prop equipment between towns no one knew. Such wasn't the case. She arrived for her first interview with well-received credentials. She was a frequent flyer and had studied the industry when she wasn't cramming for exams; she had a degree with honours and spoke two foreign languages fluently. She had letters of reference from the dean, Elixia's brother who now worked for the French Trade Commission and from the French Consul whom she met one evening at dinner, both men frequent and First-Class passengers onboard TGA.

Her flights throughout the first six months were onboard 747s in Coach from LAX to JFK, returning the same day or the day after. The second half of her novice year she worked First-Class and never looked back, frequently crossing the ocean to Paris on long weekends as a First-Class passenger.

Elixia's Les Filles du Ciel opened for business in August to a full house.

Gilligan began her second year on flight 3310 from L.A. to New York and on to Paris. Her fourth trip was in August which she worked into a week's vacation. She hadn't seen Elixia's brother since her graduation. She must have hugged him a dozen times much to his glee for the advice he'd given her five years earlier. He was shocked, at once refusing the overly generous gift. She ignored him. She was adamant and locked the gold-face Cartier onto his wrist herself. The inscription on the back read: Tu n'est pas trop mauvais pour un gars. Nor was he, she thought, too bad for a guy. She didn't think so.

He thanked her with a kiss and an invitation to the finest cabaret in France with his parents whom she knew well, proudly announcing each half-hour throughout the evening.
*
One month before the gala event she met Fred Billows in the lobby of his hotel. She'd seen him many times previously in First-Class. He liked his Rémy Martin and he liked porn. He liked little girls dressed as big girls and big girls dressed as little girls. His daughter's name was Lucy. She was thirteen. He liked her the most.

Gilligan was cognizant of the intimate perversion due to a previous flight which was seriously delayed due to strong headwinds and bad weather. Short on time and flustered he had forgotten to stow his computer into his briefcase before disembarking the aircraft. When, much too late and clearly distraught, he struggled against a relentless surge of other deplaning travellers the laptop was gone.

He was beside himself hearing that neither the captain nor the crew could help him. The plane was empty, though they went through the motions of searching overhead bins and under seats. They commiserated with his predicament; unfortunately he was a victim of his own negligence and someone else's opportunity. Such occurrences were not uncommon.

The next morning Gilligan had a vivid understanding of Mr. Billows, including that he had visited Bangkok a few months earlier. That poor girl looked younger than Lucy, her face without expression, her eyes sad and pleading. When Gilligan was done viewing the slide show, her dinner untouched and cold on the table beside her, she spent a sleepless and haunted night deleting the images, washing her prints with soap and water from the casing and keyboard.

She dropped the computer into a trash can outside the airport.

A month later he boarded once more in New York. He was drinking mimosas for breakfast, Rémy Martin between the wine he enjoyed with lunch and his cut-off prior to landing at Heathrow at five PM local time, his new computer recently loaded with Lucy and Bangkok, the same photos she had enlarged to FULL SCREEN making herself physically ill.

She had often suspected that she would one day assuage the guilt she harboured for what she'd done to her mother, never certain, that dark anxiety in large part defining her. She knew he would be onboard that day. She was ready. She had practiced what she would do and what she would not, fully aware of what that meant.

She went into the lavatory to change from her pantyhose into stockings.

He was the last passenger whose tray she cleared away.

"Another Rémy Martin, Mr. Billows?" she asked, her name tag somehow misplaced.

"Yes."

She returned with his glass on a tray, half-filled. She wanted to make a good impression, not intending to drop several canapé napkins onto the floor. The thin strip of sheer white at the bare tops of her thighs caught his eye like a beacon. She'd practiced that as well night after night in front of a mirror. He was fixated, Gilligan discreetly widening and narrowing the white gap without depriving him of the naked curves of her buttocks. She gave him the count of twenty, despising and loathing that he was ogling her the way her fathers did. She smiled up at him.

"That was clumsy of me." Enjoying my panties and my bare ass, freak?

"Sorry for not helping, I'm pretty jammed in here."

She stayed as she was, glancing at her watch, counting

ten with the second hand, allowing him an encore. "That's alright. I'm having an off day. I'm anxious for London. I've got a stay-over." She stood, straightening her skirt. "I'm sorry about your computer last time. Did things work out for you?"

"Yes. Thanks for asking."

"Germany, wasn't it?"

"Bonn. You have a good memory." He sipped too much of his cognac. "I can only hope this time the hotel's better. The secretary put me in The Gilbert. Would you happen to know the place?"

"I do, very well. They're a little out of TGA's budget for us girls so we stay around the corner and head over to the Gilbert for drinks to wind down. Maybe I'll see you there. I'll look for you."

"Or I can buy you dinner?"

He could tell she was pleasantly surprised. She wasn't certain. She was thinking. She wanted to say yes.

She also knew what he was thinking, somewhat of a no-brainer. He swirled his cognac in a cupped hand: a failed attempt at blasé sophistication. He didn't say 'may I invite you to dinner' or 'would you consider joining me for dinner', he said 'buy', as in can we eat little something, somewhere not too expensive, before I take you to my room and fuck you like a cheap whore for free instead of renting one for the night?

She said, "I know the city better than you. I think so. Why don't I come by at eight? It'll be a pleasant change. Thank you for inviting me. I know a nice sidewalk-café which isn't far from the hotel and reasonable, though after-dinner drinks are on me. Fair?" she asked.

"Yes, very fair. You've made my week. The rest is downhill from here."

You've got no idea. "Enjoy your meal, Mr. Billows," because you just made mine.

She glimpsed his way several times over the next hour. At

Heathrow she acknowledged him as he stepped from the plane into the Jetway. She knew The Gilbert, though she'd never stayed anywhere near the place. None of the girls ever went there. The hotel was a three-star filled with American jerks with expense accounts who preferred booze to comfort, a fairly good indication that his secretary saw him as two-faced.

She left the airport and went to the Queensbury. She ordered a light dinner to her room without wine and went shopping not realizing the date was July 15th. She hadn't seen her mother in seven years and Gilligan, she knew, was wrong. She would never be happy. How could she be when she couldn't even tell Elixia about Gilligan or what she'd done? How could she ever explain Gilligan or tell the real truth without pushing Elixia away? How could she explain after so long that she'd killed her father, not her mother who, because of her, was no longer the famous and capricious Miss Emma Rose?

She bought red stilettos and a red linen skirt, short and pleated. She bought a sheer red blouse and red panty-bra set. She bought a deep red, wide-brimmed hat, a passably expensive handbag, pink tinted glasses and gloves to match her hat. She bought a carving knife believing, she mused, as he must be thinking, that bigger was better. To that end, not cutting off her nose to spite her face, she bought medium as well as large condoms: silver foil for boys, gold for men. She had no idea what size a satisfactory penis should be. She didn't care. She couldn't imagine that anyone's could be satisfactory. Knowing how they looked was bad enough. She put one of each foil into separate pockets of her handbag.

At The Gilbert he was in the lobby when Collette Salazar strode through the doors, her body commanding attention. Most everyone saw her legs and her bra, no one saw her face. She'd thought of a much more appropriate restaurant for dinner, quiet, where they could talk, though she insisted on going Dutch since the place was a tad more exclusive and a ten-minute cab ride from the hotel.

Billows dismissed her offer. They strolled a block or two, hailing a cab, Collette letting him open her door to enter and exit, not making eye contact. He couldn't very well gape at what she had under her skirt and look into her eyes at the same time. She understood and was thankful.

The restaurant was charming, not quite up to the French standard, though acceptable. She chose for herself from the menu, he wasn't that erudite. She selected a garden salad and smoked salmon; he wanted chicken, she guessed, but he settled for duck à l'orange. He chose a bottle of pedestrian Burgundy by name, pointing into the leather-bound carte des vins, the sommelier cringing from behind a calm exterior.

Collette discreetly proposed a more suitable choice, a clear Pouilly-Fuissé. She'd learned a lot being with Elixia. All told the twenty plus ten seconds up her skirt onboard the plane and the two lesser opportunities to ogle her panties and thighs in the cab cost fifty pounds sterling each, 240 USD when his usual allowance, she knew, was a fraction of that. And the night was far from over. .

He was an executive. That wasn't true. He was thirty-two, despite what she'd read in his computer telling her that he was born thirty-eight years earlier. He travelled pretty much every week, he boasted. That wasn't true either. He travelled once a month, sometimes less. He was married, though not happily. They were getting a divorce. Collette thought otherwise. The woman in the photos she'd viewed weeks earlier didn't appear at all disgruntled. He had a boy and a girl. No, he didn't. He had a girl, Lucy. Not anywhere in any one of his several hundred photos had she seen a boy. She was the loveliest woman he'd been out with in a long time. That part was true, she assumed.

Her little white lie was nothing compared to his fully distorted image of himself.

She'd drafted a general idea in her mind of how she would like the evening to end, the mechanics however she would have to ad lib. She'd killed one father, not the other as much as she'd wanted to for what he did to Elixia. Perhaps now she would, in her mind. She hadn't had sex with a man since Tommy Dune forced his way into her, first making her drowsy with wine, near insensate with roofies or whatever. That wasn't sex, that wasn't love. He'd callously raped her, Elixia tenderly loved her.

She knew where to put Billows, not quite certain what to do with him once he was in, or how long he should stay in her before she called it a night. She never lasted very long with Elixia, repeatedly, though she knew men weren't that resilient and she would need time to properly manage his climax and her pain.

The evening air was compatible with a quiet stroll, he suggested. Collette understood and agreed. He needed to replace the air in his lungs that he'd lost seconds before she snatched the restaurant tab from his loose hands. His relief was tangible, thick: his argument weak and transparent. She was a senior flight attendant for TGA with an expense account to entertain certain frequent passengers of her choosing. He was too inexperienced to know better.

She paid cash, explaining that she believed he would be too timid to join her for dinner if he'd known beforehand. He thought: thank God. She thought: no paper trail to a TGA passenger dining with a redhead. Or was she a redhead? The waiter wouldn't know. He was too busy throughout the meal memorizing her tits and the full length of her legs. Either way, the least she could do was to pay for his last meal.

"Anyway the evening's young, Fred, and I did promise you after dinner drinks. I wouldn't be a very good date if I reneged on that, would I? So I'm thinking a drink or two in your room might be appropriate. If you think that's alright. I didn't quite appreciate the way those men were checking me out in the lobby. Also, I'm not one for crowds, but this one's on you."

"No problem. I have to warn you though, Collette, the room's pretty small. We are in London, after all, and I certainly don't mind if you don't."

"I'm good with it. Why ruin an exquisite evening?"

His expression said everything Collette wanted to hear. The guy was anxious. He was salivating. He was going to score with a woman nine years older than his daughter, sixteen younger than him.

The Gilbert's pub was crowded. No one noticed them hurrying through the lobby, the brim of her hat disguising her face, her distinctive red hair combed into an updo and hidden. She'd put a lot of thought into this, deciding as well that she wouldn't wear jewellery, not that he noticed her unadorned ears, neck or wrists. His obvious appreciation of her laid elsewhere.

Stepping into his room she was aghast. The ancient elevator was more spacious and no less Spartan. He had a bed, a pull-out that served as a sofa, a mini bar, matching bedside tables the size of barstools, a television set atop a small desk crowded with fliers, a phone, a menu and a tray with four glasses. The coffee maker was in the bathroom with four cups, swizzle sticks and napkins. The bathroom was the size of her walk-in shower at home.

"This is it, Collette, my home sweet home for a week, albeit not quite the Presidential Suite. That was booked."

She chuckled. Ha-ha. She wasn't wasting time.

"Fred let's set some ground rules. You shower first, and I don't like rough beards. So take care of that manly face. I'll call down for a bottle of Rémy Martin which you can serve while I'm showering."

"I have to say, I wasn't expecting this."

No, you were simply praying for it. "Call it synergy. There's a connection between us. I think so." Collette pulled away her hat. "It's been a while for me, though. So go easy. I might be a tight fit at first and I'm looking forward to giving you something you weren't expecting, not to mention a lot of satisfaction for me. I hope you're up to the challenge."

"I've dreamed of this evening for a long time. I just didn't know your name."

You still don't, asshole. Why bother with a girl's name tag when you can look up her dress and dream of fucking her?

She reached for the phone. "You're not moving too quickly, Fred. I'm not undressing until you're in the shower. Or don't you want to see me naked?"

He tossed his jacket onto the pull-out, kicked his shoes into a corner and left her, taking a robe with him. She could imagine the sick bastard in the bathroom working himself into a large, working at making himself more of a man for his ego.

Collette was nervous, convincing herself that what she was doing was no different than the waiter seeing her at the pool, if The Gilbert had a pool. She hung up the phone, laying her blouse over the chair at the desk, then her skirt. She didn't want her clothes near Billow's. Her shoes stayed on, answering the knock at the door in her thong and bra. She dimmed the light to conceal the colour of her hair, not her body. No different from the pool. She might have been a brunette, auburn, mahogany, copper or bronze. No different at all from the pool, her French accent convincing. She made no apology for the way she was dressed. If anything, she felt mischievous. No different from the pool.

The guy in striped pants and a bell cap didn't mind in the least as she leaned away from him at the desk to sign the sixty pound chit to the room. The longer she took to figure out his gratuity the better. He didn't think he'd ever seen a more magnificent body, her breasts commanding his immediate and fleeting attention. His pals in the pub wouldn't believe this. Neither would his girlfriend whose

342

rear end looked like huge dumplings compared to this woman's hypnotic and curvaceous ass. Nevertheless he was suddenly eager to end his shift and get home.

Collette added an exorbitant twenty pounds to the bill, dropping the leather folder as she twirled to face him. Her panties were sheer. She'd practiced that also, to make certain what he would see. He was a true gentleman; she thought he might be as she sauntered past him to the door wishing him a goodnight. She might have had red eyes and green hair for all that he saw of her face.

The shower stopped whistling. She heard the curtain drawn back, silence, the hair dryer, then silence, then his shaver.

She didn't wait for him. She poured an ounce, emptying the glass in a gulp, slipping into a robe, keeping her panties and bra on, her stilettos on. She didn't need him getting off on smelling her underwear.

She poured another ounce, burning her throat, her chest. She was calm. She heard the door open behind her. She poured a third ounce, reaching for her handbag and a robe, taking her glass with her. She didn't trust him, smiling coquettishly as she sauntered past him, his clothes hung carelessly over one arm, not neatly folded.

In the bathroom she leaned against the door, closing herself in. She felt as though she was locked into a porta-potty at a construction site. She ran the water, gripping the rusted knob with a facecloth, staying where she was, sliding the curtain in place. She moisturized her body with cream from her handbag without removing her make-up, daubing between her lips with oil for her not to feel pain, not for him to feel pleasure, praying to Elixia to understand. As much as she would need the pain in her mind, her body would remain unhurt for Elixia.

She emptied her glass into the sink and opened her wallet, kissing each of Elixia's pictures. She changed into fuller panties, not for Billows, for her. He was a pig, probably on his third or fourth drink. He wouldn't see anymore of her than need be.

She stepped out after ten minutes opening the door with the towel she'd dampened to make her time in the bathroom appear real. She'd practiced dozens of times. She wanted nothing to go wrong.

"You look great, Collette. And, yes, I am definitely up to the challenge."

"Fred," she opened her robe, "twirling her thong on a finger. "Do you mind if for the first time I wear my panties and bra with my shoes? I kind of have this fantasy."

He gulped. "No. I guess we both have the same fantasy."

She shrugged the robe from her shoulders, reminding herself she was at a pool. She was accustomed to American and British men staring at the beach or the pool, while Frenchmen appreciated. She refilled her glass at the desk, setting it on the table at the right of the bed with her handbag. She was right-handed.

She threw back the covers with a single motion, stripping the bed save for the bottom sheet and pillows. She wanted to appear anxious. She was anxious, to leave. She stood waiting.

He was maybe two inches taller, not yet tanned in July, his brown hair not short and not long, not dull or shiny. She eyed him with a smirk, wanting to cough a laugh when he let his robe drop to the floor. His nipples were pink, pinker than hers, his chest devoid of hair, his arms shapeless. He'd likely never seen the inside of a gym. He was neither fat nor slim, without definition other than where his gut would protrude by age forty. His legs were straight, too straight, she thought, indentations imprinted by his socks visible above his ankles. The most hair he had under his chin was a cluster of brown decorating a penis she believed might insult a hetero girl. She wasn't insulted. She'd never seen one so close and in the light, wondering why any woman would want to. She thought silver would adequately suit her need, not believing he could ever possibly be gold worthy.

The bottle was two-thirds full. She'd poured four drinks, he was finishing his fourth. She took the glass from his hand and poured him another. Her fourth was untouched.

She patted the mattress, giving him space to position himself. He was on his knees waiting.

"Not like that, Fred. I want to be on top. Deeper is better for us girls and I've got very strong legs."

He lay flat. "What the lady wants, the lady gets."

"I don't usually do this, you know. In fact you're a bit of a treat for me."

"Well thanks, Collette."

"You're welcome. What I meant was I'm more into girls. I'm very fussy when selecting a man, which I don't do very often, which is why I want you to go slow…if you can with that."

"You like girls."

She nodded. "For the same reasons you do: the way they smell, the way they feel, their moist pussies, their soft breasts, their firm cheeks I can dig my nails into . Yes. I like girls very much."

"No kidding. The same girl," he asked.

"Of course mostly the same one, unless I meet someone in-flight that I like and take her to dinner. Actually you'd be surprised how often, how many men out there really don't know their wives."

"That happens?"

"We're happening. What's the difference apart from the age? My girlfriend's in college. She's eighteen," Collette went to her side of the bed, taking a sip, bending from the hip, reaching into her handbag for the silver foil. "Hope you don't mind. I bring my own, not that I use them often. I don't. Like I said, you're a treat. So don't disappoint me. Give me something to tell her about." Collette dimmed the light once more, not too much. She needed to see, ignoring him as he put his glass by his leg and manoeuvered himself into the latex sleeve. A precise fit, she thought, snug, not too tight. Good. No pain. She straddled him, balancing, scarcely touching him. "Tell me, Fred. Did you get off looking up my skirt when I dropped the napkins?"

"You did that on purpose?"

"I did that for you. I wanted tonight to happen. I'm surprised you couldn't tell I was wet. When I stepped into the lavatory I changed into stockings and got myself off thinking of teasing you."

"I can't believe this."

"What, that I like young girls or that I was wet thinking of this?"

"Who doesn't like girl-on-girl? I mean, to hear a woman say that she got herself off..." he drained half his glass, "now that's a turn on, big time. I've got a whole new respect for flight attendants."

"I can see that."

She was nimble, compensating for what she'd never done. She pushed his hands away, telling him to lace them under his head, to close his eyes and imagine his wildest fantasy. He did. She didn't want to touch him. She kneeled to the left, putting a hand to her panties, her right leg she raised for a moment, lowering her weight as she pulled her panties to the side. She barely felt him go in, the oil doing its work.

"Whoa! You're as smooth as frigging butter."

She ignored him. "Are you like other men, Freddie? Do you like young girls, girls younger than me, like my friend?"

"Hell, yes. You could pass for a teen, no problem."

"I know. My girlfriend can pass for fourteen or fifteen just as easily. When we do the bar scene she has to show her ID." She faked a groan. "Want to know something funny? She lives not too far from me in New York...and like me she does the occasional guy. With a little different

346

make-up she could be your daughter."

"No, shit."

"I'm not kidding. On the weekends I have to force her to wear clothes. She has no shame, not that our neighbours mind when she's sunning on the patio with me...the men anyway." She faked a shudder. "God, Freddie, this is good," about as good as stepping in your wet shit.

He was labouring, straining to work his way from small or medium to large and failing miserably.

"So what are you saying, Collette?"

"Tell me. I'm curious because I really don't know. Do men really dream of doing their daughters once in a while...you know, this way? My father never saw me in my panties. I was too shy. Do you think he wanted to see me that way?"

"What normal guy wouldn't? My kid's not shy. She's popular, wears skirts that don't hide a damn thing. And her tits, what's with teenage girls needing to show their tits and their bellies these days. My guess is she's probably already fucking some pimple-faced freak in her class behind the bushes. In fact I'm sure she is. Who's a virgin at that age anymore? The wife doesn't seem to care, so what the hell. There's no law against seeing what you can. She must flaunt her ass and her crotch a dozen times a night when I'm home, sitting this way and that. So, yeah, I think about her when I'm doing the wife. Wouldn't be a half-bad idea getting rid of the wife and her for a weekend to install a camera or two. She spends a lot of time in her room. I've even thought about putting the wife to bed early a few times. The girl's kind of dumb, more like her mother than me, and she falls asleep pretty fast."

He was grimacing.

She wanted to vomit.

"That's naughty, Freddy. So a threesome with me and my girlfriend is on? I can tell her yes for next weekend?"

"That soon?" His eyes lit. "Shit, yes."

"Stay the way you are. Keep your eyes closed. Don't spoil what's happening. Let me get another rubber so we don't waste time losing momentum." She leaned to one side. "God, if she were here she could take pictures of us. Would you like that, pictures of you and me fucking, or you with her? She's so hot."

"This weekend, all day, all the pictures you want. Shit, yes, and you with her."

"Good. That's what I wanted to hear. My red panties and bra with heels is working, Freddie. I've haven't been this excited about something in a very long time."

He was on the verge. Her arms were arced in the air. She didn't wait. The fourteen inches of steel plunged into his upper chest at the very instant she jerked away from him using the hilt for leverage and balance.

He convulsed once, confused.

Collette stood over him, absorbing his disbelief into her mind, watching him speculate over the bone stem protruding from his chest, his climax coming seconds too late to fully enjoy, secondary to his unforeseen quandary, his hands grasping the smooth ebony stump.

She told him, "I stole your computer last month, Freddie. By tomorrow your wife, the one you're divorcing, yeah, well, she'll hear about Bangkok and Lucy. I'll send her a note to fill her in, telling her to expect a few hundred photos along with a few of you with your shrivelled cock all wrapped up and a hole in your chest. See? You're already shrinking from small-medium to teensy and I do hope you realize that knife will be a bitch to pull out. Thanks for that." She leaned slightly forward. "Goodbye, Freddie."

She smacked the hilt sideways. He coughed and died.

Her legs planted on either side of him, Collette pressed a warm hand against her panties. She smiled. She didn't feel pain. She'd barely felt him. She left his eyes open, made her way from the bed and went for his phone and computer. The two items were on the list she'd prepared and put in her handbag with a roll of scotch tape. She taped the list to the mirror.

She attached the power cord for better resolution, placing the laptop by his side before taking a full body photo of Fred Billows in his current condition lying beside a FULL SCREEN image of Lucy sleeping on her bed in her underwear. She climbed onto the bed centring him between her feet, gripping the handle, yanking once, twice, three times, lifting Billows a good few inches before his dead weight helped her and the blade slid out.

She continued with close-ups of his limp member wrapped in latex that was swollen with urine, his face twisted. He looked ridiculous. She captured the computer screen once more from an angle she thought wouldn't distort the image, careful not to betray her reflection in any of the photos. That was on her list as well: not to get caught.

She had imagined more blood, though she hadn't aimed for his heart. Perhaps, she mused, he didn't have one. His wife would soon not believe that he did.

She emptied what was left in his suitcase into a corner, over his shoes, placing it on the floor by the door. She went for the facecloth she'd used, covering his penis, pinching the bulbous end of the condom, facing away, pulling until the taut latex snapped free, grimacing at the eruption of dark yellow urine clotted with his ejaculate.

She clutched her stomach, her back sprayed from her red hair to her waist. She wanted to retch, her throat burning with gastric acid.

She took the knife, wiping the excess blood onto his leg. She dropped the condom into the toilet and flushed. The knife went into the tub before she added the cloth to the suitcase, putting another three check marks on her list.

She showered and douched, unbraiding her hair, soaping and rinsing twice to erase him. She left the knife in the tub with the water running for close to an hour while she added the plastic bottle and box of the vaginal rinse to the suitcase and reviewed her list. She put the panties he'd touched and her soiled bra into her handbag along with the knife, ticking the six steps and bra off her list. She left his robe and the top covers where they lay strewn on the floor; she hadn't touched them but once. She stripped the bed from under his weight, surprised by the ease, stuffing the suitcase with that, the robe she'd worn and her towel, scrawling three ticks on her list.

When she was done she dressed, ticking each item she wore from her list. She had no reason to stay naked. She poured a drink, gulped the ounce, and went to his computer to prepare a draft.

In the subject line she wrote: Your husband is dead.

In the body she wrote: He died telling me that your marriage was finished. He wanted out and dreamed each night of fucking Lucy your daughter, thinking of her each time he was doing you. He wanted to hide cameras in her room. His computer is filled with images of her and a little girl in Bangkok whom he paid for not very long ago. If you don't despise him enough at the moment, let me help you. He died expecting a threesome with me and my girlfriend next weekend. She doesn't exist, though he believed that she does and that with make-up she could look as young as your daughter. By the way he spoke while he was in me, imagining your daughter, he might not have dreamed much longer. Be thankful he's dead.

I hope I haven't ruined your summer. The world is a better place. Your home is a safer place and your daughter won't now have to live with the secret nightmares of her rape.

Images follow under separate delivery. He's at The Gilbert in London, room 329, not where he might have told you. He was a liar, which no longer matters.

My best regards, without my condolences.

Collette finished her drink, meticulously washing the computer and his phone with another soapy cloth, again ticking her list on the mirror before slipping her hands into her red gloves.

She would leave at pre-dawn. The restaurant opened at 6:30. She wasn't in New York or Paris, L.A. or Vegas. She was in London: staid and archaic, pompous and historic in culture and thinking. She would leave soon after the clocks and the phones in adjacent rooms began ringing, when showers began running and whistling, the night clerk stuck alone in his cubicle completing his audit of the previous day.

She felt good. She poured a Rémy Martin. She felt better than good. She was elated. She'd helped to sanitize the world. She poured another, a double. The outside air was warm, yet she was cold.

She tossed his glass into the suitcase with the bottle and went to her list. She wouldn't be careless. She rummaged through his pants for his wallet. Nine hundred American dollars for a week in London, what a big spender, albeit sufficient to cover her out of pocket expenses for dinner, clothing and sundry items. She pencilled ticks onto her list.

What she hadn't planned was her shower. She hadn't expected him to spray her with his piss and ejaculate after he was dead. Next time she would know better. No more showers. Again she let the water run. She was learning.

At five AM Collette made ready, tearing her list from the mirror, adding her glass to the suitcase, donning her hat and her glasses, sliding her bag onto her shoulder, noting never to raise her head once in the hall, thankful the dim morning light would make her bare breasts under her blouse less apparent.

Nothing was out of place apart from the body, its clothes and the bedspread. She checked three times, verifying her list. She was pleased. She pressed SEND on his email and phone and walked out.

Collette Salazar left with his suitcase, her eyes fixed on the carpet, her arms crossed over her breasts. She saw no one in the lobby or outside the doors. She exited and strode several blocks with a purpose, dropping her panties he'd touched into one sewer, her bra into another, the knife into third before hailing a cab, dropping her stilettos onto the street as she stepped in.

At her hotel she walked barefoot through the lobby, her arms crossed. In her room she washed and rinsed the standard hotel-issue glassware she'd taken, leaving them in the bathroom, showering once more to shampoo her hair until she felt entirely clean.

She put her panties into the garbage with her empty douche bottle and box. Her skirt and blouse she put into the empty outer pocket of her carry-on with her gloves. His bedding she folded and placed by the cart at the end of the hall on her way to breakfast. The robe and what was left of the Rémy Martin she put into the handbag that was now empty. That would go with her. She was dressed and ready for work.

At the airport she left his suitcase stripped of its ID tag in a washroom. She left what remained of her evening wardrobe in a second, the robe she trashed in a third. No one ever pilfered from airport washroom trashcans other than sniffer dogs searching for danger. Her bag she gave to an effusively thankful teenager carrying a pillow.

She passed through security with ease. She seldom smiled unless she was with Elixia or Gilligan, whispering with her eyes closed to the dark. She was tired. She was content. She felt she'd done something for her sweet and carefree mother.

On the monitors along the length of the concourse, The Gilbert was cordoned off. Apparently a murder had been committed. Further details were pending.

Gilligan Rose quickly called Elixia to tell her how much she loved her.

Her flight departed on time.

Thirty
This Year: July 09th

She served his first mimosa moments before the 380 lumbered down the runway at a mundane 170mph. She had gently squeezed his shoulder to wake him, though he hadn't fallen asleep. He was curious about contact.

John Francis Templeton Fennell was alone in his starboard side row. Adjacent to him, portside, was a businessman who might have paid for a row to himself in a smaller aircraft. He was two, maybe 250 pounds overweight, mid-forties, lethargic, sleeping, his mouth agape, his rotund gut heaving over splayed legs he probably hadn't seen in years. Fennell thought wealthy, accustomed to the good life for as long as he might live. Of course, if the plane did go down he'd either burn to death on land or drown in the ocean. No one would or could help him.

Fennell didn't have a weapon. He felt strangely naked and vulnerable without the Beretta that Deena would put under his hotel room pillow. He was dressed in Brannigan's blue suit with a yellow silk tie, blue shirt and blue loafers. He looked the part, the part of someone who was on the top rung of some corporate ladder.

Self-satisfied and self-indulgent, she thought: a totally self-infatuated prick. He would want another mimosa, or two. He would order coffee and dry toast for breakfast, no jam nor butter. He would wait an hour and order a vodka and juice. Before lunch he would want another mixed drink, then a green salad and Perrier. One hour later he would order another vodka-juice mix. She couldn't recall ever serving him dinner. She didn't think so. But, yes, another mix before landing and during this flight she would serve him dinner with a few more vodka mixes no doubt. The man was a calibrated drunk and a pedophile, a model corporate citizen one step or touch from becoming a rapist if he wasn't one already. She looked forward to killing him. She was anxious. She'd planned him for the better part of a year: what she would wear, what she say and do.

He hadn't once called her by name, not that she could remember. He didn't know her name, which didn't matter. She knew him and she wanted him badly. She wanted him with a fevered passion, more than any of his sick predecessors. For a year she'd watched over his shoulder as he ogled his daughter or daughters. He would be no different, on the verge of divorce, frustrated, his disgruntled wife leaving because of his frequent absences or cheating on him because she was bored. So why then couldn't he fuck an attractive and willing flight attendant?

She was nervous, not because of Fennell, because the fifteenth was a Friday and she'd never killed a pedophile in the States. Yet this time she would, she hoped, in New York, three thousand miles from home. She had a two-day stay over in Paris, departing on Tuesday for New York, returning to Paris on the Wednesday continuing on to Frankfurt. The problem was Thursday evening in Paris; she wanted to kill him on Friday the fifteenth which meant New York. That was her day, more important than any other, more important than Christmas with Elixia or her birthday. The day was hers to celebrate and lament alone, the day she killed her father, the day they took her away, the day she lost Gilligan for so many years, the day she last saw her mother.

The Hunt for Gilligan Rose

She never did believe Gilligan's hope, not really. She knew in her heart she would never again see her mother or dance in the rain.

Fennell, much to his dismay, and with all due respect, love and devotion to Deena, was attracted to the appealing symmetry of Gilligan Rose's very fine ass and shapely legs. She was to-die-for gorgeous. With Xara they were a knockout couple and Elixia was far from being the ugly sister. She was breathtaking. He'd seen both women with her on a few occasions. The two were sweet and innocent, charming and visually delectable. So was Rose until the fifteenth of July each year when a twisted or wounded mind usurped what he knew Gilligan Rose wanted most in life: to be normal. He knew Gilligan Rose better than any other person on the planet including de Montfort, Mendiga and the timely deceased Phillips. Had he not died, had momma Rose not butchered her husband, ten men would still be alive: an ongoing debate of morality and poetic justice versus the law that Deena seemed determined to win.

Phillips, give credit where credit was due, knew what he was doing, faking an address, buying a car in one country, losing himself in another, somewhere on a vast continent, instantly lost, found by reason of his death, buried in a grave near a home he'd never lived in. Bravo, thought Fennell, but because of you your girlfriend's kid will spend much of the rest of her life in prison, or fry. Either way, she had less than a week to play kissy with de Montfort. Mendiga she would likely never see again.

Most of all he felt sorry for Deena who, in six days, would confront and arrest her killer, would-be, could-have-been friend, whereas Deena felt sorry for Elixia and Xara. What was it with the female condition? Who was to say that Mendiga and de Montfort wouldn't hook up with each other after the trial? Two Latin lovers with something in common: Yeah, he could definitely see them working out.

He had no idea whatsoever how his day would pan out, or the following evening with the new kid at Les Filles du Ciel. She was coming towards him. Her name tag was gone, her skirt an easy hand-width shorter than on previous flights. That, he thought Deena would assert, was the male condition. He knew better. He was being an observant cop, impartial. The woman had great legs. He could easily imagine her in garters, heels and a push up bra. Hell, he didn't have to imagine. He'd watched her for hours up close and personal and practically naked on the beach, later at home vociferously defending his male right to keep his photographs of Mendiga and Deena, Deena and Mendiga. Mendiga wasn't the criminal. So what the hell and, besides, Deena wasn't all that convincing.

She was coming back. "Mr. Fennell, may I bring you another mimosa?"

"Please do. Thank you, miss."

"Coming right up," you arrogant prick.

She returned with his drink on her tray. "You look very handsome today, Mr. Fennell. Blue is definitely your colour. Did your wife or daughters pick out your tie?"

No shit. Was that a smile on her face? "My daughters insisted. They pretty much run the house." His smirk was weak. "Or they will after the divorce."

"I hear that a lot from gentlemen who travel the way you do. Fourteen and fifteen are difficult years. They want to be mature for their dad."

"Yeah, I miss them."

"It's lonely on both sides." She touched his shoulder. "Enjoy your beverage. I'll bring your toast and coffee shortly, and I would undo that tie. We're in for a long day. We won't arrive in Paris until after midnight local time. At least you're alone in your row. That's a plus. I'll join you later for a coffee if time allows and if you're not preoccupied."

He nodded, smiling, one of those noncommittal smiles.

She brought his breakfast. An hour later she brought a vodka and juice. She served his green salad and Perrier, followed by another vodka-juice mix an hour later and one before touching down in New York for a sixty-minute stopover.

He was more curious every moment. How would she hit on him? She had to hit on him. He could imagine Deena sitting at the pool wondering. He didn't see it, what Deena saw in her. She was cold as ice. The cutesy girly stuff was an act.

Half the First-Class passengers disembarked, Gilligan Rose taking the opportunity to sit in the empty row opposite his where the fat guy had slept his way across America to work through a small stack of paperwork. He wasn't timid or reticent. She didn't want him to be. She was beginning to work him, luring him into his own hotel room. He didn't think she could hike her skirt much higher, high enough for him to see the tiny silk strips at the clasps of her garters. So much for his imagination. The male condition: See a girl naked all day at the beach in the tiniest thong and any properly functioning male would still want to sneak a peek up her dress as soon as she put one on. She wanted him to look, to drool, and when she stood she didn't bother straightening her skirt. Instead she smiled at him and walked to the galley.

He wasn't expecting her to come from behind, snapping shut his computer screen.

"Mr. Fennell, I thought you might enjoy a cocktail while we're waiting. We have another fifteen minutes."

"Thank you."

He took the glass. She was letting her hand touch his. She was good. She was discreet. She walked away, his eyes focused on the slit at the bottom of her skirt when she glanced over her shoulder to see that he was. She knew.

Halfway through his drink she was sitting at the seat across from him, this time on the armrest with her legs

357

slightly parted, ever so slightly hiking the hem with her palms.

"Mr. Fennell, you'll have another passenger beside you en route to Paris. However the last row behind you on starboard is empty. I thought you would like to know. You look like a man who enjoys his private time."

"Thank you, miss."

She touched his shoulder again, taking his glass, waiting as he stood, standing, sauntering behind him while thinking how easy he would be to put down. She carried his jacket. She could imagine his story, the same one she'd heard ten times. His daughters were good-looking, too sexy for their age, there for him, taunting him in little skirts and low-cut tops, teasing him. His wife was the one at fault, though: cold, not eager to please. So, yes, what was wrong with a little peeking, a little innocent touching? Or, she remembered seeing his daughters on the slide show, photographing the oldest one naked in the outdoor shower.

He was so blatant, not bothering with thumbnails, viewing them during each flight on a full screen. She touched him again, leaving him.

Fennell couldn't help thinking, what a waste, all that quintessential female wasted on women, not to mention the other two. A male hypocrisy he had to concede, yet she was cheating on two women half a world apart, one with the other, women who didn't know their faithful lover was a killer, two women whose lives would collapse anytime soon. Shit happened.

The mammoth plane began filling with what he thought was incredible speed and efficiency. Not that he cared. He had no particular schedule whether he arrived on time or not. He never listened to the spiel. A forty-five K drop at terminal velocity somehow made life jackets and lighted aisles somewhat pointless. At altitude he opened his laptop to view a hundred plus photos of Deena and another fifty of Marie's cute tush wrapped in a stringed Rio which he'd promised to delete with Deena's and Brannigan's assurances to the girl.

He had to admit the French kid did her job like a pro, never saying no, without the knowledge of Deena's threats of castration before they left home to meet the kid at the beach. She was delightful and a little sassy; towards the end of the morning actually flipping up her pleated schoolgirl skirt for a final few shots. Not even Deena saw that one coming. The kid was okay, for being French.

Somewhere mid-Atlantic Gilligan Rose began serving dinner. He was seated in the last row and served last. She excused herself when she dropped the napkins she'd been holding under her tray. She seemed flustered, Fennell reminding himself that he was on the job and loved Archer.

She put the tray onto the seat between them, squatting, gripping the armrest of the aisle seat in the next row. She counted to twenty instinctively, talking with him without making eye contact. She was having an off day, though from where he sat he couldn't empathize. His day was quite fine, the view in the cabin far more enticing than a darkening sky. The transition from her stockings to bare her thighs was smooth, not the slightest ridge, not the slightest flaw in female perfection. The woman belonged on a catwalk when most her age were in an advanced state of decline, their mates found, the necessity for captivating beauty diminished if not obliterated by marriage and the perceived status quo of two, three or four kids.

How did she know his favourite colour was red? They were silky and lacy; a snare set between soft white strips of flesh, disappearing into what he allowed was an exquisite divide. At that moment he did feel sorry for her. She was glancing his way, making eye contact. Her eyes were sad, her smile evaporating. Perhaps she was having a bad day, which wouldn't matter much longer. Within a week she would be told when to wake, when to shower, what to wear, what to eat and when to sleep. Silk panties and eye-patch thongs would become things of the past, vague memories replaced by cotton briefs, Mendiga and de Montfort replaced by scarred dykes whose gentle caresses would be a few punches to her face. She'd be some lifer's bitch because of Thomas Dune. Inside of a year she would be far less pretty and far less tender. She'd be the one punching someone's face, anxious for a new girl, a fresh diversion from prison life.

He should never have allowed Deena to interact with her.

She dropped a handful of napkins onto the empty seat, reaching for a half-dozen others, her legs opening wider. In another life, a previous life, one without Deena, one without a killer with a killer bod, he would have asked her out on the spot. But in that scenario he would have stared up her dress by innocent and delightful accident, not because she wanted to beguile him before killing him.

She was finished. So was he. The show was over. Now what? How would a cheating lesbian hit on a guy? He reached for the tray, helping her. She leaned forward onto the armrest between them, folding her arms, sighing as though she'd lost her best friend, which she soon would...both of them. The kind of irony he could only appreciate quietly or when Deena wasn't around.

She pushed herself to her feet, managing a smile, taking her tray, disappearing into the galley.

Twenty minutes later she collected his tray. Then:

"Do you mind, Mr. Fennell, if a tired flight attendant sits beside a weary passenger?"

"I don't mind at all."

She sat, crossing her legs. "We have a couple of hours before touchdown. These eastward flights are the absolute worst."

"I have to say you look as rested as you did departing L.A."

"Thank you." She sipped her cola. "I don't believe

we've ever travelled this far together. You're either getting off in New York or boarding during the stopover for Europe. You're a busy man. May I ask what you do?"

"Industrial relations…not anything as interesting as your career but the bills get paid on time."

"I was sorry to hear about your divorce. Your daughters must be devastated."

"They understand. The situation's amicable…for the time being." He paused. "And you, married? Some lucky guy out there must think he's died and gone to heaven."

"No. We broke up a few weeks ago after a few years. He's already playing house with a brunette."

"So you're telling me he's blind or he's stupid."

"She's few years younger. You know what they say, age before beauty."

He chuckled. "She's young, but homely."

That brought a smile.

"I think so, if that counts." She slouched slightly, letting her skirt ride, uncrossing her legs, crossing them toward him. "Now I'm stuck with very expensive tickets for a Broadway play I can't use and an evening dress I can't wear."

"I can't imagine anyone leaving you for second best. You can't possibly be alone for long."

"The job doesn't help. My base is in L.A. However, I'm in Paris so frequently that I own a home there as well as in Long Beach." She patted his arm. "Not the easiest thing to explain. Then there's the stress of the whole dating thing. I'm not into becoming a notch on a gun. Ex-lovers are so much harder for a girl to explain than for a guy." She stared into his eyes. "Men are so hypocritical."

Unless they're lesbians, he mused, hot lesbians.

A portside call light flashed, beeping once. She left to pamper the passenger, returning to Fennell a few minutes later with a vodka and juice for him. She eased into her seat, slouched and crossed her legs.

"Thank you. Having a home in Paris must be wonderful. Any hopes for the French male contingent?"

"They're worse than Americans. Better dressed and better looking, true," she touched his sleeve, "present company excluded"

"Thank you."

"You're welcome, but incredibly possessive," She sipped her soda, "although I do enjoy the French way of life."

"Do you speak the language?"

He knew already.

She wasn't surprised. He was always too engrossed in his homemade porn to hear her speaking with other passengers, speaking over the PA system between LAX and JFK, JFK and wherever on more than a dozen flights. Prick.

She nodded, "And Spanish. My name is Collette Salazar. My father was Spanish."

Now we're getting somewhere. "A pretty name for a pretty girl...I mean lady."

"Girl is fine. Twenty-six isn't that old."

Neither is thirty-two.

She checked her watch. "I suppose you're anxious for that cozy hotel room."

"Yeah, nothing like a bed a thousand other people have slept and played in, though a little more comfortable than the couch in the spare room. I suppose my favourite is The Franklin in New York. I've got a weekend conference on the sixteenth, arriving Friday, flying home on the Monday," however I suspect you know that. Don't you?

She crossed her arms. She was thinking.

He waited. How much longer could she put up with pleasant banter before cutting to the chase?

"We'll be on the same flight again and I'm staying over as well. That's the theatre evening. He was supposed to meet me there, do a weekend getaway." She pressed her hand against his. "Mr. Fennell, I would never have thought to do this." But since you enjoyed staring at my bare thighs and lace panties, "but since we'll both be in the city with nothing else to do, and I've got two tickets I won't use by myself, would you consider joining me?"

Fennell was shocked. He never expected. He truly did not.

If you promise not to stab me in the chest before the final curtain "I would love to. I can't think of a more pleasant way to spend an evening. Are you sure? I mean…"

"Like you said, we'll have a pleasant evening. Call it PR. The curtain rises at nine."

"Do I need a tux?"

"A suit is fine, perhaps with a darker tie."

"The Franklin's rooftop dining room has a magnificent view of the city. Dinner first and after-theatre cocktails are my treats and I'll make sure you get home safely, wherever home is."

The Franklin, she was impressed. "Actually, I'm at the Excalibur, a few steps from The Franklin."

"Good. In that case I'll walk you home. My first name is John by the way."

"I know," and you like to see little girls in their underwear, "just not onboard…company policy. ETA Friday is two PM."

"Then you can join me for a late lunch as well."

"Oh, thank you. That would be nice, if I didn't have last minute shopping that I wasn't expecting and a salon appointment…girl stuff. I won't have time in Paris. Thank you, though, Mr. Fennell, John," she whispered, "I'm really quite excited. I suppose we never know. Do we?" Too bad you'll be late for the conference.

And a big knife, don't forget the big knife. "No. I suppose we don't. "

She combed her fingers through her hair.

He wanted to ask what made her tick, what quirk of fate made her into a serial killer. Lots of girls had deviant fathers or 'uncles'. Guys on the other hand had priests and coaches to deal with. None of them made murder an anniversary special. From a male perspective he could understand the cheating. He'd have the same problem if another woman as beautiful as Deena existed. He also wanted to know the whereabouts of Miss Emma Rose. Her kid had to know. Or she didn't and that's why she was killing, half her mind locked in a child's world filled with resentment, her father the reason they robbed her of a mother, her victims her way of killing her father, of getting her mother back.

"Well, no rest for the weary."

Yeah, you got that one right, Gilligan. "Your day's almost over, Collette."

"May I bring you another?"

"No thank you, I'm done. I need a clear head for tomorrow, stuck in a hotel room finalizing presentations for Monday. I couldn't take a chance on a delayed or cancelled flight, so I left my girls a day early. That's the worst part of the job is missing them."

She nodded, commiserating. And no doubt you miss tucking them in, waiting for them to fall asleep. "Well then enjoy tomorrow evening in the City of Lights."

"Perhaps I will, if I'm not brain-dead by then. I'm glad you sat with me. See you Friday, Collette, with a darker tie. Shall we say dinner at seven? I'll have my New York secretary reserve us a table within walking distance."

She smiled, standing, first adjusting her skirt a little higher, then down.

An hour later her voice announced their initial descent, first in fluent French, her voice sweet with flavour. Twenty-minutes after that he undid his seatbelt waiting for the crushing wave of passengers to flood by. He was the last to exit.

She wished him goodnight, calling him John. He knew better than to call her Collette at the moment.

Settled into his suite at La Marquise, his suitcase tossed onto the second bed where it would remain for the week, he opened a cognac from the minibar that Brannigan wouldn't reimburse. He wasn't into bar brands. He sank onto a Louis XIV récamier, jolting his teeth, choosing the edge of the other bed before dialling.

"You must be exhausted, sweetheart."

"I'd say more like dead, but I don't want to rush things."

"Not funny. How's Marie?" Deena asked.

"Don't know, sleeping I suppose. No need to call her at this hour. I'll see her in the morning for breakfast; do a bit of sightseeing with her, prep her for the evening."

"You be nice to her. She's new at this."

"I'm always nice."

"No, you are not. How's Gilligan Rose?"

He blew a deep breath into the phone. "Long story short, she's great in stockings and garters and I had an IMAX view of her red lacy panties and ass for about as long as it takes me to run half a mile."

"That would be in your dreams, I presume."

"No. That would be in the aisle of a 380 at arm's length."

"Really?"

"Yeah, really."

"Lucky you."

"It's a job."

"So you connected with her."

"That would be a yes. We're going to the theatre Friday evening after dinner together at The Franklin, so no cops. You all eat in your rooms, you especially. I've invited her for after-theatre drinks as well, before she kills me."

"So we're not wrong about her."

"No."

"I'm so sad for her."

"Because she's beautiful and you flirted with her gorgeous girlfriend on the beach. You have something in common."

"I didn't flirt with her."

"Oh yes, you did, which was pacemaker hot, and I'll be seeing her with the other girlfriend tomorrow. If you're sad, imagine how sad they'll be. My guess, not very; royally pissed might be a better choice. And don't think for a moment you'll be anyone's favourite either."

He sipped his cognac.

"Thanks for that."

"What are you wearing?"

"I'm in the pool, not much."

"How was the milkman?"

"Average."

"Your fault, you should be more selective."

"Be careful what you wish for, sweetheart. My father's been telling me that for a year."

"I've got you on my screen, in the pool...nice, very nice."

"You keep that thought, and you keep little Marie in her file. She's nervous enough around you, especially about tomorrow night."

"I'll be her big brother and a gentleman."

He snorted.

"Okay, that's a fennell noise. What now?"

"I was imagining Gilligan Rose's expression when she discovers two federal agents, one of them my anxious bride, are my little girls."

"You really do need counselling, sweetheart. Finish your drink and go to bed."

"Te amo."

"That's right, you do."

Thirty-One
This Year: July 10th

Sunday Johnnie Fennell woke late, placing a room-to-room call to Marie Anisette who was working hard at what she would say, drinking horrible in-room coffee, practicing and waiting for breakfast. Captain Brannigan had made very clear to her that Agent Fennell was in charge. She would do whatever he said and when. No exceptions unless she wanted to exchange a promising career for a desk job at the county sheriff's office. She understood.

Departing Miami late Thursday she'd arrived in Paris minutes past midnight on Friday too excited to sleep, too excited to eat when she finally went for breakfast. And as the day went on her excitement grew. Not exactly an agent, not an agent at all, she was a recently graduated criminologist hoping to hear one day soon that she was accepted into the academy, hoping Captain Brannigan would keep her. Very few made the grade.

She was twenty and already on a difficult field assignment. That had to count for something. She wouldn't disappoint him. Most of all she was eager about what she had discovered. Or at least what she thought was right. She knew she wasn't wrong. She couldn't wait to tell him.

At first she didn't like him. Nobody liked him. He never said hello or goodbye. She thought he was rude. The times she saw him with the captain at night, each time she glanced up from reading his case files, she saw him staring at her, making her nervous. The women in the building thought he was super conceited, the men thought he was a ...Well; anyway, they didn't like him.

None of that mattered. He was the best. Captain Brannigan had told her so once and she knew Captain Brannigan didn't like repeating herself. Deena who knew him better than anyone thought the same even though she didn't seem to like him very much the times they came in late.

Then one night Deena came in alone, without him, and Marie was called into Captain Brannigan's office. Neither woman was smiling. She wanted to die or be sick. She was going to be fired because of him and never become an agent. She knew that he didn't like the French kid.

She was told to sit. No one ever sat in the captain's office. She couldn't believe what she was hearing. She was afraid to speak because her mouth was dry. She was afraid to look nervous or stupid. She wasn't being fired. Agent Fennell wanted her as part of his team. The captain asked if she was interested. Yes or no? She would be required to pose in bikinis at the beach, possibly poses that might be a little embarrassing. She would also spend a week in Paris, France alone with him.

She didn't know. She couldn't answer and turned to Deena for help. She liked Deena who was always smiling at her and waving hello and goodbye. Deena was looking straight at her, nodding her head, telling her it was alright without speaking. She blurted a yes.

"Yes, Captain Brannigan, I will do this thing for you and for Agent Archer."

Then the captain gave her the next day off to go shopping with Deena. She had so much fun talking and laughing until: "We're meeting Fennell for a late lunch." And she thought her heart would stop beating.

He was waiting for them and stood to greet them. He called her Marie and pulled out their chairs. He was smiling and very gallant. He asked about her parents and her brother, her education and her dream of becoming an agent and didn't interrupt her once. With the casual conversation over he told her about taking the pictures and why. He would not ask anything of her that would make her nervous. Then he spoke about Paris and Gilligan Rose and she wondered how he could be so calm about being killed. That's when Deena patted her arm and promised that wouldn't happen.

He thanked her for joining their team and ordered another bottle of wine. He was laughing and telling jokes. Telling her stories about his career, stories not even Deena seemed to know. By the end of the meal they were Deena and Johnnie and she was beginning to like him even though Deena never called him Johnnie, preferring Fennell. They drove her home and he opened her door waiting until she was inside to drive away.

She thought he was such a gentleman and so very handsome.

When the day came to take pictures she was nervous. Not because of Johnnie, because she wanted to make him proud of her. He was the best and did nothing to make her feel bad. She didn't know why, she just did. When they had taken all the photos they needed she flipped up the back of her skirt like a naughty little schoolgirl and stuck out her bum.

Deena didn't stop laughing for such a long time and once each week they would meet late at the office to brief her about Gilligan Rose before driving her home. Now she was in Paris waiting for her phone to ring and as nervous as she was that first day at lunch.

She wanted to sound calm, self-assured, though she knew he could tell she was nervous. He was the best. She agreed to meet him in the restaurant in fifteen minutes and, he reminded her, she was to wear the new outfit Deena helped her select for the first part of Sunday. She hadn't forgotten, she answered. She was already dressed.

He was very debonair, she thought, for an older man, watching him pass through the open doors with so much confidence, feeling her face flush. She was alone with him for the first time.

"Good morning, Frenchie."

She knew that was his special name for her. She wasn't the French kid anymore.

"Bonjour, Johnnie."

She'd practiced saying his name free of her accent a thousand times, not yet succeeding.

He liked what he saw. She looked her age, which made him feel old enough. He couldn't imagine what he was in store for that evening. He'd seen her outfit. He'd either feel very lucky, or very perverted. He was thinking more likely perverted.

"Once again, Frenchie, Archer and I want to thank you for volunteering. What you'll be doing today and this evening is critical to the case."

He handed her a flash drive.

"What is this, Johnnie?"

"A fine collection of you posing on the beach, in the cabana and in the beachside shower, as promised. Keep them as a souvenir."

"Thank you, Johnnie. And I did promise Deena and Captain Brannigan that I would not let anything happen to you. I do not think they trust you very much." She dropped the flash drive into her purse. "But I do."

"Well, thank you again. And you're quite right, they don't. So we'll have a fun day and an evening that will look good on your service record before I put you on the plane tomorrow. The day is ours to enjoy, no work. Give me a tour of Paris and before you know it you'll be debriefing with Brannigan and Archer tomorrow afternoon. That's the tough part."

Her face lost its pinkish hue. She placed her hands in her lap as he pulled out his chair and sat, her eyes first staring into space at her left, then to her right, her dry gulps imperceptible except to him. She tried not to show that she was moistening her pursed lips, but he knew. He was waiting, not smiling, not unsmiling. He was the best. For that reason he would understand.

"Johnnie, you did tell me once that doing something that was right without permission was better than being refused permission and not being able to do what you do know is right. Do you remember telling me this?"

No reaction.

"We both know what I said. Thinking of telling me anytime soon what you've done?"

"Yes." She cleared her throat. "I did cancel my flight to Miami tomorrow. I will fly to New York from here on Thursday, not from Miami with Deena for the arrest of Gilligan Rose."

No reaction:

"I actually said "refused permission by those of a lesser ability'. I wasn't talking about me"

"I do believe, then, that I did forget that part."

No reaction.

"What exactly have you done since Friday that you believe is right?"

"The airline did also charge me 500 dollars to make this change."

No reaction.

"If I understand what you're saying, or trying to, you've done something right that has cost Brannigan 500 dollars... plus three extra hotel nights and meals, which is more like an easy seventeen hundred."

She nodded. "I think very possibly a little more than that, Johnnie. However I will pay the penalty and extra hotels myself because I do know that I am right."

"No. You won't. Brannigan will pay the penalty and extras." He put up a hand. "Let's order breakfast, after which you can tell me all the right stuff you've done in two days, Agent Marie."

She didn't think that was good. He had no expression, which she thought was worse than being angry.

He let her explain the entire menu in detail, listening attentively. He prompted her to order first, the waiter scrawling: an orange juice, a cheese omelette garnished with a medley of fresh fruits, toast and a selection of jams. She was starving. When she was finished he ordered toast without jam or butter. Then she didn't know what to do. She thought her head would explode. He wasn't asking her to speak. He wasn't asking her to say anything.

"I want one day to be a good agent like Deena. This is my dream, Johnnie."

No reaction.

"Not like me?" he countered.

"I like Deena very much." She sipped her coffee. "I do know you are good also. But why are you good? I did ask myself this question many times. You are good, I believe, because you never ask permission. That is what everyone says about you, that you never ask permission, that you are a loose cannon and a maverick. I had to investigate this word which does mean you…"

He stopped her.

"I don't ask permission for two reasons, Marie. I know when I'm right, which comes with time, and Brannigan has my back. We have history. We respect each other. You're still a little damp around the edges. She likes you, we all do. The respect comes with proving yourself and they're a hard bunch, especially the women. They don't give anyone slack. Neither will you one day. So are you going to grow an ulcer over this secret mission of yours or will you tell me how exactly you saved the world in forty-eight hours?"

"Yes. I will. Flying here I was thinking of Gilligan." She swallowed. "I do mean Gilligan Rose. How she is one day hot and one day cold, one day smiling and one day very sad. I would be this way as well to know that someone did love me so much while someone else did not. I could not imagine that my mother does not love me, or my papa. How terrible would this be for me? He calls me each night to tell me goodnight and together they kiss me through my phone."

He acknowledged her good fortune with a tilted nod. He hated this kind of talk. "You're fortunate. So was Gilligan Rose, albeit too late. Her mother killed to protect her. Or we assume that was the reason. We don't know, at least not to what extent. That said; her mother is a fugitive, an escaped murderer. Given the choice I'd stay with Mendiga and de Montfort and forget mom."

"What normal man would not? I have seen your photos of these women. This, however, is not my point I wish to make."

Her face told him that she wanted him to stop interrupting.

"I began to think of her mother. What kind of woman would not see her hurt child in seventeen years? Who would do such a thing?"

He answered, "A smart woman, one afraid of two minutes jerking in the electric chair."

"D'accord, this is true. And so she hid herself twice. She hid herself once in a place where she was at once forgotten by everyone, even by us, a horrible place, until she went away with le docteur Phillips. But where did she go? Where did she go, Johnnie? There is no record with the British that she ever returned there after her one exhibition. Why? She did not because this was not possible for her after her trial. Yet le docteur, oui, we know that he did. He bought a house that he did not live in for one day. However he is buried not far from his door." She sipped her coffee. "Phillips was very rich, no?"

"Yes."

She stopped talking as the waiter served their breakfasts. "They were together during more than one year while he made certain that she would disappear. After that year they were forgotten for sixteen more until her daughter decided that, yes, she would like to kill Monsieur Cooper. That part we do know, yes?"

"Yes."

"And now she is forgotten because, in fact, she never did exist. She did not go to prison et le docteur removed her completely from his dossiers at his clinique. So this tells us that when she did leave the courtroom she went free like a Scot."

He chortled. "We'll get her, Marie, when we get the daughter. Gilligan Rose has to know where mom's hiding out."

"I do not believe this, not after so many years. I do believe that the mother is protecting the daughter she does love so much as the daughter is protecting the mother."

"So where does the 500 dollars come into this? Give me something to tell Brannigan."

Now she was truly excited, her doubts quelled. He was listening to her, taking her seriously.

"If you want to hide in America, Johnnie, you do not go to New York or to Los Angeles. No. You do not. You disappear somewhere in the middle if your English accent is perfect enough. This is not the case in Europe with so many languages and accents. Our waiter, he does not come from here. He comes from Lyon. That one," she pointed, "she is not French at all. She is a Swiss girl. Yet you do not know the difference."

"You believe Emma Rose is here. That's what you're saying? Rose is living somewhere in France."

"You know, Johnnie, I believe, that when someone must hide, first they must change who they are. This is very easy to do when someone is rich comme le docteur Phillips, especially so many years ago when the police were not as smart as today, many of them. Some are still not so smart. You know also that in most cases these new names, the first and the last, are never much different. Joe Smith will become possibly John Simms, or Jane Doe will become Janet Dougherty. Or," she paused for affect. This was her moment, "perhaps Miss Emma Rose, the famous painter of faces, does become Mademoiselle Emmanuelle Lerosier who is a well-known artiste, who has for years lived in Nice at the south of France where she paints in her atelier a young girl peering into a mirror, one face so happy, one face so sad. The observer of these paintings is unable to determine which girl is happy, which girl is sad, which girl does stand searching into the glass, which girl does stand searching to discover her way out." Marie leaned forward. "Emma, Johnnie, is inside Emmanuelle and Lerosier does mean rosebush in French. I did speak with a gallery in Nice and did research their site. I know I am right to not have asked your permission. Johnnie, Madame Lerosier does have red hair and green eyes also. I do know she is the mother of Gilligan Rose."

"How far is Nice from here and how do we get there?"

"This is several hundred kilometres by car. We must fly, of course."

"Check the flights. Let's get there ASAP."

"We are going? Yes?"

"We are going. Yes."

She furrowed her brow, pursing her lips, waiting. "Our departure is tomorrow at ten. We will stay for two nights to return here late on Wednesday evening."

No reaction.

"You let me figure out how to write that up in the report. And exactly how much over the flight to New York are we talking here, Agent Marie?"

"I do believe four thousand more is more or less correct. The hotels, Johnnie, they are not inexpensive in Nice and I did believe you would want a car also." She jabbed a sliver of fruit with delicate precision. "I do believe Captain Brannigan will not be very happy with me."

"You leave Brannigan to me."

She beamed. "Anyway, Paris is so cold in the summer. No? Nice you will discover is so much warmer and friendly."

No reaction, as much as he wanted to smile. The morning mercury was already at seventy F.

He bit into his toast, his cold toast. "I suppose the entire week will be a little heated, at least until Friday when things will definitely cool down. You did well, Frenchie. And clearly you've spent too much time with Archer, so take the rest of the day off. Enjoy yourself. Just make sure you're ready at seven."

She shook her head. "No. I did promise Deena to take the best care of you. So I will show you my city. We will enjoy together the way that you said. How can I learn if I am alone?"

*

Les Filles du Ciel was sophisticated and glamorous, his reservation made weeks earlier from a phone in Miami routed through L.A.

The cabaret seated 700 guests at intimate tables for two. No large group was ever seated as one, raucous noise was not permitted and vulgarity carried the severe penalty of immediate expulsion. Elixia de Montfort operated an elegant club for connoisseurs of fine food and exquisitely exotic entertainment. The minimum age was sixteen. Madame de Montfort would not have her clients' expectations ruined by babies or brats.

The club was full. Marie's fake driver's permit showed that she was seventeen, though she looked the requisite fourteen. Either way, wine or anything stronger was not allowed. The French police were infamously strict in preserving the imagined purity of their youth with 7500-euro fines.

A young woman, mid-twenties, greeted them at a lectern by the door attired in a black sequined dress that was short and décolleté. Under the dim lights were hints of black panties meant to see and appreciate, a black bra, meant to see, a black beret, high-heeled sandals and clear seamless stockings enhancing very long legs meant to see.

He was oblivious to her. He loved Deena. Marie was holding his hand. She knew better. She knew of Les Filles du Ciel because of her father. She had made the reservations. She knew the women were the best-looking in all of France. The thongs came later, for thirty minutes at the top of each hour. They strolled in at 7:30.

He ordered a malt scotch, a Perrier for the kid, the kid criminologist who'd specifically asked for a private corner facing the stage. Kid, he mused. She was far from a kid. Her outfit during the day was bad enough: a short summer dress, flighty and mid-thigh, low-heeled pumps, a Gucci bag and, okay, a very short and flighty summer dress, her hair combed into a long, straight ponytail.

Not looking at what everyone else clearly appreciated was difficult. Their late day lunch was a bottle of pleasantly chilled Bordeaux with a platter of cheeses and baguettes at a café-terrasse within sight of the cabaret. His wishful thinking was that they might run into Gilligan Rose, maintaining the ruse of holding hands and starlit eyes.

This was worse, Fennell paradoxically pleased and disappointed that the warm evening air was still. Much worse indeed for a healthy man away from his woman: a sheer mauve blouse highlighting her purple bra, a short purple skirt, a very short purple skirt accentuating her bare legs, and three-inch black stilettos with thin straps spiralling halfway up her calves. Her sandy hair had that wet, tight-curl look; her eyes a bright brownish-blue dusted with pale purple, her lips pouty and glossed a deep prune; her fingertips lacquered the same shade: a gift from her favourite cop who was then swimming in her pool thinking of them and missing him.

The waitress came to the table with the drinks dressed as

invitingly as the hostess, her dress shorter and more décolleté. He was having a very rough time. He ordered for his companion, excusing himself when the woman was gone to find the men's room, leaving his companion alone.

He didn't like urinals. He didn't like public washrooms at all. That's why he paid for lounge privileges with three airlines and never left Archer in the car to take a leak in a doughnut shop. He preferred hotel washrooms that were regularly cleaned: spas for cops who didn't like doughnuts or the cops who ate doughnuts, where he could relieve himself in private while enjoying a few moments of peace and quiet and maybe a coffee in a lounge with someone he did like.

He was surprised, impressed. All except one stall were empty. How could he come to Paris and not try a foot-operated urinal, despite the white-coated monsieur in the corner discreetly disregarding him? He would. Archer, after all, had her bidet. A particular taste of the good life he hadn't acquired despite her convincing demonstration.

When he was done he stepped on the lever twice, the second time retreating to better see the rush of cascading water. He washed his hands, accepting a hand towel from the man in the corner. Each man nodding, his French limited to parlez-vous English. He searched his pockets. He had no change, giving the guy an American twenty for the total experience and leaving all the wiser with something to tell Deena.

In the cavernous hall dimly illuminated with thousands of halogen beams emitted from the high ceiling and strobes dangling midway, he was curious, or lost, or appeared that he might be. He knew precisely where his young date was sitting, meandering twice that distance to find her.

Their meal came not long after, in time for the 8:00 PM show that made South Beach and Venice Beach dull except, he allowed, when Deena was swimming or sunning. The young chanteuse's voice was enchanting, at times soft and melodic, at times strong and demanding, her eyes imploring, her eyes accusing, the perfect accompaniment he decided early on to the horde of thong-clad topless dancers in sparkling stockings and heels, their heads covered with tall, swaying plumage.

"Johnnie, you are allowed to eat while you watch them, and to blink also. No one will think you are rude."

He leaned into her, whispering, putting one hand under the table, hovering over her crossed legs, covering his mouth with the other. "You'll learn once you're an agent, Agent Marie, that we should take note of each and every detail when working a case. That's what I'm doing. I'm studying them in case one day I'm called to testify. And, Agent Marie, you should also cover your lips whenever speaking undercover. You would be surprised how many people can read what you say, possibly even our Gilligan Rose."

She covered her mouth. "You can put your hand on my very naked leg, Johnnie, if your arm is tired. I am good with this, as you say. I will not put this in my report. I will only tell Deena."

"My hand is fine where it is. The last thing I need is a stroke and Deena doesn't have to know everything."

She covered her mouth for a moment with the morsel of pheasant on her fork. "I do think you should buy Deena flowers. This will make her like you more than she does. Because you are her partner does not mean you cannot treat her nicely. She is so beautiful and kind, yet you choose to do nothing at all to make her feel like a woman. You are wrong to think this way."

He withdrew his hand, wrapping his arm around her shoulder, lightly kissing the side of her head, not unlike the other lovers seated around them.

"She knows she's a woman. She doesn't need any help from me. Everyone knows she's a woman. Believe me. The same way I'm well aware how much of your leg is bare.

Thanks for trying to kill me. Now eat your bird."

She chewed a few times, her delicate jawline barely moving, reaching for her Perrier and lemon, her eyes on the performers, the crystal goblet an inch from her lips. "Anyway, I know I am right. Think what you want."

He chortled, reaching under the table, his eyes on the dancers, squeezing her thigh not too hard. "I generally do, Agent Marie...without your permission."

*

Elixia de Montfort enjoyed her life, her job and Gilligan whose name after all these years she still pronounced as Gilligone. She also liked working the bar where she could interact with her clients and be with Gilligan whose reserved barstool was at the far end of the bar with hers.

The seats were inscribed with their names, for their use alone. At eight-thirty they swivelled from the stage to face into the mirror lined with the world's finest liquors.

"You should consider what I suggest, Gilligan. This air travel is no longer for you. Your painting is now wasted on us and our friends. You must become known for how accomplished an artiste you now are, mon coeur. What need have you of that place in Long Beach so far from me that I have seen so few times, or these long hours of work I know that you no longer enjoy? I see this in your eyes each time you leave our home."

"I promise, chérie, that one day soon I will for you and for me, for both of us...perhaps one day very soon." She leered into the mirror, at him, at the girl, surprised to see him, not surprised that he wasn't alone. "I know I should stop flying, to spend all my time with you, my days painting, my nights here with you or in our home. It's what I truly wish for. I want nothing else, but for so long you and flying have been my sole reasons for living, hating each moment apart from you, hating so many empty weeks of the year. I'm trapped, Elixia, and I can't explain. I'm not the person you believe that I am and I can't explain. I can't ever explain."

"I do know who you are. You are Gilligan Rose. You are sophisticated, as worldly as you are lovely. You are Gilligan Rose, a frightened little girl with tears in her eyes once the light is turned out. You are my rose. That is who you are. What I do not know is who kisses your tears in Long Beach, mon coeur? Who is with you to hold you so tightly in warm arms, arms that want to protect you? Who is with you to hear you whimper your name in the dark? There is no one, when all the time I am here, when all we can do is talk on the phone with an ocean between us. This is not living. This place you see in the mirror, the people behind us, I would leave this in a moment for you. This is my work, you are my life. At first, yes, so many years ago I believed this was my dream when now I do know that you are my dream. This is how you must think. I would live anywhere in the world with you and not live at all without you."

Gilligan Rose put her hand over Elixia's. "What are you telling me? You're making me afraid."

"That we must be together, that you must be a famous artiste, that you must now be known to the entire world, not simply our family, our friends and our neighbours, that I must have more of you each day of the week, not simply a home that is empty much of the year without you and a bed that we did choose together."

"I never believed you were unhappy."

"I am unhappy when you are unhappy, I am sad when you are sad when we do deserve happiness each day of the year."

"I don't want to lose you."

"Écoute-moi, mon coeur. This is not what I am saying. Listen to me. I will never leave you. You are the one who must leave. You must leave your past where it belongs. That your mother did kill your father, this is not your fault. The despicable man is dead for a reason and Salazar is no better. They should lie in the ground together along with Salazar's horrible wife. You must leave them behind. You must from this moment live with me in the present to dream of our future and remember only our past together. These fourteen years, mon coeur, are for me fourteen days. I feel I have just met you." Elixia finished what was left of her cognac. "Mon coeur, I have discovered a doctor, a good doctor who can help you forget. Please. Do this for me. We will walk this road together no matter the distance."

The silence was deafening amidst the drone of 700 guests.

"No, Elixia. I cannot and I will not. How can you possibly propose such a thing? I would die first, for the very same reason I can never be the woman you want me to be. I will never become the famous painter you believe I should be."

"Yes, you can. I know this with my entire heart."

"No, you do not know. You do not know." Gilligan's eyes welled with tears. The dark day had come, borne of a wonderful summer's evening. "You do not know that my mother is Miss Emma Rose, a famous American painter, and somewhere in this horrible world she is alive. She is alive, Elixia, living in fear because of me, because I was the one who killed my father, chérie. Me, I killed him. I killed him twice. Now do you see? Do you possibly think for a moment you can love someone who kills each night in her dreams? And that is only part of my lie, a very small part."

"Were he alive I would kill him myself, as I would kill Salazar and his wife for the way they have destroyed your life. This I told you a long time ago. If this was your secret, mon coeur, nothing at all can be worse. You were wrong not to tell me the truth, to live with this pain between us. Come. I am taking you home and do not ever imagine that I would leave you. I will not."

Elixia snapped her fingers, the bargirl a split second later instructing the doorman to have her car ready at the private rear entrance. She was taking Gilligan home.

Gilligan peered once more into the mirror, seeing him, seeing him smiling, loathing him, his arms wrapped around the young girl's shoulders. She'd gone too far in her mind to ignore what he was. Mr. John Fennell would die on her anniversary. The girl with him would go free and not be the wiser, forgetting him one day not too far into the future. His death would be the innocent girl's survival like all the others she'd saved.

Thinking of what he would do to the girl later that evening made her feel sick. If she could kill him then, she would. She wanted to so much, but she could not. Instead she slid from her stool. She took Elixia's hand, squeezing, wanting to sleep through eternity, wanting to forget, to never remember the day they took her away.

Elixia and Gilligan Rose walked arm in arm through the mystically dark club into a clear and dark night. The curtain was rising for the nine PM show.

*

Fennell and Marie walked out a few hours later, his arm around her shoulder, her arm around his waist, not certain who might see them. Not certain where Gilligan Rose might have gone. They were laughing, having a good time. Anyone passing by would see immediately that the coquettish young girl enjoyed the older man's attention. They strolled a block farther.

"Okay, hot little French girl, this is where we should kiss, a fake kiss. I don't want rumours around the office. And I should grab your bottom. You know, for some realism."

"You can pat my bum, Johnnie, a few times. I will pretend that you are my father. This is how he greets me always, with a kiss and a little patting on my bum." She added, "In a nice way however. He is a good man and not many years older than you. My mother, too, she does pat my bum. This is her way to tell me how much she does love me."

"Like your father... that hurt."

She shrugged, displaying uniquely French indifference. "I know that you do not hurt. Deena did tell me and I am counting each one. I am reporting to Deena how many times." She giggled. "Is it true that Deena did beat you up at the gym in front of everyone?"

"What! No! She tripped me when I was distracted. She tends to exaggerate, Frenchie. Don't believe everything she says."

"So she did beat you up...in front of everyone."

He liked her. She was refreshing, alert. "Well, perhaps she did a little, a very little, because I was helping her look good in front of the men."

"I do not believe you, Johnnie. Deena did beat you up." She burst into a laugh. "Kiss me, my darling, or I will beat you up."

He did, in a flash, his cheek pressed lightly to hers, his free hand skimming across a film of air between his palm and her skirt. When they were finished he smacked her ass, hard, satisfied with her yelp, mankind redeemed with a contented smile, despite which they continued walking hand in hand.

"Was that as good for you as it was for me?"

"Hmm, when I marry I will marry a Frenchman. This was not very arousing, Johnnie. This is why you live alone. You are not gentle with beautiful women."

"Beautiful women, is that right? So we're talking French women, I suppose? Or little French girls who dress like naughty little girls?"

"Yes, of course. Who else in the world is more beautiful than French women? Who else in the world can be as naughty or nice as we are?" She paused, holding him back. "I can think of only one other woman in this world."

"I know, your mother, your manufacturer."

"Do not be rude. Deena did warn me of this. No. Not my

mother. I was speaking of Deena."

"Hey, remember, no rumours." He draped his jacket over her shoulders. "You were a charming companion, Frenchie. Thank you. You played your part well. You could not have been more convincing and I suppose now that we've kissed and I've patted your bum we can stay out a while longer. I'm sorry about the wine. Will you join me for a nightcap, perhaps a cognac instead of overpriced French water?"

"Thank you, Johnnie Yes. I would like that if I can change my clothes first to look more like a woman and not a bad little girl. Also I am reporting to Deena that you are a gentleman, a nice man, not really a fennell the way that she says that you are. The other people, they are wrong also. Deena should treat you nicer than she does, now that I know you. She is your partner."

"You're right. She is pretty mean to me most days. I do my best. I just can't break through to her as hard as I try. She's pretty tough, Frenchie."

"No. She is not tough. Maybe if you smiled a bit more with her, you never seem very happy together. Invite her to a nice dinner sometime. I do know she will like this."

"When you're an agent you'll understand why. Deena and I have lived Gilligan Rose for a full year; we've had close contact with her, possibly too close. We've lied to her, which is no big deal. We're cops. It's what we do. The thing is, she's young, she's beautiful, she's rich and two women adore her. Now we're five days from putting her in prison for most of her life or a very uncomfortable chair. That's when smiling becomes a little difficult, despite how much we want her. You'll understand one day."

"I do like Deena so much. She treats me like I am already an agent and I believe she does like you more than she pretends. I saw how she did look at you when we were taking photos at the beach and at our most lovely lunch. You should buy her flowers and say something nice to her for once. She would like you for that. She is a woman, Johnnie, a very pretty one I must also say."

"She's okay for a female, I suppose." He paused, his eyes sparkling. No one was near. They were blocks from the cabaret. Gilligan Rose wasn't a problem. "Marie, do you want to know a secret, one that will get you fired if you tell anyone?"

She wasn't certain that she did. "Yes. I do."

"I'm going to marry Deena Archer in three weeks. We live together. She totally adores me."

She stood still, studying him, her quiet giggle growing into hysterical laughter and painful knots in her stomach.

"That is funny, and not true at all. Now you are being a fennell with me. She told me to expect this from you. I knew this would happen."

"Thank you for thinking so much of me."

She waved him away, then wrapping an arm around his waist for support, the other clutching her stomach.

He reached for his phone, pressing SPEED DIAL and SPEAKERPHONE. Moments after:

"Hello, sweetheart, my darling. I miss you so much. How's Paris? How is our little Marie?"

"Paris is good. We're good. Except we have a situation. Frenchie's eyeballs are bouncing on the sidewalk and I believe she's having contractions. We're on speakerphone, sweetcheeks. I told her about us, about the wedding. It sort of worked into the after-dinner conversation and somehow she thinks it's hilarious that we're getting married."

Only a short pause ensued. "Hello, Marie."

"Bonjour, Deena. This is true? You will be married to Johnnie? This is a bad joke. No?"

"No. It's not a bad joke. Yes, it's true. And yes, it is hilarious. I'm marrying the fennell."

"Mon Dieu!"

Deena chortled. "That sounds about right, whatever you said."

"Believe me, Deena; I will keep the cat in the bag for you and for Johnnie. He told me to tell no one and I will not. I promise. Anyway, who would believe me about this?"

"It's important that you don't, Marie, because of the case."

"I am so happy for you. However I am most happy for Johnnie because you will be such a beautiful bride for him."

"Thank you. Listen, Marie, we're having a simple ceremony, nothing fancy, a few friends, my friends, because he doesn't have any. I don't think he ever will. But Johnnie and I would love if you could join us on my special day. Bring a friend, a boy or girl or your brother, anyone. I'll send your invitation today."

Marie looked to Fennell who wasn't much help.

"I would like this so much, Deena. Je te remercie. I will cry all night with this wonderful news. And Deena, he is not a fennell as you call him, not that I can see so far. He is a nice man and I will go now so that you can talk with him alone. He was a gentleman all day and this evening also. He has something so good to tell you."

He shook his head, stopping her with a hand at her shoulder. "You tell her, Agent Marie. You did the work. You get to tell her. You get the glory. That's how things work."

"Tell me what, sweetheart? What don't I know?"

"Deena, we do believe that we did find Miss Emma Rose. Deena, she is the mother of Gilligan Rose, the painter. We are flying to the French Riviera, Johnnie and me, tomorrow."

"Johnnie?" Deena asked. "How, when?"

"Frenchie here promoted herself to field agent a few days ago, though between us girls she's done some enviable investigative work. It's a hunch, albeit an educated one. Chances are we'll find the woman. In the meantime let's not get Brannigan all titillated and fuzzy. If it doesn't pan out she won't have to know. The worst case: I get a couple of days on the Riviera with Frenchie for a guide. The best: we get a fugitive and a killer."

"My fiancé alone on the French Riviera, that doesn't work for me. Marie, you keep my man under control. I want a full report from you and you do have my permission to kill him if you believe you have probable cause."

"I will not let him look at any French girl, Deena. This I do promise to you."

"Punch him for me, Marie, right in the stomach…hard."

She did, seeming quite pleased with herself. "Goodnight, Deena. I will wait at the corner to give you birds of love privacy to kiss through the phone."

She left them.

"She's gone, sweetcheeks."

"Sweetheart, she's a doll. And Emma Rose, that's fantastic."

"I'm hoping. This Marie kid will be a good agent one day soon. She stepped way out of line on this one, between you and me. Brannigan would tear a strip off her cute ass." He watched her saunter away. "Let me rephrase that, her very cute ass. That said; this works, we'll get Brannigan to pull some strings to help her out. You know, the way I helped you along."

"I'll ignore that because I love you, for the time being. Did Gilligan see you together, sugar daddy and his little tart with a cute bum?"

"She must have. I saw her at the bar with de Montfort and I hit the head before they left making my debonair-self obvious. From what I could see they were having a girlie moment."

"A girlie moment, like you're having a fennell moment."

"You know what I mean, the typical touchy-touchy, wet eyes, the female stuff even straight women get away with."

"Tell Marie to punch you again."

"Something set her off. Me, I hope. Pretty sure she'll be

at home in a little bit sharpening a knife, if she isn't already."

"One she won't use, sweetheart. Now take little Marie for a nightcap. The girl deserves a quiet moment. I'm sure she's a little unnerved, and buy her some nice outfits for the rest of the week. The poor thing can't have much left to wear. That's my treat. And I do mean nice clothes, nothing trashy like she's wearing this evening and keep your eyes off her bum."

"I will, and I can't wait to see your gorgeous ass and marry you. But listen to this, this is really cool. I took a leak at the cabaret."

"You peed. You're equating your bladder with marrying me."

"No. I tried this urinal, with this guy standing in the corner, a washroom guy. The best part, I flushed with my foot, no hands. Sort of makes washing optional. Deena, sweetcheeks, we need one at home."

Deena pressed END without saying goodbye.

Thirty-Two
This Year: July 11th

She didn't look any worse in her jeans, boots and cashmere sweater, he told her, than in a micro skirt and a sheer blouse. He shrugged. So why did she bother?

Though now she knew she could punch him and she did.

They had a couple of cognacs before she went reluctantly to her room. Morning came early without too many exceptions, he told her He wanted her bright-eyed and bushy-tailed and good agents followed orders. She didn't believe him. He didn't care and when she was gone he went to the gym. It's where he did his best thinking.

The Côte d'Azur was an ideal venue for Emma Rose to disappear. She was one of 163 nationalities, one of 84,000 foreigners in a town smaller than where she was born on the shores of the Hudson. He was anxious to see her in person, to phone Deena with proof, too anxious to sleep. He was past the point of bright-eyed and bushy-tailed.

In his room sleep didn't come easily, watching Deena fade out and in on his slideshow, waking to see her randomly taunting him. He snapped her shut and took a hot shower.

At breakfast Marie was seated at a table when he arrived. She was wearing white pleated and cuffed shorts, her shoes from the previous evening and a white off-the-shoulder sweater, what she'd planned to wear home. He felt old walking towards her in his boots and blue denims. She thought he looked like Deena's prince charming swaggering through the doors.

She didn't ask. She went to him, kissing his cheeks and hugging him. She was so happy for Deena, which set the tone for most of the morning, Air France delivering them into Nice in time for lunch on the shores of the Mediterranean, Fennell telling her not to get the wrong idea about police work.

He figured three day outfits and three evening ensembles, more or less the same for him. They were, after all, playing a part and he'd come prepared to spend the week alone. Marie thanked him, declining. Knowing she was returning to France she'd given herself a budget that she hadn't used because she'd spent her first two days locked into her hotel room. Her story was a very sad one indeed, he agreed, dragging her into a boutique she knew she couldn't afford, still paying off her student loan.

She put this dress back because it was too expensive, that skirt back because she would never pay that much for so little material. He took them both. He thought the skirt was plenty big enough and made her try it on. He was right, of course, telling her to pick out the accessories, reminding her that ensemble meant complete outfit, not to chinch and not to forget the essentials she would need for three days and three nights unless she wanted help with that also. He figured 32-B and two thongs per set.

She looked at her chest, frowning, saying something in French that didn't sound quite polite as she punched him inches above his belt and sent him away to buy something nice for Deena.

The mission required seven boutiques to complete. At the eighth, his domain, he didn't need her knowing that he wore Italian straight-backs, not boxer shorts. He finished in a quarter of the time while Marie waited at a café-terrasse sipping a Chardonnay, thinking her heart would stop. He hadn't let her pay for a single item.

"Johnnie, Captain Brannigan, she will not like me for this. She will believe I am much too expensive to become a good agent."

"She won't know. Deena wanted to do something nice for you. This is her gift. Too bad she couldn't be with you. You'd still be shopping. I don't think the girl's ever been in a basement unless she's had a gun in her hand."

"Johnnie, I cannot."

He reached for his cell, pressing Speed Dial, pressing Speakerphone.

"Hi, sweetheart. Please tell me you're not at the beach drooling over all the pretty girls."

"I wish. Instead I'm here with some French broad who's giving me grief. We're at a bistro, Situation Red on the shopping spree. No quiere tu regalo esta chica. ¿Comprendes lo que digo?"

She did understand. Fennell was proving to be an excellent teacher in the spa.

"What did he say, Deena?"

"He said you don't want my gift. I disagree. Case closed. Is he treating you well?"

"Yes, he is, but I did have to punch him one time."

"Good."

"But Deena…"

"Sweetheart, any news?"

"We're dropping off the payload. Frenchie here's going to give me a tour and we'll visit the gallery after dinner. Check this out." He framed Marie on his screen, clicking the shot, forwarding the photo. "Check your email. That's what you call a French pouty face."

"Wow! Pretty sexy. I'm jealous already. You take care of him, Marie. Te amo, sweetheart."

The line went dead.

"What did Deena say, Johnnie?"

"She said to stop being difficult and relax, to show me the town and enjoy yourself. You just made her very happy."

They left the car at the hotel and strolled La Promenade des Anglais, renting beach chairs to gaze out at mega-yachts at anchor. Neither one felt like talking. Time didn't permit for much more. To the east, as far as the eye could see, on a bluff overlooking the sea, Emmanuelle Lerosier was painting a girl in a mirror. Le Vieux-Nice is where they would go first.

She'd spent hours her first day in Paris searching for rooms, one for him with a view. If it were not for Johnnie she would not be in France. He did that for her. She would do something nice for him, albeit at 410 USD per night on his expenses. Hers was a virtual closet with a view of ancient rooftops. The Côte d'Azur in July was impossibly crowded.

Seeing her room before lunch and their eight-store fashion hunt he traded keys with her and sent her to the room with a view, a spacious and elegant room with salt air wafting across her balcony from the Mediterranean. He had to stop being such a nice guy.

The gallery would remain open until ten, no reason to rush. They would eat dinner first as planned, this time with a bottle of wine they could enjoy together.

"Thank you, Johnnie for my room. I will not ask if you are comfortable in yours. I know you are not."

"You're welcome, and thank you."

"I would like to call Deena, to thank her for her extravagant gift to me. You gave me no time before. She will think I am not kind."

"She doesn't. Believe me. She likes you." He sipped his wine. She was sending a message. "You French girls have a peculiar way with your eyes."

"Yes, we do. We know that."

"Call her when we're done at the gallery. Do you think they speak English or Spanish?"

"English, yes, of course...in this place more than

anywhere else in France."

"I'm your American cousin here on vacation. Let's do it that way."

"They will not believe this for one moment. I will be your girlfriend while we are there. This they will believe more, an old American man and a young French girl."

"Don't push it, Frenchie. I can always explain spanking your tush to Brannigan and Deena."

She stopped talking, waiting.

"What now?"

"You have not told me how beautiful your new girlfriend is in her new outfit. Deena would believe this is rude of you."

"You're right, I'm wrong. You look lovely in yellow. I do have good taste. Don't I?"

"You do have expensive taste also."

Her yellow silk shirtdress was undone by three buttons at the top, two at the bottom. Her yellow satin sandals were flat, the barrette in her hair a clear citrine yellow. He just had to assume, keeping that thought to himself with a sly grin. Deena would be pleased with his work.

He checked his watch and gave her the keys. The French were insane on the road and she knew the rules better than him.

La Galerie des Maîtres d'Art was in Vieux-Nice, small, distinctive and pricey, though more than a cop John Francis Templeton Fennell was well-to-do. He didn't have to pretend.

He let Marie handle the niceties and chatter while he scanned the walls. He'd been in art galleries before, in the basement. He knew. Galleries were like restaurants. Stay out of the kitchen if you want to enjoy your meal. The oils on the walls were framed and well-spaced to afford each one the proper attention without the slightest distraction. In the basement however they leaned against the walls, stretched canvases waiting their turn, unframed and dusty or piled waist high on the floor.

When the owner approached him, Fennell gladly accepted her offer. She returned in a moment with a cognac for him and another for Marie. He had heard from a good friend about the paintings of a young girl in a mirror and his girlfriend knew where to come. He knew nothing about art. He knew what he liked and he liked the work of Mademoiselle Emmanuelle Lerosier.

"Her work is excellent, madame, to my untrained eye. I like her style very much indeed. My friend was correct in directing me to your gallery. With your permission I will take my time to appreciate her creations and to make my selection."

The woman understood: Get lost.

Whereas Marie did not understand, taking his hand the way they'd planned. What was he doing? What was he saying? The paintings were ten to 15,000 USD. She was ready to hurry out whenever he was. She could live with the temporary shame. She was a special agent like Deena, or she would be one day soon. She was working undercover, learning. That had to count for something.

Two hours later the gallery was closing. John Fennell however wasn't ready to leave. He was ready to purchase, the owner knew. Distinguishing potential clients from inquisitive tourists or idle weekend browsers was part of what she did. He was a client.

"Madame, would you kindly allow us to remain a half-hour longer, our time in your city is brief? I have made what I believe is my initial selection. However I would be greatly indebted to you were you to contact the artist to request a private tour of her atelier. As much as I am taken with what I believe is my choice, I would also prefer a painting that no one else has yet seen. Tomorrow at noon would suit my schedule if the lady would agree to receive us for a very short while. Nor would I, for a moment, neglect to consider your fee."

"Madame does not entertain visitors, monsieur. I regret to say. She is, how should I say, very peculiar."

"Please explain to the lady that I am not a visitor, rather a recently dedicated admirer of her art who hopes to become a connoisseur of Emmanuelle Lerosier."

The woman left, returning moments later with more equally generous cognacs, excusing herself to make the call.

"Johnnie, she will hate us for this, for playing with her. What are you doing to tease her this way?"

He kissed the side of her head. He liked her. She was refreshing. She would be a good cop, and honest. How rare was that?

"Let's not disappoint her right now. We're not done. We have more girls and mirrors to consider, though I am leaning towards the one which shows one girl in blue on her knees crying green tears inside the mirror, the other girl in red laughing, peering into the mirror with her green eyes wide open and sparkling." He pulled her closer, whispering. "Frenchie, these images are of Gilligan Rose. She's painting her daughter."

Her disappointment was real. "I wanted to tell you this first. I did see this right away, Johnnie."

"I'm sorry, Marie. I'm used to cops who aren't as good as you." He squeezed her. "So, do you agree with my choice?"

"Yes, I do, however I do like this one much better." The painting was of twin girls dressed in yellow, one locked into a mirror, yellow tears staining her face, her fingertips touching the fingertips of the girl looking in, smiling. "The name is a good one, Johnnie. One girl is telling the other that she wants to exchange places for a little while. She wants to be happy for a little while. This is my favourite colour, also, like my new dress."

He shrugged.

The woman returned, her lively expression telling him what he wanted to hear. Mademoiselle Emmanuelle, she confirmed, would expect them at noon.

He thanked her.

"However she does not keep her work once they are signed, monsieur. She has no need. We are her sole venue for her work. Our walls change frequently."

"I look forward to meeting her, in which case my selection is made. I will take that one of the blue and red girls and this smaller one in yellow. Will a deposit of ten thousand suffice until we return for them tomorrow?"

"Yes, monsieur, most certainly."

He gave the woman his card. "I will require crating for export, certificates and insurance."

She nodded, smiling. No kidding. He figured at twenty percent she'd just made a cool five K plus. Agent Marie didn't know what to think. She kept her mouth shut as they walked out and went somewhere for late evening cocktails. She wanted to speak. She couldn't. She couldn't find the right words. Truth be told, she was afraid. Her mind was racing, one random thought usurped by another.

Her new ensembles and shoes, more than her wardrobe budget for two or three years. She Deena did not mean for him to spend that much. His new wardrobe, the wine that he ordered was the finest and upgrading their flights to First-Class. And the paintings, the way he signed the bill as though he was paying for groceries. He'd spent more in a day what she earned in a year. She wanted to believe he was a good man, but she knew that so many others in Miami did not like him.

"Okay, what now?"

"The paintings, Johnnie, how will you take these home?"

"They'll be shipped from the US Embassy here to the Miami office, sort of like diplomatic immunity, no US Customs hassles." He grinned. "The hardest part will be keeping them from Deena."

"She will kill you for this."

"You don't think she'll like the red and blue?"

"I do believe she will not like you. You will ruin her wedding with this expense and put you in trouble with Captain Brannigan. She will investigate you for this, Johnnie."

He let that sink in for a moment, her face and her mood accentuating her unblinking eyes. She was telling him politely that he was a dirty cop. Fact was; he would be entertaining the same thought in her place. He smiled warmly, swirling his cognac.

"I have a private collection at home, Frenchie, souvenirs from each case I've solved. One is a bullet taken from the first guy I shot. His day didn't turn out too well. Another is a video of my first arrest taken from a helicopter; another is a two-ounce wafer of gold from a major heist gone wrong. At the time the wafer was worth about three grand. I wrote a cheque and got a signed receipt to avoid complications. The blue and red girls will hang in my office over those and many other curios, something I'll be showing Gayle Brannigan after the wedding. She won't question how much I paid or how. She knows I'm not a cop for the big bucks. Neither is Deena. We're very fortunate people. Enough said. Ironic though, don't you think, mother and daughter living in the same country at least part of the time over so many years?"

Her mouth was bone dry. "I am so sorry, Johnnie, I did not want to believe what I was thinking."

"Don't be sorry, Marie. I would have thought the same. It's the kind of thinking that will make you a good cop...like Deena." He passed her his phone, savouring his cognac while Marie gave a full report to Deena and piece by piece descriptions of her designer wardrobe right down to the essentials that she confirmed were indeed yellow that particular evening.

"Thank you, Deena, especially for the black one that Johnnie chose for me from you."

"Don't tell me, something short, sheer and décolleté. Is that about right?"

She giggled. "No. I did not like this one at all. He chose another, a so elegant slip dress with thin straps and a scarf to cover my shoulders and beautiful shoes. I will not wear my bra with this one, Deena."

His drink managed to stay in his mouth.

"Then make him take you for an elegant dinner. Did you hear that, Agent Fennell?"

He did, commandeering his phone before the battery ran out, walking away, returning a few minutes later to escort her to her floor, waiting at the elevator until she was in her room.

Thirty-Three
This Year: July 12th

Walking into the restaurant for breakfast Gilligan Rose was uppermost on his mind, placing her somewhere over the mid-Atlantic, supposing that her thoughts were preoccupied with him. Marie was standing.

He took her hand, spinning her around, humming his appreciation, a group of men at a nearby table applauding. She looked as good in green as she did in yellow.

"Where do you think you're going, Agent Marie?"

She wasn't her cheerful self. "Johnnie, we are still very good friends since last night? Yes?"

"We are still very good friends. Yes. In fact you're my only friend. That makes you very special."

She hugged him, kissing his cheek.

"I will confess to Deena tonight that I did kiss you. I am going shopping for a dress to wear at Deena's wedding. I did see one that I liked, and to buy her a wedding gift. However I did not tell you this. I will return before eleven."

"Give me some time for a coffee. I'll go with you. A pretty girl shouldn't be out alone with all these hungry French guys hanging around."

"No, you will not. You cannot see this dress or my gift for Deena. Besides, if a little girl can beat you up so easily, how can you protect me against these Frenchmen?"

"Good point." He sat. "You be here at eleven, no excuses."

She promised, hugging him again, not completely forgiving herself for what she'd been thinking the night before.

He shooed her away, secretly thankful for the time alone. Mother and daughter, he thought, so near yet so far, soon to be reunited in prison with ample time each day to catch up.

After breakfast he went to the promenade, studying the flotilla of yachts, wondering which one he could afford. That would be cool, seeing Deena on the forward deck of their yacht all naked and tanned, glistening in the sun. Not a sailboat, though, too much effort, too much time taken away from the delicate operation of applying SPF. Why hadn't he thought of that as a wedding gift? He might not be too late. He would call her Double Agent. He knew about boats. He'd worked his summers as a student crewing sixty and seventy-footers. He wanted fifty feet; anything more was showy, too expensive to run. He agreed with himself aloud. A sleek fifty feet would help assuage her disappointment in what he was thinking, for what he'd decided he would do.

He would wait until after Lerosier to call the boat manufacturer in the States for the dealer's number in Miami.

He checked his watch: 10:50 AM. She was strutting along the promenade, turning heads, his included. He pushed away from his chaise-longue. She was smiling. She felt better about herself. Case closed.

"Everything work out for you?"

"No. I will shop this evening also, if you do not need me. Or we can have dinner in the Vielle-Ville if you are not yet too tired of me."

"Not yet. I'm good for a few more meals."

"Thank you, Johnnie."

"You're welcome."

He took her bags. He had to admit, this case would be difficult to beat: his fiancée at home, a good-looking kid strolling with him, her arm locked into his, talking like they were close friends and not tracking a killer, a killer mom and killer daughter, estranged a few hundred miles apart.

Deena on Friday with Frenchie and a few other agents watching him in bed with the suspect, he thought, he didn't know. How else would she kill him? That was the strangest part, the most legally tricky. Deena hadn't yet killed anyone. She once wounded a guy in the leg their first month together, spun him around like a top, and that put her over the edge for a few days. People didn't just lie down and die. They went in all different directions, into the air, scraping the ground, gasping and gaping, thinking too late about a career change. Television would never capture that reality, not even close. And neither would Deena.

Marie brought him back with a pat on his arm.

"When will I have my elegant dinner in my new black dress, Johnnie?"

"Are you this timid all the time?"

"I think tomorrow because tonight I must do my shopping for Deena. I do want her to have something French to remember me."

"It's a date and Deena will definitely remember you." The girl was something special, a challenge even for Brannigan. "What does your boyfriend think about you wanting to be an agent? Is he nervous about you carrying a gun one day?"

"I do not know. I do not have one, so what he might think when he finds me does not matter to me."

"A cute thing like you doesn't have a guy?"

"No. I do not. However thank you for saying that I am cute. All the men my age and older continue to live at home with their mothers. These are not men. I want a real man, not a boy. And the older ones, they are too old. I will still be young one day and he will be dead. The others, all they want is to have sex with me, these macho Miami men, to go under my panties because I am different. I am not a girl like that. I will go to Deena's wedding alone. I do not need anyone and to go with my brother people will believe there is something wrong with me when there is not. No. I will go alone."

"And make all the other women jealous."

"Yes. I suppose. I am a French girl…and cute, also. This is what I hear."

"I haven't noticed."

She punched him.

At the hotel he gave her fifteen minutes to do whatever when she didn't have a hair out of place. He stayed in the lobby.

The drive to the atelier was circuitous and scenic. He let her drive, thinking but for a name Emma Rose would remain a free woman. Of all people Phillips should have known better.

Lerosier's expansive home overlooked the sea, hundreds of yachts and the rooftops of luxurious homes scattered helter-skelter into the deceptively steep cliff below.

Marie asked with innocent curiosity. He answered ten, twelve million seventeen years ago and nothing like Philips' never-lived-in home on the outskirts of London.

The home was gated, the exterior white stucco, the roof laid with tiles the colour of the sea, not faded and orange like the other villas. Marie spoke into the intercom, moments later Fennell whispered that he didn't believe what he was seeing. Mademoiselle Emmanuelle Lerosier was coming to the gate herself in a string bikini, suede boots and a wide smile, letting a mild wind swirl her silk robe like a whimsical cape. She was painting outside, her tan pale, her hair a deep red, her eyes a deep emerald-green and her body light years from fifty-two. He thought she could pass for an easy forty. He couldn't help thinking not bad, not bad at all.

She greeted Marie Anisette first in French, Fennell in English.

Inside she offered them ice tea. Marie accepted; Fennell did not. Her studio looked out over the Mediterranean, cluttered with sketches half drawn, paintings half completed.

"Madame tells me you that you acquired my Green Tears and my Yellow Envy. Thank you, Monsieur Fennell."

"Your work will be a fine addition to our home, mademoiselle. I'm eager to hang them."

"You are American, Monsieur Fennell. And mademoiselle you are French. You seem to me like such a wonderful couple. I wish you a wonderful life together."

"Thank you," Marie answered. She patted his leg. "We are so happy together. If only he could learn French."

Yeah, right. "We were disappointed to hear that your current work will not be completed before our departure, Mademoiselle Lerosier. I was hoping for something unseen by other eyes. May we at least see your work in progress? I would like very much to explain to our friends your work through your eyes."

He was sitting with Emma Rose, Gilligan's mother in a silk robe over a string bikini and boots. How strange was that? He'd researched her. He knew everything about her. He read every newspaper and magazine article, had copies of most of her photos. She didn't look at all like a killer, not a day older than her latest photo as Miss Emma Rose, nothing like a fugitive. Her voice had a musical quality, the way she walked almost dancing and her hands were smooth to the touch. Real hard to imagine she was fifty-two or that she'd stuck a couple of carving knives into her husband's chest. She was, he didn't know, effervescent and charming.

"Come, I will show you Forever Lost. I think so. I don't often change my titles or show my unfinished work."

The easel was set on her patio by the infinity pool, soft music playing, high stone walls affording complete privacy with only the sky above her.

"Your faces never change, a young girl with red hair and green eyes, yet they are so different on each canvas you paint. As well, your titles are emotive and compelling, as though drawing the viewer into the young girl's gloom, never her joy. I feel, forgive me if I am wrong, that the girl outside is less important."

"We are not drawn to joy, Monsieur Fennell. Joy is infectious. We must be drawn into the darkness of other minds. I think so."

"The girl, mademoiselle, looks very much like you. The resemblance is undeniable."

"This is my daughter's face when she is happy. She was always so happy, except in the dark. She was afraid of the dark. Her name is Gilligan Rose. She wants to pass through the mirror to take away Gilligan's pain, to make her feel happy again, to dance in the rain. That's what she wants most of all. I think so. She wants to dance in the rain and never be sad again. I do hope that she is."

He left that one alone.

"How old is she, mademoiselle?" Marie asked.

"She is fifteen. She will forever be fifteen. We grow old by choice, Marie. I think so. Don't ever be afraid to remain young."

Marie nodded.

"She's very lovely," Fennell went on. You and your husband must be very proud of her."

"I'm not married. I was, a very long time ago. He died unexpectedly a very long time ago."

Yeah, he did, from pains in his chest. "Your English is flawless. Are you originally from here?"

"Thank you. He was American. I learned from him."

"Votre fille, mademoiselle, is your daughter at home?" Marie added, surprising her partner. "We would love to say to our friends that we met her."

"No. She won't be home for a while, I'm afraid. Yet in

my heart, I know that she loves me. I think so." Emmanuelle Lerosier touched the cheek of the girl half-painted on canvas. "Perhaps one day I will paint her standing together. I do hate painting the mirror, each time trapping her inside, but then who would Gilligan see?"

"Perhaps she would see a face without tears," Marie answered, "perhaps a mother who loves her. That is what I hope she will see."

"Mademoiselle, we have taken enough of your time." Fennell broke in. Marie was getting as bad as Deena. "Thank you for your gracious invitation to experience your studio. I'm certain that one day soon your paintings will change, that Gilligan will find her way out of the mirror."

"I don't believe that she will. I don't think so. It's where she feels safe. She always went inside her mirror."

She walked them to her gate where she shook Fennell's hand, embracing Marie. She watched them drive away, waving, her cape once again fluttering in the gentle breeze, disappearing from their rear-view mirrors.

They went for a late lunch in la Vielle-Ville, to the Galerie des Maîtres d'Art in le Vieux-Nice. At the hotel Fennell gave himself space to make three phone calls. The first was for information, the second to purchase a fifty-five-foot all-dressed Sundancer delivered to the dealer the previous day and still in its cradle. The third call was to Deena.

There was no doubt who Emma Rose was or where she was: the hair, the eyes and the 'I think so'; 'I don't think so', the flawless translucent skin at fifty-two, her freedom abruptly over within a matter of days.

Against his better judgment, and without telling Deena, he placed a fourth call to the law firm. The man was twenty-six, he didn't live with his mother, he didn't have a girlfriend, he was becoming a good lawyer, he needed a life, he was good-looking from a female perspective and if he even thought of getting into her pants he'd be out of a job or shot with a chrome-plated Berretta or both in no particular order.

The young man was surprised. He'd thought John Francis Templeton Fennell was a shithead with a silver stick up his ass. He never spoke to anyone at the firm who wasn't a senior partner, never said hello or goodbye, never said thanks for working eighty hours a week, or kiss my ass. What he didn't know was that Fennell was a federal agent and was told in no uncertain terms to keep the fact confidential, calling from France, telling him about a to-die-for French girl who needed a date. If she needed that much help getting a date she had to be big-boned. He thought maybe not, yet he was a year into his dream job, the envy of a hundred others who'd lost out. He was royally screwed.

He asked Fennell what exactly he meant by 'to-die-for', precisely what were the terms and conditions of the evening. Fennell told him to see for himself that coming Monday. If Fennell was wrong about the girl he would pay for the dinner and throw in a Caribbean cruise for him and any other girl. If he was right Marie would have a date for the wedding. The agreement was verbal and binding. The terms were: Have a good time: The condition was: Step out of line, leave town.

Before dinner he gave Marie the job of calling Brannigan to file a verbal update. The time had come to face the firing squad for what she had done. He didn't tell her that he'd spoken with Brannigan prior to their departure from Paris to explain the kid's absence. He took the phone when she was done, Brannigan not asking for confirmation, Fennell not offering anything further. Anisette hadn't left out a single detail, though he did give her a thumbs-up while talking with the boss lady.

Later, in another dress, enjoying their after dinner liqueurs at yet another café-terrasse with a glorious view of the sparkling sea, where they'd walked arm in arm to wear off their meal because Marie didn't want passers-by to see her as the only young woman not walking that way, he was ready for whatever might come his way.

"How do you say deep shit in French, Frenchie?"

"This is very simple to answer, Johnnie. I do not. Why do you want to know such a bad word?"

"Because I have a feeling I'm in pretty deep. As Miss Emma Rose would say, I think so."

He sipped his cognac, glancing between her and the yachts at anchor. She sipped her Pernod diluted with water.

"What did you do this time, Johnnie?" She giggled. "Did you buy one of these big boats and now you are afraid to tell Deena because she will hurt you for doing such a crazy thing?"

"Yes, I did, about the size of that one." He pointed. "But that's not why I'm in deep shit. You're in a good mood... right?"

Her mouth managed to close. "Yes, I am, of course. I am on the French Riviera with a handsome man who is always joking with me, we did find Miss Emma Rose and Captain Brannigan will not fire me for not asking her permission. This is a good reason to feel good."

"Good... because I got you a date for the wedding."

He was serious.

Her smile continued, then not, fading, gone. She put down her glass.

"What have you done, Johnnie? You did not do such a horrible thing to me. I would not like you at all for this."

"I sort of did."

"Look at me, Johnnie. Do you believe that I would need your help to find someone for one day if I wanted someone so badly? How could you do this to me? And when did you do this? You have no friends, not even one at this moment, and we are in France."

"That hurt."

"I do not care. I am hurting also because you did this to me."

"He's a nice guy, Frenchie. He works at my law firm. He's single and successful. He lives alone. He's tall, dark and handsome and starting to earn very good money. And he had the same reaction: a little hostile. The thing is I'm technically his boss so he had to be cool about the situation."

"Situation, Johnnie? I am not a situation. And what are you saying? You are an agent. How can you be a boss to anyone? This is not true. I am phoning Deena. You do not need me here one more day. I am going home."

"Actually, Frenchie, I do own a Miami law firm, the best one I'm proud to say. That's a secret, by the way. I'm a lawyer, albeit with a slight conflict of interest that I'm working on and you are not going home. So why not give this guy a chance?"

"No. I will not. I do not believe you. Even so, he is doing this to keep his job if you are telling the truth...because of my... situation."

"I am, ask Deena or Brannigan. By the way, I told him you were smart and beautiful, very beautiful, and fussy, very fussy about men. I told him if I'm wrong that I would compensate him for his grief. He wants to invite you to dinner on Monday, somewhere nice, somewhere with dancing. I accepted on your behalf. He's educated, polite, a good dresser and someone you will like. Also, if he tries anything naughty I'll shoot him. He knows that. Besides, you'll have another reason to wear your black dress."

No reaction. She was learning from the best. She didn't want not to like him.

"Does Deena know of this bad thing you have done, that I cannot find my own date?'

"No. She doesn't have to know everything."

No reaction.

"Is he correct? Is he missing anything of importance?"

He shrugged. "We can pass him through an airport scanner, but fair is fair and I know he'll like what he sees," he smirked, "which is pretty much everything in that little black dress you'll be wearing."

No reaction.

"We will go dancing also?"

He nodded. "And he doesn't live with his mommy."

"I can return him if I do not like him at all."

He nodded. "Yes, you can. So are we still very good friends? Yes?"

She waited. "We are still very good friends. Yes. Because you told him I am beautiful. You may give him my number to call me on Sunday. He must ask me himself. I will know by his voice if he is a nice man."

"Yeah, about that...he's sort of calling you tonight from his office in about half an hour and he doesn't need to know why you're here. You're on a special assignment, nothing more."

She sipped her digestif. "You did buy a boat like this one, Johnnie, for Deena? And you are really a lawyer as well as an agent?"

"Yes I did and yes I am. Now let's get out of here."

She smiled. "Thank you, Johnnie, for thinking of me. I was wrong to be angry with you. I will not call Deena...not until the next time you are a fennell with me. I will do my shopping in Paris tomorrow, if you do not need me."

He thought he could survive without her, coughing a laugh, wondering what he'd done to an unsuspecting criminal lawyer in Miami. C'est la vie.

Again they walked arm in arm, Marie wanting to know everything her could tell her about her date. He wasn't much use at all to an excited young woman.

Thirty-Four
This Year: July13th

The previous evening Marie Anisette spoke on the phone for thirty minutes with Lincoln Palmer, Linc for short, with a C.

She hadn't been on date in months and the few dates she did accept too long ago to remember didn't work out: her father's fault. She had promised him before entering university and with all her heart and tears when she left their home in Chicago to work in Miami with Gayle Brannigan that she would be a good girl.

When the call ended she decided to wait until morning to tell Johnnie Fennell how excited she was for Monday evening. She believed that she would like Lincoln Palmer very much.

Just as well. Fennell was on the promenade in a nylon jogging suit, headband and Nikes paying the penalty for a half-week of excellent French wine and self-destructive French cuisine.

In Miami Deena, as much as she'd wanted to hate him a year earlier, inventing a different   reason each day to despise him, now hated being away from him. She was in for a big argument, she knew. He had his mind set. He had this thing about being right. That he was always right was another issue. This time she was right and he would have to listen to her. But that wasn't the worst.

Strangely, they fell asleep at the same time, time zones apart, Deena tired and worried while Fennell was up until

411

the early hours practicing how he would end up in bed with a female serial killer while his fiancée, Frenchie and a back-up team from Miami were taping and videoing him in the adjoining room. No more rich food, he promised, not until the week was over.

He woke at seven, tired, intent on running for an hour. The hotel had no gym. A day without a good sweat wasn't a good day. He hated running. At least in Nice, he conceded, he could check out the yachts and certain passers-by in micro-fibre shorts, tights and halter tops, most of who, for some reason, could jog faster than him. He wasn't there to run a marathon. He was on the job honing his ability to observe and recognize the minutest, seemingly unimportant details

When he was showered and dressed, ready for breakfast, Marie was in the restaurant waiting. She'd eaten, seated at the table writing a report that he would read before Brannigan. She knew that without being told.

Deena was right. He could be so annoying much of the time, and so much more gallant than most other men. She refused to speak first. She would not give him the satisfaction. She learned that from Deena.

He began, surprising her, filling his cup from her carafe.

"First off, Frenchie, the day is yours. Let's call it a paid personal day between you and me. When we land in Paris you do what you want. I'll be at the embassy sans you. I also want you to choose the finest restaurant in the city for our dinner this evening, something classy." He ordered toast and more coffee. "Now about Thursday and Friday, you listen to what I say, not Deena, not anyone else. You listen to me. You got that?"

"Yes, Johnnie, I do know this."

"Tomorrow you leave Paris on your own. I won't be around for breakfast. Take a taxi to the airport. After tonight I won't see you until after Gilligan Rose is in cuffs or dead. You have to understand that. You wanted in, and you are in, as far as I say you are. You might possibly see someone killed in New York on Friday, Frenchie. You be ready for that. You be ready to puke out your guts and to spend the night crying because you will. So far this has been a piece of cake with good food and scenery. Friday not so much and you stay out of my room when the shit hits the fan. You stay out of the way. If this works out I'll introduce you to Rose when she's the one crying. If something goes wrong I'll see you after they take her away wrapped in a bag."

"I will stay far away. I will be afraid for you, Johnnie, like I know that Deena is right now in her heart. Who does wait one year to know if he will be killed by a crazy woman? Yes, I will be afraid for you. I am afraid for you now. This is why I was angry with you last night because of Lincoln, because I do know what might happen to you. I was not angry because of him, not really."

"I'll be fine, Frenchie. Deena's got my back."

He checked his watch. Their flight was in three hours. His demeanour evaporated. No more shop talk. He sat in his seat biting into his toast, letting his mind wander, taking in everything and everyone in the dining room but her. She didn't exist.

"I know that you are teasing with me, Johnnie. So you can stop acting this way. I do agree that Lincoln does seem very nice. He sent me a photo also which I was nervous to open, until I did see him and then I was pleased. When he did see me he said 'holy mackerel' into the phone. However he did not sound disappointed to me. What does this mean, this holy mackerel?"

"It means he believes me. It also means I might have to shoot him. I'll give you a bullet to put on the table to remind him. "

"I believe he will do very well as my date for Deena's wedding. If I am right I will keep him. He asked me what are my favourite flowers and my favourite foods. This is a good indication."

"This is between you and me, Frenchie. I don't need grief from Deena."

"She will know. How will she believe I would know him without you? She will not." Marie was elated, Fennell thinking that next time he might mind his own business.

"After our dinner we will go dancing. Do you know, Johnnie, that he speaks French a little? However not badly for an American. He said goodnight to me in French, though I do believe he did practice to impress me." She thought for a moment. "Please do not tell him this."

He didn't know. He had to ask. "So…if I understand what you're saying…I'm just thinking out loud here."

She rolled her eyes. "I will not make your head bigger than what I see. No, I will not do this."

"Do I get a hug or something for my good work, or one of those cheeky-type kisses you French people seem to believe is a life source?"

"No, you do not. I will inspect him first. I will see him in person to know that you have done the best job for me. I will hug you on Tuesday if you have done well for me, if he is a good dancer and does remember my favourite flowers." She sighed. "I have not had flowers for such a long time. Thank you so much, Johnnie."

"Don't thank me. He's as desperate as you are. You deserve each other."

At that she stood. She went to him and punched him, pinching his cheek. She was beginning to enjoy punching him, the way she enjoyed punching her brother whom she wouldn't see until Christmas when he would tease her, though she would never say that to Johnnie. She wanted too much to earn his respect, to become an agent like Deena. Instead she reneged on her vow and hugged him, leaving him to his thoughts without saying a word, a dozen men and twice that number of eyes following her through the doors.

He took a deep breath, sighing contentedly. She looked fabulous in her cinnamon silk outfit and tan leather pumps, her ponytail a metronome keeping time with the sway of her skirt. He had great taste in clothes, great taste in women and yachts, and Palmer would be the first one thrown overboard twenty miles out if he even thought of disappointing the girl who was fast becoming sort of a kid sister. Not that he needed one.

The flight departed at twelve noon. He would wait until landing before calling Deena.

Marie spent her time onboard creating a profile of Emmanuelle Lerosier from her perspective, more for Fennell to read than Brannigan. She had nothing else to do until Friday, Fennell convincing Brannigan that the French kid should take part in the arrest for all that she'd done. Until that time her job was done. She couldn't very well report that she was going to dinner with Agent John Fennell in her new party dress that she would also wear to dinner with Lincoln Palmer on Monday.

*

Three thousand miles to the west Gilligan Rose was serving TGA First-Class passengers her homemade mimosas en route to Paris and on to Frankfurt. She was sixty-three hours from the theatre, sixty-six from putting a knife into his chest before midnight.

She would spend Thursday in Paris shopping for something to wear to the theatre, new shoes and gloves, a hat and sunglasses to complement her dress, two pairs of panties and a clutch. She'd decided against her white ensemble. She would wear that to the cabaret for Elixia, for their celebration. The problem was concealing the knife. How would she conceal such a big blade in such a small purse? She had an idea. She wouldn't. She would make the evening one to remember. She would make Fennell a special memory.

She had decided that John Fennell would be her last. He would be their celebration. She couldn't save the world removing one deviant a year and might well destroy her own. She didn't regret a single one, though one day she would act too slowly or he would react too quickly. She knew that not one of the wives had ever mourned her extemporaneous loss. More importantly she had gotten to the men before the touching began, before the fondling, the goodnight kisses and the pain the daughters would too late learn to understand. Those lives were saved, the ten didn't matter. John Fennell wouldn't matter either. He was the worst after Cooper, the most blatant, not once thinking to secrete his obsession with his daughters from her other passengers. On second thought maybe he was the worst, the most obscene. She wouldn't know until Friday when she might access his computer. What she did know was that his girls would be the last she would save.

Elixia was the most important of all. They had spoken throughout the night after leaving the club, Fennell jumping in and out of her torn mind as she listened to Elixia's frustration and tears, as she worried what Fennell was doing to the young girl he'd lured to the cabaret. She could imagine the worst, and she did. She would enjoy shopping for him the most, her trip to a New York pharmacy and one of those sleazy Manhattan discount stores with fast-talking salesmen where most everything sold was previously stolen.
*

Landing in Paris Fennell shooed his only friend away to spend her day on the Champs Elysée, admonishing Marie that Deena did not need anything extravagant from a kid paying off a student loan.

At the embassy the crated paintings were carried in for him, arrangements made for direct and diplomatic transport to his attention at the Miami Field Office of The Federal Task Force on Major Crime. Immediate shipment was imperative onboard an American airline other than TGA.

They didn't ask questions. The Task Force had a mandate to get things done. They were the country's best cops. Getting in their way was not a good career move at any level.

At the hotel he called Deena. He needed his black suit and a darker tie suitable for evening theatre. He got an update on the wedding; she got an update on Marie and Palmer. She thought that was sweet, more than somewhat amazed he'd been that thoughtful of a young woman's need for companionship. Then she wanted to know everything about the young lawyer she hadn't yet met.

When the drill was over, Fennell swore he would never again get involved in anyone's deficient love life or entire lack thereof. He had enough trouble with one of his own. He didn't need a pissed-off French daddy coming after him. When he ended the call he changed and went to the gym for a sweat, believing he was in for an evening of Deena and Lincoln Palmer. When he was done he crawled into bed for an hour. Marie had left a detailed message while he was gone. She was at the hair salon. She'd made reservations in his name for 7:30 at a restaurant with a view of the Eiffel Tower, romantic without being too romantic and not near the cabaret. Besides, she added, anyone who might see them would not return from Frankfurt until later the next day. She didn't want to use the woman's name. She didn't want to spoil her special evening in her special new dress.

He called her room from the lobby. A lady should expect nothing less. Marie came down a few moments later: a vision, and very much the centre of attention.

"You're making it difficult to remember that we work together, Frenchie, and that I'm getting married to a girl with a big gun. You are fabulous, kid, nice hairdo."

"This is a French braid for a French girl. People will believe you are a young-looking and handsome man eating his dinner with his lovely and sophisticated much younger daughter. No?"

"More like his younger sister."

She twirled. "No, his daughter is what I believe. Do my legs show enough?"

"Please don't do that again. I have to live until Friday."

She twirled, taking his arm. In the taxi, she sat close and took his arm. She wanted to see Paris from the Eiffel Tower with him, her arm locked into his. She would find a tourist to capture the moment. This would be her souvenir of her first case with her pictures taken at the beach.

"Do not worry, Johnnie. I will explain to Deena that I did force you to come here against your good intentions. She will not beat you up for being with me. Also, I want her to have a copy of me working with you in Paris."

"Just what every woman wants, a picture of her desirable and suave husband in Paris with some French broad in half a dress."

She punched him.

"Deena is not jealous of me. She is too beautiful to worry about any other woman."

They remained a while longer, the panorama was too special, Fennell snapping shots with his phone, photos Deena would allow him to keep, Marie's dress dancing above her knees in the slight breeze, her scarf fluttering across her shoulders and back.

When they left they strolled to the restaurant, arm in arm. Apparently she liked that.

The restaurant wasn't the most expensive in Paris, nor the least, she told him. The music was soft and the ambiance was quiet. She'd asked for the most private corner. She'd called her father in Chicago to ask where they should go, to tell him about the wedding and Lincoln. When she left Paris to live in America she was too young to know of such places. Her father, though, knew all of them as he'd known of the cabaret. He travelled to Paris often.

At the restaurant they spoke about Deena, the wedding, the day Deena decided he wasn't a fennell, the day after she'd dried off from the evening in Brannigan's office. Marie pressed a palm over her heart and promised not to tell a soul, not even Lincoln.

She wanted to speak about her date and Lincoln Palmer, disappointed. He didn't. That's what first dates were all about, he said. She would have to wait. Five days and six hours wasn't that long. Then she could tell him all about Lincoln Palmer.

They spoke about how desperately she wanted to become a federal agent, about how her father, her brother and her mother thought differently about their only daughter and sister wearing a gun and becoming an American.

"Thank you, Johnnie, for my training this week. This will help me become good cop. Thank you for helping me with Captain Brannigan also. I was so afraid she would fire me."

"She told me to thank you for what you tried to do. She didn't want to tell you herself. That's what HR is for in these situations. She feels badly, Marie, for losing you. Unfortunately you won't be working for her after September 01ˢᵗ. She can't keep you after what you did. You went way beyond what she expected of you. You broke the rules, kid. Now you have to pay your dues."

He was gloating, checking his watch, his cell set on BUZZ. At times like this he was the absolute best at being a prick. None was better.

"Johnnie, do not tell me this. No. She is making me leave my work? She is making me leave you and Deena?"

"I'm afraid so, though not until September. So you're still in on Friday's arrest. And, really, often this is for the best. You'll see. Things will work out. I know they will."

She put her crystal goblet on the table, not trusting herself. She could not have feigned a more distraught expression, her face drained of colour, her eyes liquid hazel, her deep-prune lips working hard not to quiver.

"Johnnie, you made me believe with what you said and your thumb in the air when you were talking with Captain Brannigan that she was pleased with me."

"A lot changes in a day, Frenchie, especially in this

business. But, hey, we'll see you at the wedding and you've met a nice guy. It's not all bad news."

His phone buzzed.

"It's Deena."

"Deena is calling. Does she know of this, Johnnie?"

"Of course she knows. She's the one who told me this afternoon. She wants to wish you the best in your new life. She'll miss you, but life does go on." He pressed SPEAKERPHONE. "Not too loud, sweetcheeks, we're in the restaurant. The line's open. Frenchie's here. She's not taking the news too well. Either that or she doesn't appreciate excellent French wine."

"Fennell, what have you done to the poor girl this time?"

"He did tell me, Deena."

"Yeah, I'm sure he did. He's being a fennell, Marie. Smack him real hard for this one."

Marie looked at Fennell. He was grinning his usual way, the way that she knew annoyed Deena, his lips curved slightly into a smirk on one side, not the other. She didn't understand anything.

"Deena I was so happy before. Now I am so depressed. My heart wants to stop. I believed that Captain Brannigan would one day help me."

"She has already. Congratulations Agent Marie Anisette. Brannigan pulled some very serious strings. You've been accepted into the academy. She also put your citizenship on fast-track. We can't have foreign nationals solving our major crimes. We lose you in six weeks, for a year which isn't too long. Plus you stay in Miami during that time with a position in our squad after your graduation. Good news for Lincoln Palmer, and good luck with him."

She was crying. "Deena I am not fired. Johnnie, he told me I am no longer working for her."

"Technically you're not, which doesn't mean that when you get your shield and your gun in a year you can't use

Fennell for target practice. We both will, Marie, together. Let's see if we can find his heart."

"Johnnie, I am a real agent."

"Congratulations, Frenchie." He passed her an envelope. "We thought you might like a copy of your official acceptance. The original is on Brannigan's desk. Be in her office first thing Monday morning and I would not suggest that you be late."

"Deena, I am crying. You did this for me."

"I'm crying too. We're allowed."

"So am I." Fennell added.

"Shut up, Fennell. We're not interested."

"Deena, I will kiss you so many times tomorrow for this. Do I have your permission to kiss your fennell right now?"

"If you don't think you'll ruin your meal. I wouldn't. Smack him first, though."

She stood and went to him, her face wet. She smacked his shoulder for Deena to hear and kissed his smirk, leaning across to hug him.

"Deena, his mouth is the colour of a prune."

"Say goodbye to him, Marie. Because when he gets home I'm drowning him for doing this to you."

She wiped her face. "Goodbye, Johnnie. I will miss you."

Deena didn't bother stifling her laugh, pressing END; Fennel ordered a bottle of Dom Pérignon, barely able to get a word in by the time they left the restaurant.

At the elevator in the hotel she wrapped her arms around his waist. She wouldn't see him again until Gilligan Rose was arrested or dead. She would pray for him. He told her not to bother. He wasn't a member of that particular club. She would pray for him anyway, she insisted.

He admonished her to remember his instructions to stay out of the way. She wasn't a super cop yet. She admonished him not to do anything that would ruin Deena's wedding.

Besides, she had their special gifts and could not return them.

In her room Marie couldn't sleep. She phoned her parents and her brother with the news.

In his room he phoned Deena and spoke for an hour before hitting the gym. He had things on his mind.

*

Gilligan Rose was leaving the Frankfurt Airport. Her flight the next morning would put her in Paris in time for an early lunch with Elixia whom she was anxious to see, anxious to tell that she was resigning from TGA to live in Paris and paint. The rest would come later, if ever.

Thirty-Five
This Year: July 14th & 15th

Johnnie Fennell woke late. He felt like shit, miserable, as though he hadn't slept a wink. His day was planned, as much as he could plan a prelude to his destiny. He had nothing to do but wait twenty-four hours. The kind of day he hated, the reason he once worked seven-day weeks before Deena finally succeeded in convincing him to love her, make love to her and marry her.

He would do an hour in the gym in the morning, afternoon and evening, after which he would run an hour each time and get to bed early. Toast for breakfast, a salad for lunch, something light for dinner without wine or booze and a late call to Deena. That was his day. He didn't care about the worsening forecast.

He had no need to track Gilligan Rose. She would be tracking him up close and personal the next day.

In the gym and jogging he thought about Gilligan Rose: her ruined life, her money, her soon-to-be aborted career, the lesbian girls who loved her, her life ruined as well. Hey, de Montfort, sorry to fuck up your day but your cheating girlfriend is going to prison for murdering ten pedophiles that she laid first.

He hated toast for breakfast, conditioned by vanity, he supposed. The twelve hours until his last run passed quickly, his nylon suit soaked with rain for the third time that day. He trashed it along with three pairs of socks and tee-shirts. Nothing would dry by morning.

The Hunt for Gilligan Rose

The day began with a morning that was dull grey, monochromatic, lifeless, the streets and sidewalks greasy with a constant drizzle. The afternoon was black, heavy rain pellets prancing to a staccato rhythm, streets and sidewalks glistening with the reflections of headlights, reds, greens and yellows and brightly lit storefront windows with mocking cadaverous mannequins sneering at hectic pedestrians. The evening was a living canvas of white and red streaks illuminating a dark void, a cacophony of horns blaring and thunder reverberating in the air around him, his eyes blurred and stinging from horizontal rain, his breathing difficult, his nose and his mouth taking in water.

He was glad he wasn't flying, content to know Frenchie was safe in New York with Deena and that her flight had departed before the weather turned foul. He liked the kid.

All he wanted was to sleep, to dream of his bride. She was in New York with Frenchie. The adjoining rooms were set, wired for audio-visual. The bathroom included. He made a mental note to visit the men's room at the theatre on the off chance the after-theatre thing didn't happen. Why would she waste time when she could kill him first and find some good-looking girl to cheat with in her bed?

He set his cell, called the front desk, and Deena would phone him at 12:30 AM her time. No way was he missing the flight, not after a year of tracking mother and daughter, Phillips to learn the old coot had died, Mendiga and de Montfort whom he still thought would make a very cute couple, sexy, French and Latina. What normal guy wouldn't want to see that happening?

He hadn't realized he'd fallen asleep until he woke the next morning to his cell chiming, quickly followed by some automated French girl. He believed she was automated. Anyway, he said 'merci', without rolling the R. He wasn't sure. Deena's wake-up was the one he wanted, the one that would last the longest.

Marie was sleeping, she told him. The agents were in

424

their rooms, his suit and tie were hanging in the closet of his room and his 92FS was under the pillow on the left side. He was right-handed. She would see him that afternoon in the adjoining room before he left for dinner.

The rain had abated. He wondered how the rain would sound on the boat, Double Agent, the pitter-patter of raindrops on the fibreglass deck inches over their naked bodies entwined and scented with love.

He had no reason to overdress for the return trip other than to impress her: Dockers, loafers and a sweater, cashmere of course.

He had no appetite. TGA could serve his breakfast. Rose could serve his breakfast with her legs wide open, taunting him. Possibly by then he would be hungry, or curious. He thought more likely curious.

He hated taxis, wishing Frenchie was with him to drive him to the airport. She would be a good agent, an excellent agent. Perhaps he shouldn't have teased her. Why did he enjoy being a prick? Simple: because he liked her. He teased the people he liked. He teased Deena, Gayle and Frenchie. No one else was worth his time. He hated airports. He hated airports the most when he couldn't simply flash his shield and walk through without all the security bullshit. Airlines loved cops with guns on their planes. That day though he was one of a few thousand others waiting to board flights. He was nothing, a suspect. They were all suspects without rights. Human dignity and freedom of speech had nothing to do with airports and flying. Leave your balls at the door. Do not enter. Do not ask a difficult question. Do not argue. Do not raise your voice. Do not look at me that way. Open your bag. Stand over there. You're nothing. I am. I'm important. I'm saving the nation and they're paying me twelve-fifty an hour.

He saw her. She was boarding ahead of the passengers. He tried to clear his mind. He was the last to board. The flight left on time.

"Welcome aboard, Mr. Fennell." She learned close into his last row aisle seat. "John, I'm so anxious for our evening. You haven't had a change of heart, I hope."

"We are, for sure. I haven't thought about anything else all week. I'll come for you at seven."

"I'll be ready. I've thought of you all week as well." She whispered. "We'll make the evening special. I was hoping I could sit with you for a while. Unfortunately we're full."

"I'm disappointed. I had hoped for some time with you."

"So am I, but we'll have a marvellous evening."

She squeezed his shoulder. "We certainly will."

He wondered whether she was wearing pantyhose or stockings, whether he would see her bare thighs, her panties delineating the bare curves of her ass. Perhaps he should ask her, set the tone for the evening. Why not? It's the least she could do for killing him. For that matter, she was close enough, their cheeks practically touching. No one would see. No one was interested, either sleeping or working. He could easily put a hand under her skirt, against her leg, pressing, exploring, titillating and taunting her for a change with probing fingers, making her horny, making her wet. She wouldn't mind. That had nothing to do with arresting her. Being a cop was one thing, being a guy was another matter. What the hell. He would see and feel that much and more in the hotel room. He was pretty sure the other ten hadn't stripped naked and got themselves off inside their condoms while she stood over them with a whip and a blade. Maybe he would ask her. Maybe he would drop a few napkins, whisper in her ear that he couldn't wait to see her naked, to touch her the way she wanted.

He wasn't wrong. She blew a soft, warm stream of air into his ear. She was cooing, baiting.

She served a breakfast he didn't eat. His lunch was tasteless, his mimosas too few. He couldn't get her out of his mind, her body, the evening.

Shit. They were landing. He once heard that the

expectation of one's death was worse than the actual death, being killed, being stabbed in the chest. That's what he was doing, he was anticipating, expecting his death, he was being afraid. Thus far the other guy had always died, not him, bodies flung into the air, crashing, dead, faces distorted. That was the natural order of things, not this.

He was the last to exit, Collette Salazar squeezing his arm, hugging him. She was beautiful, disarming, sensual and warm. Her perfume was sweet, not over powering. Her hair was soft, her cheek warm against his; the gentle pressure of her silk-covered breasts against his sweater unmistakable, her message undeniable.

At times like this he hated his job. Deena was right. The girl was fucked up. She needed help, not two minutes of state-supplied electrical current. He put a hand to her back, pressing, the silk smooth, her body warm, confirming the message. He thought to kiss her, thinking of Deena, debating, smiling instead and walking away.

Two PM with five hours to go. Not much time to prepare, to see Deena, rehearse, dress and leave her perhaps forever.

He arrived at The Franklin at three. Deena was in her room, the adjoining room. Frenchie was with her, the other four were in the restaurant. Neither woman was smiling. Deena was stoic; Frenchie was sombre, as cute as the day before, yet not. She was afraid for him, her fear as thick on her face as a ceramic mask. He guffawed. Perhaps she was praying. She was young. She would soon learn not to: a total waste of time.

He spent an hour with Deena reviewing Paris and Nice, Lerosier and the cabaret, kissing like lovers before the other four walked in. They didn't know. No one knew, Fennell issuing final instructions to Marie, telling her to walk through the front door of his room into the bathroom, to lie on one bed and then the other, the sofa and the chair as he watched her. He didn't trust techies: self-satisfied and self-righteous sons of bitches. They weren't the best, he was. Besides, he was the one being killed.

He approved. They didn't care. He had a perfect and unbroken view of the girl from each of the four monitors. The sound of her voice was five on five. He shut them down and went into his room for a shower and fresh clothes.

He exchanged his soiled towel with a fresh one from Deena's room, checked for his weapon and left with a thumb-up facing the primary lens. Things were happening quickly.

Deena went with him to the lobby. She kissed him hard, stealing his breath, wiping her gloss from his lips, telling him how much she loved him. He knew. She told him again, watching him cross the street to the Excalibur. That night in particular was no time for goodbyes.

Collette Salazar was in the lobby. She was radiant in a red linen dress that was strapless and mid-thigh, fashionably short for the theatre, red shoes and red bag, her ears and her neck adorned with the darkest emeralds he'd ever seen, her shoulders protected with a delicate black shawl, a black cloche encasing her red hair. Deena Archer watched matter-of-factly as the couple strolled arm in arm from sight.

Collette was pleasant, well-spoken and well-travelled, sexy, very sexy, their conversation animated, unbroken by nervous tension, their meal ending too quickly. Eight-thirty, 210 minutes before he might die.

At the theatre he wasn't interested in a performance he'd slept through once before. Instead he wondered how she would look and feel in the nude, respond to his touch, how much of her he would touch. He was curious. Was she traditional with red pubic hair as soft and as lustrous as her red mane? Or was she modern, beach-certified for the most daring thongs. He'd already seen her bare breasts. Would they feel as good in his hands as Mendiga's felt in Deena's, would her ass? Would Deena be pissed with him for knowing, for probing? He couldn't just lie there, under her, beside her, over her. Would Deena crash through the door on time? Or would she be pissed with him for being afraid, for caressing and probing a lesbian? Or would she be jealous, wanting to push him away and take his place?

Anyway, he wanted to know, he wanted to see her naked, to smell her, to experience what ten others had lived before they died.

They walked hand in hand back to The Franklin, laughing, having a good time, Collette accepting his offer of a nightcap in the bar. She felt sexy in her short dress, she told him. She was sexy, crossing her legs, taunting. Her legs were bare, soft and smooth. Shit!

The night was young, she insisted. She signalled the waiter, ordering a bottle of the hotel's finest champagne for the room. She didn't want the evening to end. She liked him. She enjoyed his company. Most men were such self-indulgent assholes. All they wanted was a constant supply of eager young pussies. He wasn't like that, she told him. She wasn't like that.

Fennell took the bottle, insisting that he pay. He was the man.

In the room she uncapped a vodka from the minibar, filling a glass, doing the same for him, kicking off her shoes, kissing him, her raspberry lips soft and full. His mind was racing. He was kissing Gilligan Rose, inhaling her sweetness, knowing that Deena was watching, wanting to cry.

He wanted to reach between her legs, to feel her moist heat, to grope her breasts, to watch her undress. Instead she went to the closet for a robe, disappearing into the bathroom, the water running for five minutes or more. He sat on the edge of the bed, reclining onto his elbows, checking for his weapon, giving a thumb-up to the farthest corner of the room. He drained his vodka, uncapping another. He hated vodka.

When she came out she was wrapped in white fleece, her belt cinched, her hair hanging in thick, dark strands. She'd transitioned from sexy to exotic. He could imagine her with Mendiga and de Montfort, getting cozy, planning her next kill. His turn had come, fifteen or twenty minutes before his death, he hoped, or fifteen or twenty before hers. She kissed him, her tongue teasing his lips. He pressed harder, squeezing her hands, hoping she wouldn't rearrange the pillows.

He reached for a robe, disappearing into the bathroom. He looked into the lens, smiling. He could imagine the four smiling faces, and the two that were not.

He showered, certain that Deena was protecting his sense of propriety, slipping into fresh straight-backs and the robe, stepping out, his hair blown dry.

She was on the bed, stretched out, her robe open, her body half covered, one breast exposed, her hip bare, her legs long, one knee raised, a single fingertip gently invading her exquisite pink cleft, her red hair gone which didn't surprise him. She was a modern woman. She was to-die-for.

"Wow, that's hot. That is really hot. I like women that way."

"I know what you like, John. You like little girls. You like to see them in their panties or like this." She shrugged the robe from her other shoulder, kneeling. "Get over here. I've waited a very long week for this."

He did. He laid by her side, facing her, watching her unwrap a foil like plucking the delicate petals of a rose, her delicate petals.

Shit, this was going too fast. "We should have a drink first, Collette. I can't say I'm used to this, something as unattainable as you in my bed."

Shit! What did he say?

"We can celebrate the evening when we're finished. I can stay the night, can't I, John? I'm not at all tired."

"As long as you want, whenever you want. I think this is

going to work out very well."

With a suddenness he hadn't expected she stripped his micro-fibre shorts to his ankles, seizing him, making him ready, slowly, precisely, humming, lowering her body over his. She had no knife. He knew he was fucked with Deena, finished, divorced before he was married. No woman would tolerate seeing her man fucking someone else unless the party was in full swing and she was busy herself.

She was so good, so tight, moist and athletic, her crescendo matching his. How could he feign shyness? He couldn't. He wanted more. He did, thinking of Gilligan and Elixia together, Xara and Gilligan, Elixia and Xara, Deena and Xara. He was living the male hypocrisy, every man's fantasy. He was living a dream. He was fucking a lesbian. He was fucking Gilligan Rose. This he was not expecting. It wasn't his fault. Deena had to believe him. Shit! She was exploding again. He could smell her. He was wet with her. She was reaching for another foil. She was hot. She was sweating. She wanted more. He wanted more, his erection suddenly cold, abandoned.

"John, roll over. Let me massage you. When I'm finished you will massage me... everywhere, John. I mean absolutely everywhere. We have to please each other completely. Don't we?"

He twisted his body between her smooth thighs, staining his hip with her pungent dampness. Deena had his back. He was safe. She was straddling his ass, rocking, intent fingers digging into his shoulders, erect nipples brushing invisible strokes onto his back. She was lulling him into another world; Deena would soon rush through the door. He was counting down, ready to twist. Her hands were pressing into the small of his back, her moist lips painting his buttocks. She was riding him. Yes, he did like very young girls. Yes he loved his daughters, hating his wife for not being like them, their nubile bodies soft and smooth, his head jerking backward, a sickening tearing sound mixed with horrible laughter, a door crashing open, a gunshot exploding, her body hurled into the air, sprawling across half the bed onto the floor, Deena wailing, his body naked.

Deena bounded over one bed to his, the two agents running to Gilligan Rose, the techies framing Marie Anisette who stood in the doorway without permission, frozen, afraid to come nearer. They wouldn't let her.

"Deena, I love you. This didn't work out so well. I'm sorry, sweetcheeks. I fucked up."

"Sweetheart, darling, I love you. We've got her. We've got her. You're the absolute best."

"Deena, I wasn't afraid. I knew you were close. I love you. I'm sorry. I didn't expect..."

She covered Fennell to the waist. "Don't talk. The ambulance is coming. We have to get you stitched up for the wedding. I can't marry you like this and I'm not letting you die. No way am I letting you die."

Her tears were dripping onto his face. They both knew.

"Deena, I'm sorry. I wasted a year. I should have quit, been the lawyer you want me to be. This wasn't supposed to happen. I'm quitting the force. I will be that lawyer, the best. Deena, you know how they say that gunshots are hot, that you don't feel the pain of deep wounds?"

"Yes, sweetheart, I do."

"It's not true. I'm cold. I'm very cold. I can't move my body and my chest is on fire."

She screamed for a blanket. "You'll feel better very soon, sweetheart."

"No, sweetcheeks, that won't happen. Please don't remember me this way. I'm sorry."

Johnnie Fennell's legs twitched once, his head jerked sideways to see her. He needed to see her one last time, to kiss her lips one last time.

John Francis Templeton Fennell died at 11:55 AM on July 15th of this year. Gilligan Rose survived with a gunshot to her shoulder.

He'd been right, of course. He was always right. Marie Anisette did see someone killed that night. She struggled to escape them, running to Deena, wailing, their tears melding, Marie touching Johnnie's warm hand one last time.

Gilligan Rose was arrested and taken to Miami. Deena Archer wasn't finished with her, not by a long shot. She wanted the death penalty. Nor was she finished with Emma Rose, alias Emmanuelle Lerosier. First, however, she would bury her 'husband', her true love, her fennell.

The funeral with honours was held five days later. Those in the squad who had once believed he was a total asshole, a pompous fool, cried at the funeral, men and women alike: Too little too late. Deena despised them all. They had waited too long to admire him, to miss him. Those from all over the country who did not know him, saluted him, escorted him to his final resting place, a uniformed formation of officers discharging nine rounds, his favourite number. Gayle Brannigan, as strong as ever, her eyes blurred, her cheeks wet, held Deena's gloved hand while whispering comforting lyrics from her favourite gospel hymn.

When the flag came, folded into a triangle, Deena collapsed. He was never a fennell, he was different. He was the best. He was hers. Why did she never tell him that? Now she never would. He would not see Frenchie's graduation; never see her walk into the squad room as Agent Marie Palmer, never tease her again. He would never see her marry the young man sitting with her, holding her hands, wiping her tears. No. He never would. He was dead, stabbed in the back by a heartless woman who didn't know him, turning grey in a silk-lined mahogany box, rotting six feet beneath her feet.

Johnnie Fennell bolted upright, his breathing erratic, his room one instant bright white, another eerily dark, his skin cold with sweat, his hair wet, his mouth dry, his body trembling, his heart palpitating, his mind infused with a blackness that he'd known too often from another time and place, another existence where inerasable evil prevailed.

He reached for the light, his watch: 4:26 AM, July 15th of this year.

One day he would explain his personal demons to Deena, once he understood where in the universe they dwelled, and when, and why they came to him as they did, whenever they pleased.

He called her. He needed to tell her how much he loved her. He needed to throw her into the pool.

The rain had not yet abated.

Thirty-Six
This Year: July 14th

Marie Anisette ate a late breakfast at the airport, not wanting to miss her flight scheduled to depart at ten, yet hoping for a cancellation. She would have preferred staying another day with Johnnie. She didn't like flying in bad weather even though the wind and rain generated by a system stalled over much of France were relatively light, not expected to intensify until midday, the pilot promising a smooth ride once at altitude over the Atlantic.

She would believe him for the time-being. She was too proud of what she'd accomplished to be nervous. She had too much to think about. She couldn't wait to see Deena, to tell her about her week with Johnnie. She was certain Deena wasn't nervous about the next evening and Johnnie, she knew, wasn't afraid of anything.

She would arrive in New York an hour later, local time, wearing one of her new outfits for Deena to see. She was also anxious for Sunday. Lincoln Palmer had promised to call her at her home, a preamble to his formal summary to his jury of one Monday evening.

The pilot's voice crackled over the drone of the jet engines. France was behind them. The sky was clearing. She glanced at her watch, resetting the time: 7:00 AM Eastern.

*

Gilligan Rose was already having lunch with Elixia de Montfort, sipping wine, waiting for the waitress to serve the

first course, lovers holding hands, weeping, planning a new future, keeping old secrets alive in a dark place where Gilligan kept hers from Xara. She was doing what in her heart she felt was right. She had waited too long: her grief and her sorrow. She was at long last following her heart: her joy and her contentment.
*

Deena left her penthouse home at 7:00 AM, departing MIA at 9:35 on American flight 1510. Federal agents never worried about long departure lines or twelve-fifty-an-hour wannabe commandos at security. They simply flashed their shields and walked through, pissing off almost everyone. Though when they passed through in European designs without a single crease, their hair coiffed, tanned, looking like not a single man stuck in line with his shoes in his hands, his belt opened, denuded of his briefcase, wallet and dignity could afford her…well, they pissed off absolutely everyone.

She arrived in LaGuardia at noon, meeting Marie Anisette for a late lunch in The Franklin's dining room. Two other agents and a couple of techies were at work in the adjoining suites

With lunch finished, when the women walked into Deena's suite, the three men and one woman stopped their work to applaud Marie. They were given a heads-up by Deena. The woman agent hurried over to hug her, to welcome her to the fold, albeit a year early. The three men returned to work. Deena's face was already plastered with prune, which she thought was pretty neat. The other female agent believed she'd never been squeezed as tightly, not even by her husband.

Deena had made a suggestion to Johnnie the night before and he agreed. Why not give the kid a clean slate? She never once asked for anything and worked twice as hard as any other intern. She'd proven herself beyond everyone's expectations. Studying cases and compiling data from behind a desk would never be good enough for her. She wanted to solve cases. She wanted to become an agent. So yeah, he was in. Why not? Besides, she wasn't that much of pain in his ass.

She promised to smack him.

Marie spent her afternoon and evening closely spying on the techies, gleaning what she could, helping them, being a gopher, learning about cameras, monitors and bugs. She'd never seen Deena wearing a gun. Hard to do in a string bikini, she thought, or with the little dress she wore to lunch the day she first met Johnnie. How silly she was to be so afraid of him.

Deena's weapon wasn't like the others. Hers was smaller, almost designer, she thought. The 92FS shone like polished silver in a holster crafted from midnight blue leather, not a black mechanical clip-on and the shiny one strapped to her ankle was like a toy. She wanted so much to be like Deena, for Johnnie to be proud of her.

He was already; Deena told her when the work was done, when the techies and other agents went to their rooms. He wasn't like that. He was more into the macho guy thing, improving slowly, making noticeable strides each day. The thing was; he had come to her in such a damaged state that he was taking more time than expected. And the shiny toy, her backup, the toy fired nine millimetre rounds.

"Deena, it is not true that nobody likes Johnnie. I do very much, and you, and my parents and my brother, and soon I believe Lincoln will like him also. I do believe Lincoln is a little afraid of our Johnnie right now. I do believe also that Captain Brannigan does like him very much in her own heart."

"Wow, Marie, seven people like our Johnnie, out of 300 million. He is making progress, yeah; just let's not tell him right away."

"Thank you, Deena, for everything. I cannot stop telling

you this. I owe you so much. To become an agent at twenty-one, this is so rare. And to have a first case so soon."

"So what's with the long face, Marie? You should be smiling, elated."

"I will smile when Johnnie is safe from her. I am worried he will be killed. I do not want to see this on these screens. I do like him so much, Deena. I believe he knows that I do."

"Gilligan Rose won't kill him, Marie. I reserve that right. She doesn't get to rob me of that pleasure. He's mine."

"You are joking, I know."

"Marie, do you see that little knob on the top of the lamp." She did. "I can hit that with this from fifty feet, every time. Her head is much bigger and the bed they'll use is thirty feet from the door. This one shoots ten millimetres. I don't miss, Marie. No one kills Johnnie except me. I'm getting married, remember?"

"I will not sleep many winks all night."

"He'll be fine. He's the absolute best, Marie, and he does know how much you like him."

"Yet you did beat him up one day."

Deena burst into a raucous laugh. "I thought I was so good. I was so damned proud that I had kicked Johnnie Fennell's ass in front of everyone, the arrogant SOB who thought he was so much better than everyone else. I stood over him, Marie, letting him stand on his own. I have a fourth Dan. I've studied for twelve years. My father insisted that I do long before I wanted to become a cop. He was afraid for me."

"Your father was smart to insist on this, Deena."

"Yes, he was. The thing is; Fennell has six black belts. He played me. I discovered the truth once we moved in together. He doesn't talk a lot about himself, not even with me. He doesn't know that I know. He's good, Marie. He is the best and he doesn't care a hoot what others think. So go to bed and don't worry about what won't happen. You will still have reason from time to time to punch him."

"Deena..."

Deena's cell chimed. She smiled, putting up a finger.

"Hey, sweetheart, you're up early. So I guess I don't have to call you." Deena listened. "I love you too, sweetheart. I'm in my room with Marie, saying goodnight. She's worried about you, about tomorrow."

Deena listened, pressing END.

"Is he fine?" Marie asked.

"He's got a big surprise for me, something in Miami that he wants to show me on Sunday." Deena recognized conspiracy when confronted with it. "What? What did he do? What did he tell you, Marie?"

"Nothing, Deena, he told me nothing."

"You're lying, Marie. You know something. Tell me."

"Yes, I am lying. And yes, I do know something. I do know I am going to my bed before Johnnie will hate me."

She hugged her friend and mentor tightly, kissing Deena's cheeks, so happy that Johnnie would not be killed, happier still that she had chosen the perfect wedding gifts.

When she was gone Deena poured a glass of wine and laid in bed, behind the louver doors of her en suite bedroom that was off-limits to The Task Force, her private place as much as protecting the equipment. She wouldn't speak with him again until he arrived.

*

John Fennell had awoken in a cold sweat before calling Deena. Once or twice a year, his demons came calling, turning his mind black, casting him into the future, the past, a different universe. He didn't know. All he knew was the power of darkness and evil struggling to invade his well-being.

He didn't go back to sleep, or remain in bed. He phoned Deena, showered and shaved, dressing in his swimsuit and joggers, opening the outer French doors of his room to an early morning of muted grey, the jagged rooftops of the tallest surrounding structures threatening to rip open a pall of pregnant clouds smothering them.

His day would be a complete bitch, not at all what he planned. He had expected a few hours in the gym, a few jogs and a few hours in the sun by the pool. So much for satellites, he thought. The one redeeming quality owned by weather people, the female contingent, was their legs and their breasts. The guys served no purpose at all.

Room service knocked on his door, bringing toast and coffee. That's what he ate. That's what he ate in the morning: toast and coffee. He would have to do something about that.

This is what he knew. He would not order a salad at lunch and for dinner he would enjoy a rôti de boeuf au jus with a bottle of good French Bordeaux. He would not jog, not an inch, not in the morning, not in the afternoon or the evening. He despised running, so to hell with that idea. He would spend his day in the gym, at the courtyard pool doing laps in the rain, getting a sweat on in the sauna instead of relaxing by the pool, decompressing, reading, whatever, and the only pussy, tits and ass he wanted to see, fondle and kiss were Deena's.

He could give a shit about seeing up Gilligan Rose's skirt. He didn't care about stockings or pantyhose, panties or bare thighs, her undeniably fine ass, her fluffy red silk or clean doorway to hell. He wanted her caught and put in prison by him: her payday for ten murders. He didn't care about de Montfort or Mendiga. The world and his quadrant of the world were too overcrowded, too full of shit to worry about those who would heal with time. Shit happened. It always would to the unsuspecting, the most innocent and naïve. They would get over her in time, find more love.

Anyway, who in their right mind would knowingly sleep with a serial killer? Maybe they would kiss and cry together, which was the least of his problems. And turning, rolling over between her legs, letting Rose ram a blade into his back? Not a chance. That was someone else's dream, her dream. His dream would blow her dream away with a single ten millimetre round to the side of her red head.

And, another thing, since when did Gayle Brannigan sing hymns? Heels and whips, maybe. She was a good-looking woman. Shit. She was very good-looking, a head-turner. He needed cold water. He needed to do laps. He didn't care about the passage of time, how quickly Friday evening would come or would end. One's future would always dissolve into one's past until inevitably ending in the present, the three intertwined, inescapable, separated by expectations driven by fear, anticipations driven by joy.

Fear driven by the expectation of one's death, yeah, that was true, though he harboured no such expectation or fear. His anticipation however was real. He was anxious to board Double Agent with Deena. He was excited. The law thing, though. How could she possibly be angry or disappointed with him? Women got over these things. Such was the female condition and she was 100 percent female. No way would she be angry, he hoped.

That evening he did not trash his jogging suit. He'd survived the day and would survive the next. He had his six ounces of red meat and his bottle of wine; he went to bed early and woke early to call Deena, not surprised at all that Frenchie was still working at becoming a good cop.

He didn't go back to bed. Time allowed; his energy flow did not. He was too pumped up. The day was July 15th of this year. He was alive and would remain that way. Damn straight.

In less than twenty-four hours Eastern Time Gilligan Rose would appear much less radiant than in his macabre dream and by Saturday morning she would be wearing a delicate shade of Florida State orange, white sneakers, white cotton briefs and a white boxed bra, her single accessory state-issued stainless steel bracelets crafted especially for such memorable occasions.

Thirty-Seven
This year: July 15th

Gilligan Rose and Elixia de Montfort woke to a fresher day, a blue sky, hearts infused with new hope, the warm morning sun beginning to dry the intimate patio of their hundred-year-old apartment, the streets below damp from the rains the day before. Crêpes sprinkled with cognac and cappuccinos dashed with a few more drops were Gilligan's breakfast favourites, always prepared by Elixia. Yet, despite the early PM flight to New York, time passed remarkably quickly. Time always went quickly for Elixia when she was with Gilligan.

This time however was different. This was the last time she would lean against the door feeling alone, feeling empty. This time Elixia didn't mind at all that Gilligan was leaving for two, three or four days, or a week, flying to Germany, Britain, the US or Japan. No. She didn't care because this was the last time. This was the final journey alone.

The Head Office of TGA was in Los Angeles where Gilligan would arrive Saturday evening. She would put her beachfront condo up for immediate sale with a broker on Sunday; certain she would wait no longer than a week for a buyer to fall in love with the view, the sand, the quiet, the décor she no longer needed or wanted, the average condo in her complex lasting no longer than a few days on the market.

Either way she would return to Paris the following

Saturday for a sumptuous dinner with Elixia, a celebration in her new white ensemble, a commitment, taking the week to finalize bank transfers, convey a very few farewells, and to whisper one last time with Gilligan that what she was doing was right. The realization that her entire life existed in France had struck her like a searing bolt. Gilligan would understand. The time had come to let Gilligan go. Gilligan Rose would set herself free.

She left her Paris home at ten with kisses and without tears, arriving at Orly near eleven with a change of clothes for the Saturday flight to L.A. and her ensemble for an evening of dinner and theatre. She had previously arranged a late day appointment with the hairstylist adjacent to the Excalibur in Manhattan which would leave ample time in her day to pass by a pharmacy and drop into a retail outlet to select an accent piece to complement her carving set.

She was on a high, drugged with adrenalin. She was determined. She despised Fennell, she'd determined, at least as much as Cooper. She would enjoy them equally. She could imagine no better way to terminate her raison d'être on earth than with her first and her last, the two worst synonymously her two best.

She saw Fennell where she expected to see him, in the preferred status Titanium Lounge, though this time she caught his attention with a discreet wave. The time was 11:30 AM and he was pouring a two-finger hit of vodka into his glass. He was smiling, smirking, and she knew why.

Good. Drink up, John. Think about me all day. Think about doing me, seeing me naked. Just don't fall asleep on me before we're done. You can't die without hurting me first. What makes your sick mind any better than the others?
*

Johnnie Fennell had time after his toast and coffee for a couple of hours in the gym. He didn't wear Dockers or a sweater to the airport. No way, not that he was superstitious. He wasn't. He wore a blue suit, white shirt

444

and red tie.

Orly was a half-hour away. He checked out from La Marquise at nine. European airport security was so much more inquisitive than the American facsimile. He gave himself time. How would he explain to Brannigan being late for his long awaited dinner and demise? He could picture her sitting in her office, her desk drawer open near midnight with her first fennell scotch of the day, waiting for the phone call from New York and her second before driving home. He smirked. He was honoured. She only ever drank when he was around. She was the best, the boss lady. They had history, a synergy mutually earned and mutually valued.

The security gauntlet was more of a breeze than he expected. He had to admit. He had a certain je ne sais quoi aura about him. He was able to casually convey 'gee, it must be terrible being you, when, you know, I'm me. Sorry about that', the exact aura that made Deena fall in love with him almost immediately, if not at first sight which she would never confess, not even during their most intimate moments. The woman had resolve. She was stubborn. Anyway, he knew better and, French or American, he hated security people and the wannabes at the Miami office were no exception.

He stepped into the lounge, he supposed, about thirty minutes ahead of her. She knew where to find him, where she had on several previous occasions. She was walking his way.

"We must stop meeting his way."

"I know. We should do something about that."

She smiled. "I was entertaining the very same thought a moment before I saw you. Are we still on for the theatre this evening?"

"Pass up heaven for another hotel room? I'll come for you at seven. You've been on my mind the entire week."

"I have a good feeling about tonight, John. You did say

after-dinner drinks as I recall and the weather in New York thus far should be ideal for a pleasant evening with a handsome stranger. I think so."

"I'm all set with a maroon tie."

"I hope you like midnight blue, a little risqué and perhaps a bit too short. I don't get to dress up very often and I did warn you."

"Yes, you did and I'm already breathing heavily. As a matter of fact I do like risqué and short, especially with deep red hair and exquisite legs." He shrugged, a sheepish grin forming. "I plead guilty to a healthy man's simple observation."

"Thank you. I'll postpone sentencing until this evening." She glanced at her watch. "I've got to run, John. We have a bunch of pre-flight checks to go through before passengers can board. I came in on the off chance that I would see you. I'm glad I did. Bye, bye."

"I'm very glad you did, Collette."

She half turned, hesitating, facing him, pressing a kiss against unsuspecting lips, smiling, sauntering into the concourse.

He emptied the vodka into the sink, reaching for a bottle of soda water. He didn't believe anyone else had to know about the kiss.

*

The flight departed on schedule, Fennell and Salazar disappointed that she couldn't join him. Friday flights were rarely less than fully booked.

He wondered about business people. No one was smiling. For the most part they were stretched out in comfy seats costing a grand an hour and they weren't smiling. What was up with that? Not one of them would have stayed in anything less than a four-star, which would be a five-star anywhere else. So they had a lousy week, were going home to lives they didn't want, wives or husbands they didn't want, or leaving French lovers they did want, lovers who were now available to love someone else. He wondered about her, the taste of her lips lingering on his. He would definitely keep that to himself.

Her attitude apart, Gilligan Rose was beautiful, sexy and smart with everything going for her except a future. She wasn't mother material, neither was Deena, though he could definitely picture Rose as a class A lover. What must she be thinking? She was leaning across his seat, serving the passenger by the window, one breast closest to him close enough to kiss, her hand resting lightly on his shoulder. So how could he not think she was sexy? She was. She smelled good. What must she be thinking? He couldn't imagine being more separated from reality. How could she possibly leave a stunning thing like de Montfort to have sex with a guy she didn't know and plunge a knife into his chest while she was getting herself off? What would de Montfort think about that, her getting laid ten times while supposedly pining for her mouth-watering lesbian lover? He thought of his dream, his hand up her skirt, her heated flesh and subsequent frostbite.

Killing someone he could understand. No big thing. People killed or were killed every day. The real mystery was the sex. Not one of the dead guys was a so-called hunk, beau or any woman's idea of an ideal catch. They were ordinary, neither Einsteins nor Spartacuses, unremarkable save for their common deviance. He'd seen forensic photographs of each one on a gurney. Much like a black and white photo, death had a way of highlighting one's flaws.

His computer stayed in its case. The girl seated beside him was seventeen, eighteen tops, cute, probably going to see grandma. The kid didn't need to worry that she was sitting beside a total pervert. Instead he asked Collette Salazar for a magazine and again she touched him, leaving no doubt that if the girl weren't sitting by the window he would have a hand resting on Miss Salazar's thigh.

How the hell would she kill him? He was far from

naïve. Quite the inverse, he was jaded with ample reason. Most people were ready, willing and able to do wrong. That was a given. Sleeping with a stranger was nothing new. Drunk or horny women got laid all the time in exchange for a few drinks or a compliment. Drop by any bar after two, three AM, tell her she's pretty, offer to pay her tab, and you get laid. But to have dinner together, sit through a Broadway show, kill a guy while you're fucking him and go home, that added an unusual twist to the natural order of things. That was cold. That could only be inherent.

She never left a trace, never a weapon, not a hair, no DNA, not even on the guys' dicks, not a smudge let alone a fingerprint. He asked her for a vodka, neat. He was becoming orange juice intolerant. She touched him again, brushing his cheek. He smiled, she smiled. He imagined her cleaning up, a devoted lesbian washing some guy's flaccid dick, flushing the condom, stripping the bed, sending photographs of her work to indifferent wives from the men's cells, never a reflection, the whole nine yards. Why not? She gave herself enough time, committing the murders hours before she left their rooms. They knew that much. She would spend hours in a room with the corpse, creating a perfect crime, extricating the weapon, not an easy thing to do, grisly and noisy, doing her best to sanitize the blade before tossing the best possible evidence in some sewer or trashcan, leaving during the morning rush to check out. Someone that good-looking never seen. He snorted. Perhaps she turned into crystal clear ice.

He thought she must have a very clean home, and a very cold one. Every man in the First-Class cabin and likely one or more women with the same thought: How would she look undressed, naked and primed? Not him. He knew. What little he didn't know about her body he assumed he was about to discover.

He pondered the irony of meeting her mother, of knowing that she wanted to kill him, of knowing that, if she did, she would kill one three people apart from Brannigan who could reunite mother and daughter, a killer duo. If that wasn't irony nothing was, which was somewhat moot because she would be dead a second later.

They landed on schedule. He was the last to exit, the last at Customs when flying TGA, when normally he would flash his ID, his blue-gold shield and walk through not bothering with the Iris Scanner. TGA flights were different because that's what she did, walking past him, this time waving at him as he stood next in line to stare into Big Brother. Yeah, this was one for the books and well worth the fifteen-grand memento for his office wall.

He wanted to give her time. He didn't want to run into her, talk to her. Besides, she had to buy a murder weapon. She was consummate, the supreme seductress. He doubted there was a man alive who wouldn't once adjust his morals and perfect marriage for a night with her. Or a woman for that matter, he grinned, an ongoing debate with sweetcheeks that generally landed them in bed.

He went to the Titanium Lounge and poured a scotch that he did drink.

*

Gilligan Rose walked into her room at the Excalibur Boutique Hotel at three, Deena and Marie with the back-up agents watching from the laptop on the coffee table in Deena's en suite.

The only man in the room said, "Good luck, Fennell. This one makes me want to feed my wife dog treats. I haven't had anything that good-looking since high school."

The female agent added, "And if you want to know why take a look in the mirror."

"Agent Fennell does not need this woman. He is much too handsome and elegant for her. Besides I have seen his girlfriend. This Gilligan Rose is homely in comparison to her."

"Fennell has a woman?" Dowell asked. "Is she

anatomically correct, or does she come with a valve?"

"I do not know what this means." Marie did know. "But I will ask him when he arrives here. He will tell you. I am sure of this."

The female agent added, "That should be interesting, Dowell. Have you ever seen Fennell at the gym?" She paused for affect. "Oh, that's right. You've never seen a gym. "What do you think, Deena?"

She didn't look at him. "I think he should get lost and do what he's paid for."

Dowell dropped onto the sofa. Gilligan Rose was undressing, tossing her blouse onto the bed. He couldn't be more obvious.

"Nah, she's good for a while longer." He leaned into the screen. "Now that's what I'm talking about. That is one nice rack."

"That's the problem, Dowell, you're talking. I said, get lost. Now, or I'm calling Fennell. Remember you're with us by default. No one else was available."

He didn't move. He was a senior officer. She didn't care. Her father was a senator and her partner was Johnnie Fennell.

Deena reached for her cell. "Fennell, yeah hi, I thought you would like to know that Dickhead Dowell thinks your fiancée is an anatomically correct rubber doll with a valve and he's getting his rocks off watching Rose do a striptease. He's salivating and won't leave. We three girls thought you should know."

Dowell snorted. Nice try. Not so amused when Deena passed him the phone. He stood with somewhat less bravado, closing the door behind him. They needed to know what pharmacy and where she would buy the knife. They needed photos of her entering and leaving the stores. And later he would photograph her with Fennell entering and leaving the restaurant and theatre.

Cynthia who wasn't his partner was there because Gayle

Brannigan wanted a second female agent on site. Marie was present as a courtesy to Fennell. Cynthia walked out behind him. Nothing would happen for several more hours. She needed sleep more than watching Rose change her European underwear when hers came six to a pack. She'd never worked with Fennell and didn't want to screw up. Letting the guy get killed on her watch would be a career faux-pas.

Gilligan Rose took her time changing into clean lingerie, slacks and a sweater without an audience. Dowell was in place across the street and Deena couldn't watch her. She couldn't help feeling the pain that would soon suffocate Xara.

Gilligan Rose was leaving her room, Marie told her, changing the subject, Fennell missing her by seconds as he came through the door without knocking. Until then Marie was more interested in the wedding, skirting Deena's probing about her big surprise like a pro.

The time was 3:30

*

Dowell reported in five times: when she walked into and out from the hairdresser, when she bought 'four-inch' condoms, when she came out with an eight-inch blade from a one-stop sleaze shop and when she got back to her room, Dowell commenting that at least she got the sizes right.

He and Fennell had equal status, Fennell the senior agent on the case. He thanked Dowell for the updates, inviting him to the squad's gym once in Miami to talk about his blow-up girlfriend. Dowell disconnected. Marie giggled, Deena rolled her eyes.

5:30. Fennell ordered room-service for two. Marie went to leave. He told her to sit her bum on the sofa. The second meal wasn't for him. She was on the clock. What did she think she could accomplish in her room? When the dinners arrived at six he went to his suite with a beer to shower and change, warning each woman in turn not to be childish.

He walked through the adjoining doors again at 6:40 dressed in a black suit accented with a blue pocket hanky, black loafers, a deep-blue shirt and maroon tie. Marie circled him, inspecting him, approving while adjusting his hanky. She reached up, kissed his cheeks, wrapped her arms tightly around him and walked out ignoring his direct order to stay.

"You have an admirer, sweetheart. The girl likes you a lot."

"She's French. They're like that."

"She's nervous about tonight, about you getting hurt. She's frightened, trying to put on a brave face for you. She doesn't want to disappoint you. This is all so new to her. Imagine what must be going through her mind. She's never been to a stake-out, let alone a sting."

He glanced at his watch. "I shouldn't keep my date waiting."

"She's in the lobby, waiting, and looking like somebody's dream girl, just not yours. She's wearing a tube dress, sweetheart. If she takes a deep breath you'll see her lunch, which you already have so don't get overly involved in your work. She's also wearing a wide hat and long gloves, definitely looking the part. The knife is in her purse, an eight-inch fold-out along with a single condom, which tells us something, and a clean pair of lacy tap pants. Yet she's wearing a sheer eye patch under her dress which is yellow if you're interested, which we know you're not. My guess is she wants to limit contact with her victim, you, if you can call a penis inside you limited." She kissed him. "Your gun's cocked. No pun intended. So make very sure she doesn't reach for that pillow. If she does, she's dead. I won't ask her twice to play nice."

"Expect me near twelve. I can't see her wanting to waste time in a bar when she can get things done and celebrate on her own or with a juicy one-nighter."

"I don't think about her anymore, the beach, Xara.

We're too close to midnight. Now I feel sorry for Xara. I can't help liking her, sweetheart."

"Don't waste the energy. Liking her won't stop her from spitting in your coffee. It'll be a double whammy for her and the Frenchwoman: a serial killer and a cheat, not to mention sex with ten men. I'm fairly certain that goes against the girl code."

"That's right, sex with ten men, not eleven." Deena patted her weapon. "I really would hate being so nervous tonight that I miss, sweetheart. Things happen in the heat of the moment."

"I have to admit that part's a little freaky. You, Frenchie and the other two watching me cozy up to a killer. That'll be a fun report to write." He kissed her. "Don't let our kid stay up too late."

He walked out. He didn't like goodbyes.

*

She was in the lobby. Her usually lustrous red hair cut straight, curtains across her shoulders and forehead, her straight-brimmed hat and evening gloves a rich Mediterranean blue complementing her midnight blue tube dress that redefined short. The sequined club dress was intended to accentuate every inch of her bare legs, front, back and in-between where a patch of bright yellow nestled between creamy smooth thighs. Of course yellow. How else would he know what he was seeing? Blue under blue wouldn't work. Good girl. Yellow was good. He liked yellow. Her stilettos were wrapped with thin straps at her ankles. She wore no jewellery, none was needed. She was the jewel, her purse a slender clutch hanging by a silver thread from her bare shoulder. Her lips were pale pink, natural, she hadn't bothered to gloss them and her nails were coated with clear lacquer. Good girl...and smart.

For an occasional killer she had an impressive MO: simple yet effective, nothing to lose or leave behind, nothing to remember except an extra pair of panties, a condom and a knife. Kill a guy, put on the gloves and do some minor housecleaning.

She stood to greet him. Not staring was a major effort, an indiscretion no one else seemed concerned with, whereas he had to make a good impression.

"Now that's the true sign of a frequent traveller, a man of schedules, on time every time."

"I struggled with myself not to hurry, not to be early. You are magnificent, Collette."

"Well, I did say short and risqué. So, do you like?"

"I like very much...very much, indeed," apart from Deena killing me if you don't.

She took his arm. Dinner was at the Manhattan Grill, a New York eatery for those who could afford thirty-dollar burgers, fifty-dollar steaks and 200-dollar wine. He could. However the best part of the meal was Dowell standing outside.

He was surprised by how composed she was, how soft-spoken, well-versed and interesting: a terrible waste. He could easily imagine him and Deena in another life, a better life, entertaining her and Mendiga, her and de Montfort at home. But shit happens and was happening big time.

She touched his hands, not too often, enough, to emphasize a point, to create a mood. She smoothed her smooth legs more often, which he thought was a matter of habit as much as sensual. Her touch wouldn't be quite the same through coarse prison denim. She was a lady, he had to admit, her manners impeccable. That would also change with plastic plates and plastic forks. She was interested in what he had to say, never once breaking eye contact when he was speaking. She was good, alluring, captivating, intoxicating and dangerous: transferable skills. She could easily earn a living as a career killer, though everyone had their day. And hers had come.

With the meal finished she reached quickly for the bill tucked into the rich leather binder, too slowly, Fennell refusing her generosity despite her expense account. Dinner and drinks were his treat per their agreement. No argument. She thanked him, as any lady would, and took his arm, neither her eyes nor her demeanour betraying the slightest admission of her failed treason.

Any passerby, any gawker who couldn't keep his eyes in his head would think they were lovers. Dowell thought he was a smug A-hole, that she was a nice piece of ass, anxious to see her again on the screen.

At the theatre Fennell was honestly impressed. They had a private balcony shared with one other couple. She sat with her hands laced together in her lap until the lights dimmed and the orchestra began, giving her dress complete freedom to captivate his male ego. Throughout the first act she leaned against their shared armrest, enthralled. Throughout the second she weaved her arm snugly through his. Towards the end of the final act she rested her head against his shoulder, running a hand as she had throughout the entire performance dreamily along the length of her leg crossed over to meet his, from the bottom of her dress close to her hips to her knee.

All the while she was waiting to kill him, not appearing the least bit nervous, during each interlude discussing the previous performance. He wanted to ask how, how could she do it. Not kill him, but pretend with such detachment. Some psycho in a white coat would have a field day with her. She was truly enjoying herself, as much as she would soon enjoy carving a hole in his chest.

So what about the Frenchwoman and the Latina cutie? Which of them did the charming and beautiful Gilligan Rose truly love, which one was the fanciful tryst, which one was passionately loved by a killer, which one would care? Wouldn't he love being a fly on the wall that day? And the day was fast approaching. Where are you? Why aren't you coming home? Why haven't you answered your phone? What's all that noise in the background? Well, it's like this.

I'm in a federal prison for killing these ten guys. Oh, yes, after I fucked them. I did have to fuck them, you know. I think so. Fucking them was the least I could do, not that I enjoyed them. And, oh yeah, I sort of have another girlfriend in L.A., in Paris. Oops. Oh, I'm sorry, that's you. The love of my life is in California. The love of my life is in France. Which one are you?

Both women would soon be subpoenaed, dragged through days of tearful turmoil, each woman despising Rose, one despising Deena.

With the final curtain came the applause, the requisite multiple encores, three times standing like puppets on a string, though he hadn't seen much of the show. He was focused on her head, her thought processes, her legs, all her legs and a deliberate splash of yellow impossible to ignore, certain the guy on the other side of her was having a stroke, praising some higher being for having put him in the right place at the right time. He probably hadn't seen that much free ass in forty years.

They decided to walk. New York cabs were usually clean on the outside. Inside, well, when your dress wasn't long enough to cover your ass when seated, and your ass was bare, walking was the preferred mode of transport. The city at that time of night might be a dangerous place, not so for him. Not for someone with a sixth Dan and an armed escort fifty paces behind.

"Thank you, John. I can't recall a more enjoyable evening."

"Ditto that, Collette."

They meandered a while, each in their private world.

"John...can we see each other again? I would like that very much. I mean you are getting divorced and I'm unattached. I don't want him back and I do like you. I do. We live close to one another in L.A. and we do see each other, what, at least once a month as things are." She squeezed his arm. "I want you to know that if you had said no about tonight I wouldn't have gone by myself. I thought you should know."

Gee, then who would you have killed? "Quite apart from your gorgeous legs hanging out from that evening tee-shirt you're wearing… yes. I would love to see you again and not to wait another month. I'm thinking this weekend in L.A., dinner by the ocean Sunday evening."

"You're on. It's a date. Now what about that nightcap, now that we've got the hard part out of the way? I'm really excited." After all, John, you are my last. The evening should be special.

"Well, we could go clubbing. You're certainly dressed for it. The problem is I wouldn't have you to myself," which is where I want you. "I was thinking possibly cocktails in your lounge or mine, though The Franklin's a little darker and more intimate," albeit not intimate enough to kill me. "That's how I would rather end the evening."

"Do you mean that?" All the others did, John, each one.

She knew. He hadn't watched a moment of the performance. He wanted her. He wanted what was under her dress, what was under her silky yellow panties. So what if the old guy across from her went home with a hard-on.

"Yes, I do, with you to myself for a little while before you fly home tomorrow. I have to say I never expected this, not from someone as lovely as you. Honestly," most women I arrest aren't a tenth as lovely as you. Sorry about that.

"Well, since I'm the woman here, let me take the lead. And believe me, I have never, never said this to anyone. I haven't. I swear. Let's have drinks in your room and watch some late-night TV. You can always kick me out if you get bored, though somehow I don't think that will happen." I know it won't, Fennell. Your cock will be a flagpole at a victory parade the minute you see me step from the bathroom.

"I'm not the neatest guy in the world. You might be disappointed." That's pretty well a given. I hope.

"Somehow I don't believe that. No. I don't think so. What's that tie worth, one, one-fifty? I was disappointed when I believed all men were creeps. I'm not disappointed now, not after this evening, not with you. I'm actually very turned on. Aren't you? And by the way, so you know, I'm very financially secure. I'm not looking for handouts, not by a long shot, and thank you again for dinner. What I want is to find a nice guy and I think I've done that. I think so." Do you think your wife will think so? Will she? What will she think when she sees your shrivelled dick and wide-open eyes?

"You know I'm turned on. I couldn't stop ogling your legs during the show. And by the way, I am a nice guy," which I know you think is bullshit. I get that. What I don't get is why. You're not the only girl who's had a rotten father.

"I know you are and I wanted you to look at my legs. I want you to want me. So why don't we get past the second difficult part and enjoy a night of wild, torrid sex? I can't say 'make love', not yet, because that got me in trouble the last time. Not that I'm saying I sleep around, John, I do not." She touched his cheek. Except for once each year with shitheads like you while I'm with someone I love in another place. "I want you to believe me. Besides, you don't have much more of me to see. Do you?"

"I hope that's not true. I'm certainly anxious to see more." I chose not to watch you showering and peeing which, of course, was recorded on video? "And I do believe you. If I believe anything, I believe that. You have no idea how I would like to know more about you."

"Can I tell you something?" All the others wanted me to.

Anything I'll believe? "We're pretty well past the point of timidity, Collette. Don't you think?"

"I think so." She snuggled into him. "I've fantasized about you all week. I mean, really, the entire week. I wanted so much for tonight to work out, partly because we do fly together, though mostly because I'm attracted to you. I have been for a long time. Now we can relax and get to know each other over time. Who knows? We might work out. I hope so. Or we might not," because you're dead. "C'est la vie. If we don't we can wink at each other from time to time onboard. I simply won't add an extra little something to your mimosas and vodkas."

"We won't know if we don't try and your mimosas are the best," much better than prison tap water, Gilligan, for twenty-five to life, no more wine, no more Dom Pérignon, no more silk panties and ultra-short dresses, nor more Xara, no more Elixia.

"But no pet names, John. Let's not pretend. We'll have some great sex first," for as long as you live, "and get to know each other second. Somehow, I don't know, sleeping with you tonight feels right for me. So, are we agreed?"

"Yes we're agreed. Yes, we are very agreed." He stopped, facing her. "Collette…"

"What? What, John?" Want me to dress like a little girl? Want me to call you daddy?

"I want to know about you. I sincerely do. I believe you're dynamic and special. Enough said, because anything else will sound trite." Like you screaming at me that you're innocent.

"You'll know me very well by breakfast, John. For starters, I have always wondered about being with a woman." The way I'm wondering about her now, the way you're thinking of your little daughters. "Does that surprise you, that I'm curious?"

"Frankly, not at all. It's the ultimate male fantasy." He smirked. Like seeing your girlfriend rub cream over my fiancée's near-naked body on a public beach, like watching Deena reciprocate with Xara. "Just don't forget me when you find one, which I can't imagine would be very difficult. Not with that body."

"Ooh, don't get me started, John. I hope you can pace yourself. I promise; we're in for a long night. Or should I say many long nights?"

"Collette, the night is going to be very long and very sleepless. I promise you."

She'd never been inside The Franklin. In New York the Excalibur Boutique Hotel was her favourite: no hassles, a quiet place to relax, intimate. The Franklin was more formal, busier. Good. So would it be in the morning.

The stroll through the lobby was unhurried, Collette with her head lowered, Dowell thinking he'd mess himself if her skirt were any shorter.

"John, you live the good life." Or you did. Enjoy your last evening.

"I try. It's a perk. Still, all said and done, I would rather be with my girls. I miss them."

That part wasn't a lie. He would miss Frenchie when she was gone.

Inside the elevator they held hands, inebriated with lust, heated with desire for one another, his arm around her vulnerable shoulders, her arm around his youthful waist, anxious, each one delirious with expectation. He wanted to kiss her as desperately as she wanted her full lips pressed against his in the heat of the moment. Neither one did, each one hungry for the other, starved, their passion tempered by some out of shape clod who'd wallowed into the elevator with them, coughing phlegm, turning purple. Fennell thinking he would kick Dowell's balls into his tonsils at the gym.

The elevator stopping, leaving him behind, they meandered to his suite intoxicated with love's urgent facsimile, neither one wanting to rush the moment.

Dowell held the door open, blowing bad breath past his lips, his eyes glued to hem of her dress she was letting ride past the fleshy curves of her cheeks until they stepped inside. This he wasn't going to miss.

*

Marie tied her hands into Deena's, sitting impossibly close. She was French as Fennell would say. The show was about to begin. Deena extricated a hand, patting the girl's knee. Fennell was good. Nothing would happen. Despite which she checked the clip in her weapon.

"I hope you will not kill her, Deena."

"I hope not, Marie. But I will if I'm too slow through the door. That's why we have to stay alert, watch every single move they make. You remember what I told you about me and Johnnie that day at the gym. He played me, like he's playing her. He is the best, the absolute best."

"My eyes will not leave this monitor, Deena, not for one moment. I will not let anything happen to our Johnnie"

"He knows that."

The other agent sat half-listening. The kid had a crush on Fennell. That had to be a first.

When Dowell walked in without knocking they ignored him.

Deena patted Marie's knee, hugging her. "Here we go. This is it, show time."

*

"I didn't mention how handsome you were this evening, John."

"Thank you. Looking anything other than inadequate is difficult beside you."

She scanned the suite, thinking much larger than most, with a separate office space, more work for her. "Your firm does treat you well."

"It's a living, albeit with increasingly excessive travel time which I shouldn't complain about…not now, not after us happening like this. I never thought a year ago that I'd be making love…sorry, involved with my gorgeous flight attendant."

"Never say never, John. Isn't that what they say? I think so."

She pulled away first one glove from her arm, then the other, laying her hat beside them on the edge of a second queen size.

"Times like this I wish I never married. I missed out. If not for my girls, I don't know. I often wish their mother was more like them, you know, that sexy kind of teenage...you what I mean."

"Yes, I do. Little girls in little plaid skirts and fluffy panties, another male fantasy right up there with girl-on-girl. We can talk about that later. In fact let's do it. Let's swap fantasies...your little girls and my big girls." She noticed the bathroom door. "John, do mind if I take a shower? And would you mind getting me a vodka from the minibar. My throat's a little dry. No kidding. It's not every day my passengers see me nude." She hesitated. "In fact would you mind showering before me? I think I would rather see you vulnerable first. I think so."

He poured 50cls of vodka into one glass, another for himself, dying for a scotch, watching through the mirror as she reached into the closet for robes.

He shrugged out from his jacket, yanking his tie from his neck, undoing the top three buttons of his shirt, undoing his cufflinks, rolling his sleeves. He'd done this before, she thought. He was cool, practiced. This one she would work quickly. Guys never minded fast when all they cared about was wet.

"Why don't you order something from the bar downstairs? What's your favourite?"

"Dom Pérignon, which isn't a prerequisite to your best sex in a long time. I guarantee you that." You are about to experience the climax of a lifetime, John. "Not that I'm bragging."

"Order two bottles. As you promised, I have a feeling we're in for a long evening."

He disappeared into the bathroom.

Fennell paying for the wine was no big deal. Dinner was

another matter, though she knew the waiter would remember her legs more than the little he'd seen of her face.
*
Deena clicked off the bathroom monitor, explaining to Marie and Cynthia that she saw no reason to humiliate Dowell.

He didn't give a shit. He was glued on Rose.

By the time the bellhop came to the door Collette Salazar had taken off her shoes and her thong, leaving the door ajar. She was stretched out on her front, facing away, her legs parted, her ass half covered, speaking French on her cell. He had heard about French women. What he was seeing couldn't last long enough. He stood watching her for five, ten seconds, maybe more, mesmerized. He cleared his throat, reluctantly, even more pleasantly surprised. She kept her phone to her ear, pushing herself onto her knees, her dress rising on cue as she backed onto the floor, talking, not paying attention, her panties on the bed, slipping the chit from its leather folder, acting a little drunk, the folder dropping to the floor, letting the kid see as much as he could as she signed Fennell's name.

She said 'thank you', tugging one side of her hem, falling onto the bed talking into the phone before he had a chance to turn and walk out, giving him the best possible view.

"How does a broad do that, completely uncover her ass and show a guy her girl?"

Cynthia answered. "Dowell, ask that kid right now to describe her face all he's going to remember is one hell of a divine ass and her, hmmm, hmmm, sweet little pussy all nice and clean which I have to believe is a little tastier than the worn out rubber one you travel with."

"Yeah, like your ten-inch purple dick."

Collette Salazar was tugging her thong into place. The bathroom door was opening. Deena ordered Dowell into the hall, threatening to call Brannigan at home, reaching for her

phone.
*
"Did you leave some water for me?"

"Take your time."

"I will. I love hot showers, the stinging water. I signed your name for the wine, which we'll split .Like I said; I don't need a free ride." She beamed. "Want I do want is a good one. I don't want you getting in trouble because of me."

"Thanks, Collette. Not a problem. That's my treat. Why don't you take a glass in with you so I'm not one up on you?"

She agreed. Good idea. Drink up, Johnnie Boy.

He went through the pretence that a 300-dollar bottle of wine deserved, gripping the cork, twisting the bottle, tilting the fluted glass, adding the wine slowly to within a half-inch of the rim. She watched him, his hands and his expression. Any other time she might have been impressed. She took her glass, expectation gleaming in her eyes.

He watched her saunter into the bathroom, checking out her ass that wasn't entirely cloaked in blue, letting her catch him, smiling. She was smiling. When she closed the door behind her, the lock clicking, he shrugged into the lens creating his best sheepish grin.
*
Colette Salazar pushed her dress to her ankles, folding the delicate fabric into a miniscule bundle, adding her panties, leaning into the mirror, cupping her breasts, turning, twisting this way and that to examine herself from all angles. She was pleased: Certainly a night to remember.

She ran the water, a facecloth between her hand and the lever. She straddled the toilet to pee without touching the seat, her hands on her knees, her face devoid of expression, patting herself dry.

"I thought I was the only one who did that," Cynthia said.

Marie and Deena shook their heads with conviction, grimacing.

"The one thing dirtier than a hotel toilet is a fold-down table on an aircraft," Deena added.

"And this old man in the hallway," Marie was certain.

They giggled.

Collette Salazar reached into the jets of steaming water, wetting her body with unhurried dabs from head to toe, patting herself dry, running a comb through her hair, wiping the counter with her towel, wiping the counter again with damp toilet tissue, flushing the toilet with her covered hand, turning off the shower the same way.

"No prints in there. We might have to dust Fennell for prints when they're done and I've got the most seniority between us ladies." Cynthia looked into Fennell's monitor. "You know, I don't see why everyone pretends to have a hate on for that guy. I know there isn't a woman in the building who hasn't fantasized about doing him ten different ways. That's why the guys don't like him. Hell, I would lift my skirt for him in a blink and tell my husband to work late, very late."

Collette Salazar picked her tap pants from her clutch unfolding them, studying them. Her last pair, Deena mused. The vial they weren't sure about until she dipped a finger into the oil a few times, massaging the excess into her lips. Cynthia commenting that it didn't get better than that on the porno channel. Marie intent, maintaining her promise, watching as Salazar slipped into her panties, peering into the mirror, whispering, everything had to be perfect, easing one arm then the other into the robe when she was satisfied.

"What did she say?" Deena asked.

Marie answered. "She has said 'forgive me, my darling. This is the last one, the very last one. I am coming home to you."

Deena pressed a hand to her chest. "Oh, shit. I don't believe this. Fennell's her last. How frigging ironic is that?

The last guy she wants to kill is a cop and the nicest guy she'll ever meet."

Collette Salazar was reaching into her clutch. She held the knife in one hand, extending the blade with the other, twisting the hilt this way and that, testing the grip, jabbing downward once, violently, fitting the weapon into her purse, smirking. The evening was very special, the first time she hadn't used a knife meant for a roast or a turkey. The others hadn't accompanied her to the theatre. However he was her last and the theatre was meant to make the evening all the more memorable. Perhaps this time she would keep the souvenir as a letter opener.

Marie didn't care what Cynthia might think. She held Deena's hand. Salazar was disappearing from one monitor into another. Cynthia went to the door for Dowell to tell him shit was going down.

In the few seconds she was out of range Marie whispered. "Deena, do not be angry with me, and do not tell our Johnnie, however I do find that your man is very handsome in his small underwear. He will be a good husband for you. You should be very proud of him. He is so hot."

Deena chuckled, hugging her, her eyes not once leaving the screen. "I won't tell him, Marie. He's conceited enough."

*

John Fennell dropped his robe. His glass already refilled twice, the wine destroyed, mixed with melting ice in the bucket. He held the bottle out to her, his back nestled into his pillow, stretched out with the duvet tossed onto the floor. He figured he would save her the trouble. He sort of had a clue.

"My fantasies about you were very accurate, John. I'm not disappointed. I hope you're not." She let him hold her glass, dropping her robe, inhaling a deep breath. "This is what you call a critical moment, John. This is where you're supposed to say something to make me feel good."

"I'm sorry. I like. I like very much. I am far from disappointed. This evening is working out better than in my dreams or my fantasies. And I've had plenty of both."

He patted the bed beside him. She straddled him instead. He might have chuckled, resisting the urge. He could imagine Frenchie holding Deena's hand. He reached for the light.

"No, please, keep the light on." She scanned him, kissing him. "I want the full affect, John. I've waited a week for this. And, really, my fingers got a little achy this week as I was thinking about tonight, thinking about you, us. I bought these undies especially for you, a little lacy, a little naughty," she smiled coquettishly, "yet fully accessible. Yours, though, might get in the way."

She put a hand to his waistband. He stopped her.

"Let me see you this way a while longer. My wife, not to speak ill of the soon-to-be dead, because I hope the future I have planned for you works out, she never wore panties like this, so soft, so silky and smooth, so sexy. I kind of have this fantasy about, you know, about…"

"…about being with a young girl in her panties, touching her through her panties, getting her off."

"She was never into games or fantasies."

"I am. Or I could be with you."

He drained his glass, half-filled with water, pouring another that wasn't, letting the white effervescence settle, adding more to her glass.

"So, women, Collette, have you ever been with one? Or were you teasing me?"

"I would like to try a woman one day soon, a pretty one. I mean, you like pussies. You've wanted mine all week. So do I." She pressed a hand between her open thighs. "I love my pussy, John. I have since puberty. She got me through the entire week waiting for you. And I know you will. So why wouldn't a woman want me?"

"I'm sure that more than a couple already do. Perhaps they're shy. I mean, how does a woman tell another woman she wants to have a trial run?"

"Do you like my breasts?"

"Yes, I do."

"Then why aren't you touching them, kissing them, squeezing them?"

"The evening will end soon enough. I'm pacing myself. I can't believe this is happening to me. This is a dream, a beautiful dream."

"You know, John, I could do a woman with you. I mean I would do a woman with you. I mean, really, you could pick up something cute and sexy, young. You're certainly good-looking enough. Bring her to your room; I could happen by, be the girlfriend or the wife surprising you. We could do that, with a young girl. I could make myself up to look younger. What do you think? Would you like that? Would you get off on seeing me do a girl?"

"I think. Yes, I think very much."

"And do you ever think about your daughters? Tell me the truth."

"What? You mean like seeing them naked, touching them?"

She nodded. "My father did, both my fathers. I was adopted after the first one died. They both wanted to see me naked. They both wanted to fuck me, John."

"Did they?"

"I think it's natural. I mean, I was beautiful as a girl, tempting in my panties. Your daughters are beautiful. Like me they probably don't think anything about running around in their undies in front of their daddy and you're a young man, young enough to pick up a girl a few years older than your daughters in a bar. I think so. We should do it, John. We should do a threesome. How's that for a fantasy, yours and mine together?"

Collette Salazar reached for her purse. "I bought these

for tonight. I've got the bill to prove I don't carry them in my purse. Hopefully one day very soon you won't have to wear one."

She leaned forward, the taught nipple of a flawlessly sculpted breast teasing his chin, his lips, her other nipple taunting his cheeks his forehead, his hands at her waist, his brain wanting the bullshit to end, wanting her to reach for the knife. He was not fucking her. No way was he fucking her. Apart from Deena who would cut his throat, and Frenchie who would help her, the DA would have a brain hemorrhage.

Yes, your Honour, it is true. However the DA's office would like the court to disregard the fact that Agent Fennell, by doing his duty, completely and absolutely and with complete disregard for his own safety and well-being, did unwilling fuck the defendant with the fullest knowledge that he was having a fucking good time...your Honour.

"Believe me or not, I've never worn one. You may have to help me." He slid down, effortlessly moving her weight with him, drinking in her beauty. "I can see someone easily falling in love with you, Collette."

This wasn't working out the way she planned, the way the others had worked out. He was supposed to be fucking her, hurting her. What the fuck was wrong with him...fucking queer?

She teased the edge of her tap pants away from her thigh, John Fennell doing what he had to; his trained eye telling him that, yes, that was in fact Gilligan Rose's glistening pussy twenty inches from his face. So near yet so far. He could also imagine her head leaving her neck.

"Johnnie, you're being a very bad boy. Aren't we supposed to be talking about young girls in panties, young women who want to share this with you in our bed and us sharing them? Can you imagine a woman kissing me here the way you want to, kissing my breasts the way you want to." She leaned into him, her breasts pressed hard against his chest. "What I want is for you to fuck me right now, Mr. Fennell. Or all future flights are cancelled. I've waited too long for this. So fuck me and I want something to remember."

His voice was a murmur. He didn't want Frenchie to hear him speaking like some festering lowlife with a rancid whore. The others would understand. She would not.

"I do want to fuck the most beautiful woman in the world as much as you want me to fuck you." He closed his eyes, squeezing her hips. "Collette, I'm thinking that when your fathers fucked you, they fucked you good, the way you like, the same way I think about my girls. They're so young, so pretty. Am I right? Did they hurt you? Did you like them hurting you?" He moved under her, thrusting imperceptibly. "Tell me. Am I right? Did your fathers come into your dark room at night to hurt you, to fuck you, to fondle your tits and your smooth ass while they were fucking you? Is that why you like girls? I know you do. Is that why you opened your legs on the plane, so I could see your silk-covered pussy? Take off your panties. Let me give you what you want, what all you whores want. You're all sluts, Collette. Let me pretend that you're young and tight and beautiful, the way you were then for them. Hurry, take off your panties. Let's get this done so I can go out and find something that I don't have to pretend is young."

She was rocking with him, as though in slow motion. She was right about him. He was the worst, worse than any of the others. She was crying. She couldn't think of anyone she could hate more.

"Fuck you!"

His eyes opened, her wrists clamped in iron-like vices, Agent Deena Archer bursting through an unlocked door, a beam of translucent red dotting Gilligan Rose's temple.

"Gilligan Rose you are under arrest for the murders of ten men, whom I'm sure you remember, and the attempted murder of a US Federal Agent. That would be me. Pleased to meet you. Now get your bony ass off me."

"Gilligan, it's me, Deena. Do as he says very slowly. Please. Let's do this right. Let's not be stupid. Gilligan, please, think of Xara."

Fennell wasn't letting go of her wrists, the blade wavering over his heart, her arms trembling, forcing downward. She wanted him dead, tears dripping onto his chest. With an abrupt twist she was sprawled onto the floor, Fennell at the foot of the bed with his weapon in hand.

"Gilligan, look at me. I'm Deena. Drop the knife before something bad happens. Believe me. I will do everything I can to help you. Let's not do anything silly here."

"I don't know you."

"Yes you do, Gilligan. Please, for me, for Xara, drop the knife."

Cynthia came into the room, closing the door. Dowell wasn't invited to the show.

"Yeah, you remember Deena. She's also one of the daughters on my computer screen that you've seen for the last year. The other so-called daughter is in the other room, also a federal agent, and I'm really anxious to get dressed. So drop the frigging knife."

She did, onto the bed, standing, Fennell facing the wall as Deena passed Gilligan Rose her dress which wasn't quite as exotic with the ruffled edges of her tap pants showing past her hem. She wiped her eyes, Fennell going behind them to dress, Deena holstering her weapon.

"I'm truly sorry, Gilligan. I am. I have to cuff you. You have the right to remain silent…"

Reading the Miranda broke Deena's heart. "Gilligan, do not say a word, not one word. That's all I can tell you."

"Stop pretending to know me. You don't know me. I've never seen you before. I wasn't trying to kill him. I was defending myself. He was scaring me. I thought he liked me. We had dinner and went to the theatre. We were on a date. At least I thought so until he started talking like a madman. I was terrified. I travel a lot. I carry a knife for protection. And if he is a cop why did he bring me here to fuck me? You were all waiting for him to fuck me. Why?"

"He wasn't, Gilligan. We needed to know how far you would go. The entire evening was monitored and recorded. We saw you in the bathroom practicing with the knife. We heard what you said, that he would be the last one. We have videos of you shopping this afternoon for the knife and the condoms and getting ready in your room across the street, in here with the bellhop. Even this is being recorded."

"I was teasing the bellhop, getting turned on, giving him a cheap thrill. So what?"

Fennell asked Cynthia to go with Dowell to the Excalibur for Rose's luggage.

"The next knife you use, Miss Rose, will be plastic. We're booked on a six AM to Miami, First-Class of course, where you'll be booked on ten counts of murder, one count of attempted murder. My best guess is that you'll see Long Beach again in about twenty-five years, if you're lucky and if you don't get the death penalty."

"I wanted to get away from you, the way you were talking. I thought you were different, a nice guy. I wanted a fling, a bit of fun that could have turned into something until you started talking like a maniac. And what ten murders are you talking about? I've been in France all week."

"No, Miss Rose, you don't believe nice guys exist." Fennell faced the lens, signalling Marie into the room. "This is Miss Marie Anisette. She's a member of a federal task force. You might remember her from Les Filles du Ciel, or possibly from my computer screen. She was kind enough to pose for me as my other daughter and be my French fling. You're a lesbian, Miss Rose, documented as such over the past year. You wanted me here this evening to kill me, to assuage an understandable hatred, to purge your mind of your demons. As agent Archer has cautioned, don't say another word. From this moment on what you say will determine your future…or the duration of that future. Leave that to your counsel who, I'm sure, will be pleased to contact your girlfriends, Miss de Montfort and Xara Mendiga, on your behalf. I imagine those ladies are in for quite a surprise."

"Don't you dare talk to me about Elixia and this Xara Mendiga, who is that?"

The time was 12:05. Cynthia and Dowell walked in at 12:35.

By one-thirty the dress, shoes and underwear were bagged along with the hat and gloves, knife, condom, oil, purse and 700-dollar theatre stubs. The second bottle of champagne was returned, the bellhop's fond memory of Gilligan Rose's feminine divinity quelled at seeing his tip deleted from the bill.

Gilligan Rose did not say another word. Dressed in low-heeled pumps, jeans and a sweater she kept her hands and wrists covered with a coat, passing through security more quickly than she ever had, keeping her head lowered, praying she wouldn't be seen by TGA crews.

When asked by Fennell whether she would like to call TGA to announce her resignation, she did. She left her supervisor a message advising that she required a leave of absence, suggesting that a few weeks would suffice. She thought so. Yes. She would return to work in three weeks.

Thirty-Eight
Miami: Federal Task Force on Major Crime

Saturday morning Cynthia and Dowell went their separate ways. They weren't needed. Their reports were written, co-signed by Fennell who put Gilligan Rose into a Miami-Dade squad car which was as simple as 'hey, you, I need your car'.

Deena and Marie rode in another, Deena in the front with the cop, Marie imprisoned in the backseat with her hands cuffed behind her like a common criminal. She hated Johnnie. She wanted to punch him so badly. She'd mentioned to Fennell that she couldn't imagine how awful Gilligan Rose must feel being handcuffed, humiliated by everyone seeing her that way.

Now she did, like Rose, against her will. In her case arrested for being French and talking funny. Deena distanced herself, calling them incorrigible children, feeling guilty that she could laugh. She saw no humour in Gilligan sitting alone, afraid, her wrists tied with cold steel when a month earlier they'd spent a wonderful day together at the beach.

Deena knew then the day would come. When Johnnie wanted something badly enough he didn't take shortcuts and he wanted Gilligan Rose. Now she was sitting in a holding cell while her mother's artwork was crated and propped against a wall in the squad room, delivered unopened by the US State Department without a single US Customs stamp.

First they needed time alone with Gayle Brannigan. This was a big deal. Gilligan Rose was a big deal and Brannigan wanted to see her. Monday wouldn't come soon enough, though he wouldn't file his final report until Monday or Tuesday, not quite certain how to explain a naked killer sitting on his parts with her compatible anatomy primed with massage oil. The videos were another matter. He didn't care who or how many saw Rose taking a leak, though flashing her pussy a few inches from his nose was something else. He didn't need the grief. Shit like that never stayed a secret very long.

Brannigan was waiting with her arms crossed, leaning against the edge of her desk. Her 'tell me something good stance'. She told them to sit. It was Saturday. Weekday rules didn't apply.

"Fennell, exactly why is this sweet girl handcuffed?"

"She's a pain in the ass, boss lady, and she's French. You can't trust them." He pinched Marie's cheek. "I was going to undo her, until she said she didn't like me anymore. I think they should stay on until she likes me again."

"Deena, are you sure you know what you're getting into? It's not too late, girl."

"Captain, it is too late. I'm stained. Who would want me after this thing?"

"Good point."

"Captain Brannigan, please, my wrists are hurting," Marie complained

"Do you like him yet?"

"No, I do not. I will never like him again. He is horrible to do this to me."

"Then I guess you've got a problem." Brannigan twisted, reaching to the centre of her desk. "Two days early, Marie. I wasn't expecting to see you today. Congratulations." She placed the official envelope in Marie's lap. "Fennell convinced me that you'll be a fine agent. Let's hope so because you'll be working under my command in a year and I don't tolerate second best."

"Thank you, Captain Brannigan. I am so grateful to you and I will not kill him for doing this to me when I learn about weapons because I do like Deena so much more than him. I know she will miss him. But, really, I do not understand why."

"Everyone likes Deena more than him, me included. Now tell me about Rose." Brannigan was looking at Marie. "I said, tell me about Rose. Or do you need your hands for that?"

"Yes, of course I do. I am a French girl."

Gayle Brannigan's laughter was a rare sound.

Almost-Agent Anisette spoke for thirty minutes, suppressing her glee. She was giving the report directly to the captain. When she finished her exhaustive account she neither expected nor asked for praise. And she got none. She didn't need accolades. She knew Deena was proud of her. Neither she nor Johnnie once interrupted, Deena leaning onto the arm of her seat listening intently, Fennell sitting indifferently, once in a while glancing at Deena. Of course she was good. She'd spent the week with him.

She couldn't wait to tell her parents and her brother, at least what she could.

"Are we in any trouble here, Fennell, with improper conduct, anything done innocently, by accident?"

"No we are not, boss lady. We've got every second recorded from different angles. She was topless for a few minutes, flashed me once through her knickers. Nice, yes" he smirked, "though I've seen a lot better…you know." He tilted his head towards Deena. "That's it. My hands didn't leave her hips except to stop the blade, which understandably has her pissed-off at the moment, not ready to talk with me. Really, I think she's more disappointed thinking of what might have been between us. You know, thinking of me all week, fantasizing, deciding whether or not to turn hetero. She feels I let her down…poor thing. Oh, yeah, she did try to get things started with a little breast action, you know, rubbing, doing that girl thing. I just wasn't feeling it. It's all on video."

Deena hurled a cushion at him. She never missed. Marie looked stunned, her eyes wide open, her lips pursed. The captain knew he'd been behaving too well for too long.

"Any woman in this room who doesn't feel sorry for Deena right now, raise your hand."

No response.

"Captain," Deena broke in, "the videos are graphic of Gilligan changing her clothes a few times, taking a shower before her date with lover-boy here, the bathroom, a little thing she did for the bellhop. I would like you to watch them at home, not here, with a private viewing for the DA when the time comes. The Evidence Room guys would have enough entertainment for a month. She doesn't deserve that, Captain."

"And exactly how much of lover-boy here should I be prepared for, apart from his little dream episode?"

Marie blurted, "You will see that he does need much more time in the gym, Captain Brannigan, because he did eat too much French food." She hesitated, borrowing Deena's scrunchy expression. "Anyway, I must say that he was a gentleman with her."

Smiles found their way into serious faces.

"Requisition a strongbox as part of the evidence package, Deena, the combination for our eyes only, no copies authorized. Good enough?"

"Good enough, Captain. Thank you."

"Does she know about her mother?"

"No, boss lady. And we should keep her in the dark until the shrinks get through with her. If the news of momma leaks out we could lose her after all Frenchie's good work."

Brannigan agreed. "Let's get her up here and let's get her a lawyer. No technical foul-ups. Understood people?"

She glanced at Marie. "And Fennell set this poor girl free."
He did, reaching for the phone.
*

Gilligan Rose sat on the bench with her legs crossed. She wasn't hungry. She'd eaten on the plane, her hands unrestricted, seated beside Fennell whom she viewed differently, who explained to her exactly how a smashed larynx would feel if she believed that trying to kill him with First-Class cutlery was a good idea, how she would live the rest of her life talking in forced whispers. He was also armed and she would spend the rest of the flight face down on the floor with her hands cuffed behind her and his foot on her neck for good measure.

Deena was seated behind her, armed, a clear shot to her back. Cynthia and Dowell were seated in aisle seats opposite them, armed. She thanked him and chortled. Beyond that she didn't want to talk with him. She felt a little embarrassed, not about the bellhop. Who cared about a bellhop? Teenage girls did worse than that every day on the internet while their mothers sat watching television doctors ranting about irresponsible parents and the innocence of youth gone bad. She was embarrassed because she believed he was laughing at her, mocking her. She had wantonly opened the most intimate part of her body to his ridicule, literally, making herself vulnerable; wanting him dead, his reaction no more ardent than if she'd opened a bag of chips instead. Now he was alive, laughing at her. She felt dirty.

He must have known, midway through her meal promising her without the slightest trace of humour, without the slightest hint of satisfaction in his voice that the video footage would be kept extremely confidential, that with the exception of her relevant time in his bathroom, her personal moments would be deleted by female technicians under female scrutiny. Such evidence was never presented in court, for the judge's eyes alone if need be, and later destroyed. She thanked him and when she was done eating he cuffed her.

She was wealthy. She could afford a good trial lawyer, not an out-of-school wannabe or a charity case loser.

They had no proof. Besides, she hadn't killed anyone. How would they know if she had? If she had, for argument sake, she would have been smart enough to kill them in different cities and countries. Polygraphs weren't a precise science, she knew that much, and to detect a lie a lie had to be told. Lies were verbal. She wouldn't agree to one. She had nothing to prove. She wouldn't say she hadn't killed anyone because she hadn't. They had nothing.

Fennell, she should have known. He was too refined, too patient. Any normal guy would have had his hands all over her legs at the theatre, under the table at the restaurant. And what guy didn't blink at two 300-dollar bottles of champagne and another 400 for dinner? She should have known. She should have run. She should have said goodnight, John, and fuck you. All week wanting him, waiting for him, dressing for him, more beautiful for him than for any of the others.

She would call Elixia; explain that she needed an extra week or two, no reason to alarm her, complications with the Long Beach condo, her job: another lie, too late for the truth. She was allowed one call. She loved Elixia. She would always love her. She'd made her decision. Elixia was the most important person in her life.

She huddled into a corner, drawing her knees to her chin, closing her eyes to the light. She wanted to whisper. She needed to whisper. How else would she tell Gilligan the truth without them hearing? Gilligan would know right away she was telling a lie. They could never know about Gilligan or Miss Emma Rose. She could never spend a day in a place of one-sided faces, not one day. She remembered her mother's faces, the day she went alone to find Miss Emma Rose and Zeke Phillips together, discovering instead that she was wealthy and that they had left her alone. She could never live in such a horrible place. How did Fennell know she was afraid of the dark? How did he know Tommy Dune had hurt Gilligan so many times, making her bleed, making her kill him twice?

Gilligan Rose was her special secret. No one could know. They had both promised not to tell anyone so many years ago. How could either one now? How could they arrest one and not the other when one was innocent and the other was guilty of constantly being hurt? They had no proof. There was no crime other than Fennell's despicable need to hurt her and humiliate her.

Fennell was at the end of a wasted year.

*

Five minutes later Gilligan Rose stepped through the door, her wrists shackled to her waist, the dual escort retreating into the squad room. In the middle of Brannigan's office she ignored Deena and Marie, focusing on Fennell.

"I've tried to calculate the cost of your trips, John. I came up with …a lot. Someone's going to be very displeased with you, besides me of course." She acknowledged Gayle Brannigan. "You must be the captain."

"Captain Gayle Brannigan, Miss Rose. Please sit down." She did. "It's Saturday, Miss Rose. The courts are closed. Unless your lawyer's playing golf with a judge you'll be here until midday Monday when the court will appoint one to represent you if you're unable to afford one."

"I am very able, Captain, which I am certain you already know. Working for me is a hobby. However I would appreciate your impartial assistance in finding the very best, discounting friends and family, naturally. I can't exactly dial 411, can I? And what lawyer will tell me he's the worst in town? I'm more familiar with the better restaurants and boutiques in Miami than I am with the best law firm. Fees are not an issue. That said, I do have a very full agenda and would appreciate being in Long Beach by early next week. To that end, if I could have that name today, I would be grateful."

"I'll get you a name within the hour."

"Thank you, Captain, and preferably a golfer. It's much too lovely a day to remain inside and I do love Miami."

"Consider yourself fortunate, Miss Rose. We're not quite up to the standards of the Excalibur or The Franklin. However we do have a far better rating than County and you will have a private room this evening and tomorrow. You can thank Agent Archer for that."

She ignored Deena. "Yes, Deena, she seems to believe she knows me. I have to say, Captain, she is very beautiful. I'm disappointed that she wasn't the one chasing me for a year. She would have caught me a long time ago."

"A fact, Miss Rose, which makes the manner of these murders and Agent Fennell's attempted murder all the more unusual."

"You mean that I'm a lesbian. Of course, you know that about me. I'm also bi-. I date the occasional guy for fun, the same way someone like Agent Archer or yourself would date a girl…for fun. You're very attractive, Captain. So you see, whoever your Agent Fennell thinks I am; we happened at the wrong time. Case closed. I thought he was coming on to me so I came on to him. We dated. Or I thought we were. Quite frankly, if I'd seen Agent Archer first, he would have been SOL." She leaned forward, leering at Deena. "I guarantee we would have been an item if only for a night, Deena. Beautiful women are like crack; once you taste us you are hooked." She leaned back. "Anyway, as fate would have it, Captain, I ended up in bed with a guy I discovered very quickly was a freak. I was scared, afraid for my life. As for the bathroom, stabbing the air, let's call what you saw a dry run. Women I'm used to, like Deena here. We're evenly matched. Not so with him. My sleeping with a guy like him… that's a euphemism, Captain…he must have said 'fuck' a hundred times… that's like a guy sleeping with a whore." She glared at Fennell. "Ever think of yourself as a whore, John?"

"No, and I would prefer Agent Fennell now that we're not dating. I do know this; this conversation is not being recorded. It's off the record. We'll disavow ours and you will disavow yours. That's fair. I know the ten men you killed were scum. That's known and is undeniable. They're not missed. We've met with their wives, all of whom received your photo albums and messages. You did a good thing. You saved young girls, the wrong way. Now you're going to prison for murder and here's something you don't know, Gilligan Rose. Had you killed me, you would have killed someone who's on your side, albeit from a different perspective. You would have sent a photo of me lying naked and dead to my wife along with my photo files of my daughters. Dirty pictures that weren't dirty at all, except in your mind. The thing is, in this instance, my wife is The Federal Task Force on Major Crime. So what would you have gained? You screwed up big time. You've already met my daughters. And another thing, had you killed me, Agent Archer would have blown your head off. You wouldn't be sitting here. The little red dot on your temple that you didn't see was approximately a half-inch across, steady, precise. She doesn't miss. A ten millimetre round passing through that dot, that's something else, that's serious damage to a hotel room. And, to answer your question, Miss Rose, I've never felt like a whore because, like you, I can afford the best. Unlike you, my job is not a hobby."

"We're at an impasse, John, with me at somewhat of a temporary disadvantage and I do believe first names are more appropriate, John, since two of your corporeal senses have enjoyed my vagina from a somewhat less than professional perspective. You did enjoy. Didn't you? I wish I could say that I envy whoever she is, your girlfriend, your wife, your occasional release. The truth is she would be happier with me. We're not all hard-core dykes." She turned her attention to Brannigan. "Captain, might I at least have clean lingerie from my luggage to see me through Monday, the pieces not collected for evidence?"

"Yes, Miss Rose, and this conversation is over. I will do my best to get you a name this afternoon. Enjoy your lunch, another area where we surpass County."

She signalled the guards through the windows of her office. No one stood as Gilligan Rose walked out.
*

The air was still. Brannigan had a way of chilling a room, Marie very much alone in sensing the temperature change. Fennell was immune, Archer learning to be immune. Brannigan liked Fennell a lot and in a week she was going to Deena's bridal shower that Deena knew nothing about. More than that, she had history with Fennell. She respected him. She liked the rude SOB that Deena was taming.

"Fennell, I take back everything I ever thought of you. If you had that woman sitting naked on you while this gorgeous...partner of yours was in the other room with a gun in her hand, you are either a very brave man or very stupid."

"Frenchie here knows, boss lady. Deena invited her."

A curious tilt of her head and: "True, Deena?"

"Yes, Captain. I feel good about Marie. I wanted her to share how I feel about, well, it."

"Marie, this is a special situation. I like these people, more than I should as their captain, may the good Lord strike me down. And I like you. So don't do anything to make me change my mind about you. This wonderful wedding is our secret around here until I say differently. I have a few issues to work out. Just because I like them doesn't mean that Agent Fennell here isn't a huge pain in my ebony butt."

"I will do nothing to hurt Deena, Captain Brannigan. I do like her so much and I am once more beginning to like Johnnie...but slowly, I must say. He was so brave also, Captain Brannigan. He is not stupid at all."

"That's so sweet. We'll put a chart on the wall. Who likes Johnnie Fennell? What kind of prize should we offer, Deena? I'm thinking a lobotomy."

Deena chuckled, Marie didn't understand and Fennell didn't see the humour.

"Captain, Frenchie here, I know she's your gofer. That said, and understood, what about double duty? It's not like we can send her home with a little pat on her French derrière for a good job done. I'm thinking let her be the go-between on this. Sure. We know that we don't always understand everything she's trying to say, but it'll pay off next year for you and will keep this Gilligan Rose thing closer to our chests...so to speak. This is a big one, boss lady. We can't let this one leak out. If somehow it does, well, I'll simply shoot Frenchie in the head and ship her body to her family with a sympathy card. Not a big deal."

Marie's mouth dropped open.

"Marie you be in this office Monday at six. Interns work nine-to-five; we work twenty-four-seven and don't pretend for a moment that you're an agent. You are not, not yet. You are on special assignment. Are we clear on that?"

Marie sprang from her seat, hugging Brannigan, hugging Deena, kissing Fennell's cheek and confessing. "I was never really mad with you, Johnnie. I knew all this time that you were playing with me because you do like me so much."

"Good Lord, strike me blind. What am I seeing?" Brannigan checked her watch, thankful. "It's noon, at last."

She went to her drawer that housed three glasses. She only ever needed three glasses filling each two-fingers deep, straight. Marie's scotch came in a paper cup mixed with fountain water.

"Has the fact that we've got a very new and very difficult situation struck any of you brilliant agents?"

Fennell raised his hand, leaning forward, grinning. "Yes, boss lady, me first, me first."

Brannigan ignored him.

Deena admitted, "I don't follow you, Captain."

"She's asked us for the best lawyer in town, and she's got the funds to pay for the best. If we give her someone mediocre any judge would toss us in the toilet and rightfully so. That's the situation."

Deena hunched her shoulders. She didn't see the issue.

"Fennell, help me out here. In everyone's opinion, who is the best criminal lawyer in Miami?"

"Bruce Turnbull, boss lady, and not just here. There's no one better in the entire state."

"That's right, Mr. Turnbull. And where does Mr. Turnbull work, for the sake of Deena and our little French associate here?"

"He works at The Summit Group."

"Yes, he does, which we all now know is owned by...anybody?"

Deena stepped in. "Johnnie."

"Yes, by Johnnie Fennell, bringing us to the difficult part."

"I'm completely distanced from the firm, boss lady, with not the slightest chance of conflict. The firm is in trust. I get a year-end bonus that I can't touch. That's the extent of my involvement."

"But trust isn't one of your strong points, so you visit the firm every so often."

"I might drop by for a coffee once in a while."

"Can you get Turnbull?"

"Yes."

"This is a rock and a hard place, Fennell."

"Pretty much, boss lady."

"We'll have to lay this out piece by piece for the DA. They won't like this one bit. You have no ties apart from coffee? You're sure?"

"None."

"And with Turnbull, our chance of conviction is?"

"We know she did it, and she knows. Turnbull will get her reduced from first to second degree in a perfect world, her world, paroled after fifteen, maybe ten, perhaps serving her time somewhere nice with fairies dancing on soft walls."

"Sweetheart, please don't talk like that. Captain, that's what she needs. She needs help, not hard time. I know her. She was raped so many times as a little girl, in the dark with no one to help her. What does that say about us? She is guilty. Yes, we know that. But like Johnnie said, she did good getting rid of vermin. So why don't we help her a little? And if the DA doesn't agree I will personally fly their entire office to Bangkok for a wake-up call. We're cops, Captain. We're supposed to do what's best for everyone. Gilligan did, for the daughters. Don't we owe her the same consideration? If not, why am I a cop? Why don't you hire bounty hunters and save taxpayers a fortune?"

Silence. When Gayle Brannigan was silent everyone was silent, including the DA.

"Fennell, give me Turnbull's private number and let's not waste time pretending you don't have it." She pointed a stern finger at Deena. "Get her formally charged and printed. Confiscate her passport, TGA credentials and driver's permit, notify the DA and let's get Rose out of here this afternoon. I don't need the extra expense. What you three have done to the department's budget would have put my kids through university, if I had any. In any event, you and Fennell stay focused and you stay away from her. No contact. You stay objective and don't go all mushy on me. Good enough, Agent Archer?"

Deena slouched into her seat, depleted, sipping her scotch. "Yeah, that is way better than good enough, Captain. Thank you, Gayle."

Gayle? Marie didn't know what to think. What she knew was not to say a word.
*

Gilligan Rose was free that afternoon not far from four o'clock on a 2.5 million-dollar bond and a GPS bracelet on her wrist, early enough to enjoy the beach not far from her time-share condo. She wasn't worried. Paris time was 9:00 PM. When she finished the call she went shopping. She had a dinner date and nothing appropriate to wear.

Gayle Brannigan went home to her husband once Turnbull left her office after viewing the videos. He left with copies of all the reports filed thus far. No one had to tell Turnbull the rules. Deena and Fennell stayed late.

Marie knew, giggling, excited. She wanted to go home, she wanted to stay. She didn't believe her week, anxious to call her parents and her brother, to tell them she was still on special assignment, nervous about speaking with Lincoln Palmer the next day, anxious about their date.

Deena didn't know. She didn't have a clue, eager for her big surprise.

He glared at Marie. "You told her. You told her, didn't you, Frenchie? You're a traitor."

"I told her nothing, Johnnie. She wanted to make me. However I did refuse. I went to my bed instead of that. I promise you this from my heart."

"She's innocent sweetheart. So what's my big surprise? Come on."

"It's not this, sweetcheeks. This is a surprise, just not for you. Yours comes tomorrow." He gently uncrated and unwrapped the paintings. "These were done by Emma Rose, alias Mademoiselle Emmanuelle Lerosier. Green Tears, go figure. What she has painted, Deena, is Gilligan peering into the mirror, happy, wanting to help Gilligan, Gilligan imploring Gilligan to help her, searching for a way to escape the mirror. Your point about her is well-taken. I couldn't think of a more appropriate memento."

"She knew, sweetheart. All this time Emma Rose has known her daughter needed help. What a terrible mother she must have been, what a despicable woman."

"You wouldn't think so to see her, a few loose marbles, maybe. We never know, do we?

"Sweetheart, what does the yellow painting represent? I can't begin to imagine Gilligan's inner torment."

"Yellow Envy: despondency conflicting with elation, one emotion suppressing the other, a constant struggle, the envy of freedom. She must have been one screwed up kid. Correction: She is screwed up. Anyway, the painting isn't ours. Green Tears is what I wanted for my office. Frenchie was set on this one. She's got this thing about yellow. So Frenchie, this is for you, a souvenir of your first case from me and Deena. Like I told you, you should always have a souvenir, lest you forget, and remembering makes you a better cop. Don't ever forget a case, not a single one."

Marie was gasping, clutching her stomach. Deena was rubbing her back.

"No, Johnnie. I cannot. I cannot do this."

He chuckled. "Yes, Frenchie, you can. Yes, you can do this. Or I will tell Palmer that you've got six toes and a big wart on your bum. Of course, being a lawyer, he'll enquire as to how I acquired that information."

"Deena, you must help me here with him. He is being a fennell with me. I was at the galerie d'art with him. I do know what this painting...."

"No. He's not being a fennell this time. You know, Marie, how you feel when you're really, really happy?"

"Yes, I do, with you and with Johnnie, to know I am now part of your team and to be your good friend also. I am so proud to know you. I do love you and Johnnie so much."

"That's right. So accept your gift. It's important to him. This is making Fennell very happy; his way of saying how proud he is of you. You did well. Believe me, that he is doing this is something rare and special. You're his partner. He's trying to say he loves you too...Frenchie."

Now she really had to phone her mother, father and brother, Fennell tolerating the squeezing and kissing as best he could.

Marie never did believe that Johnnie Fennell was a fennell. To her he was handsome and brave, debonair, and Lincoln Palmer would have a lot to live up to.

Thirty-Nine
This Year: July 21st

Saturday Gilligan Rose dined with her attorney, a late-night dinner in a fancy restaurant. The only kind he knew.

When Brannigan interrupted his golf game earlier in the day he was indeed with a judge. However a serial killer, an attempted cop killing, a mother, who was supposed to be locked in a psycho ward discovered in France after seventeen years of freedom, was impossible to resist. Apart from the fact that John Fennell was, indirectly, his boss.

He met with her, instantly intrigued, staying with her throughout the formality of booking her, leaving her for a short while to view the videos and spend the rest of his spoiled day reading Deena Archer's and Marie Anisette's versions as well as the transcripts from Emma Rose's trial. He would have Fennell's by Tuesday, which he believed. What John Fennell said, he did.

Sunday Gilligan Rose spent all day in Turnbull's office and Monday, with Gayle Brannigan's and the DA's reluctant permission, she flew to Long Beach, California with Bruce Turnbull who, once through the gate, took her passport as promised. What Turnbull did not tell them was that they would travel First-Class on Trans-Global Airlines, not expecting that the cabin and flight crews would all acknowledge her with affectionate smiles. One of the women had heard of the leave of absence, taking a moment to ask Gilligan if all was well. Gilligan assuring her that, yes, all was very well. They all seemed so taken with her.

What wasn't he seeing? She was going to prison or an institution. For how long was anyone's guess. Yet she was convinced she was going to France, completely unperturbed, not the least bit distraught, en route to the west coast. To show him what, her condo, to clean up a few loose ends? That in itself was insane. Not a good beginning. Not something he would tell a jury. What was so important? That's why The Summit Group had secretaries and investigators. Not to mention the impromptu bullshit story he had to tell his wife.

That afternoon her condo was put on the market and her car was returned to the leasing company. She was going to France, she told him, inviting him to dinner, inviting Xara, by which time Turnbull thought he might quit the law and right novels. He knew Fennell's reputation as a cop, he knew Fennell. John Fennell never fucked up. Despite which this was a legal catastrophe.

They spent all day Tuesday together, again with Xara, tears the order of the day. He couldn't believe what he was hearing about Tommy Dune, Phillips and Emma Rose, Gilligan's dark nights in bed whispering to Gilligan under the covers, the blood, the first killing and the second, Gilligan's adoption and being alone. He checked the transcripts. So much of what he was hearing was missing. The killings, that wasn't true.

"Your mother confessed."

"Mother lied."

Gilligan was weeping. "I killed my father first so he wouldn't hurt Gilligan anymore."

Xara was weeping, her face glistening.

"That's impossible. Zeke Phillips confirmed her confession," Turnbull countered.

Gilligan took Xara's hand, consoling her. "We killed our father together."

"What do you mean...we killed him?"

"I killed him second so he wouldn't hurt Gilligan

491

anymore."

"If this is true, even remotely, no court in the land would have convicted you. At worst you would have been treated, cared for. Your mother wasn't insane, your father was. What he did was criminal. And by the way, I did not hear what you just said. Let's keep this believable."

"She was in love with Zeke Phillips. I think so, though not the way I love Elixia. I wanted for so long to tell her about Gilligan and now I will tell her. Now I can tell her about Xara, and I will. She's knows that I killed my father. Telling her about Gilligan and Xara should not be that difficult. I don't think so."

He studied his watch, the second hand ticking, ticking, ticking. He needed air. He needed to escape the emotion. He wasn't acclimated to women kissing and wiping each other's tears or woeful regrets. He was accustomed to crooked cops, housewives in denial, brain-dead school kids who believed guns and knives were learning tools, lifers and repeat offenders too tainted to exist in the mainstream.

He left and went to his hotel. There wasn't enough Jack Daniels in any bar to get him through the night, or in his room where he paced until well past midnight. He wanted to believe her story; he simply couldn't get his head around what he had heard. He needed proof and more than a little. Gilligan Rose would have to face Elixia de Montfort who was already boarding her flight to Miami. Cruel honesty was a small price to pay for survival, despite which he didn't envy her. Hell hath no fury like a woman scorned; a woman lied to and deceived for so many years.

Turnbull departed LAX Wednesday morning onboard TGA knowing full-well the DA and Fennell would crucify him if he'd just made the worst mistake of his career, although he did have collateral.

Gilligan Rose departed an hour later on American, smiling. She already had an offer on the condo.

That evening he called Fennell. Thursday, with Elixia,

Xara and Gilligan, he dealt with even more emotion. When the tears ebbed they rehearsed what she would and what she would not say.
*

Sunday Johnnie Fennell took possession of Double Agent. She was in the water, fuelled and ready, outfitted from stem to stern with the latest and best of everything.

Deena refused to be impressed with his seamanship, though she did agree to get naked, a little, spending the day a few miles out diving from the transom, splashing, sunning and decompressing from the previous week.

Monday Fennell slept in. He had a difficult report to compose. Deena served him coffee and a kiss in bed, not quite finished her 'good wife' training programme he told her. Not a good time to start slacking, two weeks before the wedding. She smacked him, reminding him before leaving that the next time she saw a beautiful nude woman playing pin the tail on the donkey over his crotch she would shoot twice. The single reason he was still alive was that she'd heard him say 'I do want to fuck the most beautiful woman in the world...' and she knew he was talking about her, not Gilligan Rose. She smacked him again for whispering not quietly enough. She didn't like when he spoke that way. It was unbecoming, especially with a young woman in the room.

He understood, not really.

She left and went to a bank she'd never dealt with. There wasn't much a federal cop couldn't discover when needed, when wanted, and she wanted. She never had a kid sister to shop with, talk with, cry with, and Marie was like a kid sister to her: cute, funny, smart, talkative, very talkative and very sweet. She felt good closing the girl's ten-year student loan anonymously, swearing Fennell and the bank manager to secrecy. Marie never asked for anything, not even a coffee. She would always have her dollar in her hand, refusing charity. Good parents, Deena mused. At least now the kid could have a life.

Monday afternoon Fennell submitted his report, leaving work early, getting to the boat early. She liked the boat. She would understand. She loved him. That was a good thing. That had to mean something. She was never angry with him for very long when he was applying SPF in his inimitable fashion. And in the middle of the ocean she'd be a piece of cake, putty in his hands. Or so he hoped.

Tuesday they took the day off for more boating, preparing for the DA's inquisition the next day. Nothing would happen until Turnbull came home and Brannigan's senior agents would traditionally take a week or so between cases to clean up details, be precise, calm down, stay balanced with family, in their case mixing a little business with pleasure. She was good that way. Just don't screw up. Don't ever screw up with Brannigan. That, she did not like. What better proof was needed than the tip of a blade and inch from his chest with Rose's arms straining against his? Besides, in fourteen days they were heading to Rio.

They spent most of Wednesday with the DA's office, Wednesday evening Fennell got a call from Turnbull, a courtesy, a heads-up. A 'let's have dinner at my place' kind of call. Except that dinner wasn't being served and his place was Gilligan Rose's Horizon Heights' very expansive and very expensive three-bedroom luxury hotel suite. He suggested Thursday evening, when everyone was rested after a tight travel schedule. Shall we say eightish? Fennell thought that was good. He would tell Archer. Thank you. And John, bring the French kid. But whatever you do, do not fucking tell Gayle Brannigan unless Deena wants to marry a eunuch.

Both men pressed END. Fennell looked at his legs, his ankles. He saw the shit rising as clearly as if he was sinking into a wet dung pit. He knew Bruce Turnbull. The guy wasn't into theatrics. This was not fucking good after Brannigan told him specifically to stay far away from

Gilligan Rose. He called out to Deena.

Thursday he was fitted for a new suit, his mind distracted. He hadn't been completely forthcoming with Deena who left early for her second fitting. Her dress was elegant, yet simple and unpretentious. The adjustments were minimal. Her afternoon was spent with the caterer and the quartet she'd hired for dance music. She was home by six.
*

Marie Anisette spent most of Saturday night on the phone, telling her family about her day, that she was continuing on special assignment, that Johnnie had given her such a special gift after removing the handcuffs that he'd made her wear through the airport and locked into the backseat of a squad car, that she loved Deena and Johnnie so much, that she was going to Deena's shower. However she could not tell them anything more about her work.

Her parents hung on every word, so proud, her father worried about Monday. What did she really know about Monsieur Palmer? Not much, she told him, however she would the next day. Besides, papa, Johnnie, he would never allow anyone to hurt me.

Monsieur Anisette sounded somewhat reassured. Still, she was his only daughter and her brother was no less concerned about this unknown American lawyer who was toying with his devoted sister. He did not like the idea at all. What kind of name was this, Lincoln Palmer? A wonderful name, she told him, kissing him loudly through the phone, promising to call him soon, cutting off his threat to find and beat the indecent scoundrel to within an inch of his miserable life.

Sunday she spoke from lunch until dinner with young Lincoln Palmer. That was her day. She spent her morning dressing for the call and her nighttime dreaming of Monday evening. She went to bed early, setting her clock, her watch and her phone for 5:00 AM. She would not be late for Captain Brannigan.

Monday, her day more gruelling than usual, she approached Gayle Brannigan with a dilemma when no one else was watching the clock. She had an appointment, made before her new special assignment. The rendez-vous was very important. She would work extra hard the next day, she promised. Brannigan listened with a stern face, unyielding, asking pertinent questions, probing; getting the answers she wanted, telling Marie to go, to get out of her office, to go home and not to show up for work until nine the next morning. She would not tolerate tardiness.

That night in bed she phoned her parents and her brother, anxious to call Deena who by midnight couldn't think of another question to ask about Lincoln Palmer and Fennell wasn't getting involved.

Tuesday morning Marie returned the call from her bank manager from the day before. She didn't believe him. She didn't understand. She asked him again. What she was hearing was real, he told her. The loan was closed. She was entirely debt free.

She knew. Her mother and father had good careers, though not that good, and her brother was beginning a career. He could not help her in such a way. She called Deena. No reply. She didn't leave a message. She knew.

At home Tuesday evening in her tiny apartment she touched Yellow Envy on her living room wall, weeping. One day she would have an office with many mementos. She would. She phoned Deena again. Deena's voice was so sweet. She could talk with Deena for hours.

Deena said simply, "I don't have a clue what you're talking about, Marie. Sometimes things happen and we don't know why, quite possibly a simple gift from someone who likes you."

"No, Deena, not very simple at all. You are lying to me. I do know that you did this wonderful thing for me."

"Stop crying or I'll make you speak with Fennell. That wouldn't be so wonderful. Believe me."

"I can never repay this, Deena. Instead I will make you so proud of me. I will graduate at the top of my class at the academy and I will love you and Johnnie so much forever."

Deena chortled softly into the phone. "We know that and we'll be in the front row with your parents and brother when you do graduate. Besides, Marie, you're Fennell's partner. Everyone expects you to be good, as much as they don't envy you. He's not easy to work with." She whispered. "He can be a little frustrating at times."

"Kiss him for me goodnight, Deena, like a French girl on his cheeks. He will soon be a married man."

"I will."

"You are like a big sister to me, Deena. I do love my brother so much, however I did always dream of having a big sister also."

Deena cleared her throat. "And now you have one who's always wanted a kid sister. So you see how things work out. This is pretty cool. Now go to bed to dream about Lincoln."

"He did not call me today. Last night was so much fun with him."

"He will. Now stop crying."

"I will, but first I will kiss my big sister through my phone."

She did, a dozen times, Deena returning one. She had a kid sister, Fennell commiserating all weepy-eyed. She ended the call and smashed a down-filled pillow into his face.

"If that little prick hurts that girl's feelings I'll kick his balls into his mouth."

Fennell winced. She was serious.

The next day during her lunch break Marie bought a man's and a woman's simple and identical ruby rings. She would always be Deena's friend and kid sister. That evening she sat in her apartment waiting, hoping more than expecting. He didn't like her. That was obvious, yet she didn't understand why. They had so much fun together.

Instead of pouting she did what Johnnie would do. She went over each detail of Monday evening to understand what went wrong. What she did know was that she would not phone him.

Thursday she went to work, sad. She had really hoped she could have a boyfriend and she liked him. Little did she realize that twelve hours later would alter the way she saw the world. When she answered her phone Johnnie was on the other end inviting her to dinner, not warning her ahead of time as to why. Brannigan wouldn't be a problem. Just leave. She did.

*

She was excited. She hadn't expected to see them so soon, to give them their rings so soon.

Deena opened her little box first, shaking her head, looking to Fennell for help, wanting to feel annoyed. She knew the jeweller. The kid was being foolishly generous. Fennell opened his, blowing a quiet stream of air through his lips, suggesting that a good spanking was in order and that he should administer the punishment since he was the senior agent.

The kid had excellent taste. The silver and ruby bands must have cost the girl a full week's salary. The duplicate inscription was: My souvenir to you, your Frenchie. He pushed himself grudgingly from the table, stooping, hugging her shoulders, pressing his cheek to hers. He knew she liked all that French stuff. Deena followed suit, a little more teary-eyed, admonishing Marie that she wasn't yet at the top of an agent's pay grade.

He ordered a scotch, glasses of wine for the ladies. He had a feeling he'd be downing another before the night was through.

Marie understood. Sometimes the boss didn't have to know everything, not until all the facts were known. Tidbits of information were useless data until homogenized into credible specifics.

At times like this he wanted to revert. At times like this he missed his black suit, white shirt and black tie. Deena patted his hand, Marie creased her brow. She didn't understand everything he said. Yet this time understanding his words wasn't an issue. She saw his face. Something was wrong. He was disobeying a direct order. So was Deena. She wouldn't disappoint them. She was part of their team.

The trio arrived at the Horizon Heights at 7:55, Marie thinking that she must be the one girl in Miami who wasn't rich. She watched Deena, the way she stood, the way she walked, the way she spoke with people. Deena was confident, like the way she stood by Johnnie's door on Friday, poised, calm, one hand on the knob, the other gripping her weapon, the red beam threatening, her eyes focused on the monitor, ready to kill Gilligan Rose. She remembered not breathing, afraid for Johnnie, afraid that Deena would kill someone. Or that she might miss.

Stepping from the elevator Fennell asked once if she was ready. She took a deep breath. Yes, she was. Deena hugged her. She wasn't convinced.

Bruce Turnbull answered the door.

"Good evening, John...Deena, Miss Anisette."

They stepped in. Marie looked toward Deena. Deena wasn't impressed, so neither was she.

"Bruce, let's keep this short and sweet. I wouldn't do this for anyone else. I'll be in dirt to my shorts if Brannigan finds out about this."

"She will, John, very soon. Miss Rose will join us shortly. She's in her bedroom changing. I also invited Miss Mendiga and Miss de Montfort to join us, which is why I considered it wise to invite Miss Anisette this evening. With your fluency in Spanish and her intimacy with French nothing gets lost in the translation should there be an emotional divergence from English. You'll understand why."

"We appreciate the consideration. How was Long

Beach?"

"Time and money well spent, enlightening and impossible, difficult for Gilligan and Xara as you might imagine. Nevertheless Xara wanted to come. She wanted to meet Miss de Montfort since they have such a great deal in common." He invited them to be seated. "I'm breaking with corporate policy on this one, John, enjoying a libation...ladies, wine...John, a scotch for you?"

He answered for them. "No thank you."

Turnbull knew better. He knew what was coming and poured a substantial measure of scotch into an old-fashioned, filling two wine glasses a third full.

"This won't be your last tonight, John. We arrived home late in the day yesterday. To say we were exhausted is an understatement. On the Monday flight I was impressed by how genuinely everyone crewing on the TGA flight liked her. Yesterday, seated with Miss Mendiga, I was no less impressed."

Gilligan Rose came through her bedroom door on cue.

She was wearing a sleeveless mauve dress, short, flared, and not much longer than the one she wore to the theatre, left unbuttoned to the natural swell of her breasts, the ensemble not leaving much to imagine. Her legs were bare; her matching sandals were open and flat, a single mauve thong across her unpainted toes, another at her ankles. She wore no jewellery at all, her hair combed straight. From where she stood she might have been wearing a deep red headdress. Her eyes sparkled green, her lips coated with deep maroon.

She was captivating and exotic.

"Good evening, John, Agent Archer, Mademoiselle Anisette. I am so pleased you could join us this evening. May I introduce Elixia de Montfort, my lover? She came from France to see the man I'm accused of attempting to kill. She is, of course, more inclined towards my version of the event. She's forgiven me for thinking to cheat on her with you, John. You were my first male experience, or I should say my failed attempt at one, after my father of course. I was curious, afraid. Well, you know that. You were there. You're the one who made me afraid."

Fennell wanted to say "let's stop this shit." He didn't. "Bruce, help us out here. What does her girlfriend have to do with this?"

"She's cooperating as a witness."

"A witness to what exactly, fantasy?"

"To Miss Emma Rose being innocent of murdering her husband, the same reason Miss Mendiga is here…amongst others. However, for the meantime, Miss de Montfort, would you excuse us?"

Elixia tilted her head and smiled, squeezing Gilligan's hand, stepping into the bedroom. Gilligan Rose went into the other, stepping out moments later with Xara.

"Deena, hi, I'm so pleased to see you again. I've missed you. What's it been, four, five weeks? Doesn't time just get away from us? Agent Fennell, I'm so pleased to finally meet you. You know, Deena, being a flight attendant in First-Class I meet a lot of different types, mostly rich, well-off or well-placed. It's where I met Xara. I wanted you to meet her too, Agent Fennell, this time without the use of a telescope. And Deena, how did you enjoy your erotic rub on the beach? You never did tell me. Or should I ask how you enjoyed massaging Xara. I was right, wasn't I, on Saturday. Getting you into my bed would not be difficult at all. The hard part would be getting you out. What did I say, once you get a taste? What we would really like to know is how you could be so detached?"

"I was playing a part. We had to get into your head. We wanted to understand you. I was doing my job and let's agree, Gilligan, that you're a little detached yourself. You need help. So let us do that for you."

"Xara added, "You are quite the two-faced bitch, Deena. Do you have any idea how often we spoke about you, wanted you as a friend, a straight friend? God, we even invited you to Long Beach to vacation with us. We thought you were wonderful. How do you deal with that? How do you sleep at night? Really, thinking of you now, seeing you, remembering how I touched you makes me sick."

"I can sleep very easily because she's a killer. We needed to know why, what sets her off, what makes a devout lesbian a man-killer. Now we do. We know. We know about her father. Now we can help her get the treatment she needs, Xara. We're not the bad guys here."

"Well, I can categorically testify that she is not a killer. And I will."

"That's perjury."

"That is the truth, not a cheap lie like you massaging cream into me for, what was it, ten, fifteen minutes. You are a talented actress, Deena, or in denial. You certainly had me fooled. What happened to those photographs, Deena? Are you keeping them as a souvenir of your first girl-girl turn-on?"

"What I remember is telling you how badly I wanted to help Gilligan. I did then and I do now. So does Agent Fennell."

"She does not need or want your help. Gilligan will help Gilligan along with Elixia and me to get over this man's attack on her as well what happened with her father." She turned to Turnbull. "This woman really is making me sick. Can I go now?"

He nodded, asking her to step into the room with Elixia. They wouldn't be long.

"I did believe you were delightful, Deena. I was always so happy the times that I saw you," Gilligan went on. "And you, John, I really believe I turned you on, in bed, the way you were holding me, the way you were talking before you scared me, the way you couldn't take your eyes off my little pink diamond." She undid a more daring button, putting a fingertip to her scarcely visible birthmark. "Have you kept a copy of that for yourself, of us in bed, of me naked, of me sitting on you? I think you did. Yes. I think so."

"Let's cut the crap. Friday you were in another world. You might as well have been straddling a fence. You had one thing on your mind: killing me. Then you refused to recognize Agent Archer when all she wanted to do was help you. She's the one who got you out. She's the one who got you Bruce Turnbull. The way I see it, you had Mendiga and de Montfort hanging, a little too difficult to balance two women six thousand miles apart. So you decide to drop one. You didn't know Archer was a federal agent. So you're thinking maybe you'll get a little something local, convert a new member. Now you're three thousand miles apart, in the same country, unless you truly prefer female French cuisine."

"I made my choice a long time ago, and much too late. I have tried few different flavours, though I've never been with a cop. Well, not a pretty one anyway. You know, Deena, straights aren't the only ones who like threesomes. I think we could have worked something out." Her snort was caustic. "Mr. Turnbull, would you excuse me for a moment. I have something I would like to show them."

He nodded. Gilligan stepped into the empty bedroom.

"Drink your scotch, John, before you drop it." He refilled his whiskey. "John, ladies, Emma Rose is innocent. I will be requesting of Gayle Brannigan, the DA and the court that she be allowed to return home without fear of incarceration."

"If what you say is true, I don't have a problem with that, which raises the question…"

"In exchange for which Gilligan Rose has agreed to stand trial for the murder of her father. She's given me a detailed confession, John. We know now that her mother took the fall to protect her. Naturally, Gilligan won't serve any time."

"You're good, Bruce, the best, but this is a real stretch.

She tried to kill a federal agent while three other agents and Marie were watching. She's killed ten men. Now you're telling me she killed her old man. You get her off; I'll give you a year's salary as a bonus. I mean what I say."

"You think what you've heard is crazy? You wait. You ain't heard nothin'. I sent the Palmer kid to Nice, France on Tuesday, after his little soirée with some little hottie that's got him all dreamy-eyed. From all accounts and a lot of female chatter at the office he'll die from a broken heart if he doesn't see her again soon."

Fennell jerked his thumb in Marie's direction a few times without looking at her. "She's the little hottie."

He acknowledged Marie. "Alright, now I understand...lucky kid. Anyway, John, I had to check out your story...as an independent trial lawyer. I couldn't very well take the word of the arresting officer." He smirked. "I think my boss would have something to say about that."

"He doesn't. That's why the place is called Summit. We're the best."

"That's precisely right. We are. Anyway the kid got back today. It's all on tape. Once she knew Palmer was for real, that you and Miss Anisette were actually federal agents, she told Palmer an amazing story. You think you've heard it all being that you're street-wise and worldly, not by a long shot. Now humour me. Ladies, John, please stand."

The women did, hesitantly, curious, not Fennell.

"Party games aren't a big thing with me, Bruce."

"I need you to stand, John, unless you want Gayle Brannigan here within the hour."

He stood. He didn't like being threatened. "Let's make that half a year's salary, Mr. Turnbull."

"Please, stand together and close your eyes."

"You want me to close my eyes with Rose somewhere I can't see her?"

Turnbull's smirk was annoying.

"She gave me her word. You're safe. Please, close your

eyes until you hear differently. Give me the count of ten, tops."

They did. The pause was brief, one door opening and closing. No other sound was heard as hard as they tried.

Gilligan Rose said, "John, Deena darling, open your eyes. It is true, you know. I did kill father. Mother is quite innocent."

"Why am I not surprised? The question is, Miss Rose: Why did you wait so many years to hone your skills?"

"No, John. No Deena darling. Gilligan is telling a lie to protect me. I killed father. I think so."

Johnnie Fennell whirled as though fending off an attack, his body cold. Deena gulped air. Marie shrieked.

"John, ladies, might I introduce Gilligan Rose and her equally lovely sister… Gilligan Rose."

Elixia and Xara stepped in from the bedroom, each one hugging and kissing Gilligan, each one hugging and kissing Gilligan, stepping away, sitting together, neither one certain which Gilligan was hers.

Gilligan said, "You seem confused, John, baffled. If you would like I'll take off my clothes."

Gilligan said, "I seem to recall that you liked seeing me naked, John. Do you remember?"

"Or would you like to see Deena undressing me?"

"What I want is for you to fuck me right now, Mr. Fennell, that's what I said."

"Or all future flights are cancelled. I've waited too long for this. I said that as well."

"Do you like my dress, John? I bought it for you, and for Deena. I really do think she likes me. I think so."

"She does. I know she likes me. I think so, too."

"Why don't you drop a napkin, John? Would you like to see under my dress again? Would you like to see my panties the way you did on the plane? Not that you haven't already seen what's underneath them."

"Yes, John, would you like to see me without

them...again, the way I made my pussy glisten for you?"

"Yes, John, would you like to see my pussy one more time, inhale my scent? Or would Deena for the first time? I do think Deena would. I think so."

"Yes, she would." Gilligan was certain.

"Do you like my breasts?"

"Yes, I do. That's what you said."

"Then why aren't you touching them, kissing them, squeezing them? That's what I said."

"You must remember."

"Xara doesn't like you for trying to fuck me."

"Neither does Elixia. She doesn't like you at all."

"I've been with Elixia for a very long time."

"And me with Xara, though I can see where Gilligan could love Xara too."

"The same way that Gilligan could love Elixia."

"Seriously, John, look at my breasts to see my little pink diamond."

"And mine; don't forget my breasts, John, and my little pink diamond."

Bruce Turnbull took the floor.

"John, this is a deep bucket of legal shit. Pardon me, ladies. Yesterday Gilligan flew home with me while Gilligan flew here on American. I flew with the one I knew you didn't arrest. The one you did arrest came here on her own. How could I tell, you ask? I scrawled my full signature on the inside of her thigh where I could from time to time ascertain to whom I was actually talking. Somewhat unorthodox I grant you, and certainly not the worst assignment I've ever agreed to. She believed the tattoo might be difficult to explain on her arm or through the blouse of her uniform. The point being, John, that onboard TGA on Monday, everyone, knew this one, or this one. And yesterday they knew this one, or this one, dressed in her uniform, working the flight and serving delicious mimosas. She was working, John, when her credentials are locked up tight in Brannigan's office along with her GPS bracelet. TGA only has one Gilligan Rose on the payroll. The thing is; each Gilligan knew everyone else crewing the flights. As my father would have said, and you'll excuse me once more, ladies: this is one whack of shit, boy. These two ladies are the same lady right down to their nail clippings and I don't have a frigging clue which one is my client. My signature was removed once I was satisfied." He sipped his whiskey. "Feeling pissed right about now, confused? Don't know what to do? Miss Mendiga and Miss de Montfort, they don't know either. And, believe me, they are not pretending. These two, Gilligan, they live, breathe, and think together. They smell the same, they talk the same. They are, in fact, one woman in body and mind."

"This is bullshit. The Gilligan Rose I know speaks fluent French. Marie, you're front and centre. Help us out here and nothing simple like bonjour or salut."

Marie spoke to Gilligan for five minutes. No one interrupted.

"Agent Fennell, they are both fluent. We spoke about the weather and fashion, France, Miami and California. I do not know the difference between them or their voices. They want to tell you a story. They suggest in Spanish if you would prefer. They do know that you do speak Spanish."

Fennell stared into his glass, damned if he would refill it. "Every goddamn word ladies, in Spanish, every word you've spoken since giving me a fucking brain seizure."

When they finished he sank onto one of the scattered sofas.

"Bruce, take the other's passport and driver's permit. Confiscate their phones."

"I can't do that, John. Neither can you. You don't have a warrant. And who would you serve with it if you did?"

"She doesn't go free. No way does she go free. A whack of shit, Bruce, ya think? I'm thinking more like a fucking volcano full?"

Deena sat beside him, not touching him, wanting to squeeze her man's hand. "Fennell, watch your mouth. There are six ladies in this room, if you haven't noticed."

Marie sat by herself. She didn't want Deena thinking that she couldn't.

"Ladies, I apologize. I'm a little ruffled here." He rubbed his face. "So, Bruce, Brannigan's expecting someone in her office tomorrow for a bracelet fitting. What exactly do we do about that, amigo?"

"We listen, John. That's what we do. We listen very carefully, you and me. And if you don't refill your glass at least once you're a better man than I am. I did, as did my delightful company at the time."

He asked Gilligan to be seated, asking everyone if their drinks were fine. No one said yes. He did the honours. A few minutes later:

"John, I wasn't trying to kill you."

"Not until you frightened me."

"May I tell you a story?"

"May I? May I tell you why I was frightened?"

"I take it this is off the record?" Fennell asked, knowing.

"Yes, John, it is. I've already videoed what I need, if and when I do need it." Turnbull said. "Just get ready to gulp that drink. Agent Archer, Miss Anisette, there's a bathroom in each bedroom. Don't be shy. We'll understand. I wanted to be sick myself. I still might."

Forty
Gilligan Rose

"Agent Fennell, John, I've been a lesbian since I was in high school with a girl whose name was Wendy. Elixia and Xara know about her."

"Yes, they do. Wendy was my friend too, for a short while."

"She gave me comfort and made me feel good when I wasn't allowed to be with Gilligan." Gilligan put a finger to her lips, halting Fennell's question. "I loved her. I suppose the way a young boy loves a young girl without the obvious physical and pharmaceutical considerations."

"And eventually, for a short while, before I was taken away, I loved her too. She was soft and smooth. Her breath was sweet, her touch was tender and her kisses were delicate."

"She was everything father was not."

"I don't know why mother married father."

"Her name was Miss Emma Rose. She was very famous, though not at first."

"She painted one-sided faces: one side dark with agony and fear, one side bright with hope."

"I never asked why mother married father, or when. I was a child. I didn't care. I cared about dancing in the rain with mother…"

"And watching her paint, I loved watching her paint her one-sided faces."

"Dancing in the rain were the times I was truly happy

until I could whisper under the covers in my dark room with Gilligan."

"Gilligan and I always whispered in the dark, under the covers, about him, about the pain."

"I still do whisper with Gilligan, and talk with her on the phone. Now I can whisper about Xara."

"And I love to talk on the phone. Especially since now I can whisper about Elixia. And you."

"Yes, now I can whisper about you, John, about the way that you frightened me."

"Bruce, this is stretching my patience. One of these women is going to prison or an institution. The circus act isn't doing it for me."

"With all due respect, John, one woman is going back to Long Beach, the other to France. You have no proof of the murders other than coincidental dates which amount to the poorest circumstantial evidence at best. You have no weapon, no DNA, no photographs identifying her coming or going from any of the hotel crime scenes. All ten were also murdered out of your jurisdiction, way beyond. The best case you have is a knife near your chest after terrifying the woman, a woman plied with 300-dollar champagne straddled on top of a sixth Dan martial artist in his underwear." He sipped his whiskey. "Yes, she came on to you. Now tell me which one. Ah, yes, the one returning home with Miss de Montfort. That's obvious, of course…unless she's playing you, unless they're swapping, trying each other's girlfriend. I suppose that could happen between girls. A fellow I knew in college. He was a fraternal twin. They did each other's wives quite often before they were married…double your pleasure. The girls never had a clue. After that, who knows? They probably still do. Or perhaps the girls knew all along. Again, who knows? " He shrugged. "The point is: How will you know for sure? You won't. Or maybe Miss de Montfort comes to live here. So perhaps she did kill ten men. We'll never know. And really, who cares apart from the disciplines of our respective professions. Over the past few days I've spoken with each of the ten wives. They were surprised to hear that you might have a suspect after so many years and months. They were disappointed and wish Miss Rose well. Of course I told them she's innocent, wrongly accused and arrested for yet another unrelated incident, each ex-wife volunteering to attend the trial and speak on Miss Rose's behalf. Many of the older children, some married, would also come. Tonight blows your case out the window, John. We're talking false arrest and let's not forget possible double jeopardy or mental and physical abuse. I can tell you as her attorney that no jury will convict her and she will not do time for the father. Listen to her, John. That's all I ask. Just listen to her." Turnbull sat, reclined. "Gilligan…"

"I was born on January 15th, although I was never told why."

"I do know that mother was surprised by me because she was only expecting Gilligan."

"Mother was always a bit of an airhead. She thought that if Gilligan and I were exact twins, and we are right down to our birthmarks and bikini lines, that we should have the same name. She believed that if some stranger somewhere in the world could have the same name as me that Gilligan should have my name as well. That's what she told me."

"I didn't know the difference. I was too young."

"Until I went to school and learned that everyone believed mother was crazy."

"And that I was crazy, too, because one day I would be sad."

"And one day I would be happy."

"You see, before I went to school I could only play outside by the fence where no one could see me play with Gilligan."

"No one ever saw me play with Gilligan and that's how I went to school, alone."

"That I can remember father never worked. He was always at home with me. He liked to drink. That I do remember."

"When Gilligan went to school I would stay home and do my homework. I liked school very much."

"When Gilligan went to school I would stay home and paint with mother. I never liked school very much, not until I met Wendy which came many years later."

"I was never allowed to have friends at home, though I did have more friends at school than Gilligan."

"Father didn't like me having friends."

"So you see, I went to school on alternate days and was Gilligan's best friend."

"I was forbidden to tell anyone about Gilligan and I was always her best friend."

"So when I spoke about Gilligan everyone believed I was talking in the third person about me. They thought I was special. You know, that I was crazy: One day happy, one day sad."

"Gilligan agreed. "They all thought I was crazy like mother."

"That's when father began to like me, when I began school. He never liked me before. I don't think so."

"He began giving me my bath and drying me. He liked washing me between my legs and my bum. I didn't have breasts then."

"He liked to dry me between my legs and to dry my bum. I was too young to know. I didn't mind that he gave me my baths. He was father."

"I didn't mind either. He would sit by my bed at night in the dark, so that I wouldn't be afraid. His hand was always warm under my nightie, rubbing my back, making me feel good."

"And my bum, he would always pat and squeeze one side of my bum and then the other under my nightie to make me feel good. Often he would tell me that he loved me."

"It seems as though he did forever."

"Then my body began to develop."

"My body was changing faster than other girls."

"That was when mother and father decided to move. Father didn't like the neighbours watching mother dance in the rain. He didn't like them seeing me or Gilligan. Sometimes mother wouldn't wear very much, like the times she would wash her car."

"We moved into a bigger house where I had my own room. I didn't like sleeping alone in the dark."

"I didn't like that at all either."

"By which time mother was famous and she began travelling quite often."

"Or she painted in her studio until late each night. I remember she was always singing. She had a voice like an angel."

"Father didn't like her singing at all. I don't think so."

"Then I was older, and gradually I began taking my baths in private without father."

"I could tell he didn't like that I was bathing alone."

"By then mother was rich. She wore beautiful clothes, expensive panties and bras, lingerie and dresses. In the spring, summer and fall she would hang our clothes on the line wearing her panties and bra. She thought nothing of being carefree."

"She was very attractive. She often painted in her studio at night wearing her panties and bra. Father didn't like that at all. He believed the neighbours were peeking. I think so."

"And father wanted me to wear the same. I was the best-dressed girl in my school."

"So was I. And at night I began wearing baby dolls, or tap pants with camisoles under my bathrobe."

"That's when I would watch late-night movies with father on weekends. He liked to put his hand under my robe to make me feel good."

"One night I would lie on the couch with father, eating my chips with my Coke."

"I would lie with him the other night, though I would fall asleep early and he would carry me to bed, tucking me in, staying with me until I was asleep once again."

"I remember his hands, how they felt different when he touched me."

"Then soon I began feeling bad in the morning. That's when I met Wendy. I think so. We used to lie in the grass behind the trees at school and kiss each other's lips."

"But I wanted to kiss her lips too and one day Gilligan said that I could, though I think she liked Gilligan more."

"Mother was away more often with Zeke and father knew how much I missed her."

"He knew that I missed her and he wanted to make me feel good."

"He told me I must never tell anyone not even mother because mother would send me away."

"I began to have wine on the nights mother was gone on the weekend. He told me that if I was old enough to dress like mother, I was old enough to act like mother and that I should drink wine because the wine would make me feel good."

"And I did dress like mother, for school and for bed."

"Then he was tucking me in every night. His breath was bad though and he began staying longer in my room."

"Then he would come to my room sometime later when I was sleeping or almost asleep. I knew he wanted to touch me the way he touched Gilligan, to make me feel good the way he often tried to touch mother while she was painting to make her feel good. Yet I felt strange. He was fondling my breasts, pressing his hands under my panties."

"I began waking up naked with my panties or nightie on the floor or by my pillow, never understanding why."

"Sometimes I was sticky and I smelled, but I didn't understand why. I thought I was becoming a woman. So I asked Wendy. She never woke up naked feeling sticky, so we decided to examine each other to be sure."

Gilligan smiled a rare smile, "I touched her breasts through her blouse, and she touched mine. We liked how we felt and took off our clothes right there in the field by the trees."

"Then she let me touch her breasts again. I remember how the grass felt when I was naked. But she didn't know I was me. She thought I was Gilligan."

"I know now, and have for a long while, that I was trying to erase father. I think so. Though I did love her and didn't mind at all that Gilligan loved her too."

"Until one night father came into my room. I didn't feel very well at all. He was naked and I wondered why."

"I didn't feel very well either."

"I knew he was undressing me again, but my eyes wanted to close."

"He was inside me, not for the first time. His breath was bad. I remember wondering why he was pushing me, jerking me, like he wanted me to move up in my bed when I couldn't. He was on top of me."

"The other times he didn't hurt me as much, sometimes making me feel good because I was drunk, until the first night he came into my room naked. I don't know when. I felt his hands squeezing my breasts and pinching my nipples. I felt him inside me, pushing me and jerking me, making bad sounds. Not for the first time, but this time he hurt me. I wanted to cry. Then I wanted to sleep. I couldn't open my eyes."

"I was sleeping. His weight made me wake up. He was between my legs, hurting me again with his fingers. I think so. Then he continued hurting me for a long time. I think so. He covered my mouth and was kissing my breasts. I wanted to cry until I fell asleep. That's all I know. He was in my room twice."

"There was no light in the hall. There were no shadows.

That's how I knew. With the shadows I was safe, until they disappeared into the dark. The shadows would always disappear into the dark. That's how father came to me, in the dark. He woke me once more, though not really. He was kissing my face and my mouth. He was inside me. He was squeezing my breasts and hurting me, but I couldn't cry. I never cried. I don't think so. I wanted him to stop. He didn't listen to me so I fell asleep thinking I would tell mother that father hurt me."

"When I woke very late the next morning my room smelled and I smelled. I was naked and I wanted to be sick. My sheets were covered with blood. My breasts were blue with bruises, my vagina burned and my bum hurt. My thighs were coated with blood and his sweat."

"Father was lying beside me, naked, wearing his condom. I wanted to throw up. He was unconscious. I crawled from my bed, trying not to touch him. He wasn't father anymore."

"I looked into my mirror and all I could see was Gilligan, tortured and hurt."

"I went to the kitchen and found a big carving knife. I wanted to be sure he would never wake up, that he would never hurt Gilligan again. The blade went into him very easily. The sound he made was quite ugly and I remember the look in his eyes. He seemed somewhat startled. I thought I would be splashed with his blood like in the movies. I wasn't. I was surprised and went out into the hallway after saying goodbye. He heard me tell him goodbye and I don't believe that he cared very much that I was naked. That's when Gilligan came to me, because she knew I was hurt."

"We held each other and cried. I was also naked, my labia swollen and covered with sticky blood. I remember the strange sensation in my bum, too afraid to touch myself there. My breasts and my thighs were badly bruised."

"Yes, her beautiful little bum was covered with terrible

scratches. I was so glad that I killed him."

"But I wanted to kill him too. I went to the kitchen to find another big knife. In Gilligan's room he wasn't moving or making a sound. I wasn't afraid anymore. I wanted to kill him again for what he had done to Gilligan. If Gilligan was going to prison, I would go with her. I would never leave Gilligan alone."

"I don't remember the knife making a noise. Then he was dead, very dead. I remember that I felt nothing at all. I don't think so. I would never leave Gilligan either. Now I was as guilty as her."

"We sat together in a very hot shower to feel and smell clean, to discuss what we should tell mother."

"Then we went outside to sit in the sun with our legs wide open. The morning was very warm. The heat, I remember, helped soothe the pain."

"We were no longer crying."

"I went with Gilligan to mother's room. She was sleeping. I woke her. I told her I killed father, though at first she didn't believe me."

"I confessed also because I would never leave Gilligan alone in prison."

"She kissed me and she kissed Gilligan over and over again. She was crying. She made me take a very hot and deep bath with Gilligan to take away the smell and the hurt even though we had showered. That was when she called Doctor Phillips. That's all I know."

"So can you see, John, that I have a good reason for being a lesbian? I think so. Don't you?"

"Don't you, Deena? Do you understand now?"

Marie went into one of the bedrooms. Deena looked to Fennell for approval. He nodded. She followed behind.

"That was July 15th, the day you left." Fennell said.

"Yes. That was July 15th, the day I left."

"I didn't see mother again."

"They wouldn't let me; though I did hear from Zeke

before they took me away that father had put drugs in mother's wine."

"He put drugs in mine as well. He knew what he wanted. He wanted to rape me."

"And he put drugs in mine. He wanted to rape me also."

"That's why mother never came to help me."

"Or me. She didn't know that she should."

"Anyway, I was soon sold to a couple with money."

"My new family was also well-off. They paid a lot to have me."

"That's when I met Elixia. I ran away soon after. My new parents were bad. They would always try to see me naked, for me to see them naked and fucking. I knew the man wanted to fuck me and that one day he would. I knew the woman wanted to watch the way she watched him with others. I saw them quite often on the boat. Then one day he saw me with Elixia. That's when he told me that he did want to fuck me. That's when I left."

"What's funny? No one ever asked why a couple in their thirties would want to adopt a fifteen-year-old girl with a body that was, I must say, to-die-for."

"I was very pretty when I was young and physically mature. Why did no one think to question that?"

"Both couples were abusive?" Fennell asked.

"I slept with my light on each night. I do to this day. Shadows make me feel safe until I can't see them. He was always trying to touch me, to see me in my panties and bra."

"I do as well, prefer seeing the shadows. I left them before I was eighteen. He saw me one night, and not for the first time, by peering through my window, watching me undress. He was naked and masturbating. I left right away."

"I tried to find mother. That's when I knew she had run away with Zeke, that she was free. No one knew she ever existed. She was totally free. I knew that somewhere in the world she was dancing in the rain and thinking of me. The same way Gilligan was thinking of me, missing me."

"I tried to find Gilligan."

"Instead I was found, by a lawyer who knew where to find me. He found me to warn me and to make me wealthy. Zeke wanted me to live well, though in a letter he reminded me never to look for Gilligan, never to search for mother. When I asked the lawyer to help me, he refused very politely.

"He refused me as well. He warned me never to look for Gilligan or mother. He said that if I did mother would be discovered and sent to prison, that Gilligan and I would lead miserable lives. Better that I should know and believe that mother was fine, that Gilligan was fine and thinking of me each day."

Deena stepped into the room with Marie, the younger woman as pale as a ghost.

"I returned to France to study towards an art degree with a minor is psychology."

"I remained in New York. I have a degree in Behavioral Psychology with a few extra credits in abstract and impressionist art. I wanted to know my mother. I wanted to understand how a father could so often rape and drug his daughters one after the other, going into one bedroom after the other."

"I still don't know."

"I never will. I don't think so."

"Anyway I found Gilligan when I was twenty-one. You see, John, my heart cannot beat without Gilligan's body."

"My brain is inside her body."

"Gilligan's mind is my mind."

"I know what Gilligan is thinking."

"From three or six thousand miles away I know what she feels. I know what she thinks. That is what happens, John, after so many years of whispering so closely together in the dark."

"I love Gilligan. We are one."

"And I love Gilligan. We are each other. Don't you see?"

"I dreamed of a career as flight attendant. I always wanted to see the world, to travel, to escape, ever since mother flew me to Chicago."

"That was such a wonderful trip. But circumstances change. As much as I wanted to fly, to circle the globe, circumstances do change. I wanted to thank Zeke Phillips in a way he would understand. I wanted to compensate for father. I fund one clinic for abused children in L.A., another in Paris, which seems to make sense." She paused for affect. "You seem surprised, John. I really did think you would know that about me."

"I never gave up my dream, though circumstances do change. We all change. I think so. As much as I wanted to fly, I wanted to paint. I wanted to share that part of me with mother. I felt she would somehow know that I was."

"How's that drink working for you, John? Miss Anisette, are you feeling better?"

"Yes, I am better. Thank you, Miss Rose. I did not feel well for a very short time."

Gilligan asked, "Deena, can we continue? What you missed, John can fill in. You heard the most crucial part."

"How can there possibly be more?" Deena asked.

"There is more, a lot more," Turnbull replied, "because Gilligan doesn't know about her mother. She doesn't know about Zeke Phillips, about what happened. She doesn't know why Phillips and Miss Emma Rose abandoned her. She doesn't know where her mother lives. We do. You and I, John, we know that. You and Miss Anisette were at her home and atelier last week. Would you care to elaborate? Or don't you think these ladies deserve to reunite with their mother?"

"John, you know mother?"

"You know where mother lives?"

Gilligan gasped, inhaling loud air. "She's living in

France. That's where he was all last week with the girl.
Mother is living in France."

"John, you knew all this time and you said nothing."
She snorted. "I cannot imagine how cruel a man you
must really be."

Marie's voice was soft. "He is not cruel, Miss Rose. He
is a very kind man."

"I knew, Miss Rose. I was waiting to advise the French
police, to serve an arrest warrant and extradition papers, to
have her brought home to complete her sentence. She lives
in Nice. Her name is Emmanuelle Lerosier. She's single and
a very successful artist, every bit as successful as Emma
Rose. In fact I bought one of her paintings, one she called
Green Tears. She spoke about you. She hopes that you're
happy, that wherever you are you're dancing in the rain.
She said that. Her paintings are exclusively of you: one
fifteen-year-old locked inside a mirror, one outside peering
in. She came to her door wearing suede boots, a string
bikini and a short silk robe flapping in the wind. I suppose
the way you remember her. She looks good and she is
well." John stood to fill his glass. He wasn't measuring.
"Zeke Phillips is dead, buried in England. As far as we
know he bought a house there in order to confuse
authorities. That search never did happen. In fact, ladies,
you have Mademoiselle Anisette to thank for finding her.
Otherwise we would have had no idea where she is."

"Je te remercie, Marie," Gilligan said together.

"They are thanking me, Agent Fennell. That is all."
Gilligan held Gilligan's hands in hers.

Fennell was studying Turnbull, the lawyer unwavering.
Marie didn't care how she might look. She was sitting with
Deena whose hand was discreetly rubbing the small of her
back. She wanted to curl into Deena's lap and fall asleep or
cry.

"Gilligan," Turnbull continued, "one of our juniors met
with your mother this week. He travelled to Nice to meet

her. Your mother is expecting your call anytime now. She's anxious to speak with you. I have her number."

Gilligan sprang from the sofa and ran to her purse, practically leaving a stream of tears in the air. The purse was identical, the cell was identical.

Turnbull reached for a notepad, reciting the number.

Fennell bolted to his feet. "Bruce, that's a Miami number."

"Yes, John, though more precisely, a few floors down. She's with Palmer. He's improving his French... for Miss Anisette, I suppose."

Forty-One
Mademoiselle Emmanuelle Lerosier

Lincoln Palmer knocked discreetly on the door. Bruce Turnbull answered, stepping back. This wasn't his moment.

Emma Rose came through the doorway as though she were floating, her hand resting on Palmer's arm: elegance personified. She thanked him for his genteel manners, kissing his cheek.

He blushed, still a little clumsy with women. He knew Marie was watching him, angry with him. He'd chosen his second best suit for the occasion, the one he hadn't worn on Monday. His shirt and tie he bought the day before in Nice. Their eyes locked. He thought she looked terrible. She looked sad. She was so totally awesome. She was breathtaking, but not well. He was worried about her. He wanted to go to her to ask what was wrong, certain that she must hate him for what he did to her, the way he ignored her.

He mouthed, "Je regrette, Marie," not altogether certain she wouldn't spit at him.

She mouthed, "Je sais." She understood. He was sorry for not calling. Now she understood why.

He mouthed, "Café," discreetly eyeing his watch.

She mouthed, "Oui." She did want to meet him for coffee.

Gilligan's face was smeared with red, Emma's cheeks smeared with deep maroon.

Fennell stepped onto the expansive patio with Turnbull.

Deena followed with Marie. Palmer trailed behind since no one had asked him to leave.

Fennell wanted to speak. Turnbull had no doubt, asking him to please wait until Emma Rose filled in a few blanks. Marie introduced Deena to Lincoln who'd never been hugged by a woman wearing a gun and a shield on her belt. He excused himself for accidently touching the weapon.

"Sometimes we do accidently touch what we shouldn't and we get ourselves into big trouble. Don't we, Mr. Palmer?"

He swallowed. "Yes, ma'am, we do."

"That's right. Good answer, Mr. Palmer."

She patted his cheek. He blushed. Marie thought she would introduce Johnnie another time. He seemed very angry. She had never seen him like this.

The evening air was warm, yet Marie shuddered with a sudden chill. Palmer noticed immediately, reacting quickly, draping his suit jacket over her shoulders. Deena approved, commenting to Marie that he would do very nicely once she completed his training.

She turned her attention to Turnbull and Fennell who stood quietly sipping their drinks, leaning over the Plexiglas patio railing, facing the ocean, neither one better off than the other. Turnbull knew what inner turmoil Fennell was containing, fully cognizant of the extent to which The Task Force had gone to catch Gilligan Rose.

Perhaps she did kill those men, the reality being that too many aspects of her capture had gone wrong without anyone knowing. They'd focused on one Gilligan, the one living part-time in France, the obvious one, the one who studied at the Sorbonne, the one whose studio condo was on the twentieth floor in Long beach and not the more spacious condo on the twenty-fourth. That Gilligan Rose had one home, the one that was not in TGA's Human Resources files.

"I do want to say, John, that I'm with you on this and

not because you pay the guy who pays me. You did excellent work, all three of you. Deena, that beach episode from what I understand was incredible. Doing that took guts. I applaud you. I do. Here I applaud you. In court, however, I'm going to crucify you and John. I also applaud Miss Anisette here," he pointed over his shoulder without glancing back, "without whom that wouldn't be happening inside. John, the best you can hope for is the dissolution of Emma Rose's criminal record and a recommendation by the court that Gilligan Rose undergo treatment which will be strictly voluntary. Maybe she did, maybe she didn't kill those men, trash. Frankly I don't care either way, though my guess is that she did because you found her and you tracked her...you did. If you were anyone else, John, I'd be busting a gut right now begging for a day in court and the day after you'd be slapping tickets onto windshields, albeit ritzy windshields." He straightened. "She killed her father eighteen years ago. She's served her sentence many times over. Next time you want a real good time, you sit in a room with four women balling their eyes out. If she did put down those other ten, for argument sake, she got the message loud and clear Friday night. One is retiring, moving to France to paint. The other is shacking up fulltime with Miss Mendiga and I'm standing here between a rock and hard place. You're the best in the agency and I know it. I'm the best at The Summit Group and you know that. For those reasons this won't turn out pretty unless we come to terms, you and me."

"What are we in for now with the mother, Bruce?"

"Nothing that will shock you and Deena; however I would suggest that Miss Anisette keep her beau's jacket over her shoulders a while longer. I don't imagine the young lady is going to sleep very well tonight."

*

"Agent Fennell, you and Mademoiselle Anisette gave quite a convincing performance at my atelier. Tell me, where do my paintings hang? And are they well?"

"Green Tears hangs in my home. Yellow Envy hangs in Marie's."

"Your agency pays well indeed."

"You get what you pay for."

"Yes. I think so."

"Thank you for coming."

"I came to thank Miss Marie for finding me. If you had told me at my home that you were police officers I would have returned with you and Miss Marie whom I did think was a little young for such a worldly gentleman as you obviously are." She glanced at Marie. "I see that Mr. Palmer has taken your place. How wonderful: A fine young man and a pretty young girl."

"This isn't the family hour, Miss Rose. Or should I say Mademoiselle Lerosier? I agreed with Mr. Turnbull that I would listen, but I'm not hearing anything and it's getting late."

"I have lived a third of my life as Emmanuelle. I'm certain that if I thought for a moment I wouldn't be quite certain exactly who I am. Although at one time I did enjoy being Emma, I really never was. I was simply me. What does a name mean, or a title for that matter? If I call you John, Mr. Fennell, Agent Fennell or officer, you know who you are. And you will politely respond. I believe I will remain Emmanuelle. Yes, I think so. My one-sided faces have gone from my head so that perhaps now, Miss Marie, I will paint Gilligan outside the mirror standing together without tears." She smiled. "Yes, I do think so and you may call me Emmanuelle, Agent Fennell."

"Thank you, Mademoiselle Lerosier. Now please tell me what Mr. Turnbull wants me to hear."

"Shall we be seated? And Agent Fennell, I believe I would enjoy a glass of red wine." Emmanuelle placed herself between Gilligan, accepting the crystal goblet. "I will tell you a story, Agent Fennell, or, more properly, begin the one that my daughter Gilligan recounted with innocent omissions. You see, she never knew the beginning chapters of her life. To digress for a moment, towards the end of my story, I made myself guilty of murder for two very good reasons: a mother must protect her child and because I discovered at that very moment, seeing the knives in his chest, that I should have killed Tommy Dune the first day I brought Gilligan home from the hospital or sometime before. Had I done so, if only I could return to that time, you and Agent Archer would not have met my daughter, or her wonderful friends. Nor would you have bought my paintings and quite possibly Miss Marie might not have met Mr. Palmer. She's such a pretty girl. I can see in her eyes that her father is decent, gentle, loving and kind. She is a fortunate girl, whereas Gilligan's father was not. Gilligan's father was a terrible man."

Emmanuelle raised an open palm. She had a story to tell.

*

I was fourteen when Gilligan's story truly begins, six years before she was born. Although to tell the truth entirely, which is quite irrelevant, I must have been eleven or twelve because daddy came to me quite often in the dark to make me feel good.

Mommy and daddy were never rich, nor were they very poor. They were quite unremarkable people. Mommy stayed home. That's what I called her. I never knew her first name. I don't think so. And calling her Mrs. Rose didn't seem quite proper. She had three dresses: one for inside the house, one for daytime outside and another for Sunday. Mommy didn't really believe in God. I don't think so. I don't see how she could, though she would constantly tell me that God would come to carve out my heart the first time I did anything bad. I must say, however, that I never did see God come to the house. So I assumed at the time that I never did anything bad. Even today I don't know her name, not that I care to.

Daddy worked. I believe that he did. I think so. Though I have no recollection whatsoever as to where or what he might have done. I do remember he owned one suit for outside the house and one suit for Sunday. I remember he would tell mommy to put as little in the church envelope as possible each week. He didn't believe in God either. I don't think so. At home he would hang his tie on the doorknob of their room. He had two ties, one kept especially for Sunday. He never did undo the knots.

I never had many friends at school. I suppose because I was forever chasing grasshoppers and birds, waving my arms. I would talk to trees and twirl in circles with the butterflies fluttering around my hair. I knew the other children were laughing with their parents. I did know that and I didn't care because I could do what they could never do. I could sing with chirping birds and be sad with sombre trees. Did you know that not many trees are happy? It's true, Agent Fennell. And when everyone else was gloomy because of the rain I would run outside onto the grass with my feet bare to skip and dance in the back and the front our house.

When I was younger I danced in the rain in my underwear, running inside to dry myself with a big fluffy towel, though suddenly my body began changing. I was developing breasts and beautiful red hair where I never expected hair to grow. No one ever told me. I remember telling mommy the morning I woke with blood on my legs and at the back of my nightie. I was eleven or twelve. She yelled at me that God would carve out my heart and send me to hell the first time I would think to let a boy see my new hair, that God would see whatever I did alone in the dark, that I was never to touch my new hair and that I had become dirty like all other women.

That's when daddy began paying much more attention to me. Sometimes he would smile at me when mommy wasn't looking. Sometimes when we were alone he would pretend to spank me, patting my bum, though not very hard. Sometimes he would spank me under my skirts or my dresses, though I didn't have very many. That's when mommy made me wear my swimming suit whenever I danced in the rain. I didn't like that at all and my fluffy towel was never the same.

He began saying goodnight to me at my door, pretending to spank me, telling me I was a bad little girl when I wasn't, while mommy was doing the dishes. She did all the housework at home. She wasn't very attractive, usually making herself pretty, or trying to, on Sunday. And often she went to bed early while daddy sat in his chair in the kitchen and drank. However I don't remember what he drank.

He was lonely. I think so. He would often rub my legs under my nightie in the kitchen, patting my bum when I wasn't wearing panties because I never had panties to wear under my nightie. I had seven, one for each day of the week. Now I have several for each day of the week I wonder what Zeke would think about that. Anyway, father would put his hand at my waist and squeeze, asking me to hug him. He was daddy so I did and then I went to bed. That was when he began coming into my room, when my room was dark. I don't remember the first time, or how many times he came into my room. I do know he came often and I do remember a few. I remember the last time most of all, the night before they sent me away.

He would sit on my bed and talk with me until I was ready to sleep, rubbing me through my blanket, rubbing me through my nightie to make me feel good, saying how much he loved me, at first kissing my cheek goodnight, soon after kissing my mouth like a brother or sister might at Christmas or on a birthday, once in a while touching my breasts by mistake under my nightie. One time I woke in the night. He was sleeping beside me. I think so. Yet I could feel his fingers pressing into my new hair. I was afraid to move. I was afraid God would come to carve out my heart. I stayed awake until morning with my eyes closed. He left me without saying a word.

He didn't hurt me at all and when he was gone I tried to do what he had been doing, making myself feel good, except I didn't do very well. Partly, I suppose, because I was afraid of mommy and God.

Not long after, I suppose not very long at all, he came into my room to say goodnight. He brought me a glass of milk. Mommy wasn't well that night and he asked if he could lie beside me for a little while. He said he was tired and wanted to rest. He put a hand on my breasts. He told me it was perfectly fine for a daughter to feel close to her daddy. That God did not exist anywhere but in mommy's head. That she didn't want me to feel good. But daddy's hand did make me feel good and I went to sleep knowing he loved me. When I woke in the morning he was gone. My nightie was at my feet and I was wet between my legs. I thought for a moment that I had peed my bed and was afraid to tell mommy. Until I discovered that my bed wasn't wet and I remember that my bum hurt. I wondered about that.

The last time is what I remember the most. He came into my room in his underpants and singlet. He often roamed the house that way, scratching himself in different places. I remember not feeling well and daddy spilling my milk onto my nightie. Of course he did so intentionally. I remember him telling me I should change. I remember him pulling my nightie away, leaving me sitting on my bed naked, bringing me another, wiping me with a damp towel, making me finish my milk. He told me he wanted me to feel better, to feel good, which apparently required him being between my open legs. Of course I was naked.

I knew he had touched me there before, believing he made me feel good with his hands, I suppose, because I was always so sleepy. This time, though, he had an erection that

I could see sticking out through the front of his underpants. I'd never seen one before and was amazed he could have such a thing. He began slowly at first, not hurting, kissing me, kissing my breasts, his breath was bad, turning me onto my side, rubbing his hands across my back and my bum, telling me that this time he wanted me to see, that this was how daddies really loved their little girls. All little girls eventually loved their daddies that way.

I believed him, but this time he hurt me. He didn't go back to his room. He stayed a long time before he fell asleep. By then he was naked and I was naked when mommy came into my room in the morning.

I know now that my milk was a little more than two-percent, more like two-percent something, bourbon or whiskey, gin or vodka. It wasn't my fault. He'd been touching me for so many years. Then with the liquor it certainly wasn't my fault, though how could I tell my mother when I didn't know myself.

The day after, they took me away in a black car. I remember a man and a woman. He was dressed in a dark coat and I remember the woman's hands were cold and rough. When I turned to see mommy she was inside the house. The door was closed. I never saw her again, not once. I suppose she might have gone in to wait for God. That was the day I met Doctor Phillips. That was the day I met Tommy Dune. That was the day I saw my first one-sided face. I cried. I was fourteen. I didn't see Doctor Phillips again for several days, until my usual thirty minutes with him. I know that because he told me. My bath I had every Thursday night before the lights went out. I didn't have my first bath for almost a week and my mother didn't let me wash before I left home. She said I was too dirty to ever be clean.

Emmanuelle sipped her wine. The room was still. Not a sound. Not a breath.

My room at the institute was very small, very white and

very stark. The walls were bare. The window was high with bars on the inside and covered with grime. To see out I had to stand on my bed. I did have a bed, but I had no chair, nowhere else to sit except on the floor. I loved my room. I lived in my room for close to six years, though sometimes I would sit on the floor to let the summer sun cross my legs. That's when I would pull my gown to my hips to get all the sun and the warmth that I could. We were never allowed outside. I never really saw the sky except through my window. I never felt the rain or the grass. Not for almost six years.

We had no clothes. I wore an open gown with no underwear to hide me. They gave me one clean gown each week which was somebody else's the week before. We had no underwear, the men or the woman, eighty-two of us, because many of them, whether young or old, would intentionally mess themselves. I suppose cleaning the floor was less expensive than laundry.

My bed was made of foam stained yellow with age and the sweat of previous residents who had died. Dying was the one way to leave. I had one sheet on the bottom and one sheet on top. In the winter they gave us an extra sheet, though I never had a blanket. I ate breakfast in a big room with forty other women. I always sat on the floor in the corner. I never sat at the table because I was the youngest and prettiest girl and they wanted my gown. They wanted to pull away my gown to see my young body because I had red hair. I stayed in the corner until they brought me my lunch. The male patients came in after we left one by one back to our rooms. Sometimes the men would howl when I passed their doors. Sometimes, passing a man in the hall when I had my turn to go to the bathroom, or when a man was in there before me, he would lift his gown and want to make himself hard while making rude noises and bad faces. The men dressed in white never seemed to mind.

The next twenty hours were spent in my room where I

painted pictures of birds and butterflies in my head to hang on my walls. They were never there in the morning and I had to start all over again, painting pictures in my head. I didn't mind.

Tommy Dune was the only man I knew besides Doctor Phillips. He was an orderly who liked me. There was a nurse who saw me quite often when Tommy Dune wasn't there, mostly during the day, though we were never allowed to know time. I didn't like her at all. Without offense to these lovely young ladies with us in the room this evening, she liked me very much, more than the other women. Suffice it to say I saw more of the ceiling than her when she came to my room, which is just as well because her mouth smelled of other women and her face was fairly damaged by time. Tommy Dune liked me too.

He took care of me. He took me to the toilet which wasn't a bathroom, a little room with a toilet at the end of each hall. We all had certain times of the day to go to the bathroom. I went three times each day. We could never go more and soon after I arrived he began coming inside with me to watch me pee and, well, you know. He was a gentleman. He held my gown and helped me dress when I was finished, if you can imagine. Very soon I became oblivious to being naked. He saw me naked all the time. The nurse saw me naked and when I went to Doctor Phillips' office I had nothing except my open gown to cover my body. I never wore my slippers. They were made of paper and not very nice.

Thursday night was my bath night when Tommy Dune would sit in his wooden chair that was painted white and watch me until I was finished. He would take pictures of me, often asking me to pose. He did the same when I was on my bed.

After a while, I don't recall when, I suppose very soon after, he began shampooing my hair with soap. I had forgotten the smell and the foam of real shampoo. Very soon he began washing my back, between my legs and my breasts. He enjoyed washing between my legs the most. One time, and many times after, while I was bathing, he would take a shower, standing in the hot water making himself hard while he watched me. He liked to make himself hard in front of me. I wasn't afraid. He was nice to me. He always brought me candies and often he would bring me a clean gown to wear. He would bring me napkins for my dinner as well. That's how I made my pillows for my bed, by saving and stacking my napkins. We ate dinner in our rooms and he let me keep my paper cup to pee in when I wasn't allowed out of my room. How could I not like him? I did.

Soon after and until I left, he bathed with me. He told me that he wanted to make certain that I was clean when I knew he really wanted to make me feel good. I knew that if I let him he would bring me candy, clean gowns and napkins. Besides, he made me feel good. He never hurt me and I would always stay longer for my bath than the others. Pardon my smile, Agent Fennell. I can't possibly imagine now that I would ever think to have sex for a candy, a hot bath or a napkin.

He also made me feel good on my mattress, so many times before the lights went out. The lights always went out when he left. He turned them out from somewhere in the hall. That's what Tommy Dune did. He turned out the lights and I closed my eyes to the dark. I always closed my eyes to the dark, so afraid of the one-side faces in my little room. The faces I would see on my way to eat my meals, on the way to the nurse, on the way to the toilet, or the doctor, the one-sided faces peering out from the little windows on their doors: grey faces and green, with only one eye, a sad eye, an eye with no light behind it. That's what I hated the most: the one-eyed faces coming into my room to scare me when the light was turned out.

Then one morning a man came to my room who was not

Tommy Dune. I was naked. I never slept in my gown. I folded my gown at the bottom of my bed to keep my gown clean. I remember how surprised I was when he turned his back while I dressed. Tommy Dune never turned his back. I was even more surprised to learn from Doctor Phillips that I was having a baby. I had no idea what he meant. How could that be when I had never once asked for one?

The fact is; I was. I was having a baby. Tommy Dune, one night after my bath, wasn't expecting to stay later than he did in my room. He wasn't prepared. I might say that he wasn't dressed as usual for the occasion. He made me pregnant and this is what followed, Agent Fennell. This is the beginning of my perfect Gilligan rose.

Tommy Dune was given an ultimatum by Zeke Phillips: He would marry me or go to prison for raping a mindless idiot. That would be me. You see, at that time, Zeke Phillips didn't know me. Throughout timeless years at the institute he would see me half an hour every two weeks, never longer. Tommy Dune didn't have much choice.

How would he ever explain a pregnant idiot? The institute would close or be taken from him. To that end he doctored my file. He made me well with a few minor changes to his reports, from which time and until the wedding I lived with Zeke in his mansion platonically. I remember the first night in the bathroom, my bathroom. I had my own bedroom with such a wonderful bed, my own toilet and a bath of my own. Zeke didn't know. He began running my bath. He didn't know. He had no idea. When he turned to ask if I was fine he saw me sitting on the toilet with my top off and my underwear and jeans pushed to my ankles. I was peeing, which was natural for me by then, men seeing me naked while sitting on the toilet. He was embarrassed. I was trying to take off my running shoes and socks and he helped me. I hadn't worn clothes for almost six years.

Can you imagine? Before I left with him the nurse had

to tie my shoes. I had forgotten how. She had to put on my bra. I'd forgotten how, if I'd ever known. He helped me with my shoes, my socks and my bra. I hadn't worn one for so long I couldn't undo the clasps by myself. I've never really liked the things. Then he left me alone. I naturally thought that he would want to make me feel good in my new bed. He did not. He never did. I went to bed by myself and slept like an angel with my light on. The next morning we spoke. We spoke about everything as I sat in the window watching the trees and the birds. I remember I was crying. I had forgotten what I had missed all those years for no other reason than I liked to dance in the rain and sing with birds, because my father wanted my young body that was prettier than my mother's, because my mother had this image of God who would carve out my heart when she was the one whose heart should have been cut out for what she let happen to me.

However I wouldn't be married for several months. I wasn't ready. Can you imagine how much I had to learn, Agent Fennell? I had forgotten how to eat. Can you imagine? I had forgotten how to eat. He had to show me. In my room at the institute I ate my dinner on the floor. I ate all meals on the floor with a spoon. We were never allowed knives or forks, just plastic spoons. The times I ate meat I would use my fingers. How does one cut meat with a plastic spoon? And I would wipe my hands on my sheet because I needed my napkins for my pillow.

He taught me so much, as much as I taught him. I think so. He fired the nurse and most of the men in white and began to send home those who weren't crazy at all...like me.

He sent me to school. Do you know, Agent Fennell, that I have a degree? Did you know that about me? No. Then, why would you? You simply believed I was crazy, that I had killed Tommy Dune. You see the fact that he raped my daughters was never mentioned in court. The court never knew. No one ever knew because of Zeke Phillips. All anyone knew was that I killed Tommy Dune because I was crazy, because I danced in the rain and sang while washing my car in my bikini.

Emmanuelle put up her hand.

I still do, wash my car in my bikini.

At last we were married, Tommy and I, and soon after came Gilligan Rose who was the most perfect rose in the entire world. And then came Gillian Rose again, the most beautiful rose in the entire world and a much bigger surprise than her sister. And therein lay the problem.

You see, Zeke made Tommy Dune buy a house he couldn't afford. He was an orderly, albeit with a promotion and a bonus. Previously he was a bachelor in an apartment, at which time he was fine, him and his little black bag. He would pretend to his neighbours that he was a physician when he was not. They didn't know. Then without warning he was a reluctant husband and a father of two beautiful girls when we expected one.

I thought he would kill himself right there and quite possibly he should have. Indeed, yes, he should have. That would have solved so many problems. Had I known the future, Agent Fennell, I would have killed him myself. I mean, really, I was already insane, a bubble head. Everyone knew Miss Emma Rose was insane. I was an airhead which, then, made me insane. Wasn't I? Tell me, Agent Fennell, did you think I was insane when you met me in Nice? That's fine. Don't worry. Don't answer. The question is rhetorical. You thought I was nuts, flighty at best, you and Miss Anisette. But how are you with Agent Archer, Agent Deena? I see how she looks at you. She loves you, Agent Fennell. Don't you ever dance in the rain with Miss Deena? Or do you want to? I know that you do. Yes, I think so. I know that you do. So do you see? I'm not very insane at all. I simply like to dance in the rain and sing with the birds.

Tommy Dune knew he could not afford the girls. Or he

said that he could not. How would I have known when I had just learned to tie my shoes and clasp my bra? Can you believe I had to learn to sit at a table, how to use a fork and a knife? I had no idea. I had no idea of baptism or rules and Zeke Phillips was seriously injured.

I hadn't once considered taking Tommy Dune's name. I was Miss Emma Rose and called my daughter Gilligan because what else would I call her? You can see for yourself how lovely she is. She could only ever be Gilligan Rose. I hadn't once thought of another.

She came out from me a perfect child. The first sound she heard was my singing, though I do admit that at moments my pitch was somewhat irregular. And what would you expect, but that they thought I was crazy. And then Gilligan came out, wanting to be with her sister, when for a moment I did think that I might be crazy.

Tommy Dune was not a nice man. He was never a good man. I saw nothing wrong with calling my daughters Gilligan. That's who they were, though their father was unkind. He was ashamed of not having a son and treated them as one the few times he paid them any attention at all.

I saw nothing wrong with sending Gilligan to school on alternate days. I wanted them to be different from everyone else. I wanted them to learn more than they would in school five hours a day from books written before I was born, the way I was learning from Zeke. And now you're thinking what a terrible mother I must have been when, in fact, they were each the best in their classes and went to high school the same way, one day staying at home learning more than the one who did go to school.

That was my reasoning; Tommy Dune's was money...at first. I was slowly becoming well- known and money was much less an issue. In fact, money was no issue at all. However the law was and even though Tommy Dune never said so he was afraid of going to prison for what he had done, for making Gilligan one and for raping a young girl years ago who was thought to be crazy. Zeke Phillips never let him forget. And by then what could he do about hiding one of my girls? What he had done was illegal, which is not the same at all as both girls sharing a beautiful name.

To my shame I had no idea that Gilligan came home from the hospital as one girl. That was Tommy Dune's doing, a technical quirk. How could there be two Gilligan Rose? And remember the year. Back then computers were unknown; files were actually files with paper and handwritten notes. How was it possible to have two girls and one name? People were and still are so narrow in their thinking. I never knew, not until the day they took my daughters away. Nor did Zeke ever know, about the one Gilligan Rose, not until the day the world believed that I killed Tommy Dune. He was quite straitlaced in so many ways.

I began travelling more often with Zeke. I loved him like a father and, to him, I was a daughter. I called Gilligan each night and when I was home she would often paint with me in my studio while Gilligan sat in the corner to read her books. She read so many books.

That bothered Tommy Dune deeply, that Gilligan was so much brighter than him. And the neighbours, you see, were all well-to-do. They were lawyers and doctors, that sort of thing, while he worked in a kill room slaughtering beasts until he tired of standing in blood.

The wine was never an issue with me. Who was ever hurt by one glass of wine each week? Sometimes the law isn't right, though I never knew about the drugs and Gilligan never knew to tell me. How would she have known?

That night, the fourteenth, he put drugs in my wine. I had no idea until Zeke told me the next day. In the morning Gilligan came into my room. I felt as though my skull had been crushed. Of course I didn't believe her and when I did, when I saw him, I felt glad. I felt happy that he was finally dead, sad that I hadn't killed him myself.

I told Gilligan to bathe, to clean herself and before I called Zeke I washed the knife handles. I remembered grabbing the hilts, moving them like levers as best I could and hoping he would feel terrible pain. I did make a bit of a mess, which what I wanted.

I dragged him into our room where Zeke later helped me put him to bed, though before he arrived I told Gilligan never to say that she was raped. I made Gilligan promise. Telling would do no good. The man was dead. This way I would see them one day very soon.

You see, her life would never be the same: a fifteen-year-old girl going to school ten days a month, raped so many times by her father, one girl or the other killing her father, one Gilligan separated from the other, one half of her mind gone missing, one half of her heart gone missing. How does one live without a heart? She would no longer dance in the rain or make invisible angels in the soft grass. You see, being torn apart was not supposed to happen. Though if anyone should know, Agent Fennell, you should know the law is not always right.

I didn't see Gilligan again until this very evening. Mr. Palmer was so kind to tolerate my endless prattle during our flight across the ocean together. He is a very nice young man, Miss Marie. I had no idea until this evening that you were the pretty young girl his was telling me about.

Zeke Phillips made me insane the very way he made me well. No one ever discovered our close friendship. He convinced the court that I had regressed, that in prison I would worsen, that I had always denied having two girls, that I treated them as one, that my one-sided faces were my husband's faces and that I believed he was unhappy in life, that he could only be happy once he was dead. As a result I didn't really kill him, you see; I simply made the man happy.

I never once returned to the institute. Zeke sold the place

over a year later. In the meantime he methodically removed me. You see, once inside those walls, you do not exist. By the time the transition was complete I was Emmanuelle Lerosier living on the French Riviera. Miss Emma Rose was forgotten, remembered solely by those with sufficient wealth to purchase what quickly became significantly higher priced one-sided faces whose profits then went to Gilligan. Because who else would have had a reason to remember?

Zeke bought a house in England. He rented the place to a couple and came to live a few villas from mine. We never did live together after that. When he died I buried him in France. That was his wish: to always be with me. The grave in England is empty.

I never remarried and I never once looked for Gilligan. People would have remembered Miss Emma Rose, those who once bought my paintings. I would have made Gilligan's life difficult. Or so I believed. Missing my girls in France, or missing them from prison, the only difference was my view, Agent Fennell. Prison is prison. I would have made their lives difficult, possibly impossible. Instead I painted the beautiful face they share, one girl happy, one girl sad.

*

"And now you know the other half, John. Have fun trying to sleep tonight. With Miss Lerosier's previous permission I recorded her story, nothing before, nothing after" Turnbull reached into his open briefcase, ending the monologue. "You'll receive a copy tomorrow before we go into Brannigan's office. And I do expect an invitation. You can't have all the fun. Gilligan has agreed to join Gilligan with us as well as their mother, Miss Mendiga and Miss de Montfort. May I suggest 11:00 AM? May I also reiterate my suggestion that you do not tell her?"

Fennell stood. "Ladies I will see you tomorrow. Mademoiselle Lerosier I expect you will be a legally free woman within a few days, once your daughters are booked for the murder of your husband. That's how things work. What the judge does after isn't for me to say. Personally I'm glad you're home with them. You were very kind and very generous confessing to their murder to protect them, though I do understand why. The world is a not a good place. Your story substantiates what I know to be true. These ten dead men do make the world a better place, just not by much. However their killer doesn't make it any better at all. She should have been satisfied by killing her father. As far as I'm concerned my job is done. I caught a killer. That's she's extremely beautiful doesn't mean a thing to me, whichever one she is or both. What happens tomorrow is up to Captain Brannigan, the federal prosecutor and Mr. Turnbull. Good luck." He turned to Bruce Turnbull. "John, 11:00 is good, with a copy. It very well could be that you and I will be enjoying more lunches together after all and much sooner than expected. Goodnight, ladies."

He walked out, not prompting either Deena or Marie. They followed. Lincoln Palmer stayed. He would take her for coffee the next day.

Marie lived on the far side of town where rents weren't in the tens of thousands each month. Deena wouldn't allow her to drive, Fennell wouldn't allow Deena and he wanted another deep scotch more than a tedious drive. Marie was about to spend her first night in a luxurious penthouse looking out over the ocean.

Deena had more than enough new lingerie for Marie to sleep in and unopened boxes with European names for her to feel fresh in the morning.

Marie thought she'd died and gone to heaven. She'd never imagined an apartment as big with floor to ceiling glass walls and a patio larger than her tiny home. She thought the pool was bigger than her apartment.

She was proud. They hadn't sent her home and Johnnie

made very clear that she would not be excluded in the morning. She was fast becoming an agent for better or worse.

She whispered to Deena in the bedroom while Fennell was at the bar that she could sleep in her panties and bra, Deena whispered that, no, she could not. She would shower and change into the French-made peignoir and join them for one nightcap on the patio before retiring.

Deena went into her room to erase and the day's high heat and to change. Fennell stayed as he was, snorting when first Deena walked out onto the patio followed by Marie a moment later, refusing to tell them why. He was thinking that he'd seen quite enough beautiful women for one day.

He let them go to bed. He couldn't sleep. He'd changed his mind. While he'd been listening to Emmanuelle Lerosier and the twins, he had changed his mind. Turnbull was right without saying the words. He fucked up big time. He would tell Deena first, then Brannigan. They wouldn't know that he'd changed his mind, so the shit would hit the fan only once. Things had a way of working out.

He would become the lawyer he wanted to be. If he could obliterate a year's hard work so thoroughly without the slightest inkling, what else would he miss and when?

Forty-two
The Next Day

When Marie woke she didn't want to get out of bed. She felt like a princess. She had never seen the ocean from her bed. She noticed that Deena had put a new bikini with a fleecy robe in her bathroom the night before. Deena was in the pool, treading, miffed and glaring at Fennell who was in his robe pouring his second coffee.

"Bonjour, Johnnie."

"Bonjour, Frenchie." He passed her a freshly squeezed orange juice. "Better get into the pool quick, kid, before the water freezes. Things are pretty chilly in there this morning."

"Fennell you're a complete idiot."

"Bonjour, Deena."

"Morning, Marie. This jerk just told me he's quitting the force. Can you believe that? He wants to be a lawyer."

"Hey, I told you once before, our second night together. Don't mislead the kid."

"I thought you were joking, being a fennell…not a complete fool."

"I warned you, Frenchie. It's not even her time…must be the wedding jitters."

"This is not true, Johnnie. You are not quitting the force. I do need you and Deena so much to teach me so many things."

"And who says I'm getting married to an idiot? That wasn't the deal. I want a divorce."

"No! This is not nice to say, Deena, since I have already bought my gifts for you that I will give you on..."

Merde!

Quiet.

Fennell scanned the sky. Marie was SOL and on her own.

"Oh God, Fennell, am I having a shower? You know I don 't like all that girlie stuff."

He shrugged, stepping closer. "I don't know, but I wouldn't suggest swimming naked around two o'clock on Sunday. You might embarrass your mother, Brannigan and this one...and a few others."

He was grinning stupidly, sipping his coffee. He was falling forward, trying to see behind him, his arms out, surfacing, dripping, sputtering, accusing.

"I will not listen to you speaking like this, Johnnie. You will kiss Deena right now and you will not be a fennell with us. How can I be the best agent like you if you are not one? Now kiss her or I will tell the women at the squad that you do wear very small underwear like a Frenchman."

He kissed Deena, pushing her under the water and retrieving his cup. He stepped out smiling, dropping the sopping robe to the deck en route with open arms to hug Marie as she held out her arms to embrace him, smiling, satisfied that she had saved the day. She was smug, too smug, suddenly not quite understanding why she was in the air, sprawled, under the water, at the surface gasping.

"He does that to me every morning, Marie. He's so juvenile."

Marie parted her curtain of wet hair, the bottom half of her robe floating at her waist. "He is also so handsome."

"She's right, sweetcheeks...handsome."

Fennell went inside to prepare breakfast. Deena and Marie waded, taking turns dragging each other through the warm water. When they noticed him again the table was ready and Marie was fully apprised of the issue in Deena's words.

He was more succinct. He'd messed up. He should have dug deeper into the Rose case, been less confident than he was. He had nothing further to say. The subject was closed.

They spoke for an hour, Deena inviting Marie onboard Double Agent for a lunch cruise with Lincoln Palmer the next day. When breakfast was done they dressed and drove to Marie's home. She invited them in. She wanted to show Johnnie her Yellow Envy mounted on her wall. They were in Gayle Brannigan's office at 10:45. The captain already knew why Marie would be late. Fennell walked in last.

"Morning, boss lady. As always you are a divine vision."

"Fennell, where is Gilligan Rose and why is her bracelet still on my desk and not her wrist?"

"She's with Turnbull. They'll be here at eleven."

"She's coming with Turnbull? Why?"

"With Bruce Turnbull, her mother the famous Miss Emma Rose, Mendiga, the French woman, one huge surprise for you as a bonus, and your buddy Zakkery from Justice is also joining the party. I asked Zakkery to arrive a few minutes early. You might want to bring in more seats."

"Emma Rose. You say that as though I should have been expecting her for tea. You're keeping secrets again, Fennell. You know I do not like secrets and I certainly do not like surprises…especially your kind."

"You're in for both. Turnbull and I didn't think you should be less blown away than we were."

"Deena, did you know about this?"

"I did. And he's right, Captain, as usual. This time the full shock value is requisite. That you and the federal prosecutor are the last to know is accidental, not intentional."

Gayle Brannigan crossed her arms. "Jake Zakkery, he's a good friend. He shares my sense of humour, Agent Fennell. Be forewarned."

"He's a good prosecutor. And believe me; you won't need your sense of humour for a few days...perhaps a scotch or two. He'll probably join you. He's tough, but he's fair. He's sent his fair share of men to death row and over the years has agreed to keep that many and more out of prison. He sponsors a summer camp for underprivileged kids. He's good people, albeit a little lacking in personality."

"Emma Rose is surrendering? Don't you find it strange that after all these years she would give herself up?"

"Not after yesterday I don't. I did. Like I said, boss lady, be patient. Turnbull sent someone to get her, Marie's young heartthrob. She's not facing additional charges and we haven't arrested her. She's innocent. The daughter killed Dune after he repeatedly raped her as a teenager. She confessed. Turnbull's got the entire story on tape and more. It ain't pretty, boss lady. I hope your breakfast is deep in your stomach. Anyway, here's the thing. Chances are good that Gilligan Rose will go free and don't ask me why. You'll know soon enough and I'm taking the hit on this one, no one else."

"What is he talking about, Deena, taking the hit? Talk to me, girl."

"He's lapsing again, being an idiot. There's something about the case that we didn't see. No one did or could. Gilligan Rose is very clever, Captain, very cunning or very fortunate. The truth is we'll never really know. Like Johnnie says, just wait. You're in for the shock of your career, about to feel very nauseous and Johnnie wants to fall on his sword. He's been watching too many movies. He wants to be the hero." She glared at him. "Or he's been drinking too many mimosas."

"Captain Brannigan, Johnnie will soon quit the agency to become a lawyer. He believes he is no longer the best. Of course, you must not allow this to happen."

Gayle Brannigan waited, pensive, erupting into giggles.

"True, Fennell?"

"I've been mulling things over. Seems like good timing. Soon I won't have Deena to work with and I don't see anyone else around here worth my time."

Silence and glares from one side of the office, heightened awareness from the other. Shit was happening.

"Thank you, Johnnie, for this news. I did believe I was worth your time. I did ask Captain Brannigan to be your real partner in one year."

"That was so cruel, Johnnie. You know Marie admires you."

"That is true, Fennell. The young lady has formerly requested that she buddy up with you, which tells me she might not be that bright after all." Gayle Brannigan stared at him over the rims of her glasses, unblinking, her lips twisted into unforgiving disappointment. "Deena, you haven't told him?"

"No, Captain, there was too much going on. I was waiting until after Rio."

"Tell me what?" Fennell wanted to know.

"Gayle is leaving the squad. She's being transferred to Washington. She's been promoted. She's our new director. The new captain takes over in January."

"Gayle, this is total bullshit. You are the squad. Tell Washington to go find someone else. What do you know about being a director? You're hands-on."

"It's a done deal, Fennell. I'll be running the four divisional offices, this one included."

"A new captain, this isn't good. This isn't good at all." He rubbed his face, turning to Deena. "Thanks for keeping me in the loop, partner. Anything else you'd care to tell me? You know damn well how many years I spent training Brannigan here. Now I have to start over with a paper-pusher or some guy with a gut who's too old to aim straight. What we need here is a hard-ass and we've got her. We don't need anyone else."

"I didn't hear that Fennell because this young lady cannot marry you if I shoot you, which I don't believe would disappoint her or Marie at the moment. I also know that you have difficulty expressing your heartfelt emotion. So sit there and shut up. The new captain is a good choice. I made a good decision. She's experienced and she's capable."

"Shit, another frigging female, no doubt with a stick up her ass and a petticoat full of prissy attitude. That's all we need. Washington's turning this place into frigging a girls' dormitory. So when's the bake sale?"

"Why? What are you baking? And what do you care anyway? You're quitting. You're giving up. To do what, run over to Summit?"

"I'm rethinking my career. Not the same thing."

"Give her a chance. Believe me, you'll like her. You'll get along fine with her unless you decide to go through with this foolishness."

"And you know that how?"

"Because, Agent Fennell, you're going to marry the woman next week and we've already agreed that Marie Anisette will be your next partner. Becoming a lawyer, I don't see that happening." Gayle Brannigan paused for affect. "And this would be an excellent time to apologize to Marie for bursting her bubble. Don't you agree, Fennell?"

"I'll deal with Frenchie later. She's French. She gets pouty for no reason. And now you're telling me that I can't work with Deena, I just have to report to her. I trained her, and now I have to report to her? That won't happen. What kind of weird bullshit is that?"

"From where I'm standing you're the pouty one and if I were you, Fennell, I would stop digging that hole you're in while you can still climb out. And who the hell do you think would want you as a lawyer anyway? How many times have I heard a judge threaten you with contempt?"

"Good point, boss lady. Let's just call the subject

closed. Frenchie, we'll work something out. Let's see what happens this morning. Thank you for wanting me as a partner. You are already better than most others here, you know, because of me. Don't think they're not flapping their gums on the other side of that window about you being in here with us right now. Deena, dinner is on me tonight with champagne and candles. Congratulations, Captain. That goes for you too, Gayle. Washington will be a whole lot better with you running things." He'd spent too much time with Marie. He was getting soft. He hugged all three, Gayle Brannigan melting a little, Deena much warmer than when she was in the pool, Marie considering whether she would punch him. She did, and felt good. Then she hugged her current and future captains, so happy for Deena.

Gayle Brannigan wasn't pleased. She didn't appreciate anyone disrupting her plans or fouling her decisions.

"Marie, you did a great job with Emma Rose. What we need is fresh blood in this place, not a bunch of people running around with guns thinking they're as good as they were ten, twenty years ago without bringing something fresh to the equation. To that end I am creating a new national task force out of this office, one specifically for cold crimes of which there are several dozen throughout the four divisions. I need the best team. That means that you leave the academy in a year at the top of your class. I won't accept anything less. You will report to me directly, not Deena. You must also choose a partner you feel good with, someone you trust. He, or she, will also report to me directly, not Deena. All I need to hear is a yes and it's done. So say yes."

"Yes!"

Deena was beaming, her eyes tearing. Her kid sister would be at the top of her class. Marie was looking at her, anxious, afraid, ecstatic and excited. She ran to squeeze a surprised Brannigan, leaving her to squeeze and kiss Deena.

"Deena, you did know of this before?"

"The choice was Captain Brannigan's. I simply agreed with her. Too bad you'll only have second best to choose a partner from. I'm sure you'll find someone who doesn't run from a fight with a girl."

"I will do my best, Deena, to find someone as good as Johnnie. I do know already who I will ask. Perhaps Agent Dowell would want to work with me on these important cases. I will ask him. My mother and my father and my brother, they will not believe what I will tell them. Thank you, Deena. Thank you, Captain Brannigan."

The three were ignoring the fennell who wasn't much impressed with the female chatter he was hearing.

"Boss lady, this would be a very good time to take your seat. The show is about to begin."

Through the window he saw Federal Prosecutor Jake Zakkery taking long strides through the office. Zakkery was big at 6'4", 280 and not many months from retirement. He was no-nonsense. In front of a judge and a jury he had once conceded that Johnnie Fennell was a mental problem with a gun.

He met Zakkery at the door, neither man thinking to shake hands. He was introduced to Agent Archer and Miss Anisette after which Johnnie Fennell laid down a few ground rules. Turnbull would do the talking, preliminary questions to set the tone. No one else until mother and daughter finished their pre-recorded say. The Latina and the Frenchwoman were with them for support.

Brannigan and Zakkery agreed and more seating was brought in.

Fennell met Turnbull at the door, accepting the recordings. Introductions were brief, directed towards the captain and prosecutor who then sat listening with undisguised awe for the first time to what everyone else knew, to what Emmanuelle Lerosier and her daughter had recounted the previous day. One person was missing from the room.

When mother and daughter were finished Turnbull discreetly raised a forefinger to remind Brannigan and Zakkery. No questions until he was done, Brannigan believing she might soon throw up all over her desk.

Turnbull asked Gilligan Rose pertinent questions. Yes, she did kill her father. That was true. No she did not kill those ten men. She had wanted sex with John Fennell because he looked like a decent man and she wanted to know whether sex with a good man would feel good, or feel the way she remembered. She had to know that she hadn't been living a lie. They spoke for thirty minutes.

She asked Turnbull if she might excuse herself for a moment to visit the ladies' room. The men stood. When she returned, the questioning resumed with her answers flowing as smoothly as Turnbull's questions for the next half-hour. Gilligan Rose excused herself once again. The men stood.

When she returned they stood once more, southern men did. When she came through again seconds later they were still standing.

Fennell said, "Captain, Mr. Prosecutor, meet the second Gilligan Rose, the one your minds have been racing to imagine, to understand over the past couple of hours. In fact you and Mr. Zakkery have already heard each of the ladies speak with Mr. Turnbull for half an hour...maybe. Who knows? Would you care to tell us which of the ladies you believe was first in the office, which lady was second...Mr. Prosecutor?"

What Zakkery was seeing wasn't possible.

"Let me guess, Mr. Prosecutor. What you're seeing isn't possible? Is that about right?"

Brannigan was speechless. Not because the women were exquisitely beautiful. No. She was lost for words because of the law.

"Captain, any thoughts, like this can't be happening?" Fennell added.

"Agent Fennell, next time you're having a slow day you

go to the goddamned beach." Zakkery waited for Gilligan Rose to sit on either side of their mother. "Miss Mendiga, which of these ladies is your lover?" he asked.

"Truly, I do not know. I can only believe when she tells me that she is."

"Miss de Montfort, do you know?" he asked.

"I do not unless she tells me the truth, unless I ask of her a personal detail which I will not do. I trust her and I love her. That is all I must know."

"Miss Lerosier, surely you must know even after all these years which of these young women is which?"

"Yes, I do, Mr. Zakkery. Gilligan are my daughters. The difficulty arises in that I would have to tell you each time you see them, each time you open and close your eyes. You see, I know them by their eyes, whereas you cannot. They are that identical. I know them by their heartbeats, the way they dance and the way they sing."

"Miss de Montfort," the prosecutor asked, "will you return to France to live with a woman who is quite possibly a killer?"

"No. I will not. I will return to France with Gilligan. And if you believe I am with one, I could quite possibly be with the other. How would you know, and for how long? And be honest with me, with all of us here. Why are you wasting your time because of these ten men when they are very fine in the ground? I will return to my country with Gilligan and together we will seek help to undo the pain caused by her cruel fathers. And now that I know of Gilligan there is no longer such a heavy guilt in her heart. Now our family is larger by three. As for her first father, I would have killed him myself gladly."

"Thank you. Miss Mendiga, could you sleep with a woman who is not your lover, in fact possibly a killer?" Zakkery persisted, his voice calm, not at all flustered. "What I mean to say is that if Gilligan Rose or her sister would trade places for any length of time in order to confuse us anymore than we are, would you know and could you accept the deceit?"

She answered, "Could you sleep with someone who is not your lover? Or would you do so to save her?"

He nodded, his expression was grim. "Quite frankly I would like to answer that question. Unfortunately I am unable to as an officer of the court." He stood. "Captain Brannigan, may I suggest that these lovely ladies enjoy a coffee or ice tea in your boardroom?"

Fennell stood with Turnbull, Fennell calling out to the girl sitting at Marie's desk to escort them. When they were gone he called security at the main entrance. The Rose sisters and the mother were not to exit the building.

The federal prosecutor had trouble finding the right words.

"Very enchanting ladies, all five of them," he began. "Lesbians apart, I understand why they would be. I half wonder why the mother isn't. So let's see if I've got this right, Gayle. Agent Fennell feel free to interrupt me at any time. We put Emma Rose in what was essentially a prison for lunatics for no other reason than being a capricious and carefree child. We confined her to a room with bare walls, a bed with no blanket and a paper cup to hold her urine. A place where the state wasn't satisfied with feeding her watered-down shit three times a day so we raped her almost every night and watched as the poor girl peed and wiped her bum every day. Not content with that we sent in a nurse to do whatever the sick bitch might have done. My imagination doesn't extend that far into a sick mind. Is that fairly accurate, Agent Fennell?"

"That would seem about right, Mr. Prosecutor."

"Then Phillips makes her marry the rapist, an orderly, quite possibly with good intentions. He wanted Emma to live freely, to have her baby. In my view he should have been a patient, not the doctor. He should have known better. Then again I wasn't there. Perhaps he did do what was right at the time. Then this Dune fellow turns two girls into one. And don't talk to me about this homeschooling shit. The woman could have easily afforded tutors. She didn't, which is moot. Both girls have degrees. I sent mine to private schools for the same reason: to learn something. So Dune starts playing touchy with his girls, deciding at some point that he likes the idea of having two and he starts drugging and raping them on a regular basis. Am I continuing on the right track so far, Agent Archer?"

"Yes, sir, you are."

"I thought I might be. So now, guess what? The kid or kids kill daddy and instead of doing our job we take the low road because Phillips has good friends in high places and we send mommy back to the loony bin and hand over her abused kids to more sophisticated and wealthier pedophiles where the abuse continues and a few years later people start dying all over the place because something tipped a finely balanced psyche. And who comes along to save the day ten years after the first stabbing? Yes, naturally, none other than our intrepid Agent Fennell who was having a slow day."

"Are you with me on this, Agent Fennell?"

"You're doing very well, Mr. Prosecutor. Good to know you were listening."

"Whether Gilligan Rose did or did not kill anyone is not relevant in my view. If she did, with what we know about her, them, she would spend the rest of her life in a psycho ward. I believe she's achieved that already in her own mind. It's time for her to heal. No judge would send her to prison. I wouldn't ask for it. In fact I would refute such a sentence and I sure as hell won't ask for the death penalty even if we can prove she's guilty, which by the way is a stretch. You'll be tied up in court for five years while I'm fishing. That's because Mr. Turnbull here knows about double jeopardy and false arrest. You don't even know at this very moment who you arrested. So how would you explain that to the media? I didn't see the video and I don't want to. Destroy the thing. That's an order, Gayle. She tried to kill you, Agent Fennell, maybe. Quite frankly, right now, I'm thinking that's not such a bad idea. The maximum she would get with a sympathetic judge would be a few years. If the judge knows you she might even get a Caribbean cruise. She's not worth my time. I don't need the aggravation. Ladies, gentlemen, the court is in session right here, right now. This is not going public if we can get their cooperation. No freak show for the media at our expense. So here's what we do. We clean up the mother's file. She'll be erased one hundred percent in a day or two. One Gilligan Rose goes to France, the other goes to Long Beach. The French girl's already alluded to getting help. Therapy isn't an issue. We would never know who's in and who isn't. Hiding a twin sister from a lover for eighteen years, I can't begin to imagine. As for Dune the Justice Department won't press charges. The girls have been through enough, all five of them. The shit stops here. When the mother's taken care of we'll seal Dune's case file. Red taped, not to be opened. So let's get them in here so I can get home early and get drunk. Just two more things on a personal note before you do. You and Agent Archer did good work, Agent Fennell, and I understand you had a helpful assistant. Good luck at the academy, Miss Anisette."

"Thanks, from the three of us. What else, Mr. Prosecutor?"

Fennell was expecting a public whipping, one he deserved.

"Just that rumour had it through the grapevine that you were considering heading up The Summit Group fulltime when we at the Justice Department are having enough trouble as things stand with talent like Mr. Turnbull. Now I hear from Bruce one day last week at breakfast that you've decided to remain with The Task Force. Good move. Summit has enough good people. They don't need you. What we need are more cops like you here at the agency.

Enough said. Now let's get the ladies in here."

Forty-Three
This Year: August 01st

The sky could not have been painted a more perfect blue, or the sea a more perfect turquoise bordered with white. Mrs. Deena Archer-Fennell was the perfect accent to a perfect day. John Francis Templeton Fennell was proud of the soon-to-be Captain of The Federal Task Force on Major Crime, proof he told their guests that he really had done a magnificent job of training her. Of course, the bride punched the groom.

She'd forgiven his most recent lapse into fennellism, as did Marie, as did Gayle Brannigan because he was Fennell. He didn't want anyone else bearing the burden of losing Gilligan Rose.

The Summit Group would remain in trust until minor issues could be worked out with the senior partners, though he would retain fifty-one percent. Above all he was a cop. And, besides, who else could understand Frenchie. So, yeah, he might as well partner with her. Besides, someone had to balance the influx of narcissistic females diluting the agency.

Brannigan was proud as well and a little self-satisfied, curious to one day very soon see the wide-eyed expressions of disbelief in the squad room when the happy couple would return from Rio, when the squad would discover Captain Deena Archer-Fennell and the new Cold Crime Team of Fennell and Anisette.

Marie had a month to go before her training, so pleased

that a week earlier at the bridal shower Deena had loved her gifts the most: a man's and a woman's titanium signet bracelets with respective inscriptions 'Double Agent Johnnie' and 'Double Agent Deena'. She was also quite nervous. She'd been onboard Double Agent with Lincoln Palmer for a wonderful afternoon of cruising and swimming in the middle of the ocean. Then she went on a date with him. Then she went on another, which was fine. However each time she had called her parents to kiss them through the phone and her father was now adamant that he would see with his own eyes why his daughter was so elated. They were flying in from Chicago for dinner and Monsieur Palmer was invited. Lincoln Palmer, Linc with a C, was practicing his French which Johnnie Fennell suggested might be the problem.

Gilligan Rose returned to Long Beach with her sister and mother, Elixia and Xara. Prosecutor Jake Zakkery kept his promise. Tommy Dune was dead forever in a cardboard box that would never again be reopened. Emma Rose was free to continue living her new life as Mademoiselle Emmanuelle Lerosier, the capricious and effervescent artiste of the French Riviera, her time through to August 01st passing very quickly, spending her evenings painting and listening to her daughters and new friends.

The tears hadn't stopped, not after so many years of dark secrets, heartache and separation. That would take time.

Xara Mendiga was the happiest, her delight spreading contagiously to the four others. She had three new friends and was putting her condo on the market. She was moving in with Gilligan Rose who would soon return to TGA at the end of her leave of absence, one that she actually now did need to spend time with her new family. They would share the Long Beach apartment high above the Pacific with the love of her life and at last be a couple.

Xara phoned Deena Archer one day, to forgive her, to

apologize. That's all she wanted to say. She wanted closure. She doubted she would ever see Miami again.

Conversely, Elixia de Montfort phoned Johnnie Fennell to thank him for what he had done. He had given her back her Gilligan Rose. She was thankful and that's all she wanted to say. She was anxious for Gilligan to paint her canvases and to sit with her each night at Les Filles du Ciel.

Gilligan Rose sold her condo in Long Beach, approving the sale first over the phone. She would return to France with her mother and Elixia to paint. She would never return to TGA though she would always love to talk on the phone with her sister.

Not once throughout the previous week did mother or daughters mention Tommy Dune.

On August 01st the wedding was over at three. The reception began with mingling and chatter, music and dancing, Marie anxious to dance with the groom, advising him that he was a very excellent agent, however not so good a dancer. Gayle Brannigan had her own comments. That she would ever have thought to dance in the arms of Agent Johnnie Fennell was, well, impossible. She was happy that she would not have to miss him terribly and she told him so.

At four o'clock a package was delivered in a large crate by special delivery to Mr. John Fennell. He didn't know, yet he did. He simply didn't know why. He went to his wife, Gayle and Marie, asking that they take a moment to join him in his study. No one spoke as he uncrated and unwrapped the canvas painting.

The older woman portrayed was dressed in white. She was beautiful, her green eyes glistening with tears that were joyous and clear. Her soft lips painted red, her mouth whispering silence. Her red hair was lustrous and full, her slender arms and delicate hands with slim fingers reaching into the mirror, touching. The innocent young girl inside the mirror was dressed in white also, her green eyes filled with uncertainty and wonder. Her long hair, shiny and red, was tied into a girlish ponytail, her delicate hands taking hold. She was stepping out from the mirror.

The painting was signed by Emmanuelle Lerosier. No note was written. None was needed Emmanuelle Lerosier had named her work 'Now She Will Dance in the Rain'.

At five Johnnie Fennell was called to the phone.

"John Fennell speaking."

"I wanted to call, Agent Fennell, to congratulate you and your bride. She is very lovely. I told her so many times, though I don't believe I ever told you. I don't think so."

"Thank you."

"You're welcome, although I am the one who must thank you for returning my mother to me. That's all I wanted to say. I hope to see you onboard TGA one day and in Paris at the cabaret when I might be as well-known as Emmanuelle. We never know, do we? I don't think so."

"No, we never do. Please thank your mother for her generous memento. She made quite certain that we will never forget Gilligan Rose. Not that we would have."

"Gilligan is stepping from the mirror, Agent Fennell, taking Gilligan's hand. She's free at last."

"We're glad for both of you."

"You were right, Agent Fennell. The truth I was telling was mixed with a lie. I wanted you to know that you were right."

"Right about what, Miss Rose? We've been through a bit, you and I. Exactly what truth do you mean amongst so many unanswered questions, so many obvious lies?"

"They say a girl will forever remember her first, Agent Fennell."

"That is what they say, Miss Rose."

"Yes, though Gilligan Rose will always remember her last. That is my truth when I gaze into the mirror. I think so."

The Hunt for Gilligan Rose

Other Mystery – Suspense - Thriller Novels

By Doug Booth:

Split Verdict

The 4th Man

The Madam

Family Lies

Mother of Pearl

From Inside Her Bedroom

The Feast of Tombola

Deferred Prejudice

The Hunt for Gilligan Rose

The Fatal Diners' Club

Silent Conviction

A Christmas Killer, Comfort and Joy

Pariah In the Mirror

***

No One to Tell (Creative Non-fiction)

www.ingramcontent.com/pod-product-compliance
Lightning Source LLC
Chambersburg PA
CBHW030537020726
47494CB00005B/1399